SCORE!

SCORE!

Aarti V Raman

B L O O M S B U R Y
NEW DELHI • LONDON • OXFORD • NEW YORK • SYDNEY

BLOOMSBURY INDIA
Bloomsbury Publishing India Pvt. Ltd
Second Floor, LSC Building No. 4, DDA Complex, Pocket C – 6 & 7,
Vasant Kunj, New Delhi, 110070

BLOOMSBURY, BLOOMSBURY INDIA and the Diana logo
are trademarks of Bloomsbury Publishing Plc

First published in India 2023
This edition published 2023

ISBN: PB: 978-93-89611-22-9; eBook: 978-93-89611-24-3
2 4 6 8 10 9 7 5 3 1

Typeset in Perpetua Std by Manipal Technologies Limited
Printed and bound in India by Thomson Press India Ltd

To find out more about our authors and books visit www.bloomsbury.com and sign
up for our newsletters

To the cricket-obsessed nation that is India. And the romance-obsessed reader. This happy ever after is for you.

To my Thathu and Paati, the OG Viswanathans. I couldn't ask for better grandparents to love me.

And, as ever, to Mom, my own True North.

PROLOGUE

Email from: rajivs@iccb.in
Email to: selectioncommitte@iccb.in
Sub: Replacement of Player in WC Squad
Priority: Very High

Hello,

It is with a heavy heart that I write this email.

Zakeer Hussain was a brilliant player with a wonderful future. He was a good man, a good boy with a kind heart and dreams of being the best cricketer in the world like his idol Sachin Tendulkar. He was also thinking about settling down with his girlfriend, per his parents' wishes.

We will all mourn this young life cut so tragically short for a long, long time to come.

But as Zakeer was fond of saying, the game *always* comes first.

And with the World Cup looming closer than ever before, I believe it is time we take action and come to a decision regarding Zakeer's T20 replacement. We need an all-rounder, someone competent, just like the young Zakeer who had will and talent and so much *dil*!

His shoes are tough to fill, but we must fill them.

This is not the time for sentiment, gentlemen. Let us roll up our sleeves and present the best sixteen at the World Cup and bring the cup home. I believe Zakeer would have wanted this above everything else.

Submitting a longlist for your consideration. Let us convene soon and get cracking on the problem at hand.

It is what the young boy from Latur would have wanted.

Cheers,

Rajiv S.

(Chief Selector ICCB)

THREE MONTHS LATER

Skulking.

She was skulking.

Bee couldn't believe that her life had been reduced to this. She was hiding in the branch of an ancient tree with a pair of binoculars trained on a hotel room window. Her butt was numb from sitting on the tree. And it was raining!

For a single mad moment, she had a vision of herself as a female Sherlock Holmes with a deerstalker hat and a magnifying glass, spying on someone's cheating spouse.

Except, Sherlock was cool, *yaar*! He didn't skulk!

And neither did Bee . . . usually, in her career as a reporter. She'd worked at a couple of newspapers and was now a correspondent for Krikket-365, the cricketing arm of a sports website run by a media entertainment company.

She still remembered that fateful day when she'd interviewed with the features editor of Krikket-365, Carleena D'Silva, almost three years ago. Carleena had interrogated her on everything! Her stories at the now-defunct *Afternoon D&C*, her stint with a local sports newsletter *Saptahik Sports Illustrated*, which had risen ten times in circulation once Bee had become lead reporter, and even her dating habits and dietary preferences!

Mercifully, Carleena hadn't probed Bee too much about her last place of employment, the one that shall not be named, and for that Bee owed the woman a lot.

Scoring this job at Krikket-365 was definitely not part of the career path she'd mapped out for herself at eighteen. But it was the best Bee

Vishwanathan could do after the debacle at the 'place that shall not be named'.

Having already spent a few years in the trenches as a fresher—covering city beats, nightlife, the glamour pages, tech and science, and business—first for *Afternoon D&C* and then for 'that' publication which had almost ruined her career, Bee was determined to make senior correspondent before completing four years at Krikket-365.

Bee knew that working in the trenches was the first step to becoming a special correspondent who was sent on the coolest assignments, then becoming an assistant editor and finally the editor, preferably of the foreign bureau. Her dream job.

And she was well on her way to becoming an editor at one of the best dailies before turning forty by working her butt off.

As a cub reporter, Bee had repeatedly approached Mitra, the chief editor of 'that' publication, in hopes of securing at least a single assignment that would get her a by-line, but her pleas were routinely rejected. Hell, she had even covered sports for Mitra, especially the football World Cup, adding local colour stories to dry and boring features about who beat whom by how many goals.

But Mitra was super underwhelmed by her zeal, enthusiasm and the fact that she'd been editor of her college newspaper.

'There are hundreds like you just waiting to get your plum job,' Mitra was fond of reminding her, adding slyly that she could always leave if she wanted to or if she felt the pressure was too much or if her current job fell wildly short of her ambitions. However, if she wanted to stay, she would have to cover the local small claims court in Bandra and try to find a juicy titbit that would be run with the Indian Times Services by-line.

That too if she was lucky.

It would have made a lesser woman quit, but not Bee. She was blessed with an overload of stubbornness.

Finally, her persistence had paid off and they had given her the holy grail of assignments—politics.

Bee had been asked to do a *short* interview with Shreenath Patil, the Kennedy of Indian politics. He was handsome, charming and a real man's man. She'd always had a little crush on him. The interview could have been her ticket out of shit assignments. But one tiny question about his 'love' life had changed the geography of her life. Bee had become the mother of all memes with the words 'Patil-gate' attached to her resume for ever and ever.

So here she was—a lowly correspondent for a sports website, of all things. But beggars couldn't be choosers, and her boss, the founder of Krikket-365, was such a decent guy (a rarity in media) that she had decided to stay on, even after Carleena had left the company for greener pastures. After all, she knew it could be worse, much worse.

Now Bee was a part of the website's three-person team, but their star reporter, Abhinoy, was out with a deadly case of dengue and her other teammate, Satyarth, was getting married just when it was time to cover the T20 World Cup being hosted by India.

This World Cup was a crucial one for India. The host country was going in as more than an underdog, considering the tragedy of Zakeer Hussain's death and the subsequent shuffle-up. The bookmakers had conservative odds of 10–1 on India winning the cup.

No one expected the Indian team to do well, including the Indian media. And so when Bee, by sheer bad luck, had been assigned to cover the tournament, she didn't exactly jump with joy. Any other sports reporter would have been happy, thrilled even, to cover the cricket World Cup.

But Bee was an idealist, a reporting snob if you will. Cricket might be the lifeblood of sports in India, but it was as far away from politics or finance or business as she was from becoming a size zero. And she had been cursing herself every day for the last three years for padding her resume with the *Saptahik Sports Illustrated*'s circulation figures, one of the reasons she'd got this job in the first place.

What she had omitted to mention to Carleena three years ago was that most of the figures belonged to her uncle's company, the periodical's main advertiser. But at the time, she had been desperate enough to find an organisation that would hire her after the catastrophic 'Patil-gate'. And lying about one tiny work qualification was not such a bad thing, was it?

Of course, karma comes to collect from all those who sin, and it had come for her too.

Thus, here she was, skulking. On top of a tree. In the rain. In Jaipur!

—•—◆—◆—•—

A few minutes later, her butt vibrated.

Bee swore under her breath and, dropping the binoculars around her neck, wriggled her butt to get the phone out of her pocket. It was tricky, considering the tight spot she was in.

'*Kidhar hai tu?*' an irate female voice asked. 'We've been waiting for ever for you, babe.'

'Hey, Dhee.' Bee tried to pitch her voice to a low monotone. She didn't want anyone in the posh seven-star hotel to look out of their window and see her. Not that people who could afford such fancy hotels ever looked out.

'You're mumbling, Bee. Where are you?'

Bee rolled her eyes and considered telling her the truth. Dhee aka Dheera Chakravorty was a freelance photographer who'd been sent with her to cover the cup because she was affordable, talented and a badass.

Dhee also didn't like to be kept waiting.

'You guys go ahead with dinner. I'm stuck somewhere.'

Literally, Bee added to herself.

'Stuck? Stuck where? I hope to some hot guy's lips.'

Bee laughed before catching herself mid-laugh. Trees didn't laugh. Someone could look out and hear her. She couldn't afford to get caught.

'Something like that,' she said. 'Seriously, you guys have dinner. I'll catch up with you tomorrow. We need to get the opening shots, don't we?'

'You're beginning to worry me, babe. Please don't tell me you're at *their* hotel. You know the media has been banned from talking to them anywhere except outside officially sanctioned events. You *know* that.'

'I am not at the hotel, Dheera,' Bee replied firmly. Then she said her goodbyes and hung up before Dheera could discover the truth.

Bee figured she was telling the truth. Kind of.

She wasn't inside the hotel or even *at* the hotel. She was up on a tree, staking out the room of the Indian cricket team's captain in hopes of catching the man in an unguarded moment and getting a quick quote from him before he threw her out.

At least that was her plan.

The Indian Cricket Control Board or the ICCB was very strict in its gag order. The members of the national team, all sixteen of them, were not supposed to talk to *anyone* outside of the playing arena. The 'boys' had been told to stay away from the media.

The Zakeer Hussain incident had left the whole team shaken up and determined to play better than ever, even if they had no chance in hell of making it past the round robin.

Bee could understand their commitment and dedication. She even admired it. That was why she was here, on a tree, like a shady small-town detective, instead of being at the nice air-conditioned restaurant with her friends Dheera, Harry and Sholes, wolfing down yummy *parathas* and *rajma chawal*.

Bee had big dreams and an annoying thing called a conscience which would not let her copy-paste the press release that talked about what the team was feeling and how they were preparing for their first match. Like every other reporter covering the event had done before filing their story.

Bee might not have been overly enthusiastic to cover the World Cup, but that didn't change the fact that she wanted the scoop. She wanted to *report*.

So she was up a fricking tree outside the hotel room of the nation's favourite son, about to ambush him on the gorgeous balcony!

The curtains at the balcony doors twitched and she saw the broad back of a man as he shucked off his shirt and pants and walked into the bathroom. He was *built*!

Bee sucked in her breath. *Chance pe dance karle, Bee,* she thought even as her stomach pitched nervously.

This was her moment.

With all the stealth of a girl used to sneaking out to pub crawl with her teammates, Bee left her perch on the tree and started crawling down the bent branch that almost touched the balcony railing of the Jaipur Continental Grand.

Her binoculars swayed from side to side as she crept like a badly balanced cat burglar and quickly reached the end of the branch. Bee took a deep breath and jumped down the three feet to the balcony. But she hadn't counted on the unseasonal rain making the marble floor slippery. Her foot skidded as it made contact with the floor, her balance thrown, and she fell, butt first, with an undignified screech.

Arhan Kapoor was having a horrible day. In fact, it had been a horrible month.

Or maybe he was just horrible. Horrible, disillusioned and upset with his superiors who refused to guide him on how he was supposed to do his fricking job when no one was in the mood to play the World Cup.

Three months ago, he'd been brought in as the assistant coach of a team reeling from a personal loss and barely surviving, much less ready to participate in the T2o World Cup. As the vice-captain of the Indian cricket team, Zakeer had been an integral part of the spirit and *josh,* the lifeblood, that the Indian team was known for. He'd loved the game and was super talented, such a natural leader. To lose him to such tragic circumstances had impacted the whole team. It was dreadful just being in the dressing room. The silence was positively ghost-like.

And it was this melancholic team that Arhan been hired to manage after his successful Ranji Trophy stint with Punjab while also overseeing his family business.

The ICCB's brief had been simple. Talk to the team, pep them up and get them excited about the game again. Get them in a *winning* mindset. The media gag order was also not helping the situation. Those vultures who called themselves 'journalists' attacked his team every-effing-where—waylaying members as they boarded the bus for net practice or at restaurants they were known to frequent.

One enterprising 'journalist' had even shown up in the locker room thrusting a recorder in the showering captain Viren's face, manically asking him about India's chances of winning the cup.

As if the brief press conference they'd given in Mumbai before the start of the tournament wasn't enough! All of it was enough to give Arhan a migraine the size of planet *Mangal.*

His ex, too, was calling him non-stop because finally Madam wanted to get back together, which added to his foul mood as he walked into his hotel room.

Arhan mentally reviewed his schedule for the next day, the opening match between India and Bangladesh—a breeze if the boys could just pull it together. Today had gone off well. He had had a breakfast meeting with the manager and coach, followed by a quick session with the playing twelve. Then they had all proceeded to the venue for warm-ups. Practice had gone off well. Zakeer's replacement, Prithvi Narayanan, was blending in decently and so far no one had done anything too untoward.

But Arhan knew—from a lifetime of watching, playing and now coaching the game he loved the most in the world—that this Indian team was missing that spark, that *junoon,* which was crucial to make champions out of them.

It was a tragedy and he didn't know if he could help them win . . . or help them in any way at all.

Arhan was basking in the warm jet of the shower and wondering about possible talking points for tomorrow, his headache receding under the flow of water, when he heard a loud scream from the balcony.

A woman's scream.

He cursed, ducking his head under the shower to wash off the shampoo. He grabbed a towel off the heating rack, wrapped it hastily around his dripping waist and stumbled out of the steamed-up bathroom.

He couldn't believe his ears. He couldn't really believe that someone was in his room.

'Dammit!'

Arhan walked towards the balcony, blinking rapidly to clear the water from his eyes. He opened the balcony door, felt the steady patter of unseasonal rain in the desert state of Rajasthan and cursed some more.

The woman was real. There she was. In the balcony of his room.

The woman was unsuccessfully trying to stand up.

Arhan ran to her, one hand firmly holding his sodden towel in place, and hauled her up without any finesse.

The woman gasped.

He didn't care. He dragged her inside, registering the softness of her flesh in a distracted corner of his mind, and flung her on the first available surface, which, unfortunately, turned out to be his bed.

The woman sprawled there, trying to catch her breath, shaking dripping hair out of her eyes as he took in the incriminating evidence dangling around her neck.

Binoculars! She was a stalker or worse!

'You have,' he began in an ominously quiet voice, 'exactly sixty seconds to tell me who the fuck are you and why the hell I should not call security. Now!'

Bee gulped.

Her brain computed several facts all at once.

First, she was *not* in the captain's room, because Viren Kaul was five feet something of stocky bluster. This man was tall, well, tall-*ish,* with a gym-toned body.

Second, he did not look like any Indian cricket team member that she knew of. So, he was either management or her information had been entirely false.

Third, he was in an influential position because he had a double room all to himself. With French doors and a balcony! So that most possibly made him management.

Bee flipped through the pictures in her brain, trying to place him while her heart pounded in her chest and her breath came out in gasps.

As she tried to stare up at the growling man in all his semi-naked glory, she did the only thing she could. She put her hand in her pocket and . . .

Bee started popping.

The man's incredibly hazel eyes narrowed as the sound echoed like a gunshot in the super-quiet room.

'What the . . .' The man stared wide-eyed at her.

She started popping faster, her fingers going *ping-ping-ping* on the bubble wrap; she could feel the plastic crinkle and turn limp. The sound managed to calm her a bit. Bee noticed that even though he looked mad enough to murder her, the man before her was awfully sexy. Even his toes, big, with neatly clipped nails, were sexy. She had a thing for clean feet.

'I am Bee,' she said. 'I came to meet Viren Kaul. This is just a mistake.'

The man narrowed his eyes. 'I don't believe you.'

Bee felt a tiny snake of lust slither through her. She darted a quick glance at his thick wrist holding the towel in place on that very fine hip. The snake slithered some more, squirming with heat.

Bee gulped once more and started popping faster until she ran out of wrap.

'What the hell . . . Is that bubble wrap?' he asked, amazed, as he finally caught on to the sound.

Bee slid the limp plastic out and showed him the burst bubble wrap. 'I do this when I'm nervous. It's a coping mechanism. My therapist says it's an essential part of my strategy to avoid panic attacks.'

He stared at her.

'Groupies go to therapists? *Kya din aa gaye hai*,' he murmured, almost to himself.

Bee had a strange buzz in her ears and missed his comment. She put the wrap back in her pocket where it belonged, feeling the tiniest bit calm.

'I am sorry,' she said quietly. 'I thought this was Viren's room. Honestly.'

'Did he ask for you?'

'What?' Her startled eyes shot up to meet his. 'No, he doesn't know I am here. I just wanted to talk to him.'

'Yeah, I bet you did.'

As the man took in her bedraggled appearance, Bee became aware of her hair, dripping and dishevelled with leaves stuck to it. Her jeans were hopelessly wet and showed a tear and her jacket was torn from when she'd caught it on the bark as she'd climbed up the tree. She'd worn eyeliner, but it had long since washed off in the rain, along with her lipstick, leaving her with a bad case of raccoon eyes.

In that moment, Bee looked like Vidya Balan in that epic scene from the movie where she played an unhinged courtesan.

'Viren sure has weird tastes.' The man rubbed one hand over his face as if trying to scrub the strangeness away.

Unfortunately, that was the hand holding the towel.

Bee shrieked but watched in fascination as the towel slid down the man's thigh in agonizingly slow motion. Her mouth stayed open while her eyes took on a hungry gleam.

Dheera, Harry and Sholes—her colleagues who knew her pretty well by now—would have called it her '*mujhe chahiye*' look. It usually made an appearance around a plate of *pani puri*.

The man's gym body was well-earned if his . . . equipment was anything to go by. And oh my, those thighs looked like they could climb mountains. In fact, *he* looked like a very lean, very solid mountain.

It took a second for the man to grasp the situation. He cursed aloud as he quickly turned, bent down and picked up his towel.

Bee couldn't help it. She craned her head to get a better look at his backside. However, she quickly scrambled back on to the bed as she felt him glower at her. The snake of lust turned into an agitated butterfly that was very aware of her own vulnerability.

She was in a semi-naked stranger's room, on his bed. He was strong, which meant she couldn't escape him if he decided to attack her.

Quite suddenly, she wished she'd brought along her trusty can of pepper spray instead of the bubble wrap.

'Sorry, sweetheart. I don't roll that way,' he said, straightening. He cinched the towel in place with a knot that pulled the skin tight over his six-pack abs.

Bee shook her head, a mixture of fear and desire rendering her speechless for the moment. This was not how this night was supposed to go.

'I-I don't have a problem with whichever way you roll,' she said. It absolutely figured. The first man to twang her hormones in ages and he played for the other team. 'To each his own.'

'What?' Incomprehension clouded his handsome face. 'What are you talking about?'

Bee shrugged, a delicate movement of her shoulders, projecting non-judgmental sincerity from her pores.

'It does not matter to me, sir,' she said. 'Gay or straight, we love who we love.'

'Of course, we love who we love . . . *O tori!*' The man chuckled

She could hear the undercurrent of sarcasm in his deep laughter. It added to her inexplicable attraction to impossible men.

'What?' She frowned as she leaned forward.

'It's just funny that you would have no problem with *me* considering, you know, you are who you are.'

'I am who I am? Who am I?' She was puzzled.

The man smiled nastily. 'Viren must be someone special for you to come in through the freaking balcony. Good for him,' he said suggestively.

'Good for . . .' Bee gasped as the full meaning of what he said hit home.

She scrambled to her knees on the bed, the binoculars swinging wildly on her chest. She impatiently turned them around to her back, righteous anger turning her ordinary brown eyes into gold. Or maybe that was just the romantic lighting in the expensive room.

'You filthy-minded moron. What are you talking about?'

'I'm sorry. That was impolite of me.' Now it was his turn to shrug delicately, affected nonchalance radiating off him.

She didn't buy it for a Mumbai minute.

'You're insane!' she spat out, hopping off the bed in the wake of her righteous anger. 'It is sexist, idiotic men like you who give men the world over a bad name. Thinking I am a-a-a starstruck groupie just because I snuck into a hotel room to meet a dude! Whatever happened to thinking the best of people?'

The man took her by the arm and marched her to the door.

'What is a man supposed to think if some woman drops into his balcony from nowhere and says she is in the wrong room?' He spoke through clenched teeth. 'Especially when she herself admits that she was here to meet some other guy? Granted, you don't look like a groupie, but that could just be the rain. Who am I to judge?'

He sounded so cold and ruthless that Bee saw crimson.

Before she could stop herself, before she even thought about it, her hand curled into a fist and she punched his nose. His head snapped back as something squished and cracked with a sickening crunch.

Bee gasped as enormous pain radiated from her fingers to her wrist and then shot up her right arm. She hadn't realised that punching someone would hurt the puncher! She felt like shit even as the pain numbed her fingers.

The man looked shocked. Horrified. Blood fountained from the broken cartilage as he held a hand up to his bleeding nose. He couldn't say a word, but his hazel eyes conveyed his rage.

'I'm sorry. I'm so sorry,' Bee babbled, horrified at herself. Then, she backed out the door and continued, 'That looks bad. You should put some ice on it.'

The man mumbled something incoherently.

Bee said, 'Well, I think I better leave. I'm so sorry for . . . I bet that's going to swell.' She nodded at his bleeding nose. 'You should have a doctor take a look at it ASAP.'

The man jerked his head in the direction of the lift.

'Glow,' he growled.

Her adrenaline-charged brain interpreted it as 'Go'. Bee didn't stop to think twice, knowing full well that her victim's mercy could turn the minute he lay his hands on a phone and called hotel security to have her disbarred from the premises forever.

—⁃✦ ✦⁃—

Bee snuck out the same way she had entered the hotel, using the service entrance in the back alley; she had befriended a line chef in one of the hotel's world-class restaurants to get info on the Indian team's position. She was resourceful like that. And yet some buff, half-naked guy had rattled her. Enough for her to start popping bubble wrap!

It did not sit well with her.

Bee shoved her hands into her jacket pockets, the binoculars safely tucked inside so no one would think her weird or worse, a stalker, and exited the hotel via the 'employees only' door of the Michelin-starred restaurant.

The alley was overflowing with dustbins that held the refuse of the four restaurants serving the hotel's guests. The air smelled like rotting garbage and cigarette smoke.

Bee wrinkled her nose and ducked her head as she ran away from the hotel. The rain had thankfully stopped and the roads were muddy. Her sneakers squelched on the asphalt and the sound echoed in her head, much like the punch.

She couldn't believe she had attacked a grown man—a man so much stronger than her—and come out the winner. But the smidgeon of pride she felt was soon overshadowed by shame and regret. Her mother would kill her if she found out what Bee had done.

Besides, she could have handled the whole situation better—even though he'd called her a groupie—considering how hot he was.

Bee recalled that slo-mo moment when the man's towel had slipped and he'd unwittingly flashed her in all his glory. She hummed appreciatively as the snake of lust reared its head once again.

She would have loved to meet this guy under less weird and more clothed circumstances. She was sure they would spark.

Then, Bee's breath whooshed out and she fell for a second time that night. Someone hurtled on to her back with all the force of a wrestler.

Bee narrowly avoided getting her face squashed in the mud by turning her cheek to the side.

She screamed. '*Oye, dikhta nahi kya?*'

The sound was lonely in the deserted alley. She raised her head, blinking mud and spit and dirt from her eyes, and tried to find her attacker. All she saw was a black-hooded blur exiting the alley.

She sat up, her body aching and her head ringing with pain and reaction. Bee stood up on shaky legs, thankful that she hadn't sustained any worse injuries than a scraped cheek, which was already stinging. She took a hesitant step and her knee throbbed from encountering the chilly night air, thanks to the unfortunate tear in her jeans sustained a few minutes ago.

She bent down to check for further injuries when she spotted a small black object lying on the road.

A phone. One of those cheap models available for less than a grand. The person must have dropped it when they had collided against her.

She scooped it up; the phone was icky with dirt and muck. Bee smeared the dirt away to find the screen was scratched and the phone dead. She looked up and down the alley again. It was completely deserted. She debated throwing the phone away, but good manners prevailed.

Someone's important contacts and messages were probably stored on this device. She couldn't just leave it lying around.

Bee stuck it in her pocket and started limping away as fast as her bruised knee would take her. Today was so spectacularly not her night, she wouldn't be surprised if lightning struck her down.

—·◆ ◆·—

'So, where were you last night and who were you doing it with?' Dheera asked her the next morning at the breakfast buffet at the Sawai Mansingh Stadium.

The press had a special buffet room all to themselves since the ICCB didn't want to scrimp on any publicity they could get for the tournament, without allowing the media to actually talk to the team.

Dheera piled on fluffy *aloo parathas* next to three Amul butter chiplets. It was serially unfair that she could eat anything she wanted and not gain a gram, even though she had two cute little munchkins while Bee, who had never given birth, had to watch everything she put in her mouth.

Bee raised her brows at Dheera's loaded plate. 'You are going to fall asleep before the first powerplay is over if you stuff yourself like this.'

Dheera chuckled. She poured herself a mug of thick coffee and they wandered back to their table.

Tall and statuesque Dheera was dressed like any pro photographer in comfortable cargo pants, a white *ganji* and a jacket to add some severity to the outfit. She was Bee's counsellor on the days she desperately needed one.

Sholes and Harry were already seated, eating breakfast as if it was their Last Supper. Their plates were twice as full as Dheera's. They'd added scrambled eggs and toast to their thick *parathas* dripping with butter.

Harry Singh and Karan Sholekar were fellow second-stringers working for lesser-known publications who'd been invited by the ICCB to cover the tournament, all expenses paid.

The four of them had become friends because of their non-seniority status.

Bee stuck her fork into her fruit bowl, which sat in solitary splendour on her tray, and tried not to think of gooey butter.

'Bee hooked up with some guy last night,' Dheera announced suddenly. 'And she won't tell me who he is. He's also the rough types from the shoddy make-up job I can see on her face. So, Karan, Arjun.' Dheera pointed her fork at the two men respectively. 'Go and beat the crap out of this monster.'

Bee spat out her mouthful of watermelon.

Harry and Sholes gave her concerned glances.

'Dude, is she serious?' Harry asked.

'Why would you hook up with some random guy? Aren't you engaged or something?' Sholes questioned.

Bee glared at Dheera, her mind winging back to the monster she *had* roughed up. She wondered what her friends would think of her shitty behaviour.

Dheera shrugged as she dug wholeheartedly into her scrumptious breakfast.

Bee speared the watermelon again and chewed it methodically before she answered. 'I am not engaged. I was just chatting with that MS from the US for two weeks! And you're all nuts. Especially you, Dhee.'

'I can totally see the bruise on your cheek, babe.' Dheera laid a sympathetic hand on her arm. 'I get that you're embarrassed and don't want to make a big deal of it, but the guy is scum and his balls need to be fried in oil. Right, boys?' Her steely glare was enough to make the two men vehemently nod their heads.

Harry side-hugged Bee and said, 'You're like our *chhoti behen*, na? We have to take care of you. Tell us where this fucker lives, and we'll go break his balls.'

Bee almost groaned in frustration. She pointed her fork at each of them as she spoke.

'No one molested me. No dude hurt me because I didn't *hook up* with any dude.' Unbidden, a memory of the naked man's hazel eyes, right before he dropped his towel, flashed before her. She continued, 'I did do something dumb though because I am an investigative reporter and I wanted to prove it to my boss.'

'What did you do?'

Bee grinned as she remembered her madcap impulse from the night before. 'I tried to break into Viren Kaul's room to get a quote from him about the opening match today.'

'You did what now?' Dheera asked.

'You heard me. I tried to get a candid quote with the Indian captain by sneaking into his room. Except I ended up in the wrong guy's room and . . . anyway, I didn't meet the *kaptaan* so I left the hotel. Then I tripped and fell on the road on the way back when someone pushed me out of the way.'

When her friends continued to stare at her unconvincingly, she elaborated a bit more but didn't mention the semi-naked guy or slipping towels or bubble-wrap popping or broken noses.

Sholes stopped eating altogether while Harry's mouth hung open, giving the entire table an unattractive close-up of his half-chewed *paratha*.

Dheera punched her in the same arm she'd squeezed sympathetically a moment ago.

'Stupid girl,' she said clearly. 'Who the fuck do you think you are, sneaking off to do candid interviews when you know the team is under a media gag? You could get fired, you know.' Dheera's eyes widened. 'Or worse, Kaul could get fired and we'd be without a fucking team captain.'

Bee shrugged. 'I weighed that against the odds of being the only reporter to actually talk to the team and the scoop was worth it.'

Harry shook his head. 'You're crazy, dude. Remember Patil-gate?'

Dheera snickered as she relished her *parathas*. 'Which sexual position was his favourite? Do refresh my memory, love.'

Bee scowled at her. 'That was not the question I asked regardless of what the internet says, so stop torturing me. You all know I asked him his position on improving sex education in Maharashtra and the copy editor fucked it up!' She sniffed as she was forced to recall the embarrassing incident that had almost ended her journalistic career.

'Besides, this is a completely different scenario,' she continued. 'I was just following my reporter instincts. Isn't this what we are trained to do?'

Sholes resumed eating. 'Nope, you are paid to write about cricket, so do that. And only that!' he stressed. 'Don't do stuff like this again, Brigha. Your parents will have a heart attack if they find out you got fired. Again. And arrested for breaking into a sports star's room.'

Bee stuffed a grape into her mouth and glowered at Sholes. 'Do not call me Brigha again. You know I am petitioning to get my name legally changed to Bee! Brigha is a horrible name.'

Sholes grinned in silent apology.

Bee continued stubbornly. 'And I was neither fired nor arrested. What would have happened if Sachin had not given in to his instincts and stood his ground after Waqar Younis beaned him with that bouncer in that first test in '89? History would not have been made. The cricketing world would have lost its God even before he was born.'

'Your point being?'

Now Bee pointed her fork at the ceiling. 'You have to take chances. Great things happen when you make them happen.'

'I suppose you're very proud of having got a bruised cheek to match Sachin's broken nose?' Harry could be sarcastic when he needed to be.

Bee grinned. 'Why not?'

'For a person who claims to not like cricket, your tendency to instantly spout cricket facts and twist them into a moral science lesson is impressive.' Dheera chewed slowly.

'Blame it on my cricket-crazy family.' Bee shrugged and then turned towards Sholes. 'You guys have no nose for news. Why the hell did you become a journalist in the first place?'

'Free food,' Sholes promptly replied.

'Sexy ladies.' Harry winked at both of them.

Dheera snorted, but she did toss her mile-long hair back.

'And you guys call me crazy.' Bee finished her fruit bowl and gulped down her coffee. 'Anyway, I just realized something.'

'What?' Dheera asked. 'Don't go climbing trees in the middle of the night without your friends? In fact, no tree climbing. Period.'

'No,' Bee said. 'Waqar Younis must have felt like a God breaking Sachin's nose with that beamer. You never forget your first.'

There was a particularly smug look on her face that no one understood. The other three merely shook their heads and continued with their calorie-laden breakfast. Bee smiled and settled for a second cup of coffee.

Arhan was escorting his team to the back entrance of the Continental Grand and on to the bus parked almost at the pavement as a gaggle of reporters and cameramen followed them like lemmings. Even the *hatta-katta* WWF-type bouncers were not enough to deter this horde intent on getting something from this year's most controversial and talked-about cricket team.

'What are your chances of winning today, sir?' One reporter called out.

'Do you think the toss will affect the outcome of the match?'

'Which position is Prithvi coming in at? Is the mood in the dressing room too depressed for the team to be in a winning mindset?'

Viren stiffened in reaction.

Arhan pressed a reassuring hand to his shoulder. 'Don't listen to them. They're not worth it. You can't let them get into your head. The team needs you,' he finished.

Viren took a deep, controlled breath, straightened his dark blue Team India jacket and stepped on to the bus. The rest of the team followed. No one looked back as strobe flashes exploded and reporters kept yelling questions about team morale and toss decisions and a hundred other things.

Arhan shut the door of the air-conditioned bus with a definitive thump.

It was a relief to get out of the shining noonday sun.

The match was at 4 p.m. Even though, traditionally, opening day matches were played in the second half, the organizers had expected iffy weather when they were deciding the schedule and they didn't want the first match to get washed out. Last night's sudden downpour just proved their point.

His boys, on the other hand, were less than pleased to play in the sweltering sun for the first time in months.

The ride to the Sawai Mansingh Stadium would take about thirty minutes and Arhan intended to make full use of that time to talk his team up and get them in the right frame of mind.

This was a relatively new practice since the head coach usually handheld the players. But Arhan was a lot more hands-on than his predecessors had been, and the coach was too busy cosying up to his newest floozy to bother too much over breach of protocol. Besides, the team enjoyed hanging out with him. Being a has-been cricketer had its perks. 'Everyone have a good breakfast?' Arhan asked once the bus started moving. All of them were talented, deserving of their places in this Indian team and yet . . . they looked dispirited, lacklustre.

Depressed.

'Yes,' they answered in unison.

'Great. Because you can't load up on the calories during lunch since we'll be practising. Getting a feel of the ground. Is that cool?'

No one bothered answering.

Arhan noticed everyone sneaking furtive glances at each other.

After a beat of silence, Karthik Mukesh dared to ask what everyone was thinking. 'AK, what the hell happened to your face?'

Arhan touched his bandaged nose and the accompanying black eye gingerly. He felt homicidal anger at the female who'd played him, then punched him!

It had taken him a considerable amount of 'creative truth-telling' before the hotel's doctor patched him up. Well, creative truth-telling and three two-thousand-rupee notes had done the trick.

And, by God, if he ever saw that woman with the lethal hands, he was calling security first and asking questions later. A smart man learned his lessons the first time around.

'I fell and broke my nose in the bathroom, man. It's embarrassing. Let it go.' He parroted the lie he had peddled to the hotel's doctor.

'You're taking painkillers, right, AK? The doc checked you for everything, didn't he?' Karthik persisted.

'Yes, I am fine.' Arhan smiled and the gesture stretched the skin of his broken nose over the splint. The smile turned into a wince. He touched his nose again and said, 'Nothing hurts more right now than this nose and my ego. If we are done playing doctor-doctor, can we get down to the serious business of winning this match already?'

Instantly, the temperature in the lumbering bus dropped by ten degrees. Each and every player looked out of the window or fiddled with his phone. They had no interest in listening to him anymore.

'Look,' Arhan began quietly. 'I know, okay? Zak's departure is hurting us all. But we can't let it affect our game. The media has already written us off in this tournament. We are the has-beens, the players with broken hearts and morale. We aren't expected to win a single match.'

'We are *not* going to win a single match. We are depressed and underprepared, no matter how much we practice,' the captain said equally quietly. 'I don't understand why they are even making us play, bro. Especially since we all petitioned to be excused from this tournament.'

The other players nodded in agreement and looked accusingly at the assistant coach like they did each time Arhan broached this subject.

Arhan's migraine started acting up again as he recalled the manager and coach's strategy session with the selection committee—the one place he had no voice.

'The boys will rally and pull through.'

'It's a multi-crore broadcast deal. The sponsors will pull out if the defending champs don't play.'

'He was just a boy, *yaar*. What's the big fuss about? He's been dead for months now. Tell them to buck up and move on. How can they still care so much?'

Arhan had wanted to smack all those unfeeling *choots* who didn't get what it meant to be part of a team. How there was no 'I' in 'team'. The current team had been poised on the edge of glory when Zakeer had died unexpectedly. They needed time to recover. Arhan, along with the team's counsellor, had already raised these concerns, but they had shut him down cold.

'Think of all that sponsorship money. Gone. No, no. We can't excuse them from playing. Make it happen, Arhan.' The head of the ICCB had ordered and that had been that.

Short of forfeiting their salaries and their positions, which would kill all their careers, these men were stuck playing the tournament. And not a single one of them was happy about it. Not even the replacement, Prithvi, who was staring into his phone and pretending his presence was completely normal and not the result of another man's death.

'Just do your best, guys,' Arhan said, knowing his words were inadequate. 'I have no pep talk prepared here. Zakeer is dead. Nothing I can say or do will bring him back.'

Everyone flinched at his stark words.

'I am just hoping that we respect his memory and put up a decent fight before getting knocked out of the cup. I don't have a problem if you guys think you can't win under the circumstances, but Zakeer would have hated knowing you all think of yourselves as losers.'

Viren grunted. 'Don't commit emotional *atyaachar* on us, AK. It's not fair.'

Arhan shrugged, feeling the weight of a hundred worlds on his shoulders.

This whole situation was so messed up; he didn't know how to deal with it except to take one step at a time and not think too much. But it wasn't his ass on the line as the teams lined up on the ground and he knew that.

'Life's not fair. Do the best you can. God knows, I want to go back home as much as you guys. Just to get away from the speculation about my nose.' He winked and grinned, not allowing the wince to show. There was enough sorrow and pain on this bus already.

Some men chuckled and looked a little more alive than they had five minutes ago. Arhan understood asking for anything more from them was foolhardy, so he stopped talking and looked out the bus window.

The Sawai Mansingh Stadium has been home to some of the most scintillating victories since its inauguration in 1969. Tonight's opening match of the T20 World Cup was no exception.

The match began with a toss win for Bangladesh, who decided to bat first; a smart decision since this pitch always hardens as the day slips into evening, and chasing is not the best way to win matches in Jaipur.

After a lacklustre practice at the grounds, the Indian cricket team stepped on to the pitch nearly three months after the tragic death of their teammate and vice-captain Zakeer Hussain. Their body language was slow and pitchy, and they conceded far too many runs in the first powerplay.

Minnows Bangladesh took full advantage of India's lethargy and made hay while the sun shone. Their innings score stood at 180–4 after the first 20 overs were bowled.

The team that went back to the dugout once their fielding was done looked small, already defeated. It was not to be.

'Hey, what are you doing?' Harry nudged a muttering Bee as he sat down next to her on the bus that would drive them back to their hotel.

Bee shrugged. 'Writing copy in my head.'

'Don't you carry your laptop in your big *jhola*?' He gestured to the Fendi hobo bag that her cousin had sent for her from New York as a belated birthday present. It even had the original 'F' metal hardware and Fendi stamped on the lining and zips. It was roomy and stylish and Bee felt very grown-up whenever she carried it.

She nudged him back. Hard. 'It's a Fendi. Stop insulting my handbag.'

'God, what a finish!' Dheera sighed as she slid in next to Harry.

The backseats were already filled with other media persons and the driver turned and asked them if he could move it now. They all nodded.

'I was sure India was going to tank this one and I'd be able to go home when they also lost the next two.'

'Where is your patriotism, Dhee?' Bee spoke absently.

She had no particular interest in whether India won or lost. This gig had lost its charm the minute she'd sucker-punched a hot guy on the nose. Now she just wanted to go back home before he found her and filed an FIR.

'Cricket is an unforgiving sport. But did you see Karthik's sweet cover drive in the end? Worthy of Kohli, man,' Sholes said, awed.

They all chuckled and started rehashing the thrilling chase the hosts and defending champions had given Bangladesh after the first 4 wickets had fallen in the opening 2 overs. How Karthik Mukesh, the wicketkeeper, had come in and saved the day, along with rookie Prithvi Narayanan and how their quick-fire 50-run partnership had steadied the sinking ship. India had taken it to the wire with this one and won the match with a boundary off the last ball when 3 runs had been needed.

It was an opening match to die for.

'I hate that asshole AK though. He just took the boys away from the venue and loaded them on to the bus like cattle after the mandatory press con was done. And such a short conference that was,' the guy from *Indian Express* complained. 'Surely, after today's win they would have wanted to talk to us in detail.'

'AK anyway thinks too much of himself, doesn't he?' Harry said.

'Hey!' Dheera jumped in, blowing a bubble with the gum she was chewing. 'Arhan Kapoor is a fine, fine cricketer with an exemplary record, and we should all be so lucky to have him managing this ragtag team. I've heard he rides with the team and even practises every day with them.'

She suddenly had a dreamy expression on her normally droll face. 'Must be how he is so fit.'

'Who are you talking about?' Bee asked curiously. 'Who's Arhan Kapoor?'

'Arhan Kapoor, babe. You saw his bio in the press packet, didn't you?' Dheera prompted.

Bee shook her head. 'I know the stats of the playing squad, thanks to my brother, so I didn't open the damn thing.'

'Go back to your room and break it out,' Dheera advised. 'Arhan is a stud. And an *adarsh beta* too.'

'Hang on! Is he the same Arhan Kapoor who played for Punjab? The guy who was supposed to play for the national team, but then his dad passed away so he went back home to take care of the family's bankrupt business?' Bee asked slowly.

Her brain sorted through all the information that was stored in there thanks to her family.

'Yes. That's him.' Sholes nodded approval. 'He joined as an assistant coach a few months ago. Even guided the team to an overseas series win after Zak's tragedy derailed us.'

'Google him now,' Dheera advised. 'You're going to love him.'

The driver dropped them at the hotel just as a police Jeep pulled up to the entrance.

Bee hopped off the bus, stretching cramped muscles. She whipped out her phone and checked her messages—three from her brother and one from her uncle, all about the match.

She had just brought up the Google app when a man from the front desk hailed her.

Bee walked towards the marble reception counter as the others headed to the elevator bank. She gave them the go-ahead and they filed into the lift.

The wiry young man, whose name tag read 'Dinesh Singh, Desk Manager', looked anxiously at her.

'I'm afraid I have some bad news for you, ma'am.'

Bee's heart sank.

Oh no! Had that man found her? Or was it her folks? Did someone die?

Her head swam with all sorts of dire scenarios. Automatically, she shoved one hand into her skirt pocket and started popping.

Pop. Pop. Pop.

'What?' she asked. 'What is it?'

The desk manager looked startled at the strange noise coming from the woman but answered in a calm voice. 'There's been an incident in your room, Ms Vishwanathan. It looks like a burglary though nothing has been stolen, not even your laptop. But the police would like to talk to you anyway. We're so sorry, ma'am. So very, very sorry.'

Bee continued staring at him in shock while bursting the bubble wrap.

Pop. Pop.

Pop.

'Madamji, how do I spell your name?' the inspector asked.

His English was patchy at best, but he was trying laboriously to sound correct, and she appreciated it, even if she felt clobbered.

Bee answered with a smile. 'It's a very long name, sir. You can just put it down as Bee Vishwanathan.'

Her Hindi was flawless, as flawless as any Mumbaikar's Hindi could be. Her folks might have come from the Coromandel Coast but she considered herself a child of Mumbai.

'No, madamji, it is an FIR. We need full name. It's procedure, you see.'

Bee took a sip of the tepid water she'd been given solicitously and said, 'It's just better if I write it down then, sir. It's . . .' She took a deep breath and mumbled, 'Brighabhujaambaa Vishwanathan.'

She closed her eyes in sheer embarrassment at having to whisper that horrible name out loud. And, as always, she wanted to kill her Paati, her grandma, for sticking her with so many syllables.

'*Madamji,* what?' The man did a double-take as he tried to wrap his head around that mouthful of a name, especially on this pint-sized woman.

'I am petitioning to get it changed. I have sent a notice to the Gazette and everything,' Bee said hurriedly. 'Why don't I write it down for you?' She tried to smile, but it felt fake.

'No, *madamji.*' The inspector shook his head, 'I will do it. You can just spell it for me, yes? Birga . . .'

Dear gods! Yesterday she had turned into a felon and almost been mowed down on the road and today her place had been vandalised. The fates were coming after her with a vengeance. There was just no other explanation for it.

Bee shook her head and spent the next five minutes getting her name right. The interview proceeded smoothly thereafter.

The inspector, Vikram Singh, was a portly *paan*-chewing version of Inspector Clouseau. Other than the fact that the *chaw-chaw-chaw* of his jaws working non-stop pounded into her head like machine-gun fire, he had been quite helpful ever since he'd taken her to the manager's office, sat her down and explained to her the facts, such as they were.

Fact one, someone had broken into her room and turned it upside down.

Fact two, this was a common occurrence in low-end hotels where security was not as tight as it should be.

Fact three, the most important, nothing of value had been stolen. Even her expensive laptop had been left untouched.

Twenty minutes later, Bee was still reeling from the inspector's advice to not file an FIR because, fact four, it was a clear case of vandalism— probably by a former employee—and not robbery because nothing was stolen. There were no CCTV cameras, and the desk manager swore on Amba Mata that he did not see anyone come in. Plus, and this clinched the deal for the inspector, her bathroom window, which faced the street, was broken.

The inspector had helpfully offered to get her an upgrade to a suite since the hotel did not want any negative publicity from the *mediawale*.

It was a win-win for them all, according to Inspector Vikram Singh as he asked her to think it over before calling for his flunky. He also gave her his card with his personal phone number so she could call him for any updates, any time.

And then he left, expressing his sympathies for her tragic situation.

Bee took a deep breath, longing for her trusty bubble wrap, except she'd run out of bubbles while talking to the desk manager. She really needed to carry more of it around. But her anger-anxiety issues had only escalated since she'd arrived at this blasted tournament and it was just day one!

Bee sat in the air-conditioned office letting Dinesh Singh's words wash over her as he pleaded with her to not report him to corporate. He added that he would upgrade her to their best suite, free of cost, and have all her meals comped at the restaurant. Bee smiled weakly and made appropriate responses while she tried to process what exactly had happened.

Finally, she exited the manager's office and bumped into Dheera, who was pacing the lobby anxiously, looking for her.

'Babe.' Dheera hugged her tight, bending almost in half. 'I have been dying to see you, but those fucks at the front desk refused to let me in. "Police matter," they claimed. What the hell happened? Are you okay?'

Bee sighed and hugged her back; Dheera's genuine concern helped ease some of the cacophony of sound and confusion in her head.

'I am fine. My room has been vandalised. Nothing was stolen apparently, not even my laptop. I guess I should consider myself lucky.' She couldn't help the bitterness from leaking out. Her room had been destroyed. Someone had rifled through her stuff, either with deliberate malice or for no reason whatsoever.

But, apparently, it was no big deal because nothing was stolen!

'Yeah, you should!' Dheera exclaimed. 'Imagine if you'd been there when the bastard had broken in.' She shuddered. 'No questions about it. You're going to stay with me from now on. Okay? We can bunk together.'

Bee smiled, though it felt a bit hollow. 'I've been offered a suite by the hotel. And all meals comped.'

Dheera chuckled. 'That's great. Then I'll move in with you. I just don't want you to be alone anymore.'

Bee shrugged. 'We'll figure something out.'

'Of course, we will. We're not going to let anything happen to you. You need to call Satyarth and give him the lowdown. And your parents.' Dheera frowned. 'Have you talked to them?'

Bee shook her head. 'I am not calling Appa. He'll just break out my *janam kundli* and tell me that my *Mangal* is in retrograde, so it's causing this recent rash of misfortune. As for Satyarth . . .' She heaved a sigh, thinking of her immediate boss. 'I'll call him soon. Just not now.'

'Of course, darling. Take your time.' Dheera soothed her. 'You need a stiff drink first. The boys are waiting at the bar. And hey,' her eyes brightened in fierce mother-hen mode, 'we'll get free drinks with your new celeb status.'

Bee laughed at that. It didn't feel so unreal now. 'Why don't you join them? Put everything on my tab. I'll come soon.'

'But—'

'Dhee, I'm not upset or anything,' she said gently. 'I just want to be alone for a while. Process everything. I'll be there soon, I promise.'

Dheera hugged her again. 'No moping or popping, okay?'

'Yes, boss.'

Bee had no destination in mind when she started walking down the main road.

Jaipur, like most overcrowded cities in India, was loud and colourful and had a plethora of sounds and smells that assaulted even the most jaded traveller. It wasn't exactly on the cleaner side, but there was a certain old-world charm to it, left over from when the Rajputs ruled this princely state with fierce loyalty. The pink marble buildings were not visible in the night light, but the hawkers selling their wares on the pavements offered a strange comfort to her.

Life remained the same even when everything about it had changed. She honestly had no reaction except bewilderment and sharp anger towards the vandal who'd destroyed her room for no apparent reason.

She did not have any enemies; she was neither that popular nor that good a journalist. And after last night's bizarre events, she was almost exhausted on the mental front.

Yet . . .

A part of her understood that this wasn't some random, senseless act of violence, no matter how much the local police wanted her to believe otherwise. But then what possible grudge would someone have against her?

She was no one.

Just a poorly paid mouthpiece of press releases and half-facts at a corporate-run news website.

Like all the other 'journalists' here.

It was inexplicable and yet it had happened.

Bee gripped the hair at her temples in frustration.

When she looked up from where she had been standing, morosely kicking tin cans and watching them roll, she realized she was back in front of the Continental Grand. The Indian cricket team was inside, probably celebrating the day's victory.

Bee stood up straighter, squared her shoulders and walked in, channelling her inner badass. She was going to turn this terrible day around. She was going to get that candid interview she so desperately wanted. She was going to prove to herself that she belonged here, at this tournament, on the press corps.

Her phone buzzed. Amma. She ignored the call and nonchalantly climbed the pink marble steps. When she'd been assigned to cover the Mantralaya for two months, she'd learned that acting confident got her inside the government building more often than flashing her press card.

So she did just that.

The snappily dressed *durbaan* gave her a salute and let her in. She smiled back and said, 'Good evening.'

The mezzanine was a hive of activity. Tourists and team staff were scurrying into restaurants and on to elevators while the hotel staff helped them. The gorgeous lavender suede sectional beckoned her. Bee wanted to lay her tired aching head on it and snooze her day away.

Except she was on a mission right now.

She approached the front desk and located a clone, albeit a refined version, of Dinesh from her own hotel. Hitesh was also young and wiry. He also craned his neck and stared down her low-cut T-shirt.

'Hello,' Bee leaned against the desk, pressing her chest to the edge so that the clone's eyes went there automatically. It was a small price to pay for information. 'I am looking for Viren Kaul's room. There is a parcel for him from my employer. Can I get his room number, please?'

She smiled, pouting a little and batting her lashes in what Dheera called the 'Katrina Move'. The effect was to make her eyes appear wide and innocent while drawing attention to the berry juiciness of her lips. Bee cursed herself for not having put on lip-gloss before coming in.

'It is against hotel policy to give out guests' information to anyone, ma'am.' Hitesh looked exactly where she wanted him to look. 'But you can leave your parcel here and we can send it up to Kaul sir's room. That should be fine?'

Bee's smile turned into a scowl of distress, splitting the tender skin of her chapped lips. 'Yes, that would be totally fine. Except I am supposed to take the receipt of delivery from Kaul sir or my boss will kill me. It's an extremely fragile *Ganpati ki moorti* that has been blessed by Mahadev Baba.' She leaned in some more. 'For good luck, you know. My boss is Kaul sir's . . . aunt's cousin. And Kaul sir is expecting it today.'

Hitesh looked conflicted. Bee knew instinctively that he was cricket-crazy too and wanted India to win; she had rarely met an Indian man who wasn't. She could see the indecision shimmering in his eyes. But he had a job to do.

She just hoped his insane desire to be the hero to save India in the World Cup would win over this minor fireable offence at the workplace.

'I can understand, ma'am, but—'

'What the hell are you doing here?' An unamused, cold male voice snapped behind her.

Bee whirled around and looked at the devil with the nose guard.

Shit!

Her day had just gone from bad to *barbaad*.

7

Arhan could not believe this woman's nerve. She was back at the scene of her crime.

He had to hand it to her though. To show her face around here, especially after punching him and breaking his nose, showed chutzpah, something most people didn't have.

He grabbed her by the elbow and shuffled her to an empty corridor behind the reception counter, which led to the unused business centre. To her credit, she followed him quietly without any fuss, although there was a certain fighting light in her eyes.

He moved out of punching range while still looming in front of her, which was easy since she was a tiny thing really. He could put her in his pocket and carry her around. But, somehow, she had managed to punch him!

Arhan growled. 'Explain yourself. Fast Before I actually file an FIR this time.'

Bee smiled sweetly and dug into her roomy bag before holding up the inspector's business card. 'Shall I dial or do you want to do the honours?'

His eyes narrowed and she was sure he would strike her. He looked murderous enough to do so.

Bee braced herself against the wall behind her. The marble felt cold on her back while her 'victim' blasted her with his body heat. She was clearly depraved because she found his stubbly, stubborn-jawed, murderous face hot!

Bee stood straighter while Arhan plucked the card with two fingers and examined it. Then, he shot a superior grin at her and asked, 'You know everyone, I'll give you that. Is he one of yours?'

'One of my—' Bee gritted her teeth and took a deep breath before she did something unthinkable. Like, break his broken nose again. 'Let me clarify this, once and for all. I am not a groupie or a hooker. Even if I were, you could not afford me.'

Surprisingly, he grinned. A full-out stretching of his facial muscles, which gave him an air of such boyish innocence. Bee gaped involuntarily at the transformation.

'You never know, madam. I could afford you if I wanted to.' Arhan leaned in even closer. 'I am loaded after all.'

'I am going to scream if you don't back off,' Bee said through gritted teeth.

He moved his face an inch away. Somehow, it just made him seem closer than ever. To an onlooker, the two of them must have looked like a couple having an intimate moment.

It was hot and annoying at the same time.

'You could try,' he said nonchalantly. 'Then you'd have to explain why I am bothering you in the first place. Which would involve me telling everyone and their mother how you accosted me in my room while I was naked. Do you really want me to tell everyone you're a starstruck groupie?' The question was casually posed while his damned eyes laughed at her.

Her eyes flashed with unholy fire. 'I am *not*—'

'I know. But then who are you? And why are you so interested in Viren?' He seemed genuinely puzzled now.

'I am a journalist,' Bee answered stiffly, her skin tingling from where he was still touching her arm. She was furious because she loved it. 'I am covering the cup for Krikket-365. I just want five minutes with the captain.'

'You're a reporter.' His disgust was clear in the way he spat out the word 'reporter'. 'That's worse than being a groupie.'

He stepped back from her, folding ripped arms over his chest. He looked her up and down, from the frizzy mess of her hair to her pink kurti with a red flower at the cleavage. She wore her favourite paisley long skirt with trusty Kolhapuris, perfect for style and comfort.

'And you dress like neither.' The look in his eyes was derogatory to the extreme.

Bee instinctively looked down at her clothes. It was her boho-chic look and she hated that he made her feel cheap and dowdy.

She rolled her eyes and snatched the inspector's card away from him, not wanting to give him the opportunity to make good on his threat.

'Thanks for the fashion tip.' She shoved the card into her bag. 'Clearly, you've spent enough time with groupies to know how they dress. Good luck with that, by the way. Wear an umbrella next time. You never know what you'll catch nowadays. Goodbye.'

He hauled her back to the wall, his fingers biting into her arm. A sharp gasp escaped her as she tried to struggle away from him.

'What the hell? You can't touch me without my consent.'

'But you can say whatever insulting thing that comes to your mind without needing mine?' he observed. 'Isn't that right?'

Her eyes widened in real distress.

Even though he was dressed casually—in his lucky ripped jeans and Wankhede Boys sweatshirt that Sachin had gifted him ages ago —Arhan knew he must look menacing. He hadn't shaved so his beard was acting up big time. Plus between the black eye, the nose guard and the looming, she was bound to think he meant her bodily harm.

He felt the slightest spurt of admiration because she stood her ground even so. He wanted to move away and apologise because his mother had raised him right and he really did not make it a practice to scare provocative, insulting reporters.

'You're not as bad as you're pretending to be right now.' Her strained voice quavered at the very end, belying the toughness she was trying so hard to portray.

Arhan smiled. There was actual menace in that smile. His eyes were blank, dangerous, but he stepped away from her because he really was not that person. 'I am worse, Miss Journalist. Stay away from my boys. They will not be fodder for your gossip rag.'

'It's Krikket-365,' she hissed. 'The second-largest sports news website in the country with a reach that rivals most TV news channels. It's not a gossip rag.'

Arhan shrugged, nonchalant.

Something he said must have struck her right then. 'Hold on,' she said. '*Your* boys? Do you know the Indian cricket team? Are you staff? Management?'

Before he could answer, a female voice wafted over to where they were standing. 'Arhan *beta,* could you tell these nice people at the front desk that I don't want a suite? I am quite all right with the double room they've allotted me.'

Bee's head whipped to the newcomer. If she had to describe her in one word, it would be 'regal'.

From the top of her flawlessly coiffed, perfectly coloured hair, the pearls-and-diamond choker gracing her neck and the folds of her designer chiffon sari down to the gold rings glittering on her toes, she looked like a gracious, albeit slightly bemused, queen.

Bee gasped as recognition hit her. She instantly bowed her head. 'Maharani, you're gorgeous!'

'Thank you, my dear,' the Maharani replied with a smile. 'Although, the title's no longer legally allowed.'

Arhan muttered something under his breath that sounded suspiciously like 'kiss ass' as he walked forward, dragging Bee along with him.

Her head was reeling again.

So *this* was Arhan Kapoor? Dheera's stud, Sholes' asshole?

The asshole stud bent down and enveloped the petite woman in a warm embrace. 'It's wonderful to see you, Ranisa. We weren't sure if you would make it.'

'You all invited me so warmly. How could I refuse?'

Ranisa gestured to the middle-aged rotund gentleman standing solicitously next to her. He had ridiculous sideburns and Bee noticed instantly that he was the chairman of the ICCB, Arhan's boss.

'Sir.' Arhan tipped his head in deference to Rajiv Shastri's august presence.

'Arhan, good game tonight. Good game,' the man boomed out. 'Clearly, your presence in the dressing room is making a lot of difference. *Badhiya hai!*'

'They are an outstanding lot, sir. It's got nothing to do with me,' Arhan said modestly.

'This is the best thing about you, Arhan,' the Maharani said. 'You're so humble. Now, be a dear and help out with this suite situation. Rajivji here is insisting on keeping me in style.'

'You are style-worthy, Ranisa.' Arhan kissed the tips of her fingers and Bee watched the regal old lady's eyes shine. 'Also we need your entourage to be in one place with you, yes?'

'My dear, I have come all alone. The estate requires all hands on deck at the moment. So it's just me this time.'

'Still, Rani sahiba,' Rajiv interjected. 'We can't put you up in a double room like an ordinary commoner, could we? How would that look in the media?'

Bee saw Arhan give her a covert glance.

'Nonsense, Rajivji. I am as ordinary as any of you,' the Maharani said sweetly. 'Don't lump me in with royalty, will you?'

The chairman and Arhan gave the Maharani identical smiles, peasant to royalty, and then Rajiv moved away, attending a call on his phone.

Ranisa smiled politely at the young woman hovering just behind Arhan, looking avidly at them.

'Now who is this pretty lady you were canoodling with in dark corners, Arhan?' She chuckled, a lovely, lilting sound.

'I wasn't canoodling—'

Bee cut short his answer by extending her hand and introducing herself. 'Hello, I'm Bee Vishwanathan. A reporter for Krikket-365. I'm covering the World Cup for my website. It's a pleasure meeting you, Your Highness.' Arhan's mouth tightened as Bee added defiantly, 'Considering the day I've had.'

'I'm Kalavati Devi Chauhan from Jaigarh, my dear. Not Your Highness.' Kalavati Devi shook her hand, a brisk shake that was somehow innately feminine. 'I do hope everything is all right with you?'

Unexpectedly, tears filled Bee's eyes. She was really overwhelmed by the events of the past two days. She gamely swallowed the hot ball in her throat and said, 'It's nothing. I'll get going now. It was amazing to meet you.'

'Nonsense, my dear. You clearly look rattled. Tell me, Arhan, where are your manners? This young lady is upset and you're skulking in a corner with her.'

Arhan bowed his head, but Bee knew it was an empty gesture.

Kalavati Devi extended an unwrinkled hand, tennis bracelet glittering, and said, '*Chalo*, Bee. Have a cup of tea and tell me everything.'

And so it was that Bee found herself having tea with a queen half an hour later.

8

Arhan had never before seen ingenuity of this level in action.

Bee Vishwanathan, apparently a reporter for Krikket-365, was a revelation.

Just yesterday, she'd snuck into his room, insulted him and punched him hard enough to break his nose. Today, she'd charmed the hotel's duty manager into almost letting her meet Viren with that bullshit story about the Ganpati statue.

And now she had somehow managed to finagle an invitation to tea with a queen!

Did nothing faze this woman or was she just plain lucky?

And what the fuck kind of name was Bee Vishwanathan anyway?

Arhan sipped his rapidly cooling Oolong, with two sugars, lots of milk and a dash of cream, and watched Ranisa hold court.

'I was invited by the cricket board to be an unofficial part of this cup,' Maharani Kalavati said in response to Bee's question. 'They thought I'd add a touch of royal glamour to the proceedings, I guess. It seemed like a good idea to get away from the day-to-day running of the estate and so here I am imposing my old lady presence on these young lads.'

Bee laughed or rather she bellowed. The wickedly sharp sound registered in Arhan's brain as yet another negative about her.

She tucked her hair behind her ear. 'I don't think anyone will dare call you old or think you were imposing yourself anywhere, Your Majesty. Your presence is too powerful for that.' She crossed her legs nervously and gulped the tea down. 'Shit, that's hot!' Her eyes rounded in dismay. 'Oh no. I'm sorry for cursing, Your Majesty.'

'It's okay, my dear.' Ranisa laughed, a low mellifluous sound. Nothing like Bee's guffaw.

Bee uncrossed her legs because she seemed to realise one did not do that in front of royalty either. She tucked one ankle behind the other just like the Maharani.

Arhan watched her cross and uncross her legs and felt a grin tug at his lips. She might be a ruthless news vulture out for the next big story but she was certainly entertaining.

Kalavati said, 'When I first married into Maha Kunwar Sahab's family, I was given an etiquette training course for about three months before they even let me out of the palace. Propriety was drummed into my brain. Appearances are everything, you see.' She chuckled at the fond memory now, comfortable sharing inconsequential confidences with a total stranger. 'I remember my mother-in-law, the Maharanisa, would ask me to parade in her bedchamber with *War and Peace* on my head as I walked in four-inch heels, back arched, posture straight.'

'She sounds like a piece of work.' Bee sipped her tea. And then, as her remark registered, looked horrified. 'I deeply apologise, Your Majesty. I did not mean to insult your family.'

'It's quite all right, my dear,' Kalavati said. 'She was an old crone intent on causing trouble in her son's marriage, but . . . she's gone now and I am still here.' There was a battle-hardened glint in the grande dame's otherwise mellow brown eyes. 'You still have not told me about the terrible day you've been having.'

'There's nothing to tell, Your Majesty. I spoke without thinking.'

'It's true,' Arhan chimed in. 'She has no filter.'

Kalavati looked at him calmly. 'As a queen who has always had to pause and reflect before opening her mouth, I envy Bee her ease of thought. There is nothing wrong in saying what's on your mind. After all, honesty is the best policy, isn't it?'

'Yes, Mr Kapoor. Isn't honesty the best policy?' Bee asked sweetly, sipping tea, with her pinkie sticking out, just like a real lady.

'I agree that the truth is always better than lies,' he answered. 'But sometimes, you need to know when not to open your mouth and vomit it all out.'

'Now that I cannot disagree with,' Kalavati murmured. 'Appearances are everything.'

Bee wisely did not argue with her.

Arhan stood up. 'Well, as entertaining as it has been catching up with you ladies, I am afraid duty calls. I need to watch post-game tape and make notes.'

'Of the match?' Bee couldn't stop her curiosity from shining through.

Arhan chose to ignore her remark and instead inclined his head, nodded at them and left.

'Such a beautiful boy,' said Kalavati as she watched Arhan leave. 'So well-mannered and responsible. He would make such a good son-in-law.'

Bee held her snort in. The man jumped to conclusions based on appearances and had the worst possible opinion of strangers. He was neither well-mannered nor responsible. But who was she to contradict a queen?

'I am sure, Your Majesty,' she said.

Kalavati sighed and placed her cup back on the saucer, the edges aligning with each other in perfect symmetry. 'I wish life worked smoothly on royal command. But you are digressing from your story again. Do tell me, my dear,' she invited.

And since this time it was more a command than a request, Bee was forced to narrate the whole sorry saga of her room being vandalised and the cops refusing to do much about it.

'The good thing is I've been upgraded to a suite at the hotel,' she concluded. 'My friend Dheera is insisting on staying with me so I don't have to worry about being mugged in the dark. The bad news is that I have to call my boss and my parents and tell them about this incident. They are not going to like it.'

Bee toyed with the rim of her cup, her finger making a 'zing' sound against the delicate china. 'It's a small thing, of course, but I was scared for a minute. I mean, vandalism in broad daylight. How is a woman supposed to feel safe?'

The Maharani reached over and gave her wrist a firm squeeze.

'I have a solution to your particular problem. Why don't you stay with me?'

Bee's mouth dropped open in shock. 'I beg your pardon?'

'You could stay with me,' Kalavati repeated delicately. 'I've left my companion at home so I need someone to engage with while we travel from city to city for this tournament. I think you'll do marvellously well at that.'

'This is a very kind offer, Your Majesty, but I couldn't possibly stay with you,' Bee said automatically.

'Why not?'

She sighed, trying to be logical and polite. 'It's not just me who is unsafe, right? Today it was my room, tomorrow it could be someone else's. We don't know what the burglar, or whoever, was after. There are other female reporters who could be in danger too.'

She wanted to add how it sucked that this was the state of their country, but held her tongue.

See, I do have a filter, Mr Kapoor, she thought smugly before continuing, 'Plus, it smacks of nepotism of the highest levels. Lastly, it's just not right.'

The Maharani shrugged. 'Why is it not right?'

'Because . . .' Bee struggled to find a polite way to reject a queen.

'If you need any more incentive, I am invited to dinner with the players regularly. You can talk to them as much as you want.' Kalavati smiled genially as if she helped total strangers every day.

'The ICCB won't agree to it. Especially Arhan Kapoor.' Bee grasped at straws. 'None of the players will want to talk to me either. Breaking the media gag order is a fireable offence.'

Does the queen realise what she is offering me? Bee wondered. A chance to mingle with the very people she needed to mingle with, in an informal setting. An opportunity to observe them, talk to them and use it all to write brilliant copy. She could dig herself out of the black hole that was Patil-gate. The offer was so unbearably tempting. She was just afraid of the invisible catch.

'Other teams are staying here too, you know,' Kalavati said. 'You could write about them from an insider's perspective. Don't they have a term for reporters who get to stay with an army platoon during wartime?'

'Embeds,' Bee supplied. 'It's what they call reporters who get to report from within a unit.'

How exactly could she ask royalty where the *kala* was in the tempting *dal* that she was serving so generously without sounding offensive and insulting? Especially since the woman had been nothing but kind and gracious.

'Then that's what you'll be. Embedded with me. And you'll be safer here than you would ever be in a second-rate hotel.'

'Can I think about it? It's not fair for me to slide into five-star luxury while the others suffer in a hotel with terrible plumbing,' Bee said and then clapped a hand on her mouth. Oh god! She'd just mentioned plumbing. The Maharani was surely going to take offence at that!

The Maharani chuckled. 'I'd help out everyone if I could, Bee. But for now I hope you will accept an old woman's offer of companionship. This is the first time I have been all alone in years.'

Bee could feel her reservations melting. The Maharani sounded so sincere. Who was she to deny a lonely old woman some companionship?

She'd be a fool to pass it up. And Brighabhujaambaa Vishwanathan was no fool. She was pragmatic and ambitious enough to recognise the opportunity staring her in the face—exclusive insider access to the tournament.

'When you put it that way,' Bee said slowly, 'I'd be honoured to accept your offer of companionship, Your Majesty.'

The Maharani smiled, kind as ever. 'Please call me Ranisa. I have a feeling this is going to be an exciting time for all of us. Now let us tell Arhan and his people the good news before he downgrades me from the suite to the double room. I am sure you will want your privacy. He can send someone to sort things out back at your hotel.'

And that, Bee thought darkly, *was the catch—close proximity to a six-foot hunk of a surly brute who thought being a reporter was worse than being a hooker.*

—•◆ ◆•—

'So explain this to me again,' Dheera said as she helped Bee stuff clothes into her ruined duffel bag. 'How the hell did you manage to get an invitation to live with a freaking queen when yesterday you told me that the hotel wouldn't even let you on to its premises?'

Bee surveyed the clothes, bedding and toiletries tossed on the floor of her hotel room in dismay. It looked as if a tsunami had hit, upending everything.

She shrugged. 'I don't know. One minute, I was arguing with that *man* and the next instant the queen was inviting me to tea with her and telling me about her soap opera-style mother-in-law. It was . . . surreal,' she finished.

'Man?' Dheera's frown prompted her to elaborate.

'Arhan Kapoor. Your stud. He is horrible by the way.' Bee wrinkled her nose in displeasure.

Dheera's frown turned into a glare. 'Don't talk crap about AK, Bee, unless you want to be lynched by a mob of adoring women. We all love him. He is hero material.'

Bee rolled her eyes as she shoved shampoo and conditioner into her toiletries bag. She had no idea what anyone would want with the Herbal Essences conditioner that she'd bought on sale from the local beauty store. Trying to find the logic behind the vandalism was depressing. She was secretly glad she was getting out of here.

'The man needs someone in his corner,' continued Dheera.

Bee remembered, with unnerving clarity, how he had backed *her* into a corner and loomed over her like she was some wench on a pirate ship. All he'd needed was an eye patch and a mole on his tanned cheek to complete the image of a ravaging buccaneer.

'Why are you panting?' Dheera asked her.

'What?' Bee focused her attention back on Dheera. 'I wasn't panting, I was letting out an angry breath. That man is insufferable, Dhee. I don't know what you see in him. He was grinning like a madman as he watched me babble on to the queen.'

'I find that hard to believe. Arhan is known for always being kind and polite. You must have done something to set him off,' Dheera declared.

'Blame the woman, won't you?' Bee surveyed the messed up sheets and the table lamp smashed to smithereens next to her untouched laptop bag. A shiver of acute revulsion crawled through her.

Why would someone do this to her?

'I am not blaming you, babe.' Dheera gave her a half hug. 'I am actually glad you're getting out of here. Plus I still get to keep your suite. There are rumours of a bathtub and a heated towel rack in there. And a bed that's like a cloud. This place, however, gives me the creeps.' Even indefatigable Dheera shuddered as she looked around.

Bee bit her lip, placing her laptop bag on her shoulder while Dheera took the duffel and they walked out of the room. 'I wish I could get you in there with me too. I don't like thinking of you, the only other woman reporter, being alone in this horrible hotel. It's extremely unsafe.'

'Don't worry about me, honey,' Dheera reassured her. 'I have Harry and Sholes to guard me. They've agreed to crash in the suite with me. I am sure any thief would think twice before attempting to take on all three of us.'

Bee stepped out of the room and locked it firmly behind her. Outside stood Harry and Sholes, looking worried and, for the world, like two stocky but fierce big brothers who would beat up anyone for their little sister.

'You're okay?' Harry asked as he took the bags from them.

Bee would have normally protested but it felt nice to be taken care of, just for a minute.

'Yes, boss. I'm completely okay.' Bee leaned on him and Sholes, who was scrolling on his phone now that he'd ascertained Bee was fine. Sholes gave her an absent pat on her arm and continued scrolling.

Harry, on the other hand, was more concerned. 'I think you should stay with us. Sholes and I will keep you and Dheera safe, won't we, bro?'

'What?' Sholes looked up. 'Oh, yeah. Absolutely. Guard you with our lives.'

Bee laughed while Dheera glared at him. 'Say that again with a little conviction, will you? Now I'm afraid to have you as my roommate.'

Sholes gave her the middle finger and Dheera responded with a sharp jab to his potbelly.

He yelped and glared back at her.

Bee sighed and said, 'I am going to miss hanging out with you clowns. Come over for lunch every day. And don't forget about me, okay?'

'You're just staying in a different hotel, sweetie,' Dheera reassured her. 'Not moving to Mars. I'll see you tomorrow for breakfast at the grounds.'

'Yes, absolutely.'

They'd reached the parking lot where a luxury car with the hotel insignia waited for Bee, engine idling. The driver helped Harry stow her meagre luggage, including her 'I'm Bringing Sexy Back' backpack, in the boot.

Then Bee squared her shoulders and gave Dheera one last hug.

'Play nice with the team and get the story of your life out of this,' Dheera spoke low in her ear.

'I *will* get the story of my life out of this,' Bee promised.

Bee drove away from her friends feeling oddly abandoned, even though she was the one choosing to move away.

9

The Continental Grand lived up to its reputation of keeping its guests in the lap of luxury. Bee's room in the cymbidium suite she was sharing with Maharani Kalavati Devi of Jaigarh was unreal, to say the least. She had seen many TV shows where the bedrooms had miles of curtains and a bed that looked like heaven and a bathroom that was actual heaven but even in her wildest imaginings she had never thought she'd live in one.

When Bee had checked in, the queen was already in her room, taking a siesta before dinner.

Bee didn't know the protocol for entering a royal's bedchamber. Should she knock, curtsy and then announce herself or was it the other way round, she wondered as she watched the bellboy stow her hot purple backpack in an ornate marble armoire. The bag, along with the rest of her luggage, looked incongruous in these opulent surroundings.

The thought grounded her.

She tipped the bellman fifty rupees and he smiled, saluted, bowed and left.

Bee unzipped the backpack and removed her laptop. She switched it on and immediately connected to the hotel Wi-Fi. The suite came with unlimited free internet.

First, she typed a quick email to her employers explaining her changed circumstances, emphasising the embedding status. Then she called Satyarth.

With a little bit of creative truth telling, which included avoiding any mention of how she had punched the assistant coach and broken his nose, she was able to convince her immediate boss to let her focus more on the day-to-day lives of the players during the tournament rather than merely reporting on the matches. Finally they decided that unless something super-exciting happened, they would use the press releases for match commentary while Bee focused on in-depth columns of her experience on- and off-field with Team India.

Her talk with her boss was a cakewalk compared to the next conversation she needed to have. Her family.

Deciding to bite the bullet at once, she texted her brother Aggy to come online so they could all video chat before she had to go down for dinner.

Her brother replied with a thumbs up and 'C U in 15'.

Bee quickly changed into comfy clothes—yoga pants that flapped around the knees and a ratty oversized T-shirt—and was typing up her match notes when the familiar sound of an incoming video call rang in the room.

'Here goes nothing, Bee,' she muttered as she hit Accept Call and waited for her family to appear.

Back home, Amma, Appa and Aggy crowded around the little screen on the netbook, the connection surprisingly strong once it settled.

Bee felt a wave of such intense love that tears pricked her eyes.

'Hey, guys,' she said.

'Bee, we were so worried! You didn't answer your dad's post-match texts. You know how he gets if he doesn't talk to his cricket expert,' Amma chided.

'Yeah, I know, Amma. I was just caught up in a work situation,' Bee said.

'This does not look like your room at the Savoy,' Aggy piped up.

Saddled with Aghora Sarma Vishwanathan—her family was batshit when it came to picking out names—her brother had gone out of his way to avoid the family legacy. His mohawked hair was blonde at the tips and he had a plastic plug in each ear. In the first year of his doctorate at Mumbai University, Aggy Vishwanathan looked every bit the wacko genius Bee had always known her little brother to be.

Bee hesitated for a second and then plunged ahead with the truth. 'I don't want anyone to worry but there was a small incident and I had to shift hotels.'

Three horrified faces stared back at her from the laptop screen. Then the barrage began.

'What happened?' Appa asked with his customary brusqueness.

'Are you all right? Were you assaulted, *kanna*?' Amma almost shrieked. 'I told you, you needed to take pepper spray, but you said,

"No, no, it's too expensive. I'll buy it with next month's salary." Now see what's happened!'

'Bee, what's up?' Aggy, the calmest of the lot, asked. 'You seem okay. And this room looks like a freaking palace. Did you get kidnapped by a Rajput or something?' He even winked to let her know he was cooler than their folks.

Aggy had been by her side through everything—bad breakups, catfights, Patil-gate. Once, they had snuck out to smoke pot on the building terrace and even had a terrible tongue-piercing adventure together. He was actually pretty cool.

'*Pesaama iru*, Aggy! I mean it, shut up,' Appa said firmly. He turned to the screen. 'Start talking. Now, young lady.'

Since it was his I-mean-business voice, Bee started talking. She recounted the adventures of the past day and a half with as little drama as possible while her family ran the gamut of expressions as they listened—from shock and anger to dismay and fear, followed by anger again and severe concern.

'Then the Maharani invited me to stay with her in her suite and it means I am kind of embedded with the team. You know, like war correspondents who get to report from within a unit. I get to report from the centre of the action, which is great for my column. So you can see that everything's worked out okay,' Bee concluded brightly.

'You're coming home right now. No questions asked,' Amma said firmly.

Shanti Vishwanathan wasn't your typical, garden-variety Indian mom. She had let her daughter make truly awful decisions, trusting in her capacity to fix things to carry her through. She had supported her, encouraged her and, in every sense, been the perfect mom a woman could ask for.

So when she ordered her to do something, Bee found it hard to say no.

'Your Amma is right, Bee,' Vishwanathan Govind, her Appa, said. 'I warned you that this trip was not coming at the right time for you. *Guru* is acting up in your career house and that is never good. You should have stayed home and—'

Bee rolled her eyes. 'Appa, give it a rest. I don't believe in that horoscope crap and you know it.'

Bee looked straight at her mom. She had never felt the need to have many friends growing up because she'd had Aggy and her mom. They were a unit. And it was better than any school or college bond. So she addressed her mom with all the love she had for her.

'I know you're worried, Amma. I understand that. I am being extremely careful. I can't help it if some random idiot decided to go mental in my room. How is that my fault?'

'You just told us you were climbing trees in the middle of the night while it was raining. You could have fallen and hurt your back. And you broke into some stranger's hotel room!' Amma started ticking off all the high points one by one. 'What if he hadn't been a gentleman? What if he had attacked you? What if you didn't have your bubble wrap with you and you'd had a meltdown right in front of that nice man? Why don't you *think* before you act, Bee?' Shanti demanded.

All logical questions that she had no answers for except murmuring, 'Amma . . .'

'You know things are serious when I say they are, right?' Aggy said.

Bee turned an exasperated eye on him. 'Not you too, Aggy!'

'Yeah,' he said. 'Me too. Arhan is a decent guy. We all know that about him. Viren, not so much, which you would know if you bothered reading the papers once in a while! Worst. Journalist. EVER!' Aggy punctuated.

'Hey, I read,' Bee protested. 'I just don't read the one-sided fear-mongering trash that passes for news nowadays.'

'Whatever. I also think it is best you came back. I'm sure Satyarth would not have a problem with that, considering the traumatic experience you've just had.'

Aggy was more stubborn than the Nandi bull when he had to be. He was also fiercely protective of his sister.

'No.' Bee shook her head. 'I am not blowing up my one chance to make a mark at this job. Not after what happened with the politician.' She was sure of nothing else but that.

'I am safe, you guys. The only reason I even told you anything is because I didn't want Dhee or someone else accidentally spilling the beans. All of you can be so melodramatic. I was just trying to be honest with you. But I am not coming back.'

'I could write an email to Satyarth,' Vishwanathan said grimly. 'He's your boss, isn't he?'

Bee was horrified. 'You wouldn't, Appa!'

Of course, he would.

He'd done exactly that when she'd been interning at a PR agency while finishing her bachelor's. The whole office had a great time teasing her about her dad and his email stating how he was concerned about his daughter's health and safety because she was working all hours of the night.

Needless to say, the management had allowed her to go home at a reasonable time after that. But for the duration of the internship, she was stuck with the moniker Daddy's Little Girl. It was one of the reasons she hadn't pursued a career in PR. The humiliation had taken away the charm.

Now too he grumbled when she stayed out late, but at twenty-nine, there wasn't much he could do to make her stop.

'Of course, I will. In fact, I think I will just call him up and give him a piece of my mind right away.'

'Appa, you'll get me fired,' Bee said, desperate.

She had forgotten how crazily overprotective her family was. They were normal parents, usually, but when they started interfering with her job, all appreciation went out the window.

'Maybe you can quit and come back,' Amma suggested.

Bee gasped out loud. 'Amma! You did *not* just say that.'

Unexpectedly, Shanti touched the netbook screen and said in a quivering voice, 'You're my *kanna*. My little girl. I worry about you. Of course, I will say it if I think your life is in danger.'

Bee sighed. 'Dammit, Amma. It's not fair when you start crying. Trust me, I am fine. Promise.'

'Brigha—' her dad began.

Bee snapped. 'My name is not Brigha anymore. And, before you say anything else, I know you called yourself Vish Govind when you were at work, which was a smart move, career-wise. I cannot be Brigha, so I am changing my name.'

'You can call yourself whatever you want but you will always be my Brigha. And you will listen to your mother and come back home right this instant.'

Bee set her lips in a mutinous line, mirroring his posture and expression.

'No, Appa.'

'Brigha—' The light of battle was clear in Vishwanathan's eyes, the very eyes he'd passed on to his headstrong and bewildering daughter.

'I am staying here, covering this damn cup and writing award-winning copy like a professional reporter. So please support me like you always do. Please?'

The screen exploded with noise as her family yelled back. Words like 'immature', 'ungrateful', 'no daughter of mine' floated towards her but she muted her laptop and just glared at them.

Thankfully, there was a knock at the door. She unmuted her family and said quickly, 'I have someone at the door. For God's sake, behave yourselves.'

Bee opened the door and saw the Maharani, looking rested and resplendent in another chignon, chiffon sari and pearl-diamond choker combination. The woman had fabulous taste in clothes.

'Evening, Ranisa.' Bee swept into a curtsy.

'My dear, Bee.' The woman gave her an affectionate squeeze on her arm. 'Aren't you ready for dinner? We need to go down in 10 minutes. I just checked in to see how you were settling into your new quarters.'

'It's perfect. Ridiculously perfect.' Bee smiled widely. 'The bathroom is to die for.'

'Wonderful.' The Maharani's eyes went to the laptop screen where Bee's family was ogling at the regal presence. 'Is that your family?'

'Uh, yes,' Bee said. 'But you don't have to—'

'Lovely. I will just introduce myself to them, shall I?' Kalavati swept into the room as if she owned it and gestured to Bee to pick the laptop up.

When Bee reluctantly lifted the laptop and held it at eye level, Kalavati folded her hands and inclined her head. 'Namaste. I am Kalavati Devi Chauhan from Jaigarh. It is very nice to meet you all.'

Aggy was surreptitiously trying to edge his Mohawked head out of the screen.

'Yes, Your Highness, I mean, Your Majesty, I mean . . .' It was rare to see her composed, unflappable mom stumble around.

Bee grinned behind the laptop.

The Maharani waved it away. 'Please, stop. I despise such formalities. I am so glad to have your daughter as my companion for this trip. I miss my daughter so much.' As the Maharani blinked away tears, Bee's eyes widened. 'She's recently bereaved, you see, and she didn't want to travel with me.'

Finally, Bee's torpid brain put it all together.

Zakeer Hussain, the dead vice-captain, was the queen's son-in-law! The queen's daughter, Princess Ujwala, had eloped with him just a few months ago. It was in all the papers. Even Bee had been forced to read the headlines.

'Royal's Daughter Runs Away with Superstar Cricketer.'

This explained why the Maharani was present at the tournament. The ICCB needed to express a show of sympathy and grief while still keeping the game alive. What better way to do that than to ask the grieving, royal mother-in-law of the recently departed vice-captain to be a part of the tournament!

It was such a genius move, Bee couldn't begin to comprehend the machinations behind it.

Her family, meanwhile, was making appropriate sympathetic noises.

The Maharani waved them away graciously. 'It was an unfortunate tragedy and I am hoping that my daughter begins healing soon. Until then I am so glad your daughter will be here to give me company. An old woman like me, in this all-male camp . . . it becomes lonely, you see.'

'Of course, of course,' Amma stammered. 'It's only that we were worried about her, especially since she was robbed.'

'I wasn't robbed, Amma,' Bee said loudly. 'Nothing was taken from my room.'

'Your parents are right to be worried,' Kalavati said gently. 'They love you and want you to be safe.'

Bee couldn't argue with that.

Then the Maharani turned back to the screen. 'I have top-notch security, ma'am, who guard me and those around me with their lives. I can assure you that no one will harm a hair on your daughter's head while she is with me.'

'But we would feel better if—' Vishwanathan Govind began.

'Sir, I have a daughter too and I understand perfectly well what it feels like to fear for the safety of our children, especially when they are so far away from us. After all, in today's troubled times, women are so unsafe.'

Everyone made mutual clucking sounds that grated on Bee's nerves.

'But your daughter is a brave and smart woman,' Kalavati continued confidently. 'She won't do anything that will endanger her life. Not to mention the ringside view of this cricket circus that she will get. Why not let her have her chance?'

Now it was her family's turn to fall silent.

From behind the laptop screen, Bee silently mouthed 'Thank you' to the woman. One did not argue with queens, did they?

'Well . . .' Shanti began, in a tone that signified defeat, 'if you think she will be safe, Your Majesty, then I suppose there's no harm.'

'I do think she will be safe.'

Bee turned the laptop towards herself. 'See, she does. And now I have to get ready for dinner. I'll let you know when we can talk again. Okay?'

'Goodbye, everyone,' Kalavati said, ever the gracious hostess. 'Have a wonderful night.'

The family mumbled appropriate goodbyes and the chat ended.

Bee shut her laptop with a huge sense of relief.

She found Kalavati Devi regarding her with soft eyes. 'Your family really loves you. You should not worry them.'

'I'm just doing my job,' Bee replied just as gently. 'I know they love me and that worrying about me comes naturally to them. But I wouldn't be a very good reporter if I always did as they asked.'

Kalavati stayed quiet.

Bee continued awkwardly, 'But thank you for saving my ass.'

She bit her tongue! Crap! She had done it again. She had properly cursed in front of the queen.

The Maharani laughed. 'No problem, my dear. I am used to difficult daughters whose asses need saving from time to time. Now, why don't you get ready? We are late for dinner. And one must never keep the hosts waiting.'

—◆ ◆—

As Bee went down for dinner with the Maharani, she was still thinking about the gorgeous bathroom from where she'd video called an extremely envious Dheera as she got dressed. Bee had even set an early alarm for the next morning so she could have a proper bath in the claw-footed tub. Living in the lap of luxury definitely had its perks.

But there was a flip side to all this luxury, and Bee was made brutally aware of it during dinner. Good to her word, the Maharani had ensured Bee dined with the team—all the stars and athletes she'd seen and heard on TV and radio growing up.

But the entire time Arhan Kapoor presided over them like an anxious father. He had let slip that she was a journalist even before she'd introduced herself, so while the lot of them were particularly polite to her, no one made an effort to actually talk to her. It wasn't as if she was being isolated; the Maharani was too forceful a presence for that. She just felt like an accessory, occupying space but not really required.

It didn't help matters at all that Arhan Kapoor kept glowering at her as he sipped his chilled beer and dissected the match with his team.

As the evening progressed, it got progressively worse because she was reminded by the queen, yet again, that she couldn't use any direct quotes from the conversations she overheard. Suddenly, writing award-winning copy seemed as impossible as reaching Mars.

If Bee had thought that gaining entry into the inner sanctum would automatically grant her access to this exclusive world, she'd been proven mightily wrong by Arhan Kapoor.

10

India's win in the opening match had given it the much-needed 2 points to stay in the group.

The next three matches in the other groups went off as expected. Sri Lanka trounced Canada in their opening salvo. Zimbabwe and New Zealand battled it out till the last ball with the more experienced side emerging victorious. And, finally, Pakistan played the strong, crowd-favourite Australia in a lopsided game where the Aussies demolished Pakistan's pacing attack by posting a total of 350 in 20 overs.

The three matches were all played at the Sawai Mansingh Stadium and Bee split her time between the VIP box with Kalavati and down in the sticks with the rest of the press corps.

Dheera, Harry and Sholes met the queen and came away highly impressed. They were also invited to lunch with the queen, which turned out to be a raucous affair. Dheera had even worn a sari with a spaghetti strap blouse!

Outside of the hotel and during match time, whenever she was hanging out with her people or the Maharani, Bee had a blast. There were no more mentions of the break-in and the press corps hotel had apparently pushed for the installation of CCTV cameras after the incident. She was glad her stuff being mauled through had awoken the management to the need for better security.

The matches were all routine drama, all good fun to write about. But Bee wanted the scoop. She wanted to write about the underlying tensions, the little rituals, superstitious and otherwise, that this new Indian team had before their first round-robin game against Ireland.

The round robin required the teams to play each other once within their own groups. After that, the first two teams from the four groups would advance to the next stage—the quarter-finals. From there, it was a bloodbath—knockouts with no second chances.

For now, match after match was being played across Jaipur, Kolkata, Delhi, Mohali, Chennai, Bengaluru and Mumbai and twenty-one days of exciting, nail-biting T20 cricket were underway.

The potential to dig deep and come up with some truly insightful news, especially from the Indian dressing room, was immense, untapped.

Bee was frustrated and she complained daily to her brother, while faithfully relaying ball-by-ball replays to him and listening to his opinions, passed down from her dad, of course. She used it all to pretty up the standard press release copies the media was given after each match. Unlike Team India, the other teams gave elaborate press conferences and she was lucky enough to wedge her way to the forefront of the Aus-Pak match and get a couple of insightful comments from the young captains of both the teams. But her column, optimistically called 'Bee Embedded', was glaringly bare of any Indian comments and quotes. Even Satyarth was beginning to question her wisdom of getting close to the team and had started making noises asking her to go back to the press corps since she wasn't cutting it.

Bee knew she couldn't outright ask the Maharani to help her and declare a royal decree for the cricketers to start sharing with the embedded journalist. Mostly, Bee felt as if she was in enemy territory and even though it wasn't wartime, it might as well have been. All because of one man—Assistant Coach Arhan Kapoor.

—— ◆ ◆ ——

'What are you doing?' Arhan barked the night of the Aus-Pak match. It was his favourite phrase around her.

Prithvi Narayanan, the newbie she'd sat down next to during dinner, actually moved his chair away a discreet two inches at Arhan's question.

'I was trying to have a conversation with Mr Narayanan,' Bee replied.

Arhan looked at Prithvi and the poor guy moved one place down so Arhan could take his seat.

He glowered, as usual, his nose made prominent by a cute Band-Aid.

'I'm ninety-nine per cent sure you're stalking me,' Bee said to cover up her reaction to him.

'Leave Prithvi alone,' Arhan said brusquely. 'He's young and nervous. You don't actually have permission to interview him.'

Bee shot him an affronted glare. 'Hey, I was just making polite conversation—'

'Which will magically find its way into your column tomorrow.'

Bee huffed out a breath.

'I have had a chat with the board,' Arhan said casually. 'They're aware of this situation and have left it to me to handle it as I see fit. I have half a mind to have you banned from sitting with us.'

Her jaw dropped. 'You wouldn't.'

'For the good of my team, of course I would,' he replied grimly. 'Don't mess with me, Bee. Don't try and catch Umang Yadav in the elevator. Or chat up Viren outside the gym. In fact, stay ten feet away from them at all times. These men are here to do a job, a difficult and high-pressure job under extremely tragic circumstances. I will not have some pretty woman coming in and making things harder for them. Are we clear?'

I don't care that he thinks I'm pretty!

'Are we clear, Ms Vishwanathan?' Arhan asked again, a little forcefully.

'Should I also shine your *jutti* while I'm at it, Mr Kapoor?' Bee asked acidly.

She was acutely aware of Prithvi, who seemed to be nonchalantly digging into his dinner, intently listening to their conversation. This was beyond humiliating. Red crept up her neck, heating it up.

'You can, actually. I'll have them sent to your room.' Arhan raised his eyebrows, looking completely serious.

'You can go to hell,' Bee said pleasantly through gritted teeth. Pride made her add, 'I solemnly swear that I won't come within spitting distance of your soldiers.'

'Thank you.' Then he literally dismissed her and turned towards Prithvi, his demeanour changed, instantly affable. 'Prithvi, I want us to go down to the nets half an hour early. I'll throw grounders with you so your fielding catches up to the more experienced players. We'll work on it together. *Theek hai?*'

'*Theek hai*, Coach sir.'

Then Arhan was gone, leaving Bee frustrated and annoyed and *hot* because he'd called her pretty. She was upset because she knew she should regard him as the enemy. In fact, he was the general of the enemy camp. Yet every time he appeared, his eyes smoky with repressed anger and a voice that was beginning to send a shiver down her spine, the lust snake grew . . . longer and wider until it sat snug in the middle of her belly, like a fat python that had swallowed a fox.

Something had to give.

And it did. The next morning, right before they were all to leave for Bengaluru for the next leg of the round-robin matches.

11

Bee was late for breakfast because she'd stayed up too late surfing the internet for any gossip she could find about Arhan Kapoor in a perverse burst of curiosity that she could not explain. As a consequence, her morning routine had suffered by a good half an hour. Not to mention the extra ten minutes she'd taken to toss all her stuff into her bags because she had to catch the media bus that was leaving well before the team bus. The team had a private jet; the media would rough it out in coach.

A text from Dheera telling her their bus was due to depart in thirty minutes had Bee debating whether she should skip breakfast altogether. The Maharani took her breakfast in bed so Bee did not want to disturb her. But her stomach rumbled loudly, making the decision for her and she jogged downstairs to grab something to eat.

The breakfast lounge was nothing short of a wedding spread. Continental, English, Indian and American vied for attention on various tables laden with delicacies.

Bee picked up her customary cup of fruit—mango, musk melon and grapes—and, for extra energy, added a bowl of cornflakes, sprinkled liberally with sugar, and poured enough milk to float a battleship.

'You're drinking that, ma'am?' Viren asked casually.

Bee shot a startled glance over her shoulder. The fricking Indian captain was in line behind her!

She breathed through her mouth. 'Yes.'

'Nice.' He smiled.

He was a little taller than her, of average Indian male height. Yet there was an undeniable power in him. It wasn't as contained as with Arhan who made breathing difficult when she was near him, but the captain had presence.

'Every time I'm in one of these places, I am reminded of the dining halls at Hogwarts. Food just appears magically in front of me, even food I can't eat,' Viren remarked.

Her *kajal*-lined eyes widened. 'You know Harry Potter?'

He smiled again earnestly. 'Even though I am a sportsman, ma'am, I do crack open a book occasionally.'

Viren replenished his fruit cup with twice the amount of fruit she had in hers and he loaded up on fluffy egg-white omelettes that made her mouth water. His security hulked behind him, massive giants who probably ate omelettes by the dozen.

Bee shrugged sheepishly. 'I didn't mean to insult your intelligence, sir. I am just surprised that you were able to reference it so quickly.'

'Sir?' Viren quirked his brow like The Rock. She should have found this gesture sexy because every single female in this cricket-fanatic nation did, but there was something missing . . . well, not quite.

'Do I seem that old to you, Ms Vishwanathan?'

Bee peeked a look at where Arhan was sitting at a nearby table. Viren's anxious 'dad' was silently glaring at her from his premier table, telling her to get a move on.

Bee resisted the urge to stare right back at him. She hadn't struck up the conversation with Viren, he could surely see that.

Couldn't he? Well, too bad!

She laughed louder than she meant to at Viren's question. 'No, it was a mark of respect and you know it. Or are you deliberately trying to bait me like Steyn did Tendulkar before every ball in the third test in 2011?'

'And what did Steyn tell Sachin?' Viren asked, curiously.

'I believe it was, "I will get you this time."' She scooped some fruit into her mouth, continuing absently, 'I don't believe he got him as many times as he wanted though. At least, not in that match. Though he did get 50 wickets with his 5 for 75, it did not include Tendulkar.'

Viren's smile went from amused to impressed. 'You seem to be very knowledgeable about the game.'

'I grew up on it. I am Indian, you see,' she explained mildly.

'Still,' Viren insisted. 'I don't know many women who can quote the bowling figures of a test match played years ago.'

'Personally, I enjoyed Cronje's SAF team much more than I do today's,' Bee said thoughtfully. 'This team is more unified and has realised its potential greatly but there was just something so romantic about Cronje's team, you know? It had just returned to international cricket after years of Apartheid *and* was taking on India and Australia.'

Viren's jaw dropped wide open.

'What?' She looked down at her chest, then at the tray. 'Did I drop something?'

Viren shook his head as he guided her to a seat at his table. Bee sat down without thinking.

'No, like I said before, I just haven't met many women who can hold valid opinions on cricket that do not involve gushing over a cricketer's looks or batting shots.'

She grinned. 'Who says I don't gush? But the game is what matters in the end. The precision with which decisions are made and executed on the field. The sheer beauty and talent of some of the men who play. The legends who have made cricket what it is today.'

'You have favourites?'

She shrugged. 'I'll get lynched if I reveal my favourites. But I could quote their career averages and you could guess?'

'You know the career averages of cricketers?'

'Ouch, Mr Kaul,' she said. 'Why wouldn't I know the career averages of cricketers or, for that matter, any sportsman I liked?'

'So, you like cricket?'

'It's worshipped as the second religion in our home,' she answered promptly. 'It was only because of my Paati's—I mean my grandmom's —intervention that we don't have a picture of the '83 team on our puja wall.'

There was a burst of laughter and Bee realised she held the attention of several of the Indian team. But Arhan stolidly plodded on with his porridge, not even raising his head. She felt a pang of annoyance that his rejection was having a greater effect on her than all the appreciative laughter.

'Ms Vishwanathan is going to quote the career averages of her favourite cricketers and I'm to guess their names,' Viren informed his teammates.

Similar looks of shock dawned on the other players' faces.

Okay, this is weird. Have they not met even one female cricket columnist or just regular women who play the game and are good at it? Isn't the Indian women's team one of the best in the world? What is with all the surprised looks?

'In fact,' Bee leaned forward determinedly, her fruit cup forgotten, 'I'll not only give the career averages but also career bests. I'll warn you guys, not all of them are Indian—'

'Don't you have a press bus to get to?' Arhan interrupted her moment of glory with a growl.

Bee cursed herself mentally for being drawn into a friendly contest with the enemy camp. She shovelled her food in with no finesse whatsoever, ignoring Arhan.

'Don't be silly, AK,' Viren said casually. 'Ms Vishwanathan can come with us. We have plenty of room on the plane, don't we?'

'She's press,' Arhan said. His eyes made it plain he thought of her as a *rakshasi*, destroyer of all that was good and holy.

But this time Bee stared back, challenging him. Her heart beat faster at the casual way in which Viren had said 'she can come with us'.

'We have orders from management to not talk to any press during this tournament,' Arhan said quietly.

'Arre, Sirji.' One of the bowlers, a teenage trailblazer who was touted to be the next Shoaib Akhtar, said, 'We aren't talking to the press, Coach Sirji. We are talking to Beeji, na?'

'Please,' Bee said before she could stop herself, 'don't make me sound like a Punjabi grandma before my time. And, of course, I am Bee, your walking-talking cricketopedia, not press.' She even made a show of unclipping her press badge and tucking it into her bag.

At the icy look Arhan gave her, she shrivelled up a little on the inside but smiled gamely on. If he wanted her off the plane and away from the men who finally wanted to talk to her, she wasn't going to make it easy for him.

'See?' Now the vice-captain, Suresh Vijay, took up her cause. His Tamil accent was prominent in just that one word. 'She's not press, Arhan. She's just a fun person to hang out with and learn from.'

Bee did not understand the about-turn this team was making right in front of her, but she was not going to question her good fortune.

The men were thawing. They were talking. She didn't have to use quotes to make her copy interesting if she could just get a sense of who they were in real life. This could work.

Arhan opened his mouth as if he wanted to say more but then he thought better of it.

Bee waited for his refusal with defiant eyes that she wisely hid in her cereal bowl.

'I'll make a few calls to get permission. If the bosses say okay, she can come with us.'

The team cheered and whooped as if something truly amazing had happened and Bee grinned as well. She quickly texted Dheera.

Kaul invited me to fly with them. Yay! Wish me luck.

Dheera's reply was instantaneous. *Who did you* bajaao *to get this invite?*

Bee grinned and replied, *FO.*

Then she sent another text. *It's a funny story. Tell you when we meet.*

The bowler seated next to her, Shomprakash Banerjee, asked her very seriously, 'Viren Sir just told me that you know every cricketing stat on this planet. Is that true?'

Bee chuckled. 'By God, no. But I know the ones worth knowing.'

Opposite her, finishing the last of his oats porridge, Arhan Kapoor's fingers tightened around his spoon. She felt a spurt of irrational pride at his obvious displeasure.

This victory was indeed sweet. And life in enemy territory was not so bad.

—◆ ◆—

'Largest wicket haul?'

'Jim Laker. 1956 Ashes; 20, n-no 19. Too bad Kumble couldn't do it twice in Delhi in '99.'

'The highest score by any batsman?'

'Lara; 501, not out; 1994 versus Durham. Although people debate it as the highest since it was in first-class cricket.'

'Then, the highest international score is—'

Bee answered quickly, beating Prithvi Narayanan, 'Lara again. Against England in Antigua, 2004; 400, not out. Although I personally preferred the 154 which won West Indies the match in '99.1999.'

She leaned back in the plush recliner seat of the ICCB private jet. She'd read about planes like this in old romance novels. This was back when she was young and dumb enough to want to read about alpha males. Only presidents and billionaires were given such treatment. Or royalty like Maharani Kalavati Devi, who was safely ensconced in a seat at the very back with her pashmina shawl draped around her as she napped. Her bodyguard, a Jason Momoa-type named Kartar Singh, was standing at attention behind her. He wore a red turban with his all-black suit and shades—a strange mix of modern and traditional that he seemed to pull off.

Bee could not believe she was actually here, on this plane.

When Satyarth had called her into his tiny excuse for a cabin and told her she would be travelling with the media team that would cover the T20 World Cup, it had seemed like a death sentence to her. She didn't particularly enjoy cricket even though she was in the business of writing about it. Tennis, especially Nadal, was her favourite. She also had no experience covering live games and with the media gag order imposed by the board, there was no way she would be able to write anything worthy of a by-line.

But how the tables had turned!

Fortunately, her first column about India's match on day one had been well-received. She'd even got a few encouraging comments when the article had gone live on the website. That felt good, morale-boosting.

But now, after spending some time with the 'boys', she was rapidly revising her opinion of the game and, particularly, this team. They were young and decent and were beginning to show sparks of the spirit befitting an elite sports team. This was evident in the competitive spirit with which they barraged her with questions, each vying with the next to come up with a stat she couldn't provide.

So far she'd been able to field them, but her knowledge was not inexhaustible.

'Guys,' she said. 'I have a really stupid request.'

'Yes?'

'My Appa and brother Aggy would absolutely die of shock if I told them I am travelling with you guys. They'll demand proof. Would you mind . . .'

Instantly they all looked at the assistant coach who was tapping away at his laptop, his headphones dangling around his neck while his phone buzzed. She wondered if he was getting a headache from all the chatter around him while he tried to work.

Then she remonstrated herself for thinking about him.

'What?' He looked up, arching his neck as if driving away the kinks. 'If she isn't going to post it on social media or sell it online, I don't suppose I can stop you hooligans, can I?'

And so, ten minutes later, Bee's ordinary smartphone became the proud owner of a selfie with the entire Indian cricket team.

Arhan waited till almost everyone had disembarked at the private airfield near Bengaluru's international airport. It was one of the many ways in which they avoided a mob frenzy.

Bee was struggling with the overhead hatch where she'd stored her bag. He opened it for her, standing close to her, and felt the warm give of her spine. He immediately moved a step back.

'Thank you.' Bee's smile ended even before it began.

'You're just a trained circus monkey to them,' he said without preamble.

'I beg your pardon?'

'Your new besties with whom you're taking selfies? Your buddies who are crowding around you like you're Ms Cricketopedia. They'll lose interest in you in a minute once they remember you're a reporter —the enemy.'

Arhan watched with narrowed eyes as she groped around in her pants pocket for something. He heard the mumbled words 'stupid bubble wrap' but didn't pay any attention.

'I am not the enemy and I am certainly no monkey,' Bee managed when her search proved futile. 'We all know Google can do what I just did in point nothing seconds. They treat me as a person, something you are incapable of doing apparently.'

'They look at you and see a hot item who can talk their language,' he said bluntly. 'You're a rarity, an anomaly in their universe. But the novelty will wear off quickly enough.'

Her chest heaved in indignation and Arhan forced himself to only look at her furious face.

'You are an arrogant jerk and I sincerely do not know why these lovely men even like you. And I wish . . . I wish . . .' She made a sound between a scream and a growl and then, before he could react, reached up and pulled his nose. Hard.

Arhan leapt back as if she had punched him again, murderous rage turning his eyes to slits.

'You . . .' His fists ached with the need to pop her one.

'Go on,' she said, standing her ground. 'Do it. Hit me. I don't expect anything better from someone like you. Talking down to me, intimidating me in front of your 'boys'. Is that how a gentleman behaves?'

Arhan actually saw crimson wash over his eyes. 'If you were a man,' he breathed.

'If I were a man, I would have taken Viren's bat and beaten you silly by now,' Bee retorted. 'If I were a man, you wouldn't have a problem with me, Coach Sir.' Her tone turned scathing, stinging. 'If I were a man, you would have a drink with me and we could amicably sort out whatever issues we had. But I am not a man. I am a woman. And I am damn proud of it.'

She took her bag from the hatch and shoved past him. Arhan stumbled back a couple of steps and glared at her, silent and colossally mad.

'Don't you dare forget it, Arhan Kapoor. I am a woman and I could break more than your nose if I wanted to.'

Arhan stroked his poor, abused nose which was hurting unbearably now and wondered if this woman was put on God's green earth just to wreck his life.

'This match is so boring,' Dheera complained the next day as they sweltered in the hot sun at the M. Chinnaswamy Stadium.

England was playing Zimbabwe and the overs were trickling by sluggishly. The heat was making it impossible for the players to deliver an exciting match. The English pacer Simon Broderick had already ripped apart the middle order of the opposition and now Zimbabwe was struggling to retain wickets while scoring runs. It wasn't easy for the underdogs.

'Shouldn't you be down there with the others, using your wide lens to capture the next Jana Vishwas Bank Maximum Sixer?' Bee nodded towards the grassy knoll behind the boundary stands where a bunch of photographers had set up their equipment to get the best output. They wore caps, plus there were umbrellas to shield them from the sun. Still, most of them had chosen to move out of the shadows as they would spoil the shots.

'I'll leave this box when England wins the match in double-quick time and I get to return to my room and take a shower.'

'Dheera,' Harry snickered as he shovelled popcorn into his mouth with all the finesse of a baboon. 'Krikket-365 is not going to pay your minibar bills if you turn in sub-standard work. Someone is bound to talk.'

Dheera shot him an eff-you glare after tipping her glasses up.

The batsman on strike struck a boundary through deep cover and the fielder dived desperately to catch the ball before it bounced past him. The crowd roared in approval. Everyone stood up to watch the action, even though there was a TV screen in the press box that relayed the match via satellite as with every household in the world.

'Good one,' Sholes said as he scribbled something in his notepad.

'Show me that pic again,' Dheera demanded of Bee. 'I still can't believe how lucky you are, you jerk. Hanging out with the team, cracking jokes, taking selfies. You're living the dream, you know.'

Bee rolled her eyes as she scrolled through her picture gallery, bringing up the appropriate photo. She looked at it with fresh eyes along with Dheera. The team were all dressed in casual sweats and shorts or track pants. There was a camaraderie in the picture that shone through. And then, there she was—wild hair tied back with a Bandhani bandana, wearing loose orange pants and a scoop-necked yellow tee, a pixie-like grin on her face as she stood squashed between sixteen supremely fit men.

Those two hours she'd spent with the team talking about cricket, the best things about the game, had seemed to give them a sparkle that had been missing at the press con conducted before they left Jaipur.

It was a sweet feeling even though Bee knew she was being naïve and arrogant in thinking her presence mattered that much.

'Too bad Arhan didn't pose,' Dheera said.

'Not really.'

Bee had popped a considerable amount of bubble wrap on her way to the hotel in Bengaluru, stewing over Arhan Kapoor's latest unfair accusations and hurtful words.

Trained circus monkey, my foot!

She wished she had done more than pull his broken nose. She should have kneed him where it hurt the most. Not that her exit had been less than spectacular but she wanted to cause him more than just physical harm. She wanted to hurt his ego and heart like he had hers. He'd taken a wonderful professional highlight and tarnished it with his unkind claims.

'Hey.' Harry put a sweaty arm around her shoulder, a few seconds later. 'What's up, babe? You looked pissed off.'

'Nothing. Here, you can ogle at your gods too.'

Bee passed him her phone and he squinted at it, out of the glare of the sun, making all the appropriate admiring noises. She let it all filter out of her brain.

It was Sholes' turn next. He looked at photo and said, 'Salil Achrekar looks tired. Must be his shoulder injury acting up again. *Pata hai* if he is playing tomorrow?'

Salil was an accomplished middle-order batsman with an uncanny ability to catch a ball in the air. He'd thrown his shoulder catching an 'uncatchable' during India's last series before the World Cup.

Bee shrugged. '*Pata nahi*. We didn't talk about the team or the matches or anything related to the cup.'

'Weird. I thought you would be pumping them for information since you'd wormed your way into their forty-inch chests,' Dheera muttered sarcastically.

'It's not like that, honestly,' Bee protested. 'I wasn't trying to worm my way into anything at all.' At Dheera's disbelieving look she elaborated. 'Staying with the Maharani means I have to behave with a certain level of dignity too. According to her, "appearances are everything". So I can't be a grasping, quote-hungry reporter-vulture when I am around the team.'

'I see.' Harry nodded wisely. 'Catch it, man!' he yelled suddenly.

The English fielder caught the ball an inch before the boundary line and the crowd went wild. They all clapped and cheered as this meant the match would end that much sooner.

Harry turned to Bee and said, 'So what? You're going to "incept" them into giving you interviews?'

Bee chuckled. 'As if! I am neither smart nor feminine enough to incept a man into doing anything, Harry. Besides, even if I wanted to, the Night King would smell a plot a mile away and would gobble me up before I could even think of a word!'

'The Night King?' Sholes asked.

'Arhan Kapoor,' she answered grumpily.

'*Chup kar!*' Dheera cut in. 'Arhan is a gorgeous, sweet guy. He is not this jerk that you keep making him out to be. Secondly, all women have the power to make a man do anything they want.'

At this, three-quarters of the press box turned their heads away from the match to look at Dheera with varying expressions of incredulity. She held her hands up in the universal gesture of surrender and said, 'I didn't mean you guys, obviously. You all will never do anything you don't want to do.'

'Absolutely!' The guy from the *Time* said.

'Right on!' The *HP* guy muttered.

'Fuck, yeah.' One of the popular bloggers from *Cricbizz* added.

Dheera whispered to Bee sotto voce, 'Every one of them will do what you want. You just need to know the tricks.'

'No, thank you.' Bee was emphatic in her refusal.

They watched the match in silence for a few minutes.

Then Bee tipped her sunglasses down her nose, leaned towards Dheera and said, 'Can I really incept any guy I want?'

'Sure you can, baby doll.'

An image of Arhan Kapoor's infuriatingly superior face rose at the back of her mind. His delectable mouth spewing hateful junk. It would serve him right if she made him do something he didn't want to.

Like, kiss me.

Bee sat up straighter.

No, not kiss me!

Now, where did that thought come from?

Bee shook her head to clear her mind. She looked back at Dheera and said, 'Teach me, *mere aaqa*.'

Dheera winked. 'Listen closely, Princess Jasmine . . .'

—·◆ ◆·—

At around the same time, Arhan was at the nets on the Modern School grounds. It was a holiday so there was no mob of cheering students to interrupt them. He'd decided to practise with Salil Achrekar to see if the ace fielder was fit to play the next match. Achrekar had been desperate to come on to the field, so Arhan had padded up and was swinging his bat as far as it would go.

One of the understudy quickies, Ashok, came at Arhan, who middled the bat and held his stance, watching the ball for as long as he could.

The quickie released the ball. It came hurtling towards Arhan at the speed of a bullet, a streak of white.

A bit of a reverse swing is all that's required, if I have judged Ashok's follow-through action correctly.

The ball made contact with his bat as he heaved and swung it right at the cover where Salil was in position. Achrekar dived for it but the ball went sailing past him.

Four!

Salil winced as he sat up and Arhan walked over.

'Are you okay?' Arhan squatted next to him.

'I'm okay, Coach Sir. *Bas ek minute*. I grazed my elbow.' Salil showed him his latest injury.

'Is your shoulder still bothering you?'

'Sir, I—'

Arhan squeezed the player's good shoulder and looked him square in the eyes. 'You have a solid five years left in the game if you continue playing as well as you almost always do. Don't destroy your future for this tournament.'

'But, Sir, Hasmukh Sir told me that I'll have to play the next match.'

'But do you want to?' Arhan asked him gently. 'Are you fully confident you can?'

Salil's usually animated face fell and he shook his head.

Arhan gave the guy a hand and they walked back to the nets. 'I'll talk to Hasmukh; give him the update. You focus on healing. Akshar's working with you specifically, isn't he?'

'Yes.' Salil nodded enthusiastically at Arhan's mention of the team's head physiotherapist. 'He has a new hot compress-cold ice method he wants to try with me after practice.'

'Great, go for it now. I think we can call it a day.'

Arhan waited till the player was out of earshot before dialling Hasmukh Kanstiya, the selection official responsible for this tournament.

'Hey, AK, what's up?' Hasmukh answered.

'What's this *chutiyapa* I hear about Achrekar playing tomorrow?' Arhan asked, without preamble. 'His shoulder is still sore. It needs to heal.'

'I know, *yaar*, but the big bosses think he needs to get off the bench and play some real cricket. We will need him in the later stages when we make it to the semis, *na*? He needs to be on the field, get into the right mindset, if we are to win.'

'We aren't sure of *making* the semis, Hasmukh,' Arhan spoke through gritted teeth. 'I won't have a player's health jeopardised this early in the tournament.'

'*Arre*, we won't be sending him just like that. He'll have his shots and pills. He'll be flying as high as a kite as he scores.' Hasmukh snickered.

'Listen, Kanstiya, I want to talk to Shastri about this. We aren't going to send Salil out to play unless I have assurance from Akshar that he is absolutely fine,' Arhan said grimly. 'I won't risk his career over this tournament. The ortho guys want to take a look at his X-rays ASAP.'

'You can take it up with Akshar, but I know he will agree with me. He knows what's good for the team.' Kanstiya said as he hung up.

To Arhan's frustration, this was exactly what happened. Over the next fifteen minutes, Akshar Shekhawat cleared Salil Achrekar to play even though the young man was not a 100 per cent fit.

And there was nothing Arhan could do about it.

13

A CUP SPLIT WIDE OPEN

We are almost at the end of the first leg of the tournament where the matches have been fast and furious with every shade in between.

Today's final Group A match between Sri Lanka and Pakistan demonstrated a level of skill and sportsmanship that has not been seen in a T20 match since the third-edition IPL final when Chennai Super Kings beat Royal Challengers Bangalore hollow by coming together in form just before the semi-finals.

After India's unexpected, but not surprising, loss to Ireland by 52 runs because of a batting-order collapse that was triggered by Salil Achrekar's on-field injury during the Irish innings, Group B has become a battlefield.

The conclusion drawn early on was that Group A would emerge with clear winners, considering the in-form Sri Lankan and Australian teams. However, Pakistan, with a spectacular bowling display that bundled the Lankans out for less than 72 runs, the previous lowest T20 WC total, has not only changed this perception but also made an emphatic statement that they are throwing their hat in the ring too.

Fast bowler and Pakistan captain Junaid Akmal led from the front with his brilliant bowling figures of 4–1–16–5 (0W, 0 Nb). He systematically attacked the opposition with clever field placements and even better bowling.

At the beginning of the match, held at Kolkata's Eden Gardens where many a clincher has been played, he opted to send the Lankans in to bat because it seemed the smart thing to do. Overcast skies meant the match could be washed out due to bad weather, and having an easier total with a quick fall of wickets would only work in Pakistan's favour.

Sri Lanka's Arjuna Gunasekara and Ranjith Fernando—considered one of the world's best opening pairs—swaggered on to the field with the confidence of posting a defendable total.

Ten minutes and 6 balls later, the tides had turned.

The pitch stayed dry even though lightning cracked on the field in the form of Rashad Murtaza, the very able wicketkeeper-batsman whose name will go down with the all-time greats like Dhoni, Gilchrist, and Sangakkara. His keeping was impeccable, his reading of the ball sublime and his reaction time, especially when he stumped the last wicket, was less than 0.08 seconds—a record previously held by MS Dhoni. Murtaza is yet another example of that classy breed of batsmen who bat even when they keep and not the other way round.

Meanwhile, in Groups C and D, things have been going as expected with England and South Africa flattening New Zealand and Zimbabwe, respectively. Unfortunately, Zimbabwe has become somewhat of a punching bag for the playing three ...

'Are you done, my dear?' Kalavati's voice interrupted Bee's flow, bringing her into the present. Since she had sat down to work, Bee had barely looked up from her laptop, her fingers flying as her thoughts crystallised in a rare display of cohesion. She had on noise-cancelling headphones and hadn't heard the Maharani knock.

Bee quickly saved her current column since she had till the next day to file it, closed her eyes and stretched her kinked muscles.

She had been writing a filler piece, a stream of consciousness post to lighten the high dose of info-heavy articles on cricket she'd been sending, complete with stats, quotes and figures.

The reading audience had been impressed with her Jim Laker comparison when the Australian spinner Greg McDonnell took 10 for 10 in the Aus-Canada match, and when she'd written about the Steyn successor of South Africa eating up Zimbabwe.

Bee smelled Elizabeth Taylor's White Diamonds, the Maharani's signature scent.

They had continued rooming together in Bengaluru and Kolkata despite Bee's protests that she belonged in the press barracks. One didn't really say no to quasi-royalty as Bee was rapidly learning. Especially not to someone as forcefully regal as Maharani Kalavati Devi.

'Oh, Ranisa. I am sorry I didn't hear you. Is it time already?'

'Yes, my dear. You just have enough time to shower and get dressed if you move now.'

'Crap! I forgot to set an alarm.'

Then she swore once more in her head as she realised she had cursed in front of the Maharani yet again. 'Pardon my language, Ranisa.'

The Maharani chuckled. 'It is admirable to see your dedication to your work, Bee. Now, if you could be just as dedicated to being on time. Appearances are everything, you know, and being punctual tops that list.'

Bee nodded and hopped off her perch on the comfy chaise lounge in the presidential suite at Kolkata's Park Grandeur. The view of Park Street was amazing as were the glittering lights that marked the city skyline with Victoria Memorial in the distance.

She had fallen in love with the chatty colourful vibe of Kolkata the minute she'd stepped off the tarmac and landed in a barrage of mixed banter.

'Yes, Ranisa. Give me thirty minutes and I'll be ready.'

The Maharani wandered further into the room, checking out Bee's outfit for the evening. She'd laid it out on the bed before sitting down to finish her column. It was a silky LBD, a piece she'd picked up from a consignment store in South Mumbai. The bodice was a drop waist with a sheer back, which, of course, meant no bra. The sleeves were tiny puffs of fabric piped with silver lace, echoing the sweetheart neckline that exposed an extra bit of cleavage. The skirt hit her just above her knees and flared slightly to give the dress a feminine edge.

Bee had decided to pair the dress with her favourite red stilettos, the only pair of heels she'd brought on this trip since partying was not a priority after game day. She also planned to carry a ridiculous excuse for a clutch, a tiny coin purse that she had borrowed from Dheera just for the evening.

All this preparation was for the reception for the players, which was being held in the hotel ballroom. The media was not invited. But Bee was going as the Maharani's plus one.

'It's great that the tournament sponsors have tied up with the Autism Centre and are auctioning off team memorabilia to raise money for a good cause,' she said as she stripped in the plush bathroom.

No matter how much time she spent in there, these hotel bathrooms always gave her a little thrill. This one had a sunken bath with shower jets that rained temperature-controlled water. The mirror was a floor-length oval set in a gold frame that stood next to a granite counter inlaid with gold-veined marble, or so the brochure in her room claimed.

Like every other middle-class working woman, she'd already stashed multiple little lotion bottles and a hand-embroidered hospitality kit into her bag.

'Yes, my dear. It is,' Kalavati called out absently. 'It's even more wonderful that they've asked me to be a part of this beautiful cause.'

When Bee emerged from her shower in record time, she saw the Maharani laying out a long blue velvet case next to her dress on the bed.

She stopped towelling her wet hair and asked, 'What is that, Ranisa?'

The Maharani looked up and winked. 'Diamonds are a girl's best friend. Especially if they are surrounded by other gems.'

She flipped open the jewellery box and nestled inside was the world's most exquisite bracelet. Delicate diamonds were punctuated with sapphires, rubies, garnets and amethysts.

It was dazzling.

Bee whistled soundlessly. 'That's the piece you're auctioning tonight?'

The Maharani nodded. 'Yes. And I would be so happy if you would wear it till it is auctioned.'

Bee's mouth dropped open in blank shock. 'No way!'

'Yes. Would you please do me this favour, my dear? It would be far safer in your hands than on the display table with the other memorabilia.'

'I would be honoured,' Bee said faintly, 'but wouldn't you want to do the honours yourself? It's a royal heirloom, isn't it?'

'If my daughter were here, she would be wearing it. But she's just . . .' A shadow passed over the older woman's face and coloured her usually warm eyes with sorrow.

'This beauty has been in the family for generations. I am sorrowed to part with it.' The Maharani's lower lip trembled under the carefully applied lipstick.

'Oh, Ranisa.' Instinctively, Bee reached out and hugged the Maharani.

Even with the heavy silk sari and jewellery, the woman felt feather-light to her. The Maharani awkwardly patted her back before stepping away.

Clearly, PDA is not in the royal protocol handbook.

'I would love to wear it and honour your family's tradition.'

The Maharani blinked rapidly and said, 'Thank you, my dear. I know you will not let me down.'

———◆——

'Presenting Her Royal Highness, the sovereign monarch of the princely state of Jaigarh, Maharani Kalavati,' the announcer bellowed in a booming voice.

The doors to the ballroom opened and the Maharani swept in, cocooned in a phalanx of bodyguards and accompanied by a secretary who had flown in especially for the occasion.

The announcer looked enquiringly at Bee as she attempted to walk past him.

She muttered uncertainly, 'Bee Vishwanathan of Andheri, Mumbai?'

The announcer droned on, 'And her companion, Bee Vishwanathan of Andheri, Mumbai.'

Bee's neck flushed as she walked in through the imposing doors of the ballroom under the scrutiny of what felt like a thousand eyes. She dared not look up as she hurried after the Maharani's entourage and attempted to blend in with them.

The Maharani came to a halt at the centre of the room and turned to Bee. 'I need to meet the organisers and talk shop with a few acquaintances, my dear. You will be bored silly. Go on, get out there. Mingle, dance, drink some champagne. We will let you know when the piece needs to be displayed. It won't be till after dinner.'

Bee shrugged, gave an entirely unconvincing smile and wished desperately for some bubble wrap to pop. This social gathering was way out of her league. She knew no one here. Who the hell was she going to mingle with?

Her phone buzzed. It was Harry messaging from Dheera's phone. *Have fun. Hook up. If possible, take hot selfie with team and send! xoxo - H&D.*

She rolled her eyes and typed a quick sarcastic reply. She missed them enormously. If Dheera was here, she would openly rate the suit-and *bandhgala*-clad men mingling in the room, holding expensive crystal tumblers and talking knowledgeably about the state of the Union. The women were all in *desi* designer wear, polished and sophisticated but with the haughty look that only comes from wealth and breeding.

Bee felt insanely out of place . . . and invisible.

'Ms Bee!' It was the Pakistani wicketkeeper, Rashad Murtaza.

They had interacted briefly when she'd asked him a toughie at the press con after the SL-Pak match and he'd had to scramble to answer.

'Mr Murtaza, lovely to see you here.' Bee oozed extra warmth since she was grateful to see at least one familiar face.

Rashad, in an emerald-green *sherwani*, looked young and dapper and very handsome in an Arabian sheikh kind of way.

'No, Ms Bee. It is you who is looking lovely.'

Bee leaned in closer and said in Hindi, conspiratorially, '*Kaafi* boring party *hai na?*'

The man's eyes shone bright and he smiled. *'Haanji, Beeji.'*

'Please,' she said as she led him to a small crowd of men that she'd just spotted. It was the Indian cricket team, huddled in a corner. 'Call me Bee,' she invited.

She tapped Karthik on the shoulder and said, 'May we join you?'

His face instantly brightened and he smiled genially at both her and her companion.

'Terrific! Guys, Bee is here,' Karthik said. 'And Murtaza Bhai too. Hey, you guys were good on the field against those Aussie bastards, *haan? Bajaa daali.*'

'That last wicket, with the bails flying? Terrific,' Prithvi commented.

Rashad shrugged, pleased and embarrassed to be the centre of attention. Bee squeezed in next to him, holding on to her glass of champagne, not feeling so out of place anymore. She was with her people after all.

——•◆ ◆•——

'Do one more, one more, please,' Abhijit Shahane, the Indian opener, begged half an hour later.

Bee rolled her eyes and gulped down her second glass of champagne. 'Aren't you guys tired of me boring you with all these mundane match details?'

The Aussie captain, Royston Martin, shook his head. 'Are you kidding, Bee?' he slurred. 'You may as well be the single hottest woman on the planet because not only do you know the game, but you also *understand* it.'

He was even drunker than she was.

Bee grinned, flushed and tipsy, buzzing on champagne and goodwill. 'Thank you, Mr Martin. That's not sexist *at all*.' Her voice dripped with sarcasm.

There was a crowd of about fifteen men surrounding her by now. They laughed uncomfortably. She looked at their eager faces and sighed. 'Fine. One more. That's it.' She raised her empty glass in a toast to the Australian captain.

'It's the last over of the 1999 World Cup semi-final. South Africa versus Australia. Klusener's batting, Donald on the non-striker's end, Fleming's bowling.'

There were whistles and catcalls at her dramatic opening.

'Bang! Bang!' she said. 'Fleming goes for two fours, off the deep extra cover. Mark Waugh can't stop them. One run needed for South Africa to qualify for their *first-ever* World Cup final. For the third ball, Steve brings all the fielders inside the thirty-yard circle. The single needs to be stopped. At any cost.'

She could replay the scene so clearly in her head.

The Australians in yellow versus the South Africans in green. The sun shone brightly while the players sweated it out in Edgbaston. The crowd and commentators on the edge of their seats. Her family had been catatonic in front of the twenty-four-inch BPL colour TV that had ruled Indian living rooms before flat screens were born.

'Damien Fleming yorks it out; Klusener plays it to short mid-on. No muss, no fuss. Darren Lehmann moves in like a cat and is faster to the ball than Donald. Allan Donald starts to run, but Lance Klusener doesn't. Donald is out of his crease. Lehmann misses the direct hit for Donald. South Africa survives the ball.'

The players were hanging on to her every word. She exchanged her empty champagne flute for a tumbler off the tray of a passing waiter, taking a sip— it was whisky, a good blend, warm and smooth.

Bee continued her narrative. 'Donald looks up at the heavens and smiles. Klusener the Zulu is cold, unmoved. Fourth ball in and still

1 run needed. Fleming bowls another yorker, just outside the off stumps. Klusener digs it out somehow. The ball rolls past the stumps at the non-striker's end. Klusener starts running like a maniac. Donald watches the ball go past him and so doesn't see Klusener. He doesn't know he is supposed to run too. Klusener yells, "*Run!*"' Her voice rose.

'Donald realises he has to move. Mark Waugh gathers the ball and rolls it to the bowler trying to affect a run-out at Donald's end. But Donald hasn't moved from the non-striker's end, so it should be the end of the play.'

She took another pause, another sip. 'Fleming sees the Zulu has charged from the striker's end and is halfway across the pitch. He underarms the ball slowly to Gilchrist so it reaches the wicketkeeper's hand instead of throwing it or taking the stumps off the non-striker's end. There is no one at the striker's end. Donald cannot cross half a pitch in one step.'

Bee paused and everyone waited with bated breath. 'Adam Gilchrist, my favourite, favourite player *ever*, uproots the stumps and the stadium erupts in chaos. That's the day I saw my father cry for the first time ever.'

Bee finished off the whisky while a resounding round of applause greeted her narrative.

She smiled self-consciously and took a small bow. It was weird, crazy actually, the way all these men were so fascinated by her memory and recall.

'You are a goddess, Bee!' the Aussie captain declared as he came forward and kissed her cheek.

She blushed. 'Thank you, but it was nothing,' she said, pleased, buzzing on a different high now.

'Maybe we could . . .'

The Aussie captain's warm blue eyes swam in front of Bee as she found her arm in an iron grip and heard a familiar voice whisper in her ears, 'Why don't you come with me before you cause an international scandal?'

14

Arhan had met many charming, fascinating . . . hell, beautiful women in his life but he had yet to come across a creature as infuriating and taxing as Bee Vishwanathan. The harder he tried to keep her out, the further she managed to barrel in, all guns blazing.

It was enough to drive a man—*him*—insane. And why did he care that her dress had no back and little skirt to speak of, which made him want to—

'Hey!' the exasperatingly worrisome creature interrupted his disturbing train of thought. 'Can you not drag me off? What will people think?'

Arhan stopped dead right where he was. Unfortunately, it was the dance floor and the band had struck up a slow-paced number. He put his arm around her waist and smoothly brought her half a foot close in a parody of a dance move.

'Are we playing statue-statue?' Arhan asked, softly, placing her hand on his shoulder. 'Move.'

Bee moved. 'What's your problem?' she bit off, finally.

'You are,' he replied instantly. 'What were you doing with those men?'

Bee grinned, stepping up to him and linking her arms around his neck.

He stiffened against the intimate gesture.

Damn her!

'I was just playing my part, Mr Kapoor. I am a trained circus monkey, remember?'

He didn't dignify her snide comment with an answer. Instead, he continued glaring at her, his hands on her waist.

How do women apply makeup so expertly that their ordinary brown eyes become all liquidy and golden? Makeup was the devil's own invention!

He looked away from her eyes to her plumped-up lips . . . and had this extremely explicit vision of leaning down and tasting their plumpness.

Big mistake!

When that didn't work, Arhan scowled and looked further down.

Wrong again, pal!

All the blood surged towards his cock as he saw the neckline that delicately displayed her breasts with a teasing hint of cleavage. More explicit visions crowded his head and made him realise, belatedly, why he'd actually dragged her away from the crowd of adoring men, and why he turned into an unrecognisable caveman every time he was around her.

He wanted her to himself.

His hands tightened around her body of their own volition.

Bee gasped and looked up at him with a confused expression. He shook his head slightly, trying to dislodge reckless thoughts of his hands roaming all over her. Failing spectacularly, he made himself look around at the dancing couples and nodded stiffly at someone he knew.

'What are we doing here, Arhan?' Bee sighed exasperatedly.

He looked at her and exhaled. 'I don't want you to mistake what I'm about to say. You need to watch yourself around these men. Not all of them are . . . gentlemen.' He tried to keep all emotion out of his voice, though it was hard.

'Hey,' she said indignantly. 'They all behave very well with me, unlike you, you jackass. I was just having a conversation with them. Fostering international relations.'

'You were holding court,' he retorted, 'which is even worse. You know very well you had them eating out of the palm of your hand. They were ready to make you their Draupadi.'

He regretted his little outburst as soon as the words were out of his mouth. He clamped his mouth shut and closed his eyes tightly, kicking himself mentally for saying something so phenomenally offensive.

What the fuck is wrong with me? What the hell am I saying? This is not what I meant at all!

'I didn't—'

But before he could complete his sentence, Bee stomped her stiletto on his foot. He stumbled and hobbled in place, shooting daggers at her.

'If you have such a problem with me, stay the hell away!' She spoke in a low voice, trembling with rage. 'I don't need you to come "save" me like some fucking knight in shining armour, you know.' She started to walk away but then, a beat later, she turned to face him, stepped closer and said, 'I definitely do not need lessons in etiquette or a character certificate from you. It's truly mind-boggling the way you manage to insult me every time you open your mouth. Everyone else might think you're the best thing since *aloo parathas* but I certainly don't.'

With that magnificent speech, she stalked away, her delicate hairdo wobbling with the force of her pace.

Arhan watched her retreating back. Her gleaming bracelet caught his eye, making the blood rush back to his head.

I can't let her walk away from me, not like this.

He limped after her, desire and shame twin daggers in his gut.

Bee's chest heaved with each deep breath; she was trying to clear the vermillion haze from her eyes.

Arhan Kapoor brought out the worst in her. Their last few meetings played in her mind like a movie reel.

Amma would die of shame if she ever found out that I broke someone's nose, called him names and have now possibly crippled him. Even if he deserved it!

As if on cue, her phone chirped, signalling an incoming text.

It was a quiet corner so Bee leaned against the cool marble wall and thumbed her phone open. But before she could see who was texting her, a figure stepped in front of her, blocking out the light.

'What the—'

She looked up to see Arhan staring down at her. For the first time that night, she really saw him. He wore black dress pants and a white shirt with a red tie—a very basic outfit. He should not have made her breathless but, unfortunately, he did.

She noticed that he was panting as well. They both stood still for a moment, breathing deeply, staring at each other.

Before she could open her mouth to yell or do anything, Arhan mumbled, 'I'm sorry. For what I said right then.' His voice was low, almost toneless. He placed one large palm against the wall, right next to her ear, his face inches away from hers. 'I'm sorry . . . for being a total jackass. There's no excuse for it. None.'

His words surprised her. She looked in his eyes and saw a reflection of what erupted inside her every time he was near.

Attraction. The lust snake reared its head inside her and hissed in anticipation.

Arhan leaned in closer, enclosing them in a bubble where only the two of them existed. The sounds of the party, everything, faded away, leaving only Arhan in her field of vision. It was heady, intoxicating. But what was more intoxicating was the way he was looking at her, with unabashed desire, as if he wanted to swallow her whole. It made her bold enough to lean a little back, so she could look him in the eye.

'Why are you such a jackass to me then?'

He smiled, devastatingly handsome and completely unaware of it. 'Maybe because my seduction technique belongs on a school playground.'

Bee did not want to smile though her lips twitched at the sincere self-deprecation. 'Maybe? I think most definitely, Mr Kapoor.'

'The weird thing is . . .' Arhan hesitated, the first time she'd ever seen him look so earnest. 'I didn't even recognise it till now.'

'Recognise what? That you've been absolutely horrible to me for no reason?'

'Oh, I have plenty of reason, Ms Vishwanathan.' He touched his still slightly bruised nose.

'Not fair! You called me names first. And I've apologised for that,' she said defiantly, pointing at his nose.

'Again, I apologise. You don't know the things I have seen travelling with the boys, the situations I have found them in. Anyway, I digress. Refresh my memory, Ms V, did you really apologise for breaking my nose?' He placed his other hand on the wall next to her, enclosing her.

But this time Bee saw consideration in his stance, on his ridiculously pretty face. She knew that if she said the word, he'd move away, be a gentleman. And she knew this because she'd watched him around everyone else and he was always unfailingly decent, be it with waiters or support staff or random fans.

He was horrible only to her.

'You can't punish me because you like me,' she said softly, waiting for him to deny it. 'That's gross misuse of power.'

He nodded, miserably. 'I know. Would it help if I said I've been in deep, deep, *deep* denial about it?'

'About what?' she asked nonchalantly. She was enjoying teasing him.

Arhan's face cleared, taken over by pure desire. It was like watching a spotlight come on during a day-night match. His eyes were ruthless with purpose.

Bee's knees went weak as he came closer, his breath warm on her face. Her heart thudded loudly. She desperately wished for bubble wrap but could only clench her hands, which quite urgently wanted to touch Arhan 'the fricking enemy' Kapoor.

'Can you forgive me, Bee?'

Her spine melted at his sincere words even though her self-respect wanted to take a stand against him.

He can't get away with being so mean to me with just a few kind words.

'Can you?'

Bee turned her head away, the breath knocked out of her.

Arhan stepped away immediately and oxygen rushed back in.

'I'll stay away from you,' he said quietly. 'If you can, please do forgive me.'

Bee smiled weakly at him. 'I'll think about it,' She didn't want to think about it.

He nodded. 'You do that.'

Arhan turned to leave when Bee reached out and tugged at his wrist. He looked curiously at her. 'Yes?'

'I've thought about it,' she said, bringing him closer.

He came to her without much resistance, his hands landing on her waist. She put her hands on his chest, clutching the lapels of his jacket.

'Bee . . .' Arhan murmured.

Bee took a huge gamble and asked boldly, 'Tell me, honestly, why did you drag me away from the Aussie captain?'

They looked at each other for a charged moment, hazel eyes clashing with golden brown. Desire and tension crackling between them.

'Because,' Arhan said thickly, 'I wanted to do this. '

Before she could blink, his lips were on hers, as if swallowing her whole. Then they gentled and feathered a soft kiss on the corner of her mouth.

'Tell me to stop, okay?'

She didn't.

His hand, tentative and questing, brushed against her shoulder blades and slid down her naked back, setting off fires everywhere he touched. Bee realised he might not be the grade-A enemy she'd termed him. In fact, Bee dragged Arhan closer, clutching his shirt, as the scratch of his stubble melted her from the inside out.

She placed a hand on his face and kissed him back, voraciously.

The kiss went incendiary in seconds as he slammed her against the wall, his hands moving up and down her body, devouring her.

Her brain was empty of thought. It felt wonderful. His lips moved to her neck as she pressed his nape closer to her, his black curls deliciously soft against her fingers. His hand slipped inside the low neckline of her dress, and she shivered. She hadn't realised calloused fingers could be unbearably arousing.

Bee made a sound, a cross between a moan and a sigh. But it was loud enough to penetrate the fog of lust that had shrouded Arhan's brain.

'Let's get out of here,' he said thickly against her neck.

Bee tried to nod, but her head felt too heavy, the pins that held her delicate updo digging into her scalp. Her skin felt too tight for all the raw desire coursing through her. He ran his tongue down her neck, where a pulse beat strongly in an echo of her heartbeat.

Bee held on to Arhan, her knees losing strength.

'Bee, let's go,' he whispered again, breathlessly.

In that instant, the lights went out in the big ballroom.

Arhan instinctively shoved Bee behind him, as he turned around and tried to peer into the darkness.

She poked him in the back with sharp nails. 'Hey, what the hell are you doing?'

'I am trying to protect you,' he answered.

'What did I tell you about me not needing you to save me?'

'Shhh!' he whispered.

He could feel her roll her eyes, even as he ordered his brain to start functioning and stop imagining hot, wild sex with Bee Vishwanathan. It was difficult but he managed it somehow. His pulse calmed down, oxygen rushed into his brain and, finally, he could think clearly.

He could hear a cascade of rising chatter, mostly in Bangla and English.

'Everyone calm down!'

'Bhoy peyo na! Shaanto. Shaanto!'

'Stay here,' he ordered.

At the mutinous look on her face, he changed his tone, 'Please stay here, Bee. I'll check what's going on. Do not move, please.'

Bee watched Arhan walk away, taking with him that magical lethargy that had possessed her the second he'd confessed his attraction, turning her into a puddle of gooey lust. She felt logic and common sense trickle back into her.

Bee moved away from the wall, following the loudest sound, her legs wobbling a little.

The lights came back on just as she reached the first panicked knot of guests, and the decibel level in the room increased exponentially. Her head pounded, the pins digging into her scalp. She blinked a few times, trying to adjust to the blinding lights after the sudden darkness.

She looked around but couldn't find Arhan anywhere. Instead, she spied the sign for the bathroom. She needed to get out of the ballroom's rarefied air and regain her equilibrium.

The bathroom was a sinful extension of the ballroom—wall-to-wall shag pile carpeting, massive urns that held potted palms and a marble counter on which stood two wide glass bowls with faucets that glittered in the scented air. The counter offered everything from perfume to condoms.

Admiring the full-scale service of the hotel, Bee walked over to the gilt mirror and stared at her mussed reflection. Her gloss was eaten off, her lips looked bruised. Her sophisticated updo was smashed at the back, probably when Arhan had shoved her against the wall, his hands driving her mindless. Knowing she didn't have a choice, Bee removed the bobby pins and let her hair cascade around her shoulders.

Now she looked like the wild heathen he'd once accused her of being.

Bee wet a tissue and wiped her hot face and neck, reapplied her gloss and tried to brush her hair into some semblance of style.

The heavy doors opened and another guest stumbled in. She wobbled on pointy heels and adjusted her golden gauzy *dupatta*. With her artfully tousled hair, defiant red lipstick and slightly deranged eyes, she looked in worse shape than Bee.

'Are you all right?' Bee was concerned.

The woman focused on her. She was beautiful, with almond-shaped eyes, an evenly proportioned face and a size zero figure.

Her dress was subtly slutty. She wore maroon velvet cigarette pants and an A-line kurta in the latest Pakistani style that flowed to the ankles. But her kurta was more like a jacket, showcasing her 36 D breasts that were covered in a gold bikini top held together by a knot in the middle, exposing her flat, firm stomach with a bar through her belly button.

'Yeah, I'm all right,' the woman muttered.

Then, her heavily made-up eyes narrowed and she ran towards Bee. She held Bee's wrist in a vice-like grip, her nails digging into the skin. 'Where the fuck did you get this?'

Up close, even her designer perfume couldn't mask the vodka fumes emanating from the woman. 'Did you *buy* this? Is the auction over?'

'What?' Bee tried to tug her hand away. 'No. I am just showcasing it for the Maharani till they announce the bids. I can't afford to buy this.'

Bee knew the first rule in dealing with crazy drunks was to keep your voice calm and soothing and not make any sudden movements.

'The Maharani.' The woman's lovely face contorted into a grimace. 'That witch.'

Bee gasped.

'So you're in the queen's circle now. Be careful, babe. You can get in, but you can't get out. And this . . .' She pressed the bracelet deeply into Bee's wrist, causing her to yelp. 'This is as fake as the Maharani's affection.'

Bee stared, speechless.

The woman's eyes filled with tears. 'I couldn't . . .' Her voice broke. 'I couldn't. And I am so sorry . . . so sorry.'

The door opened a second time and the Maharani stepped in, imperiously.

Her usually calm face crumpled into a mask of distress as she looked at the weeping woman. *'Hey bhagwaan, Ujwala. Thu khatro pidhoro hai! Thane katri vaar kiyo hai ke logon mein maari hasi ni—'* She stopped mid-sentence when her eyes registered Bee's presence.

Bee couldn't understand the exact words but she knew disappointed mom-speak, having heard it enough times herself.

So this is Princess Ujwala.

'Bee, my dear. Could you please not let anyone else in? I need to speak to my daughter alone.' The Maharani switched to English.

Bee nodded and the princess let her go. Bee gently unclasped the bracelet and gave it to the woman, pressing it into her limp palm.

'This is yours,' she said quietly before escaping the intensity in the room.

Her world had just been rocked by the weirdest conversation ever.

The events of the evening had left Bee famished so she moved towards the buffet and was loading up her plate when the Aussie captain homed in on her, all blonde-haired, blue-eyed charm. She mentally rolled her eyes but pasted a pleasant expression on her face.

After the upheavals of the last half an hour, she was in no mood to make polite conversation. All she wanted was a quiet corner in which to devour her *bhapa ilish* and rice. If the steamed fish tasted half as delicious as it smelled she would enter gastronomic heaven.

'We were searching for you, Bee,' he drawled on, cupping her elbow in an entirely masculine gesture of possession. 'When the lights went out, I was so worried about you. Where did you disappear to with Arhan?'

'I—'

'We didn't disappear, Martin. We were dancing. Didn't you see us on the dance floor?' Arhan asked as he appeared at her other elbow.

The Australian gave her a questioning look. She smiled a what-can-you-do smile.

Arhan placed an arm around her shoulder, ran a thumb over the soft skin. Bee shivered inwardly.

The Aussie shrugged good-naturedly and said, 'Cool, mate. I didn't know that's how things were.'

'That's not how things are.' Bee smiled placidly at them and shrugged Arhan off smoothly.

Arhan grunted next to her but she ignored him and continued addressing the Aussie captain. 'I'd be happy to talk about the '61 Australia-Windies match with you, Royston.'

'That'd be heaps cool, Bee. Maybe some other time? We could even discuss how my boys could beat Arhan's boys,' he said as he backed away.

Bee turned to Arhan the minute they were alone. 'Don't ever speak for me, please.'

Arhan sighed. 'That wasn't . . . Where were you? I asked you to stay put, didn't I?'

'I went to the bathroom and I didn't realise I needed your permission. Now let me eat in peace.' Bee sat down at the closest table and Arhan promptly settled in next to her. She gave him a belligerent glare. 'Dude, can you breathe somewhere else? I can't eat with this much testosterone swirling around me, and I am famished.'

Arhan narrowed his eyes, ready to deliver a blistering retort when the Maharani appeared at their table.

She had red-rimmed eyes. 'Bee,' she said in a wobbly voice that sounded exactly like her daughter's. 'Could we please talk?' She gave Arhan a tattered but regal smile. 'Alone.'

The Maharani swept Bee into a tiny anteroom off the ballroom. It was tastefully decorated with velvet tapestries, antique vases and an uncomfortable chintz-covered settee. Bee dutifully sat down next to the Maharani and tucked one ankle behind the other. Some habits were beginning to rub off.

The Maharani touched Bee's vibrant hair. 'You look much better this way,' she said. 'Don't ever listen to me and put your hair up again.'

Bee smiled and discreetly picked lint off the settee, hoping to God she wouldn't slide off. It was extremely slippery and her balance was not what it usually was. She could still feel Arhan's hand gripping her hip.

Bee was in desperate need of some bubble wrap.

'I am deeply troubled that you witnessed that painful scene between the princess and myself.'

Bee didn't bother to correct the Maharani that it was the princess who had been rude to her, not the Maharani. As it was, she was in obvious distress.

'It's nothing. If I had known the princess was in attendance I would never have —'

'I didn't know myself, dear. Ranawatji, my assistant, did not see fit to inform me that Ujwala had decided to tag along for this event. I shall have some stern words with him over the matter.' There was an unyielding glint to the queen now. Then, her distress returned. 'I am so sorry, Bee. My daughter was inexcusably rude to you. If there is anything I can do to make it up to you . . .'

This is a night of unexpected apologies.

Bee leaned in and squeezed the queen's knee. 'Please, ma'am. It was nothing. Your daughter meant no harm, I am sure.'

The Maharani closed her eyes. There was utter weariness in her posture. 'I am not sure about that, Bee. I thought . . . by now she would be over the terrible tragedy that has shaken our lives. That she would at least have recovered enough to not cause embarrassing scenes in public. I guess I was wrong.'

Bee leaned in further. 'I don't blame her. Your daughter is obviously grieving her lost love.' She added unwisely, 'I'm sure she will get over it in time.'

The Maharani's lips quivered, showing the merest blurring of maroon colour outside of their natural shape. 'You don't get over the death of someone you love, Bee. You just learn to endure it. I still miss Kunwarji so much. Every day. Especially during trying times like these.'

Although she'd never experienced this kind of everlasting love, Bee's heart went out to the woman. She seemed to be on the verge of a breakdown. Bee cast around for a topic to take the Maharani's mind off her problems.

'Well, if things keep going the way they are, Team India's trying times will beat everyone else's, ma'am. The Aussie captain was just trying to pump me for information about our boys.'

Rani Kalavati blinked slowly and focused on Bee's grim smile. 'I hope you didn't reveal sensitive information, my dear.'

Bee chuckled. 'Believe me, even if I had wanted to, *he* wouldn't have let me.' Then, sensing the Maharani's confusion, she added, 'I mean Arhan.'

The Maharani's eyes cleared and gentle humour filled them. 'That boy takes his job very seriously. He would have made an excellent prince.'

A shaft of something hot and green pierced Bee, even though she was sure that wasn't what the Maharani was implying. She gamely plodded on. 'Yeah, I bet. He is certainly autocratic enough. Although I admit, he would look sexy in a *pagdi*.'

Bee bit her lip at her thoughtless remark but the Maharani laughed. 'I wish more people were as honest as you, my dear. As for Team India, I don't think we need to worry about them being eliminated just yet.'

'The bookies have stretched the odds 18–1 now. It's going to take a miracle for India to qualify, ma'am.'

The Maharani gave her a sphinx-like look. 'Stranger things have happened. It's cricket. Don't underestimate our men.'

Bee wisely kept her rebuttals to herself and allowed the Maharani her delusions. After all, the poor woman needed them, considering the rude troll she had for a daughter.

The auction was in full swing by the time the Maharani and Bee returned to the ballroom.

The crowd of eager guests was going at it, trying desperately to outbid one another for a bat signed by the Aussie team. The figures were mind-boggling.

Bee was starving so she loaded up her plate once again with the fish and mouth-watering murgh dum biryani and raita, the likes of which she'd never had before.

She watched the whole hoopla from the very back of the ballroom, inhaling *roshogullas*. After having three of the softer-than-a-baby's-bum *gullas*, she decided that the only way she could conceivably eat again was if she walked up to her room on the fourteenth floor.

She needed the exercise; it was a necessity now.

Arhan was nowhere to be seen and she was fine with that. Just because they'd had a singeing make-out moment didn't mean he was going to be her undying Majnu. Nor did she want him to be.

Bee slipped out of the ballroom, while the Maharani's bracelet was being called for auction.

It had been fun playing dress-up for a night, like being Cinderella. Nothing had gone the way she'd planned, and she definitely had stories for Dheera.

Bee traipsed to the emergency exit, slipped out of her heels and started climbing the stairs. Seven floors up, her lungs were burning and her calves were aching and she was seriously considering her position on workouts.

Bee took a few deep breaths; a stitch on her side was causing her stomach muscles to cramp. She put a hand on her cramping abdomen and sat down on the stairs for a moment.

The elevator banks on the other side of the door pinged, signalling an incoming lift.

'Screw it,' Bee said, gathering her shoes in one hand, and ran to the door.

She pushed it open and reached the elevator just as the doors were about to close. She pressed the button and the doors opened. Bee slumped against the mirrored panel of the lift, gratefully pressing the button for her floor.

She barely had the energy to step out when the doors opened. Bee rummaged in her purse for the key card to the royal suite and was surprised when the door opened from the inside and someone stepped out. Someone in a black hoodie and a cap that covered their entire face.

Bee's eyes widened as her shoes dropped to the floor.

The intruder's black eyes turned deadly. He whipped out an arm and dragged Bee forward. Then, he slammed her against the wall, face-first.

Bee's breath went shallow as an elbow pressed down on the back of her neck, squeezing her windpipe efficiently.

A monstrous voice whispered, '*Kidhar hai?* Tell me where it is.'

Tears gathered in Bee's eyes and she squeezed them shut. The elbow went in tighter while Bee tried to claw her way out of the hold.

The intruder was not very tall, of average height, but he was all muscle, immovable. He yanked on her loose hair now, tugging it from the scalp.

Bee gasped out loud in pain.

'Where the fuck is it?'

'I . . . I . . .'

The elevator dinged open again and the intruder cursed, foul and long. Then he slammed Bee against the door, her temple hitting the edge. Her eyes rolled into the back of her head. She slid to the floor unconscious as blood trickled slowly down her forehead.

16

'I really think your dad is right and your *Mangal* is going to get you killed,' Dheera said the next morning.

After she'd come to last night, Bee had called Dheera to her room and together they'd cleaned up the wound and fashioned a cute butterfly bandage. Then Dheera had crashed with her.

Bee groaned and turned on her side, snuggling under the 300 thread count sheets. Her body was one long bruise and she didn't want to breathe, much less talk. She just wanted to sleep.

'I also think we should definitely call the police and the Maharani and your make-out buddy Arhan. I hate that you want to keep this quiet. This is a crime, woman!' Dheera yanked the covers away from Bee who groaned some more.

'You're a tyrant, Dhee. I made a grave mistake befriending you!'

'Get up! We need to talk to the authorities.' Dheera was using her mom voice, the same one she used to subdue her two toddlers. 'I can understand why you didn't want to make any fuss last night. The Maharani had a rough night and the hotel staff was busy with the charity gig and blackout. But I really don't get why we can't call your make-out buddy now.'

'Arhan is not my make-out buddy!' Bee let out a growl of frustration.

Her stupid brain immediately flashed back to Arhan grabbing her and kissing her like a goddamn hero from a romance novel. And she'd loved every second of it. Every hot, scorching, improper second.

'We just had a moment . . . a really, *really* hot moment, I'll give you that. But that's all it was! And as for the authorities, no, Dhee! I'm still on thin ice with Satyarth. He'll take me off this assignment if I go to the police and it leaks out.'

Bee shuddered. 'Not to mention my family will lock me up!'

'Brigha!' Dheera jumped on the bed, held her shoulders and shook her trying to knock some sense back into her friend. 'Get a grip. Your life is more important than this assignment. I am beginning to agree with your folks that you need to be locked up.'

Bee glared at Dheera.

Her friend continued sombrely, 'You're full-on crazy if you think I am going to just let you get attacked and do nothing.'

'Dhee! You're hurting me.'

Dheera let go of Bee. 'Take a shower. Get dressed.' She was uncharacteristically grim. 'We have an appointment with the police. I've already mapped the route to the station on my phone.'

'Dhee, please. I *can't* talk to them.'

'It's either them or your parents, Brigha. You decide.'

Bee flopped back on to the downy pillows and cursed the fates for always putting her in the wrong place at the wrong time. She also vowed to never eat a *roshogulla* ever again.

The damn things had almost got her killed.

—⋅◆ ◆⋅—

Inspector Paramjit Thapar was part of the special branch that had operations in every city in India. He had ten years of hardcore experience dealing with criminals so, naturally, he had a low opinion of mankind in general.

He was very good at his job because of this very opinion. It meant he trusted no one.

When two well-dressed, designer-bag-toting women walked into the Park Street police station, Inspector Thapar was chatting with the station head, enjoying a cup of masala tea with ginger and two sugars.

Like everyone else in the vicinity, he watched their progress with interest.

The older, taller one looked effortlessly beautiful. The other woman was wearing a purple kurti with bright pink harem pants; she was a walking beacon, unmissable.

Then the tall one whipped off her glares and Thapar saw the determined eyes. He immediately snapped on his invisible armour.

'We'd like to report a break-in,' the determined one said in pure Bangla. 'At the Park Grandeur.'

The officer on duty perked up a little, tucking in his potbelly in the presence of females. 'Madams, why don't you sit down first?'

The older woman whipped out a badge from her bag and flashed it at Sub-Inspector Brijmohan. Thapar watched as the man's eyes bugged out, as did his belly. 'Madam! We will give you any help you want. We can even lodge an FIR.'

The younger woman fidgeted with her phone, rolled her eyes behind her glasses and said, 'This is such a waste of time. These guys are not going to help us. Let's just leave. Please.'

Thapar decided it was time to make his entry. He hated it when people acted with prejudice against the force. He gulped down the rest of his chai and stood up, smoothing the lines on his suit jacket so it fell neatly.

Bee looked up at the man who was walking towards them and her spine straightened automatically.

The man was of average height, same as her attacker, and slim. He obviously wasn't a part of the workout brigade, of which Arhan was a devoted member. Yet, there was something about his wiry build that had Bee thinking twice about underestimating him.

He extended a rough hand. Bee saw that a part of his index finger was missing.

'Chief Inspector Paramjit Thapar, special branch. How may I help you?'

'Bee Vishwanathan,' she said, 'Reporter for Krikket-365. We're covering the World Cup matches.'

'Lovely. I read your column, Ms Vishwanathan. Your analysis of the Aus-Pak match was spot on. If they had played the original eleven instead of replacing the spinner with the fast bowler, they might have even scored a 100 in their innings.'

'Obviously Royston Martin read the pitch wrong—'

Dheera cleared her throat, loudly. Bee's enthusiasm waned.

Thapar nodded at Bee's bandaged forehead. 'Did this happen during the break-in?'

So far Bee had managed to keep the butterfly bandage hidden behind a lock of hair. She was impressed and a little apprehensive at his comment and attention to detail.

The inspector was sharp and had a keen eyesight.

Dheera nodded. 'Yes, she was bleeding profusely when I arrived at the scene.'

'I see.'

'It was extremely bizarre, Inspector Thapar,' Bee began earnestly. 'I am not even sure the attacker meant anything by it. Nothing was stolen and the rooms were left untouched. My companion has lots of expensive jewellery in her safe and none of it was disturbed. I think they just made a mistake and I was caught at the wrong place. That's all.'

'Why don't you leave it to the police to draw their conclusions; you just tell us everything that happened, okay? But first, please sit, get comfortable. Have some *bader cha*. It's the best in the world.'

Thapar drew out a couple of chairs and gestured to the ladies. He snapped out an order in precise Bangla and the female havaldar on duty scurried out only to return with a ledger. Another flunky rushed in with steaming cups of tea.

Dheera was impressed while Bee's apprehension increased. This man had clout. He wouldn't be as easy to manage as the policeman in Jaipur.

Shit! I'll have to tell him about Jaipur.

Bee sat down, gripping her Fendi tote tight, desperately wanting the bubble wrap that she'd stowed inside. Of course, Thapar would think her emotionally unstable if she started popping in his station. So she accepted the tea in the earthen mug and sipped on it.

The inspector had been correct. It was delicious.

'Now.' He leaned back against the creaking chair that the in-charge inspector had vacated in deference to him. 'I hope you've had that wound looked at. Head wounds are very tricky.'

'I took first-aid classes before my pregnancy. I made sure it wasn't anything serious.' Dheera was back in her mama bear mode, defending her cub.

'Be that as it may, it would be better to take Ms Vishwanathan to a hospital and have her properly checked out.' Thapar was deliberately mild.

'I am *fine*, Inspector,' Bee said. 'After I woke up, I made sure to check for a concussion. No dizziness, no nausea and I can recall my name and ATM PINs. I have been checking every two hours.'

Thapar leaned forward on the desk. 'You fainted?'

Dheera gave him a grim look. 'She was knocked unconscious. This is a very serious matter, Inspector. My friend here is trying to brush it off but you don't let her, *thik achhe?*'

She then started on a barrage of Bangla, some of which Bee caught. Words like 'dedicated', 'determined to be successful' and 'job' she could make out. The rest of it was lyrical gibberish.

Thapar held up his hand.

'I believe I would like to hear from Ms Vishwanathan herself. She's a reporter. She can give us the facts. Whether we lodge an FIR or not can be decided later. Is that fine with you, Ms Vishwanathan?'

Bee smiled in resignation, finished off her chai and said, 'Please, call me Bee. Everyone does. And I will tell you everything I know.'

Thapar leaned back in his chair, the hinges creaking under his weight. 'Wonderful.'

17

The flight to Chennai was scheduled for noon.

The emergency staff meeting was still underway, even though they had to leave for the airport in thirty minutes. Everyone important was there: the captain, support staff, management and the official selector, Kanstiya. He had flown out to Kolkata at an ungodly hour just to get to this all-important meeting called by, of all the people in the world, Arhan Kapoor.

Thus, it was to Arhan that he addressed his comments. 'Look, I was only following orders,' Hasmukh Kanstiya defended himself. 'The board was keen to have an anchor in the middle and Salil has proven in the past that he can play despite injuries. How was I to know that he couldn't do it this time?'

'Because I said so. Specifically.' Arhan replied, deadpan.

There was an air of dangerous calm about him. He had conducted business with four-penny vendors and shaken hands with the country's best leaders when they had visited his sugar-processing plant in Ludhiana. He had learned the value of keeping a poker face while coaching a flagging Punjab to their first-ever Ranji Trophy final last year. In short, he knew how much to say and how much to show.

Kanstiya shrugged. 'You're not on the board, AK. I have to take into account its decision. You can't hold that against me.'

Arhan smiled. It was a nasty smile. His players knew that smile meant the *taandav* would commence shortly.

'I have an injured player in my already broken team; there is a very real possibility that he might never play cricket again. And it's all because of *your* decision to uphold the board's directive. You chose to listen to the board members, who sit in their air-conditioned offices and watch the match on their flatscreen TVs, instead of heeding my advice. I am *here*, with the players. We play the game here. We live the game here. You fucked up.'

'Hey—'

'You. Fucked. Up,' Arhan repeated. He looked at a stoic Viren who gave him a small nod. 'This team, *my team*, needs to heal. They need to fall back in love with the game. Practising for ungodly hours at the nets is not going to give them a winning mentality. Actually winning will.'

'Look, Arhan. I get your point,' said Balvinder Lakhani, a board official.

He chewed on his odious pan-flavoured candy and smiled sympathetically at Viren who was glancing at his watch, the latest from a brand that he endorsed. The time was nearly 10.20 a.m. They needed to leave now if they were going to make the scheduled Chennai flight.

'But now, cricket is as much about the drama as it is about the sport,' Balvinder said. 'Technical-vechnical is all you, the boys . . . We have to worry about price points and ad buys and player contracts, which are to be renewed next year. We need to worry about revenue . . . and revenue comes from advertising which comes from sensational cricket as well as the drama behind the scenes.'

'So one man's career going down the toilet is entertainment for the rest of us?' Arhan demanded.

'Well,' Balvinder emphasised, 'if you want to be crude, yes.' The board member turned to the head coach, Garry Marshall, who was suspiciously silent during this entire exchange. However, it was this silence that spoke volumes about his commitment towards the team. 'Garry Bhai didn't have any problem with sending Salil in, did he?'

Garry shrugged. 'I leave the big decisions to the big guys and the micro-management to Arhan.' He gave a toothy Aussie grin to his assistant who was silently vibrating with rage. 'You're a fine lad, Arhan. I would not be able to do this without you. But there's hardly any point in wasting our time now that the game has been lost. We need to chalk it up to a loss and move on. Look to the next game.'

'You want to make money, Lakhani sir?' Arhan hoped his poker face was still holding. 'You want to give the paying audience theatrics and showmanship. Let the fucking team *win*.' He almost growled the words out. 'They have the potential for it. Give us a measure of control over what goes on in the damn dressing room instead of letting us just be a mouthpiece for the board. I can't keep propping them up with empty pep talks anymore. It's shallow and selfish.'

'Hey, we're doing fine in the dressing room,' Garry said. 'Aren't we, Viren?'

The captain measured his words carefully as he answered. 'Arhan is not completely off-base in wanting more autonomy and allowing us to play our natural game. The players will be more confident about their roles if they were assured of their place on the team. This game of musical chairs makes for low confidence, and this reflects in our game. No offence.'

'Well.' Hasmukh shifted uncomfortably in his seat. 'I can understand where you're coming from.'

'Awesome. We would love it if you could pass on the message to those sitting above you as well,' Viren said.

'I have another concern here,' Arhan spoke quietly. This time, he addressed Akshar, the team physiotherapist. 'I need assurance that Akshar will not repeat the disaster from day before yesterday and jeopardise a player's career for the sake of one match.'

'Arhan, I honestly thought he was good to go,' Akshar protested.

The physiotherapist was a silent, bespectacled man with a soothing demeanour, always immaculately dressed in formals. He also had the slightest trace of an accent from his time abroad. 'Salil was in good form. No pain whatsoever, and I supervised his injection and supplied him with pills as well. He should have been able to play.'

'He had a rotator-cuff injury, Akshar. You know how serious those are,' Arhan retorted. 'Playing through the pain is one thing. Playing when a body part has completely broken down is quite another. Why the hell did you certify him to begin with?'

Akshar shrugged, glanced away. 'I was just doing my job, what my bosses told me to do.'

'Your commitment needs to be to my *team*!'

'My commitment, financial and medical, is to the ICCB, Arhan,' Akshar answered promptly. 'With all due respect, I answer to them. And when they asked me if the guy was good to go, to the best of my medical knowledge, he was. I am sorry I miscalculated. It won't happen again.'

To his credit, the man sounded sincere.

Arhan sighed. 'I hope we have all learned something from this meeting, gentlemen. We have a team that is in need of encouragement on all fronts—physical, mental and spiritual.'

'Maybe we need Mahadev Baba ki Ganpati to win the tournament,' Garry drawled. 'Or we could all sneak off into dark corners of hotel corridors for some "physical" encouragement, am I right?'

Arhan swivelled his head and shot his boss a cold look. 'What are you talking about?'

Garry looked at his immaculately buffed nails, gleaming pink with health and zero physical exertion. He might have been a great Aussie captain in his time, but he'd grown lazy and complacent with age. Now instead of runs, he preferred to count the dollars in his bank account and the fake extensions in his girlfriend's hair.

'Nothing at all. Just that fraternising with the enemy is an interesting way of keeping them at arm's length.'

Arhan forced himself to chuckle, feigning nonchalance. 'If you're referring to the reporter, you don't have to worry about it.'

He was very aware of Viren's startled and disapproving glance and willed him to keep his mouth shut, which he thankfully did.

These people did not need to know exactly how things stood with Bee and him. It was his personal business and he wanted to discuss it with his sexist, chauvinistic superiors as much as he wanted a hamstring injury before a match!

As expected, the men laughed, winked and let the matter go.

Except for Akshar Shekhawat, who was looking intently at his phone, a frown on his usually placid face. Something was the matter with him. Arhan vowed to take time out and get to the root of it at the next available opportunity.

Finally the meeting was adjourned with nothing much accomplished.

Kanstiya gestured for Arhan to wait after everyone else had filed out of his suite. 'You think you're winning points by doing this, by flexing your muscles. But you're not.'

Arhan wasn't surprised by the comment. 'I am just trying to do my job.'

'You're here as a favour to someone. On a trial basis.' Kanstiya was blunt. 'The minute we find you wanting, you're out. Once upon a time, you had a bright future in this game and it's only because of your sentimental value, which the audience laps up, that you're here. *Bhoolna mat*, Arhan.'

'Funny,' Arhan murmured, plunging his hands into his pants pockets, 'I thought I was here because I was the only man for the job.'

'We can find ten Arhan Kapoors before your flight takes off for Chennai,' Kanstiya said quietly. 'Don't think we won't do it.'

'I understand that. But you need to know something too. As long as I am the assistant coach for the Indian cricket team, I am going to try my absolute best to do right by my boys and help them win.' Arhan was as blunt as Kanstiya had been, and even more deadly serious. 'If you have a problem with that, take it up with the people who hired me in the first place. I am sure Rajiv Shastri, who comes over for dinner to my house every time he visits my *pind*, will be only too thrilled to hear your fascinating observations.'

Then he left before he could do any more damage to his career and Kanstiya's rapidly turning red face.

———+◆ ◆+———

'I am telling you, we made a big mistake by talking to that Thapar guy,' Bee whispered to Dheera two days later as they were making their way back from a press con. They blended in with the crowd leaving the press con hall and met up with Harry and Sholes.

India was yet to scrape through after losing to Ireland and everyone was talking about how the fire of the opening match had pretty much fizzled out as the league matches had progressed. The sure-fire winners kept advancing, with Australia leading the juggernaut. India was nowhere in the picture; most of its players were not even battle-ready. No one was blaming them, but when the host nation played poorly, it did not make for a large or receptive audience. The TRPs were tanking and the organisers were having a confab with the board.

Bee was privy to a lot of inside information, thanks to her proximity to the team, but she couldn't use it anywhere because of the breach-of-trust issue. She was also reluctantly beginning to think the game mattered more than reporting on it.

'Why would you say that?' Dheera asked, loudly. 'The cops have been super helpful.'

Some of their fellow journalists gave them a surprised look.

Bee glared at her friend and dragged her off to a secluded corner, leaving Harry and Sholes behind, lost in their own world and talking excitedly about the latest win—West Indies beating Ireland—strengthening India's odds of making it to the next round.

'Could you control your volume, babe? We don't need the whole world to know our business, okay?'

Dheera shrugged, the movement shifting the Leica DSLR, with a wide lens attachment, hanging around her neck. She removed the strap and strung it on her shoulder.

'Listen, Bee. I don't know why you're so upset. That Thapar guy is cool with you flying to Chennai, *na*?' Dheera was the voice of reason. 'Most of the time, these cops don't let you leave town in the middle of an active investigation. He isn't even looking into the Maharani's affairs, not that it would be easy to inquire into a queen's affairs without raising alarms, even for the special branch, know what I mean? All he wants is for you to try to recall anything unusual about the break-ins.'

'Well, I gave him all the information I could about the stupid attack. I wish that it had never happened and that I was living inside bubble wrap.' Bee was understandably distraught.

'If wishes were horses, pigs would fly,' Dheera said. 'I don't regret involving him at all. You need the authorities on your side. This is getting out of hand. First, someone breaks into your room, then he assaults you. What's next? A quick knifing in a dark hallway?'

'You make it all sound like a conspiracy, Dhee.' Bee chuckled. 'I hardly think I am the target of a professional criminal who is involved in some nefarious activity and doesn't want me in the picture. I am sure it's all just a coincidence. The only good thing is people are doing a lot of "poor baby" around me and they don't even know about the second incident yet!'

'If this were a paranormal romance, I would say there are no coincidences, only vampires, and no fate, only werewolves,' Dheera grumbled.

Bee looped her arm through her friend's. 'You're Team Edward all the way, aren't you?'

'Forever,' Dheera agreed. 'I can't believe you're leveraging a life-threatening incident for your job.'

'It wasn't life-threatening, Dheera.'

'What's not life-threatening?' Arhan asked as he appeared in front of them, almost out of thin air. Almost immediately, his eyes narrowed in that all-too-familiar angry look Bee knew so well and he spat out, 'What the fuck is wrong with your head?'

Arhan was in a foul mood when he caught up with Bee. A headache had made a permanent home in his frontal lobe. One of Akshar's assistants was making noises about checking out his eyes in order to rule out the need for glasses.

Arhan knew that poor vision was not his problem. In fact, he saw all too clearly. He saw a team falling apart despite a world-class batting and bowling order, injuries notwithstanding! He saw men dispirited and upset because their motivation was failing them every time they went on the field without Zakeer Hussain, the unofficial team mascot. They weren't even trying anymore, self-fulfilling a prophecy of failure. The win against the Bangladeshis had come by only because, even on their worst day, India could beat one of the minnows, even if the minnows gave a tough fight.

Arhan knew of no cure to heal a mourning team. And yet, it was his job to keep trying to motivate them to win, to get them into a playing mindset, a winning mindset. It was starting to feel like an impossible task.

It did not help his cause at all when half his brain continued to obsess over Bee Vishwanathan and the scorching kiss they'd shared. Right before she had flounced away from him without so much as a goodbye.

A man had his pride.

It was this pride that had made him keep his distance, keep his cool. He hadn't knocked on her door the night of the kiss, even though every bone in his body had wanted to. He hadn't sought her out on the plane ride to Chennai. He'd been a gentleman, the one she had so rightly accused him of not being. The fact that she hadn't talked to him either or texted or acknowledged his existence in any way had riled him up some more. But now he wanted some answers from her.

He'd waited till after the press con to seek her out, knowing full well she wouldn't miss such an important meet. But she'd disappeared again with that photographer friend of hers, adding to his headache.

Thus, he was in a foul mood when he finally caught up with her.

A small bandage graced her otherwise perfect forehead at the right temple. She'd done an admirable job covering it up with a careful tik-tok pin placement. And her outrageous neon pink tee shirt and cargo shorts with the ever-present casual *Kolhapuris* were a distraction of their own.

But now he knew this woman. Knew her intimately, if not biblically. So he knew where not to look.

'Well?' he demanded, resolutely looking at the forehead. 'Are you going to tell me what's going on or do you need me to jump through more hoops?'

Dheera's lips pursed at Arhan's tone, but she said nothing. It was Bee who answered, 'I'm not the one who makes people jump through hoops.' She gave him a scathing glance. 'Case in point.'

Then, she brushed past him and stalked away, removing bubble wrap from her shorts pocket. Dheera stayed where she was.

Arhan gave a growl of mingled frustration and inappropriate lust.

'I am going to give you the benefit of the doubt,' Dheera said.

'What?' He was still watching Bee depart. She was hard to miss in her crazy outfit. It was difficult to acknowledge that she was the same svelte, poised creature who'd exploded in his arms a few nights ago.

'You can put your tongue back in your mouth now,' Dheera said, exercising remarkable patience. 'She's gone.'

'What?' He gave the photographer a myopic glance, his migraine gaining epic proportions. Desire was not the most pleasant of additions to an already terrible headache. 'You're her friend, aren't you? I've seen you both hanging out with Harry Singh and Karan Sholekar. They are decent guys, they wouldn't hurt her. So what happened?'

'This is exactly why I'll give you the benefit of the doubt,' Dheera said. 'You seem to care about Bee even though you choose a very *gadadhari Bheem* way of showing it. And, sometimes, she does need someone authoritative to talk to her. I think you could be that guy.'

'Authoritative? Me? With her?' He rubbed a hand down his face, pinching the bridge of his aching nose. He had no interest in going up against Bee's right hook again. 'You have me confused with some other guy.' He searched his memory bank for the woman's name. 'Dheera, right?' he finished.

Dheera nodded.

'Bee will never listen to me about anything, Dheera.' Arhan bit off the truth. 'But I need to know what's going on. Why is she hurt?'

'You need to make her listen to you, AK,' Dheera said stubbornly. 'Bee doesn't realise she is in way over her head and maybe you could make her see reason. God knows no one else can. If nothing else, maybe you could hold her down after sex and tell her she needs to be more careful.'

Arhan was mortified to hear that Dheera knew about them. He could feel the blood creeping up his neck and over his ears; he felt hot under the collar of his blue Team India sweatshirt.

'Dheera, I—'

She waved a hand to dismiss his next words. 'Forget about it. She is like my little sister. She tells me everything. At least this means now she won't marry that MS-from-the-US Iyer dweeb. Focus on the problem at hand, Arhan.'

'Which is what? You still haven't told me.' He looked at her, confused. 'And what is an MS from the US?'

Dheera huffed out a breath. 'You should have a talk with her. You clearly have a lot of catching up to do. And remind her that her folks are one call away if anything else goes wrong. Maybe she'll take the threat seriously if it comes from her make-out buddy.'

18

Bee was pissed. All the bubble wrap in the world was not enough to help her anger subside. Her thumbs ached from popping continuously so she switched to the next calming tactic—reciting cricket facts to herself. Some people counted prime numbers, she thought of cricket. It was an unfortunate by-product of being born into a family that revered cricket as much as mathematics and since she'd *sucked* at maths, her survival technique had been to learn all about cricket, as much and as fast as she could.

Besides, now that she was spending all her time on the cricket pitches, so to speak, she was beginning to understand why 1.4 billion people were crazy about the game. It was glorious on a good day and God-like on the best!

Jeff Dujon is the only wicketkeeper to have played more than thirty tests and never lose a series.

Lasith Malinga got 4 wickets in 4 balls in international cricket, against South Africa.

Shane Warne turned the ball a whopping 38 degrees to Andrew Strauss during the Ashes 2005 test series.

I am still so pissed I could punch Arhan all over again.

'Bee,' Suresh Vijay, the team vice-captain interrupted her thoughts, steadying her as she almost slammed into him. 'Are you talking to yourself?'

Bee tried to clear her head. Suresh Vijay was not the recipient of her anger, Arhan Kapoor was. She smiled wide, even though it felt fake. A surprised Suresh took a step back at the teeth-baring smile.

She toned down her smile to civil. 'I am fine, Suresh. It's nothing. How about you guys? The result was favourable, wasn't it?'

The vice-captain shrugged. 'With West Indies winning this match as expected, we only need to beat them to go through. But I am not so sure about that, Bee. We need more motivation and—hey, what happened to your head?' He reached up to brush away the lock covering her bandage and instinctively switched to Tamil. 'Did you see a doctor? It looks pretty serious to me.'

Bee smiled again, this time with a lot more warmth. 'I am fine, Suresh. I am more concerned about the team. This lacklustre form is not going to win anyone the finals, is it?'

Suresh looked upset and worried, but he knew better than to open his mouth. A gag order was a gag order after all.

'You're not spilling team secrets, are you?' a cool voice inquired as Arhan strode up to them.

Suresh gave him a sheepish grin. 'Sorry, AK. I didn't mean—'

'Never mind.' Arhan had the audacity to wink. 'She is smart enough to get anyone to talk. Even me.'

Suresh shrugged again, pointed at her forehead and left with a quiet 'Take care'.

Bee, not in the mood for another confrontation, elbowed Arhan in his stomach and attempted to walk away. He pulled her back and caged her against the wall and said softly, 'I believe the last time we did this, the consequences were vastly enjoyable for the both of us. Want to try again?'

To her everlasting horror and shame, tears filled her eyes as she stood inside Arhan's warm yet imprisoning hold.

Arhan looked flummoxed, as if he'd never seen women cry before. But Bee knew he had grown up with three sisters.

'Are waterworks your Kryptonite, Coach sir?' She was justifiably bitter.

Bee tried unsuccessfully to get him to move while tears ran down her cheeks and finally settled for wiping them away, glaring at him through red-rimmed eyes. She looked adorably pretty with her tomato red nose and trembling lips.

'Do you want your bubble thingy?' he asked cautiously.

She huffed out a breath.

'Well?' He pressed tentatively.

'It's all popped out.' She sniffed.

'Hurray for the environment.' His smile turned sheepish when she glared at him with watery eyes. 'Seriously, you need to find an eco-friendly method to deal with your . . . issues.'

She stopped crying. 'Well, thank you for your concern. It's touching how you care more about the sea turtles than about me.'

He sighed, loud and gusty. 'I'm sorry, Bee. I keep fucking it up with you.'

'Yeah, you do . . . because you're a jerk. I thought we had established that.' She sounded morose yet cute while saying it, so he did what he wanted to and kissed her tomato nose. Quick and sweet.

Bee blinked. 'What was that for?'

He shrugged. 'No reason. I just felt like it.'

'I ran out of bubble wrap because of you. You and your foul mouth have ensured I have no more bubble wrap left.' She gave him a sour look. 'Your mother should have washed your mouth with Vim when you were a kid.'

Arhan grinned in pure mischief. 'She tried, but I always ran away. They called me PT Usha *da chotta pra*.'

'Bra?'

'*Pra*, Bee, P-R-A,' he said, spelling it out. 'It means brother.' He tried for a charming smile.

'You think you're so funny.' She rolled her eyes and some of the stiffness left her shoulders.

Arhan put a careful arm around her waist, leaning away from her hands. When she didn't immediately attack him, he took it as a good sign and led her to a nearby bench. He made sure that he was sitting close enough so he could put his arm around her again if she needed or wanted him to.

Because he certainly needed and wanted to.

'So?' he said. 'Who's this MS-from-the-US Iyer dweeb Dheera warned me about?'

'What? No!' Bee grumbled. 'I am going to kill Dheera for opening her big fat mouth.'

Arhan's lips twitched. 'You have a thing for mouths, yeah?'

Bee kept silent.

'Your friend is worried about you,' he said gently. 'She thinks you're playing with your life. And if you're getting hurt like this, I'm afraid I have to agree with her. You're being stupid.'

Bee was indignant. 'You don't even know what's going on. You don't know what Dheera was talking about and you're already passing judgment on me.'

He bumped her shoulder companionably. 'I know you, Bee. You climbed a damn tree in the rain to score an interview with my captain. You're capable of anything. Most of it brave and/or stupid.'

Since she couldn't deny his observation outright, she chose to ignore him, rummaging in her tote for more wrap. Just in case.

'Will you tell me what happened to your forehead, sweetheart?'

It wasn't the term of endearment that caught her off-guard. It was his patient, almost meek, tone. Arhan Kapoor, king of all that he surveyed, was never humble. He wasn't even *nice*, even though he kissed like a very nice boy.

She knew she was trapped as soon as she looked at his concerned face with all that sexy stubble. Her spine melted just a little at the thought of feeling that beard on her skin again.

His eyes were admirably patient.

'Would you believe it if I tell you a door hit me?' she asked. At his continued stare, she slumped her shoulder against him. 'Fine. But, if I tell you the truth, you have to promise not to freak out or tell the Maharani or my boss. They'll all want me to go home.'

'I—'

'Promise me, Arhan.'

His chest swelled with the force of his gusty sigh. 'Fine, I promise.'

'Okay. Here goes,' Bee said, and proceeded to recount everything for him—the attack when she went back to her room in Kolkata, calling Dheera after she came to slumped outside her suite, the visit to the Park Street police station the next day, meeting the interesting yet scary Inspector Thapar.

'The inspector was helpful,' she concluded. 'He told me it was all right to continue with the tour, and that they would discreetly question the hotel staff and review security footage and get back to me if they found anything. Since nothing was stolen, it's not really a priority but I was hurt, so I guess they will take this incident a bit more seriously than the police in Jaipur.'

Arhan scowled. 'Jaipur? What happened in Jaipur?'

She scowled back. 'Weren't you there when I told the Maharani about how my room was broken into the day of the opening match? Nothing was stolen then too, but the cops were not as helpful as Thapar. I even showed you the inspector's card, remember?'

'Oh, that was for real? You weren't making up a sob story to score an interview with Viren?'

'Do you have such a low opinion of all reporters in general or am I the exception?' Bee asked, slowly, inexplicably hurt at his crass dismissal. After all the time they had spent together, Bee had figured out that Arhan didn't like reporters very much. In fact, she'd never met a sportsperson less inclined to talk to the press, so she wasn't surprised, but the hurt she felt was new.

Arhan Kapoor should not have the power to hurt me.

Arhan had the grace to wince. 'I didn't mean to—'

'Oh yes, you did. I'd just like to know why so I am not ambushed again.'

He was quiet for a long time. Bee stood up. She was tired of being around him. Agreed, it was more exciting than a rollercoaster, but she didn't need the drama at this point in her life, thank you very much.

As she walked away, Arhan caught her wrist, in a classic filmy gesture.

'There was a woman—Jasleen Karnal. She came to our home in Ludhiana at my dad's *chautha*,' Arhan spoke in a low voice. 'We thought she was mom's friend since she was close to her age. Mom thought she was an acquaintance of my father, so she was warm and gracious even in her grief. It was a wake so everyone assumed those present were close to the family and that woman ended up talking to our next-door neighbours. The next day, the headline read "Local Sugar Factory Owner Commits Suicide over Loss of Mistress". The by-line was Jasleen Karnal.'

Bee sucked in a sharp breath. This was horrible! And absolutely callous on the journalist's part to have exploited the family's grief. She couldn't blame him for his antipathy towards her profession now, could she?

'I am sorry, Arhan,' she said as she sat down next to him.

'I know you're not like that.' He said softly, and in a gesture that squeezed her heart, he entwined their fingers together, brushing his thumb over her knuckles. 'I know that. And I am sorry I've been so difficult with you. I just couldn't understand my feelings.' He looked into her moist eyes.

She seemed to be waiting eagerly for him to continue but he shook his head, not completely ready to share yet, and changed the topic back to her safety. 'Whatever you're mixed up in sounds serious, Bee. You really should think about going back home.' Sincere concern radiated from him.

Bee's heart turned to mush again, even after she'd sternly ordered it not to. 'It's not that simple, Arhan. This is my career we're talking about. I am finally getting somewhere with this column. My boss is recognising my contribution and I am not bothering your team anymore. I have enough material with the other teams talking to me.'

She held up a hand before he could have it out with her again. 'I get it. I am not going to ask anyone to disobey a gag order. But you can't ask me to leave either. I am not going anywhere.' Bee was intractable.

Arhan was not completely convinced. 'Bee, it's not about the gag order—'

'I do believe it was all just a big mistake,' she continued slowly. 'I am sure the police in Kolkata will confirm my theory any day now. I don't have anything of value for anyone to steal.'

'Are you sure about that? Did the attacker say anything to you? Anything at all?'

'No, I . . .' Bee paused as all of a sudden she remembered the intruder's question.

Where the fuck is it?

She'd been too caught up in her terror to even think about it at the time and in all her subsequent accounts that little significant detail had got lost.

'Yes,' Bee said slowly. 'He asked "Where the fuck is it?" Twice. But I don't know what the fuck "it" is.'

'Are you sure about that?'

'Positive.'

He raised his eyebrows, questioningly. 'Are you sure you're not just looking to pack me off?'

She gave him an insouciant grin. 'I am not that easy to get rid of, Coach Sir.'

Arhan's lips quirked at the mockery, making him look boyish. He drew her closer, giving her all the time in the world to pull back if she wanted to.

She didn't. Instead, her eyes fluttered shut in anticipation and surrender.

He kissed her on her injured temple.

Bee's eyes sprang open at the unexpectedly tender kiss.

'This MS-from-the US Iyer dweeb,' he prompted. 'What's the scene with him?'

She chuckled at his peeved tone and kissed his stubbled chin. The friction was delicious. Bee turned to face him fully. 'There is no scene with anyone. I am not doing anything with him. He is no one, just some random guy my parents wanted to set me up with.' '

'So I don't have to worry about this guy moving in on you when I'm not watching?'

'Will you be watching me?' Bee only half-teased him, aware of a shift between them in the last few minutes. Their animosity had turned into something intimate, sweet. At least, she hoped so!

Arhan's eyes shadowed, the toll of the past few days showing in them for the first time. 'Won't I?' he murmured. 'You're a walking, talking item number of a complication, Bee Vishwanathan.'

She exhaled and pouted. 'That is only borderline offensive, which is a vast improvement for you.' She pulled her hand away from his, even though it felt so nice nestled in his big palm. 'I have to leave now. I have to prep for my interview with the Lankan captain and meet the Kiwi fitness coach after.'

Arhan grinned. 'What scoop are you angling for with Arjuna Gunasekara? He's not that easy to *patao*, you know, Oxford-returned lawyer and all.'

Bee shot him a withering glance. 'You know as well as I do that Arjuna could have been a lawyer like the rest of his family but he picked up the willow. Anyway, I can hardly *patao* him.'

Arhan shook his head. 'How *do* you know so much about cricket, Bee? You're one of the most technically sound columnists I have ever encountered.' He gave her hand another squeeze. 'I mean that sincerely.'

Bee shrugged. 'Try growing up with a cricket-crazy dad, brother and three uncles. We had stats quizzes before the Border-Gavaskar Trophy and Ashes if they fell during school vacations.'

'It must have been an experience.'

Bee smiled softly and Arhan felt his heart clutch the slightest bit.

'Sometimes it was just short of World War Three.'

'Well.' Arhan kissed her hand. 'I'm quite glad cricket was drummed into you.'

Bee looked around, leaned in and kissed him quickly on the cheek. His eyes rounded in pleasant surprise.

'So am I,' she whispered.

19

The gym facilities at the Chennai Grand Intercontinental were only slightly above acceptable for an athlete like Arhan. His daily regimen consisted of a three-mile run, followed by push ups and a go at the elliptical. On alternate days, he added some light weight training to the mix. Unlike the fanatical workout brigade, he didn't have separate leg, abs or chest days. The time he spent on the ground with the players, sharpening their game and going over drills again and again and again was something else entirely. That was play, and he loved it.

He'd always loved being outdoors, playing any game as long as he didn't have to break open his books and do maths or learn verbs. The years he'd put in getting his MBA had been their own kind of prison. Even when he had rebuilt his dad's company from the ground up, he'd managed to get in his three-mile run, waking up as early as 4 a.m. to do so. He had been considered the resident crazy in his hometown, running around in white track pants with nothing but a *ganji* to keep him warm.

When he'd helped fund the technical college on the land left to him by his grandparents, the first thing he'd done was install a running track. Sports were encouraged in the state of Punjab as a whole, so the move had been appreciated and lauded by the then chief minister who'd come down for the inauguration. The college was now in its fifth year and was holding its own in academics and, more importantly, sports. It was the one thing, apart from coaching Punjab to a Ranji win, that Arhan was truly proud of.

As mindless rock music poured into his ears, he heard the steady rise of his heartbeat, his own breath puffing out as his feet pounded the treadmill set to the highest level. It was too late at night for anyone else to be using the gym as all the players were pretty much tuckered out from practising on the nets or playing actual matches.

The Kiwi team's coach had invited him for a sauna sit-down a few minutes ago and he was contemplating taking the bloke up on his offer. A sauna sounded wonderful after this workout.

Just then he saw Akshar enter the gym, distracted, looking intently at his phone.

Arhan waved at him but Akshar didn't even bother acknowledging him.

That was weird. Akshar wasn't deliberately rude, ever.

Surprisingly, Bee's journalist friend Karan Sholekar walked in next. He made a beeline for Akshar who was lacing up his shoes on one of the benches. The journalist sat down next to the physio who jumped up as if there were rats crawling up his ass.

Karan stood up too. He showed Akshar something on the laptop he was carrying to which the physio shook his head, vehemently.

Karan went closer to Akshar, almost threateningly as he invaded his personal space.

Arhan casually shut his phone off and tried to lip read. The benches were on the opposite side, quite far away, so it was almost impossible, but whatever was going on didn't look good at all.

Finally, the journalist walked away, exiting the gym. Akshar looked worried as he slowly finished lacing up his shoes.

If Arhan was right, the next visitor into the gym would be Bee. Because Ms Vishwanathan was always where she shouldn't be, chasing a quote from the Indian cricket team. Fulfilling his silent prediction, Bee walked in and collided with Sholekar. Arhan watched with narrowed eyes as the man almost shoved her back in his haste to get away.

Arhan stopped the treadmill. Bee hadn't seen him yet. This gave him an opportunity to watch her unobserved, something he only felt mildly guilty about.

Arhan watched with interest as Bee walked over to the New Zealand fitness coach, shaking his hand and keying in notes on her phone.

The Kiwi coach gestured to Akshar, who was working out next to him.

Arhan got off his machine, wiping it down with disinfectant tissues in record time. He casually ambled over to where the two men were exercising on stationary bikes while Bee leaned against a third, listening to them, her phone on record mode. She was nothing if not professional.

'Hey, Edward.' Arhan nodded at the fitness coach.

'Hello, Arhan. Sorry, mate. This young journalist here wanted a few minutes of my time. Could you hang around till I finish with her?'

'You should be careful what you say to these reporter types, Edward. They are all vultures,' Akshar said, expressionless.

Bee looked at him, surprise writ all over her face. Arhan moved in front of her, instant protective mode activated.

'I am sorry you feel that way, Dr Shekhawat,' Bee said politely. 'But, just like you, we also have a job to do—to report on the tournament as honestly as we can.'

'Yeah, right.' Akshar gave her a contemptuous glance. 'This is off the record but it is not like you actually report the news, only sensationalist *bakwaas*. If it were up to me, I would ban the media from all cricket venues in totality.'

'I didn't know you felt this strongly, Akshar,' Arhan said quietly. He was acutely aware of Edward Banner, the Kiwi coach, watching them with a bemused expression.

'Well.' Akshar glared at him, defiance clear in his stiff posture. Bee had stopped recording and was just watching Akshar curiously. 'I do. And if you know what's good for you, you'll stay the hell away from them too. They're fucking evil.'

With that, he hopped off his bike, brushed against Arhan, barely nodded to Edward and stalked out.

Arhan debated between going after Akshar and talking to Bee. A second later, he took Bee's arm after making his excuses to Edward and led her out the door. 'I'm sorry about that.' At her cocked brow, he added defensively, 'Your friend, Sholekar, riled him up before you came in. It's the reason he was acting so weird. Do they know each other?'

She shrugged. 'I don't think so, but who knows? I think there's a fatwa out on me, anyway. Physios, cops, assistant coaches, attackers—everyone wants a piece of me.' She winked. 'Maybe my *Shani* is sitting on my *Mangal*.'

Arhan rolled his eyes at her blasé comment. Then, he turned grave. 'Did you think about what the attacker could want from you?'

'Not really,' she admitted. 'I have been immensely distracted by this hot guy I am seeing.' She nudged him with her shoulder.

'Is that what we're doing? Seeing each other?' He spoke idly, as he towelled down.

'We're not?' Bee asked tartly.

'What do you think?'

'I think you're avoiding the question.'

He grinned sexily at her, placing the towel around his neck. 'I avoid nothing.'

Arhan moved in closer to her, their bodies brushing and she stood on her toes, their lips aligning as she felt his musky scent coming off in waves.

She was hot and bothered and he kissed so well when he put his mind to it. Her hands moved from his hair to the towel around his neck and something about the fabric on her fingers triggered the memory of their first meeting. Her stumbling from the tree and seeing him in nothing but a towel . . . the towel slipping . . . her punching his nose and running and falling again on the road and finding . . .

It!

Bee's eyes snapped open. 'I have to go.' In an instant her feet were back on the floor.

Arhan nearly collided with the wall. 'Hey, give a guy some warning.'

'I think I know . . . I have to go,' she repeated, distractedly. She gave him a quick peck on the cheek and ran off.

A bemused Arhan guzzled down a bottle of water and, wiping his sweaty neck, decided to pay Akshar a visit. He'd been a jackass to Bee and she'd forgiven him for it, even when she didn't have to. Akshar owed her an apology.

Maybe we could co-author a book titled Don't Be a Jackass to Reporters. Arhan's humour was restored on the way to the physio's room.

—◦— ◆ ◆ —◦—

Back in her hotel room, Bee fished around in her tote and finally extracted the phone that had slipped into a tear in the lining. Removing it widened the tear in the bag, but it seemed a small price to pay.

Bee sat down on the edge of the bed and examined the phone. It was a tiny black thing that fit in the palm of her hand. It had an old-school keypad and a small display screen, now scratched—a very basic model that was available at any store for around a grand.

It wasn't a smartphone and, as she unscrewed the back and looked at the SIM card, one of the Big Three, she understood it to be a burner phone.

She tried to think back to the night she'd found the phone. There was a man in a black hoodie who had knocked her down. Maybe he was the owner of the phone. Maybe it was the same guy who'd come after her in Jaipur and again in Kolkata!

The idea seemed a bit far-fetched, sure, but no more far-fetched than an ordinary woman like her being attacked. Twice. What were the odds of that happening, even in a country as potently unsafe as India?

Okay, my theory is entirely possible.

Bee scrolled through the phonebook but found no contacts. It was the same with text messages, no messages were available. The phone was wiped clean as if it had never been used.

But it was the only strange thing she possessed that could possibly cause this much chaos.

Think, Bee! It's a phone. And what do people do with phones?

They made calls.

Bee pressed the green call button and a single number flashed on the incoming call list. She pressed the green button again. The call connected and it started ringing.

Her heart thudded with anticipation and fear. Something extremely weird was going on and Bee had to get to the bottom of it. The phone rang seven times. Eight. Nine.

'Pick up, pick up,' she whispered.

'Hello?' said Arhan on the other end.

'Arhan!' Bee shrieked. 'Is this your phone?'

There was a pause at the other end. Long and tense.

20

Finally, Arhan answered wearily, 'It's not mine, Bee, but I am looking at the dead body of the man who owned it.'

'Where are you?' Bee whispered, head buzzing. Dizziness and anxiety clutched her stomach in tight knots.

'In Room 1804. On the eighteenth floor. Can you come over?' He sounded uncharacteristically grim.

'I don't think that's the best idea, Arhan,' she said, thinking fast. 'There's a dead body there. In fact, you should get out of there too. Come to my room.'

'I know there is a dead body, Bee,' he said. 'I am looking at it. I can't leave. The police will be here any minute. They'll find it suspicious if I am not at the scene of the crime after I called them.'

'Oh hell! I need my bubble wrap.' She got up and hunted for the emergency wrap she kept in the nightstand drawer. It stared back, limp and all used up. 'Oh double crap!'

'Can you keep it together?' he whispered urgently. 'Can you please just get here? I don't . . . I can't be alone,' he said softly.

Bee had never heard him sound this vulnerable.

'Sure. Yeah. I'll come. Hang on.' Bee dumped the phone back into her bag, burying it deep inside the lining and ran out of her room, thanking providence that the Maharani was out having dinner with some dignitary or the other. She was sure even she could not have morphed 'I am going to meet my sort-of boyfriend in a hotel room that has a dead body' into a convincing lie.

The elevator took forever to show up, and Bee jiggled the limp wrap in her pants pocket as she waited for the right floor number to flash. She got off on the eighteenth floor and counted the doors to room 1804.

Bee knocked, her heart pounding like she'd climbed the stairs instead of taking the elevator.

'Who is it?' Arhan asked.

'It's me. Bee,' she whispered.

He wrenched the door open and drew her in, nearly dislocating her shoulder in the process.

There was a single bedside lamp glowing in the room. Bee blinked to adjust to the almost darkness. It looked eerier now that she knew why she was here.

'Where . . .' She swallowed. 'Where is it?'

'Under the window, near the bed.' Arhan nodded at the double bed, which took up most of the room.

He looked pale under his stubble like he was about to puke. Bee took his hand and wrapped her fingers around his. Arhan squeezed back. Hard. She could see that he was rattled. Anyone would be.

They moved closer to the bed and Bee got her first good look at a dead body. It was the Indian team's physiotherapist, Akshar Shekhawat. He was splayed on the floor, arms akimbo, eyes open in a rictus of terror, his mouth open in a silent scream. A small pool of blood stained the floor around him, presumably from a wound at the back.

This was unbelievable.

Bee felt sick. She buried her face in Arhan's shoulder. He held her tight, sinking his head in her hair, his breathing harsh and deep. His fingers dug into her back.

'Bee,' he said.

'It's okay,' she managed. 'It's okay.'

They drew back and looked at each other in shared fear and confusion.

'I think I might need your bubble wrap too,' he said.

She embraced him again, trying to offer him whatever comfort and strength she could. 'Did you call anyone other than the police?' she asked.

He shook his head against her shoulder. 'I wanted to talk to Akshar because of the scene at the gym. I know him, Bee,' he tried to reassure her. 'He is never rude to anyone, especially women. So I thought I'd check in and see what's up. I tried calling him but he didn't answer, so I came down to his room. The door was open when I knocked. I entered and . . .'

Arhan shuddered, and Bee hugged him closer still.

'It's okay. It's okay,' she said again and again.

Akshar's dead gaping eyes were imprinted on the back of her eyelids. *It is not okay! Not at all!*

But Arhan knew that already. She didn't want to make it worse for him.

'Did the police say when they were coming? Did you talk to hotel security?'

'I meant to call them after the police but then you called and —'

'Call them now. They need to be here too.' Bee pushed him towards the phone on the bed stand and he dialled reception.

'Hello,' he said. 'I am calling from room 1804.' Arhan gulped, she could see his Adam's apple move. 'I need to report a death. Could you send somebody up?'

The police in Chennai were efficient and thorough. Within minutes of arriving, they had cordoned off the area with yellow tape. The body had been photographed and dispatched in an ambulance. Procedure was followed to the last letter. Akshar would only be declared dead by medical personnel in a hospital.

There was a chalk outline where the physiotherapist had lain and Bee couldn't look at the space without wanting to vomit. She sat next to Arhan as he answered the same questions over and over again.

Yes, he had called Akshar at around 11 p.m.

No, Akshar hadn't picked up.

Yes, he had used the elevator to get to the eighteenth floor.

No, there was no one else in the floor's lobby when he'd walked in.

Yes, the door was open when he'd knocked.

No, he hadn't disturbed anything when he entered, but he couldn't be sure if anything was missing, stolen or taken.

Yes, he had found the body like that. Exactly like that.

No, he didn't know if Akshar had any enemies. The man was nice, decent.

Yes, this was a nightmare.

They grilled Bee too but she had absolutely nothing of value to offer, save corroborating Arhan's timings. He didn't mention anything about Akshar owning a burner phone so she kept quiet about having one too.

An hour later, Bee ran a bath for Arhan in his hotel room four floors up while he paced outside, wearing a hole in the plush carpet.

Hotel security had posted a guard outside his room at the police's request, although she wasn't sure if it was for his safety or their security.

The hotel manager was hysterical at the idea of a death in his hotel. The media was already clamouring for information. A huge crowd had gathered in the courtyard as the news leaked out. Traffic was in a snarl outside the hotel and no one knew what to do. It was utter chaos!

Bee stepped out of the bathroom and looked at Arhan. 'Hey,' she said. 'Get in the bath now. The water's warm enough.'

'I feel sick,' he said.

'I know.' She went up to him and rubbed a comforting hand over his back. It was sweat-slicked even though they were in an air-conditioned room. He gripped her forearms, a wild look in his eyes.

'I just saw him! I just saw him at the gym and now he is . . . now he is . . .'

'Shhh . . .' She soothed him, leading him by the hand to the bathroom. 'Just get in the bath, Arhan.'

Just then Arhan's phone rang, a loud noise in the room. He startled, almost vibrating in apprehension. The hotel extension rang next.

Arhan gave her a panicked look.

'I'll talk to them. You go take a shower.' She was firm, like her mom always was during a crisis.

His phone displayed Balvinder Lakhani's name.

Bee answered it with apprehension. 'Hel—'

'Arhan, *kya chal raha hai*?' Balvinder boomed. 'Let me in right now! Why is there a guard outside your fucking door? Are you a suspect? Everything is fucked up, Arhan. We need to talk right now!'

'Arhan can't come to the phon—'

'Who are you? His bloody secretary?' The man used a few more unflattering terms that made Bee's blood boil.

But this was a trying time for everyone, especially the people affiliated with Team India, and she needed to cut him some slack. One of his men was dead.

'I need to talk to Arhan right now,' Lakhani said in a menacing tone, 'And I mean *now*!'

Bee let out a deep breath, clenched her fist and started making popping motions in the air.

'Arhan is in shock,' she answered coldly. 'He's just seen the dead body of his colleague and friend, and he has spent the last hour answering endless questions from the police. You need to show him some consideration, Mr Lakhani. He will talk to you in the morning. Please let him rest for now.'

'But—'

'I understand your worry and concern. But, as I just told you, he is in considerable shock and—'

The phone was snatched from her hand, and Bee turned to see Arhan wrapping a towel around his waist while tucking the phone under his chin. 'Sirji, yeah, the media is going to eat this up. We need to do immediate damage control,' he barked.

He paused, an eyebrow arched, and listened to Lakhani talk.

'Yeah. I am cool. I am good. The police asked me a hundred questions. I answered them all. It shouldn't be a problem. I'm more worried about the team. How is the board going to handle this?'

Bee's mouth dropped open in abject shock. What happened to the guy who looked ready to fall apart in her arms just a few seconds ago?

This Arhan was hard, implacable. He was naked in a towel but he might as well have been wearing a suit of armour. He stood like a warrior going into battle.

His eyes scared her. They were bottomless, ruthless.

Arhan turned away from her, pacing again. Not in agitation this time, but with purpose.

He continued talking to his boss in confident tones, thinking aloud on strategy and damage control and a plan to not let this upheaval affect his boys, affect the game and their chances of winning the cup.

Bee sat down at the edge of the bed and waited for him to finish the call.

When he finally disconnected, he picked up the hotel extension, which had just started to ring again, and answered with a terse, 'Arhan Kapoor here.'

He listened to whoever was on the other line and said, 'If you guys put any reporter through to this number, I will personally make it my mission to destroy your career.' Then he slammed the phone down and, apparently thinking better of it, placed the receiver off the hook, next to the phone on the stand.

Arhan ran a shaking hand through his wet hair. Water trickled down his spine and she followed the progress of the beads with her eyes.

He turned to face her. His frown disappeared, the hard cast to his face softened the slightest bit.

'Hey,' he said.

'Hi.'

'Sorry about that. I needed to talk to him before he decided all of this was my fault and fired me.'

'Why would he do that?'

Arhan shrugged, corded muscles on his shoulders shifting sinuously with the movement. 'It's what anyone would do in his place, Bee. Blame it on someone else. This is a nightmare. A terrible, very public nightmare. I don't know what we are going to do next.'

'Well,' she said slowly. 'Your people could cancel the tournament. I don't think anyone is going to be in a playing mood after this. Least of all, the Indian team.'

He stared at her as if she had sprouted two heads.

Bee shrugged defensively. 'It's practical, isn't it? Your team's physiotherapist is dead. He could have been murdered. I don't think the team will be able to cope with the loss of yet another member.'

'Do you understand the sheer scope of loss the ICCB would incur if we cancelled the tournament?'

'Do you understand human beings and their feelings?' she retorted before she could stop herself.

He stopped moving towards her. The familiar stiffness was back in his body, as was the distant, mistrustful look in his eyes. The tenuous peace that they'd established scattered like morning mist.

'Am I back to being the enemy?'

'I think you should leave,' he said carefully.

'What?' She stood up, bouncing on the heels of her feet.

'You're a reporter . . . the media. I just instructed the front desk to not allow anyone in. And the board is probably already slapping a gag order on me. How would it look if they found you here with me?'

He sounded reasonable-*ish*. That was the worst part. That he believed his own twisted logic.

'And you care more about what the board or the hotel staff thinks than me?' She was incensed.

He didn't answer.

Bee walked out the door.

But she immediately walked back in, placing the burner phone found on Akshar's person on the bed stand next to the disconnected receiver.

They hadn't given the burner to the cops. It hadn't been a well-thought-out decision—withholding evidence from the authorities —but it was already done. She could even hazard a guess as to why Arhan had done it. He'd answered a call from the phone she had when he'd come to find Akshar. He'd been trying to protect her from getting involved in the investigation.

Bee wished she could feel kindly towards him for it.

'I think it's too late to give this to the authorities now.' Her voice simmered with unexpressed rage. 'I would suggest you bury it in the bedding or something, but hey, what do I know? I am just a bloody reporter.'

Then she stalked out of his room before she did something stupid. Like, break his nose . . . again.

Or cry!

21

Arhan couldn't sleep.

He lay on his bed, staring at the ceiling where the myriad lights of the city, red, orange, pink and blue, whirled on and on like a kaleidoscope.

The migraine had become his best friend and he couldn't muster up the strength to take a pill to get rid of the pain.

He could still see Akshar's dead eyes staring back at him from the foot of the bed . . . a nightmare!

Arhan had naïvely thought he'd suffered through the worst. His dad had died and he'd lost out on playing for India. Then he had endured a small-town scandal while trying to keep his family sane, ensuring the family business stayed afloat and making enough money so that they could move out of said small town and never return.

He'd slaved like a dog, running the sugar presses at night because he couldn't sleep. And he'd emerged triumphant at the end of it all. The sugar business had benefitted from his decade of hard work and was now ably looked after by his younger brother and his brothers-in-law.

Getting his younger sisters married had been a bitch in the aftermath of the scandal. Small-town gossip was ruinous to young girls' marriage prospects but he had managed it all.

Now he thought he could finally do something for himself. For the game he loved more than anything else.

At thirty-three, he knew he couldn't play for the country. Nevertheless he'd made a place for himself in cricket, first with Punjab and then the national team. He had jumped at the opportunity to coach the team, even one as fractured and broken as the current eleven. Because he *loved* the game. Loved India and sincerely believed greatness was just one game away with the present team.

When Zak had passed away and his duties as coach had doubled to include counselling and hand-holding the players before every match and appearance, he didn't mind. He loved this team enough to do what was best for them. He wanted to be a part of a winning combination.

He was selfish. He wanted to *win*. Even if it was as the assistant coach of Team India.

But Akshar's death had royally screwed up the chances of that happening.

Arhan considered raiding the minibar for whatever alcohol was in there but thought better of it. He had no appetite and drinking on an empty stomach was bound to create problems he just wasn't capable of handling right now.

He'd switched off his phone because his aching head couldn't take the ringing anymore. And he had no desire to talk to anyone.

Especially not Bee. Bee who had accused him of not understanding human beings.

Of course, he understood human beings. He was human, wasn't he?

But, unlike her, he also understood big business. And cricket was, at its heart, a very profitable business with thousands of crores of rupees riding on this tournament.

This latest cloud of scandal was going to affect the TRPs and viewer responses if they didn't spin it right.

He knew this. The chaps running the board sure as hell knew this. His disastrous Kolkata meeting had proven this. And Arhan was nothing if not pragmatic.

Shit! He was pretty sure Lakhani would want him to talk to the team. Get them through one more disaster on their way to the quarter-finals.

His stomach rumbled.

Arhan got out of bed, went to the bathroom and vomited everything he'd eaten that day. When he crawled back into bed, sweaty and shaking and weak, he lost the battle with himself.

He dialled reception and asked to be connected to Bee Vishwanathan's room.

When she picked up on the first ring, he knew she hadn't been able to sleep either.

'Hi,' he said softly. 'It's me. Please don't hang up.'.'

She was silent. Ominously. But she didn't hang up.

'I was angry. Upset. Akshar is dead and my boss is breathing down my neck and I did not need you telling me what was morally right and wrong. I do understand the consequences.'

She remained silent.

'Akshar is . . . was my friend,' Arhan continued, with a little desperation. 'We have chilled out together after matches. He was so helpful with the guys. They really looked up to him.'

Bee breathed out; he could hear it over the phone.

Arhan closed his eyes. He was exhausted, unutterably weary. He felt like shit, probably looked like shit too, and he had screwed up pretty badly with the one woman who understood what he was going through at this exact moment.

How could he fix this?

'I am sorry,' Arhan said wearily. 'I am fucking sorry, okay? I shouldn't have said those nasty things to you. I acted without thinking. I am stressed and I am upset and I took it out on you. Because you were handy and available.'

'That's a shitty apology,' Bee said finally.

'What do you want me to say?' He was at his wit's end but still so glad he had her to talk to.

'I don't know, Arhan.' She sounded tired too. 'I don't have all the answers. I can't sleep either. I keep thinking . . . maybe that could have been me. In Kolkata? When I was attacked. Maybe I would be dead too. And I am scared out of my mind. There's not enough bubble wrap in the world to make this okay,' she whispered.

Arhan sat up straight as a different kind of terror struck his heart.

She was right. She was absolutely right. She'd been attacked too. What if the attacker had pulled a knife on her or, God forbid, a gun! She would be a chalk outline on the floor now!

How did I not think of this before?

Sheer fear made him ask, 'Would you consider going back home?'

'That's not fair, Arhan. You know you can't ask me to leave if the tournament is not cancelled.'

'Have you eaten?' he asked instead, meekly. He knew she was as rattled as he was and had probably skipped dinner.

'No. Have you?'

'I just threw up,' he confessed, feeling the rancid acid burn in his oesophagus even now. Even after he'd thoroughly brushed his teeth. 'I can't get him out of my head.'

'Me too.' Her voice was rusty as if she was swallowing back tears.

It hurt his heart just like it had when he'd heard his mother wailing after seeing his dad hanging from the ceiling fan, bowels empty, neck snapped. As if something was essentially wrong with his world.

Arhan rubbed at his beating, aching heart. 'Don't cry, Bee.'

She sniffled and said, 'I am not crying. I am a reporter and a strong, calm woman. I don't cry.'

He chuckled. It was a terrible imitation of the real thing. 'No. You start bursting bubble wrap or punch half-naked men and break their noses when you're upset.'

'I also recite cricket facts to calm myself.' She didn't dispute his accusations. 'And you totally deserved to get punched, then and now.'

'Next time I'll just punch myself when you're around and save you the trouble.'

She sniffled again. 'Don't act all cute. I am still pissed at you.'

'Can we talk even if you're pissed at me?' He knew she wasn't as upset with him as she had every right to be. He was profoundly grateful for it. He settled deeper into the bed, feeling a layer of peace and well-being steal over him as he imagined Bee in her own bed, in the Maharani's suite.

'Maybe.'

Finally, he asked what he had been dying to for a long time, 'Bee . . . is your name really Bee?'

'It will be as soon as the petition comes through.'

'What petition?' He was intrigued.

'You have to file a petition with the Gazette office to legally change your name. The due process takes three months. Then you take out an ad in two newspapers saying your name has been legally changed to so and so and, voila, you're a new you.'

'Are you serious?'

'Yeah. I can't believe it either. Three whole months! Bloody corrupt bureaucrats, the lot of them.'

'Why do you want to change your name though?' he asked, curious.

'Obviously because I don't like it, duh!'

'What's your real name, Bee?' he asked, even more intrigued now.

'If I tell you I will have to kill you,' she shot back, without thinking, as usual.

The silence that followed was awkward and protracted.

'I am sorry, it just slipped out.' Bee apologised, 'I have no filter sometimes.'

'Sometimes?' Arhan said softly. 'So . . . cricket facts, huh? What kinds of facts do you have, Ms Cricketopedia?'

'Did you know Matthew Vaughn is the only international player with the most hundreds to have been dismissed the least number of times in test cricket in the '90s?'

'Really? And who's been dismissed the most?'

'Sachin.'

Arhan's jaw dropped. 'You're joking!'

'Nope. Sachin was out ten times in the '90s.'

'And which matches were these?'

Bee racked her brains for a minute and said, 'I think it started with . . .'

And they spent the rest of the night talking cricket and ignoring the dead body in the room.

—⊢◆ ◆⊣—

In a police station across India, a printer spat out a sheet of paper detailing the murder of Dr Akshar Shekhawat, licensed physiotherapist for Team India.

It was picked up by the on-duty havaldar and handed over to the special branch officer who had asked for all information regarding a woman named Bee Vishwanathan.

Her name had come up in this report as well.

At dawn, Inspector Paramjit Thapar was on the first available flight out of Kolkata to Chennai.

This case had just become interesting.

22

Bee could remember dozing off with the phone dangling from her fingertips, listening to Arhan's deep, infinitely sexy voice recalling a childhood memory of a hard-fought match full of twists and turns and a no-ball or two that he had played in his *pind*.

They'd talked cricket—nothing else—after he'd rendered the world's worst apology. But somehow, over the four hours they'd spent together on the telephone, she'd forgiven him.

She also admitted the ugly truth to herself. This wasn't just attraction. She really and truly *liked* him. With a capital 'L'.

It was awful, of course.

There was no future here, considering he had a business in Punjab and a job with one of the world's best sports teams while she was firmly and forever a Mumbai girl. Hell, there was no present, but her hormones and heart had spoken.

As a result of the events of the evening, her dreams were a mix of the ghostly and the erotic.

In one particularly sexy and frightening sequence, she was watching Arhan's towel drop in movie-time slow motion while in the background, someone was skulking, wearing the black-hooded Ghostface mask from *Scream,* creeping in closer with a knife.

And then somehow, she had been stabbed à la *Psycho.* That's when she'd woken up with her heart in her throat.

It had taken thirty minutes of deep breathing exercises for her to get back to bed and, even then, her dreams were restless, horrific.

As a result, Bee was not in the best of morning moods when Paramjit Thapar called.

'Yes?' She looked sleepily at her alarm clock. It was 9.50 a.m.

Damn! She needed to be in the stadium's media lounge by 11 a.m. for the day's debriefing from the board. Arhan had specified the time in front of her during their dreamy conversation last night.

'Good morning, Ms Vishwanathan. It's Inspector Thapar. From Kolkata. Hope you remember me?' The slightly gravelly voice of the inspector registered in her consciousness.

Bee sat up straight. 'What? Of course, yeah. Yes, I do.'

She rushed about, trying to untangle her day-old jeans from the wardrobe and find a matching T-shirt while brushing her teeth and trying not to make inappropriate noises on the phone.

'Excuse me,' she said and, muting the call with one hand, spat out the toothpaste before gargling vigorously. Then she wedged the phone in the crook of her neck as she flossed. She quickly unmuted the call and said, 'Thanks for holding, Inspector.'

'No problem. Could you meet me for a quick cup of coffee, Ms Vishwanathan?'

Bee knew it was an order disguised as a request so she gave the only answer she could. 'Sure. Give me fifteen minutes, Inspector.'

—⦁ ◆ ⦁—

Fourteen minutes later, Bee was sitting in a corner booth of the hotel's all-day café, sipping on an espresso.

Thapar sipped on green tea. He looked the same as before, competent and casual . . . confident.

'Is there any update on what happened at the Park Grandeur?' she asked.

'No, ma'am. Unfortunately, we questioned the staff on the floor, housekeeping, busboys, even the elevator guard. No one remembers anything.'

Bee didn't know if Thapar found that suspicious.

'We even checked the security footage,' he continued, 'but there was no one with the description matching your attacker. They might have come in wearing something else.'

'But they left in the hoodie. I saw that bastard getting on to the elevator in the hoodie,' Bee protested.

'Ms Vishwanathan, I have your statement here that says you passed out the second your head hit the door's edge. How could you know what the attacker wore or possibly took off after you fainted?'

The inspector looked apologetic, but he was ruthless.

Bee pursed her lips as she considered Thapar's theory. *Dammit, he was right.*

'Fine,' she conceded. 'If there isn't any news regarding the break-in, why do I have the pleasure of this conversation?'

'Because we heard of Dr Shekhawat's death last night and it's an awful thing to have happened. An awful, awful thing.'

Bee had always wondered at every public servant's ability to fake sympathy when the reality was something else.

'It's awful for the Indian cricket team and its board.' A touch of ice entered her tone. 'I am just a reporter covering the cup.'

'Yes, but you were with Assistant Coach Arhan Kapoor at the scene when the first respondents showed up, weren't you?'

'I came in later,' she emphasised. 'I know nothing. I haven't interacted with Dr Shekhawat at all and I just went there because Arhan called me freaked out of his mind.'

'Funny,' Thapar said, his tone thoughtful. 'It's very funny that Arhan Kapoor would call you, a reporter, rather than his boss or someone else from the team. Don't you think so, Ms Vishwanathan?'

Bee cursed inwardly. She sighed, ran a hand through her hair and said, 'We are . . . friends, Inspector. That's why I called him. He sounded really freaked out so I went over. End of story. Now would you like to know exactly why I called him or is your imagination good enough?'

Thapar's eyes narrowed. 'I thought he called you, Ms Vishwanathan.' *Fuck!*

Bee licked her lips and said, 'One of us called the other, Inspector. You'll excuse me for not remembering the very exact sequence of events.'

'I understand, Ms Vishwanathan. And I do believe my imagination is good enough.'

'Do you need anything else or am I free to go?' Bee asked politely.

Thapar finished his tea and rested the cup on the table before saying, 'Nothing for now, ma'am. I am at Hotel Dharma International in Velachery. I'll be at the stadium during the match. If I do think of anything else, I might want to talk to you there.'

Oh, man. He was staying on? What the hell kind of case was this that the special branch had dispatched one of their own itni jaldi?

Bee knew what the acceptable answer was. 'Of course, Inspector. Anything for you.'

—┼─◆─◆─┼—

Arhan gulped two ibuprofen and washed them down with a glass of orange juice as he watched the half-time coverage of the match in his makeshift office at the stadium. It was no bigger than a cleaner's closet and still vaguely carried the scent of phenol but it was his own space.

He could *think* here without anyone interfering.

The press meet had gone off as well as expected—it was more like watching a car accident in slow motion. The hound dogs were out in full force asking precisely the kind of questions the board, and he, didn't want asked.

The team was seriously rattled and they had a match that night. He'd scheduled his pep talk with them for 6.30 p.m.

But getting them into the stadium was going to involve disguises and props.

If it wasn't for the sponsorship money and player contract renewals, which ran into hundreds of crores, he would have advised the management to cancel the tournament. To hell with the consequences.

But when crazy money and the careers of the best sportsmen were involved, finer feelings went out the window and you did what you had to do.

He didn't want Viren and the rest of the men to be cheated of their just dues.

His headache receded the barest bit as he watched the anchor garble on about the number of sixes that the Kiwi batsman, Brandon McConnell, had hit in 2 consecutive overs—9, close to a world-record.

McConnell's run-scoring had improved New Zealand's chances of winning this match and sneaking into the knockout rounds beginning tomorrow. India's match against West Indies was the last important league match. Most of the other teams were finalised.

His laptop made a pinging sound.

He'd turned off the ringer on his phone to get away from everyone and their mother and was in no hurry to do anything but brood. Wearily, he pulled up his email account.

It was a mail from his younger brother, Lucky.

Heard about Akshar. What the hell is going on, bro? Mom is worried sick. She thinks you're going to be next. Call when you see this. We are worried too.

Family—you couldn't escape them or bury them in a ditch.

He speed-dialled three and waited for Lucky to answer.

His brother picked up on the first ring. 'Bhai, what is going on? The news channels are all speculating about an insider murdering the physio. And they suspect senior management, according to the police reports. *Kya hai yeh sab?*'

'Fuck-ups, as usual.' Arhan rubbed a hand over his face and found a bushy beard. Damn, he really needed to shave. 'The police have just released the autopsy report. Apparently, it's not a head wound from a blunt object that caused the guy's death. Although at first glance it definitely seemed like it.'

'Are the media right then?'

'I can't tell you anything more, Lucky, without breaking a hundred confidential laws. It's a total mess. My head is going to explode,' he admitted.

Lucky was family, his brother in crime in so many childhood capers, that it was easy to confide in him.

'Calm down, *bhaisaab*,' Lucky said. 'I know things look bad right now, but I'm sure it's nothing. Whatever it is, it has nothing to do with you or the team. You need to focus on getting the boys ready for their final match. We have a pool going about India making it through to the round robin!'

'You and your gambling! You disgust me, Lucky!'

Lucky chuckled. 'Hey, let me remind you, you used the seed money from my winnings eleven years ago when we needed to buy that new pressing machine for the factory. Where was your disgust then?'

'Buried under the need for money,' Arhan answered promptly.

'Anyway, the media can speculate all they want but I know for a fact that it wasn't you who killed the poor bastard.'

Arhan was laconic. 'Thanks for the vote of confidence but why would you say that?'

Lucky answered, 'Because you may be a bastard, Arhan, but you're too chicken to be a murderer.'

'Fuck off.' Arhan ended the call with Lucky's laughter still echoing over the phone.

Two seconds later, a knock sounded on the door and Bee slipped in, looking absurdly pleased to see him.

'Hey, how did you find me?' he asked.

'Your boss told me you'd be here so I thought I'd catch you before —'

Bee stopped and stared. The room was a mess. 'What is this place? Why are you here?' She wrinkled her nose. 'What is that smell?'

'It's phenol. Is there anything you wanted or did you simply come here to harangue me?'

'*Harangue?*' She grinned and moved closer, taking care to not brush up against anything. There were cobwebs on some of the items stacked in the room. 'That's a GRE word there. How do you even know how to use it?'

The look he gave her was the equivalent of a droll smile. 'I did attend university, you know. Even got an MBA. I have a family business to run.'

'Oh yeah, sugar factories.' She bumped hips with him as she settled on the only clean surface in the office. 'I cyberstalked you.'

Bee held up her fingers, counting off facts about him. 'You own three sugar factories in Punjab. You have now diversified your portfolio to include year-round farming and renting the fields out to government agencies for crop-testing, which I think is a super-smart move. And you built a college in your village.' Bee winked. 'Colour me impressed.'

Arhan looked mighty cute as he tried to not be embarrassed as she listed all his accomplishments.

'Seriously. What's up?' he asked. 'Why are you here instead of hanging out with the vultur —' He stopped mid-word and changed tack quickly. 'I mean your press buddies.'

She crinkled her nose again. 'They are my buddies, you know, and really good, honest people. Like you. You've got to stop treating them like the Hezbollah, dude.'

'Why don't we agree to disagree on this issue and you can tell me what's going on,' he suggested.

'You're learning.' She smirked.

'Bee.' His patient look turned slightly annoyed.

'All right, all right.' She idly ran a nail down his arm. 'Inspector Thapar from the special branch is probably going to want to talk to you at some point today. We need to get our stories straight before he does that.'

'Inspector *who* from *where*?' Arhan was bewildered. But he had slipped an arm around her waist absent-mindedly and was hugging her close.

His embrace felt so *good*. If she played her cards right, he could probably become her make-out buddy, like Dheera kept saying. 'Remember I told you Dheera made me report the assault at a police station in Kolkata?'

'Yeah . . .'

'Well, this very intense policeman was at the station and he apparently followed up with Akshar's death report. He called me this morning and said he was in town. So I met him for coffee at the hotel and he asked me questions about Akshar's death.'

Arhan stiffened imperceptibly at Bee's words.

She continued talking. Fast. 'If he came down to talk to me, he definitely wants to talk to you. You're the prime eyewitness, Arhan. We need to be sure that we tell him the exact same thing. This guy cannot be fooled.'

'He is a cop, Bee,' Arhan pointed out. 'We don't *want* to lie to him.'

'No, of course not,' she said. 'But we are withholding information and evidence from the authorities and that's pretty much a motive in cases like this and you'll end up in jail.'

'What evidence? Withholding what information? We told the police everything,' he said, running a hand through his hair.

At his perplexed look, she said, 'Remember the phone I called you from? And the one you answered in Akshar's room? They're evidence and we still have them both.' She spoke slowly, as if to a child.

'Then let's turn over all the evidence to him. Right now.' Arhan was emphatic. 'I don't want to keep Akshar's secret phone with me anyway. Let the police do their job.'

'You should have thought of this yesterday, Arhan,' she said bluntly. 'Now if you show up with two untraceable burner phones, we're both screwed. You *and* me.'

'But why can't we just give them both the phones and tell them we forgot about them because of the trauma of seeing a dead body? Which is the truth,' he protested.

'You think they will just believe us? And what about the board? Do you think they'll just allow you to continue with your job coaching the team if they knew you were in possession of a suspicious burner phone connected to the team physiotherapist's death?'

He hated that she was right. 'But it is not mine. It's Aksha —'

'Do you know what the police will do to you to get a confession? The third-degree torture they'll use if they suspect you? And they will suspect you.'

'Do you cover crime or sports?' His protest was feeble, half-hearted.

'I am a woman of many talents. But seriously, Arhan.' Bee was urgently grim. 'We need to concentrate and line up our act.'

'Can't we just destroy the phones?' The logic was faultless in his head. 'No phone, no withholding of evidence, no crime. And definitely no motive. No one can link us to anything if the phones don't exist. One chuck into the ocean at Marina Beach during high tide and we're home free.' His eyes brightened with relief at the simple solution.

'Yo, genius!' She tapped his forehead twice. 'Did a cricket ball hit you really hard when you were a kid and you lost your common sense?'

He gave her a hurt look. 'There's no need to be mean.'

'I'm sorry.' Bee sighed. And kissed him. Soft and sweet, like he had kissed her not twenty-four hours ago.

He blinked. Just like she had. As if he couldn't quite believe what had just happened.

'Someone hurt me pretty badly for this phone, Arhan,' she said quietly. 'They most certainly had a hand in what happened to Akshar and I am a hundred per cent certain they will not rest till they find the phone or silence us. And when they find out we don't have the phone, what do you think they'll do to us?'

Arhan sighed. It was a deep sigh that came from his diaphragm.

'This is a mess I wish I could hand over to someone else.'

'Arhan.' Bee was gentle, surprisingly so.

Arhan looked at her.

'I am sorry,' she said. 'I know you don't want your life complicated by all this, *some* of which I am responsible for. But trust me when I say this, going to the cops will get us arrested and destroying our only clue as to what's going on will definitely get us killed.'

'What wonderful choices,' he muttered.

'This sucks, I know.' She squeezed his arm. 'But we have to make the best of our situation and right now that means getting our stories straight so Thapar doesn't get on our trail while we do some real investigation.'

'You sound very impressed with this Thapar guy. Who is he?'

'Do you remember the inspector from that Vidya Balan movie?' Bee asked.

Arhan nodded. 'I think so . . .'

'Well, he exists in real life,' Bee said bluntly. 'And he wears unwrinkled cotton shirts and speaks at least three languages, as far as I know. He isn't one to mess with, trust me.'

Bee waited with bated breath for Arhan's reply.

'All right,' he said finally. 'Let's do this.'

23

The roar from the MA Chidambaram Stadium, located at the edge of Marina Beach, rivalled the roar of the waves crashing against the shore. India had just finished batting the West Indies.

The beach was practically deserted. The coconut vendors were gone, jumping over the fence and trying to sneak up trees. Standard match-game fare.

The stadium was full to bursting in the light of the shocking death of the team's physiotherapist.

There was a manic energy in the air that nauseated Arhan as he and Lakhani sat in the latter's Jaguar for an impromptu 'meeting-sheeting'.

'Look, *bete*,' Lakhani said. 'You're doing a fantastic job with the boys.'

Balvinder Lakhani chewed on his trademark betel leaf candy. His *paan*-scented breath percolated the AC confines of the sedan.

Arhan wanted to gag. He rubbed the bridge of his nose. His migraine had started the national anthem very softly right by his pituitary gland. 'Thank you, sirji. It's all due to your generosity.' He kept his tone compliant, mostly because his energy was depleted from the events of the past few days, a lack of nourishment and missing Bee.

Weird, she is living rent-free in my head.

'You were a damn fine player, Arhan *bete*,' Balvinder began, 'but you're an even better coach. You understand how the business side of things works and yet you have the capacity to touch the boys' hearts. I do believe they will lose their *hosh* and *josh* without you.'

'With all due respect, sirji,' Arhan said politely, 'we have an exceptionally talented and hungry team with the skill to make it to the very end. Please don't take anything away from their accomplishments. Why, just today, Dashrath Singh's lofted shot on Merrill's bouncer showed a steady temperament and accurate reading of —'

'*Haan, haan.* They play well. *Maloom hai.*' Lakhani paused and chewed on his candy. 'But recent circumstances are going to devastate them, Arhan. That *choot* Akshar—' Lakhani took a deep breath. 'I swear to you, Arhan, there is nothing more selfish than dying in the middle of a big tournament. Imagine if the sponsors had pulled out and the TV people wanted their money back.'

The man's potbelly shuddered. 'This is a worse fiasco than what those West Indians pulled and then Sri Lanka had to fill in during the test series. Good thing we taught them a lesson today.'

'Sir, the West Indies is still fighting for better player contracts. It's not their fault their board is not as rich as *Kubera.*' Arhan repeated the oft-made statement, incredulous that anyone could be this clueless and ruthless at the same time.

'Look, you should play the game for the love of it, *bete.* Not for money.' Lakhani puffed out his unimpressive chest as he tapped out a cigar from a gold-encrusted case, all gung-ho and patriotic. But Arhan had it on good authority that the man would sell the tricolour for the right price.

He resisted the urge to twist the *bandhgala* collar of Lakhani's bespoke suit till the man's pale face turned the shade of the *paan* candy he was so fond of chewing.

But more than anything, even more than choking this nutjob official, Arhan wanted this pointless conversation to end.

He wanted to leave.

He wanted food.

He wanted to talk to the team and go over strategy sessions before they headed out to Dharamshala to play the next leg.

He wanted Bee Vishwanathan, inexplicable as it was.

Arhan shifted restlessly in his seat.

Lakhani laid a hand on his shoulder and he tuned back in. 'You need to talk to them and keep them focused. We have a lot of responsibility with this tournament. The default on the satellite rights fees alone will be enough to bankrupt the board if we don't deliver a super season. Are you getting my point?'

'Yes, sirji. I'll do my best. But you must also understand. Akshar was a very important part of this team. His loss is going to impact us all.'

Lakhani shrugged, a deliberately blasé gesture. 'Dedicate the rest of the cup to him if you want. But don't disappoint me, Arhan. I took a huge bet on you when your good friend Kapil Srivastav arranged that meeting at the CCI and begged me to consider you for this position.'

'I understand that, sirji. But—'

'No buts, Arhan. Make it happen. *Chak de phatte*, as you Punjus say.'

Lakhani's phone trilled, the latest Bollywood item song and he thumbed it open and started talking rapidly in Sindhi.

Arhan laid his aching head back on the comfortable leather rest and wondered how his dream job had turned into a living nightmare.

—◆ ◆—

'Mr Arhan Kapoor?'

Arhan stopped on his solitary walk to the hotel elevator bank and turned to look at the voice in question. Average height, lean but muscular under his suit jacket and an unwrinkled cotton shirt.

The inspector had found him.

Arhan smiled politely. 'Yes, how can I help you?'

The man flashed his badge at him. 'Inspector Paramjit Thapar, special branch. I am here to head the Shekhawat investigation. I was wondering if we could talk for a little bit? I have a few questions for you, Mr Kapoor.'

Arhan mentally waved goodbye to peace. 'Absolutely, Inspector Thapar. Anything to help close the case. Akshar is a wonderful friend and a good guy and I—'

'Was,' Thapar said.

'I beg your pardon?'

'Akshar *was* a good man. Allegedly. And you *were* his friend. Again, allegedly. But he is dead now. Allegedly murdered. So that means someone had motive enough to kill him.' Thapar paused and studied Arhan—his unshaven face, his tattered jeans and the navy blue sports coat with the Team India logo that he wore with casual elegance—before continuing, 'Do you know of anyone who might have such a motive, Mr Kapoor? Since you were such good friends with him.'

Arhan shook his head, no hesitation. 'I absolutely do not, Inspector Thapar. I am sorry but I need to sit down, have some coffee and aspirin. My head is killing me. I hope that's fine?'

'Of course.'

They walked over to a coffee shop just off the hotel mezzanine and settled outside under a colourful awning.

'Did you catch the match today, Inspector?' Arhan tried to make polite conversation.

'Unfortunately, no. I was going through the crime scene and medical reports.' Thapar lit a cigarette.

'Do you mind?' Arhan nodded at the smoke. 'I have a headache.'

Thapar shrugged and put it out, right in his water glass where the limp cigarette floated like a forlorn carcass. 'Tell me, Mr Kapoor, would you lie to the police?'

Arhan understood then why Bee was so freaked out by this particular cop. He seemed immune to everything but the law. And he had the look of a bloodhound.

'Absolutely not. I am a law-abiding citizen, Inspector. I have nothing to hide.'

'That's what she said.' Thapar snickered at his joke.

'Who?' Arhan spoke absently as he swallowed his headache pills.

'Bee Vishwanathan, your . . . friend? Lovely woman. So intelligent and charming . . . and such a deep knowledge of sports. It's no wonder you're dating her. You are dating her, aren't you?' Thapar said, taking a shot in the dark.

'What?' Arhan jerked his head. 'Yes, yes. Of course, I am . . . we are together. Bee is the love of my life.'

He could have bitten off his tongue the minute the words left his mouth because Thapar's sharp eyes narrowed at the statement. 'I don't believe you, Mr Kapoor.'

'I'm sorry,' Arhan said. 'We are dating, of course. That's not a lie. But Bee's not the love of my life.'

Arhan saw a faint sheen of sweat appearing on the man's throat. Maybe he was human after all.

Thapar smiled faintly at Arhan. 'Police *se jhooth*, Coach Sir? On the first question?'

'Would you like to place your order, sir?' A waiter had appeared, looking expectantly at them.

Arhan could have kissed the server for appearing at the right time. He shook his head discreetly to clear his mind of the previous conversation with Lakhani and focus on the one at hand.

'Coffee for me,' Thapar said. 'Black, two sugars. And a chocolate chip cookie.'

The waiter turned to Arhan. 'Congratulations on the win, sir. We were all cheering like crazy here.'

'Thank you, your support means a lot,' he replied automatically. 'I was wondering if you guys have any real food here. Sandwiches, omelettes, pasta, anything quick and hot. I am famished.'

'Absolutely, sir. What would you like?'

Arhan rattled off a few dishes and asked for a glass of iced tea half-filled with Coke. When the waiter looked confused, he clarified, 'Half iced tea, half Coke.'

'Yes, sir.'

They checked their phones in awkward silence till the waiter deposited their beverages on the table. Thapar raised a brow at the murky brown drink in front of Arhan.

Arhan, on the other hand, took a healthy swig and felt more human than he had in hours. He shook out another two aspirins and gulped them down with some more of his Coke-iced-tea.

Thapar sipped his coffee. 'I watched you play,' he said. 'A Lancashire county match. Against Surrey, I think. I watched you make that century in 54 balls. You were classy. Elegant. Textbook.'

'Thank you. I remember that innings very well.'

The memory of those halcyon days didn't hurt Arhan as much as it used to. He had developed shields that protected against the pain of not actually playing the game he loved so much.

'You could have come back when they drafted you in the T20. I know you have the talent. Half the country knows that. And you have friends here, don't you?'

Arhan shrugged, fiddled with the straw on the glass. Watched it make squiggly bubbles, the Coke fighting with the tea. Aspartame, the sweetener in Coke, chased headaches away as effectively as aspirin, a cure he'd learned in Lancashire.

'I had to make a choice a long time ago and I needed to stick by it. There is also the question of mental and physical fitness that every sportsman needs to understand about himself. While I am a reasonably fit athlete, I have lost the ability to be a fit cricketer now.'

'Why? You've still got a few years in you, don't you? You're just thirty-three.' Thapar probed idly.

'People retire from the game at my age, Inspector,' Arhan said softly. 'It would be ridiculous and childish of me to expect some sort of glorious and short-lived comeback that would indeed make for sensational headlines but would not lead the country, the game or me anywhere. I am happier where I am.'

'Coaching?'

Arhan nodded. 'Coaching. I understand the passion for cricket, being a former first-class cricketer. I can also sympathise with the business side of it, being a businessman now. But cricket is as much about cold-hard cash as it is about the heart, and I try to provide that balance to my players. So they can play the best possible game on match day.'

'Impressive. Idealistic. Did Akshar Shekhawat share your idealism?'

Arhan blew out a breath as the food came. Platters full of eggs, toast, butter chiplets, a sandwich loaded with veggies and meat, and a decent-sized pizza with the cheese sizzling on the crust. When he'd loaded his plate, he held his knife and fork and nodded at the food. 'You're sure you don't want anything, Inspector?'

'Absolutely not.' Thapar invited. 'But please go ahead.'

Arhan pounced on the food before answering the cop's question. 'Akshar was one of the most qualified physicians we've had on retainer. He graduated from Columbia and interned with the New York Yankees before coming back home. The team was fortunate to have someone with his technical and medical know-how on their side.'

'That's wonderful. But you didn't answer my question.'

Arhan paused in the act of spooning eggs on to his plate. 'Akshar was a doctor, a man of science. But he was a sports doctor. He understood the grandeur and the fairy-tale reality we sometimes live in.'

'Fairy-tale reality?'

Arhan made a swinging motion with his fork. 'If MS Dhoni's sixer at Wankhede in 2011 was not a fairy-tale moment, I don't know what is. Look at the stats' books, Inspector, and you will find them littered with many such instances. Akshar loved that about the game as much as I do. That's why he was able to keep the guys going, physically at least, when sometimes they would have thrown in the towel.'

'That's wonderful.' Thapar conceded.

'He was a good man,' Arhan said simply. 'A stand-up professional and a team player. We never had any undue complaints from the team, including the second-stringers, about his practices and techniques.'

'So you're saying he didn't have any enemies?'

'I have no idea what your definition of an enemy is,' Arhan said, a little exasperated.

'Someone who had motive enough to pump this *good man* full of xylazine and watch him die.'

Arhan stopped midway while chewing a bite of the sandwich. 'Xylazine? Horse tranquilliser?'

Thapar nodded. 'It's confidential for the moment but toxicology reports suggest trace amounts of xylazine in Akshar's bloodstream.'

Arhan swallowed with difficulty. 'So . . . it's murder then.'

The bite of the delicious tandoori chicken sandwich turned to ashes in his mouth.

Thapar nodded. 'Yes, it is murder. A planned, pre-meditated murder, considering the murderer used a syringe specifically after coming up to Akshar Shekhawat's room with the intention of killing him.'

'That's awful,' Arhan said. 'Why would anyone want to kill him?'

'That's exactly the question I am asking you, Mr Kapoor,' Thapar spoke softly, his eyes like a striking cobra. 'Didn't you argue with Akshar just hours before, at the gym?' Thapar took out a small diary from his jacket pocket and made a great show of consulting his notes. 'Edward Banner told me so when I spoke to him.'

Arhan stiffened. 'Then you'll know that Akshar also spoke to a reporter, Karan Sholekar, at the gym right before "allegedly" arguing with me. It didn't have anything to do with me or Bee Vishwanathan. I've already told this to the police at the scene.'

'It was nothing that Shekhawat insulted your girlfriend . . . the supposed love of your life?' Thapar didn't wait for Arhan to deny it. 'Maybe it wasn't, maybe it was. Maybe you followed him back to his room. You argued some more. Maybe you lost your head in a moment of anger and jabbed him with enough tranquilliser to kill a 500 kg horse?'

'That's ridiculous.' Arhan's voice went dead low. Underneath the table, he curled his fingers into a fist that ached to punch the smug cop. 'Apart from the impossibility of procuring the poison, are you actually accusing me of killing Akshar just because we had an argument?'

'Often enough arguments are reason enough to kill someone, Mr Kapoor.' He finished his coffee.

'You must be a cynical man, Inspector, if you truly believe that.'

'I have seen things that would leave you shrivelled up in horror. The hate mankind has for itself. One more thing.'

'Now what?' Arhan asked coldly, warily. Bee had been right on the money about this Thapar guy. He was relentless. And unforgiving. Not a person to mess with.

'Your doctor, the so-called *sant* physio from Columbia, was addicted to online poker and pornography. He was heavily in debt to rummybaaz. com. Did you know that?'

Fuck!

Arhan shook his head, while his heart hammered in his chest. Akshar earned almost eight figures, working as a primary physio for the team. How could he be in debt?

'That's not true. Akshar was a family man. His kids call me uncle. He doesn't watch online porn.' But the words were hollow-sounding.

'Everyone watches porn, Mr Kapoor. Let's not kid each other.' Thapar was all business now. 'It's the gambling thing that's tricky, isn't it?'

'I . . . I wouldn't know anything about that,' Arhan confessed.

Arhan's father had taken his own life after plunging the family business into massive debt. Of course, he'd done it to expand their business and not because he was addicted to women and gambling. But the bottom line was that Arhan knew how debt could shatter a person and break apart a family.

'Well, I do. Money, Mr Kapoor,' Thapar answered his own question. 'Money can make a man do stupid things. Money and sex. So you need to think back as much as you can and let me know if you find anything —*anything*—slightly suspicious about Akshar's activities.'

Thapar tucked a crisp five-hundred-rupee note under his empty coffee cup. 'You'd be surprised at the things people do that you wouldn't suspect them of, Mr Kapoor. I'll take your leave now. Getting a cab here at this time of the night is impossible.'

Arhan sighed. 'I'll ask the driver to drop you off. Just give me a second, please.'

Thapar waited while Arhan spoke to the on-duty driver and signed for his food. He then walked the cop out of the hotel. They waited at the hotel entrance for the driver to bring the car around.

'Inspector,' Arhan murmured, 'you seriously don't think any one of us here could have had a hand in Akshar's murder, do you?'

'It's not my job to draw conclusions, Mr Kapoor,' Thapar said. 'I follow the evidence and it usually leads me to the perpetrator. People are not as clever as they'd like to be.'

The car purred to a smooth stop at the entrance and Thapar got in. He glanced back and Arhan saw ruthless determination on the cop's face.

'But I will promise you this,' Thapar said. 'Whoever killed Akshar Shekhawat will hang for it. And not just because this nation will bay for the bastard's blood but because I hate criminals, Mr Kapoor. I fucking hate them. You have a good night.'

24

'I hate criminals, Mr Kapoor. I fucking hate them.'

The inspector's words buzzed in Arhan's head as he rode the elevator up to his floor, his laptop bag and jacket curled up like little puppies at his feet. He was swaying with exhaustion and was suddenly afraid.

Thapar had shared some disturbing facts about Akshar.

Arhan had the distinct feeling that very soon Thapar would ask him for his alibi for the time of the murder. And he had none.

He walked out with his stuff and was fishing in his pocket for the key card when he stumbled.

'What the—'

Arhan focused and saw Bee's *Kolhapuri* chappals blocking the way to his door. She was curled up on the floor, fast asleep. One arm pillowing her head, body curved into an 'S'. Her nostrils flared with little puffy breaths.

She looked so adorable and innocent. Worlds away from the horror he'd just been a part of.

Arhan bent down, put his things by the door and scooped her up into his arms. She made a snuffling little noise and instinctively snuggled closer to his chest, her arms around his neck. He was immensely distracted by her warm breath against his throat and his own weakened defences that demanded he kiss her awake right now, distance himself from everything Thapar had just told him.

Bee tightened her hold around him and sighed.

Arhan opened the hotel room door with great difficulty and deposited her on his bed. He drew the covers over her. Then he went back out, got the rest of his gear, hung up the Team India jacket on its special padded hanger and stripped.

A shower was out of the question tonight. He didn't want to wake Bee up.

So he brushed his teeth, splashed some cold water on his face and got into bed.

He gave his sleeping Bee one single wistful glance. Then exhaustion caught up with him and he dropped off like a stone.

—·◆ ◆·—

Bee woke up next to a sexy sleeping Arhan. She fluttered groggy lashes open and saw Arhan's nose squashed against hers.

His usually unsmiling, flat mouth was partly open as he emitted a soft snore. His lashes, she noted with envy, were longer than hers.

Why does God do that? Give guys sexy lashes.

She raised one finger and lightly traced his stubborn jaw, feeling the scratchiness of his beard pleasantly tingle her skin.

Arhan Kapoor wasn't ridiculously handsome, not Fawad Khan-handsome, but she certainly felt . . . gloopy around him. Like the inside of a melted chocolate cupcake from LPQ.

And he had integrity and spine. She found that incredibly desirable.

He'd been so uncomfortable with the whole burner phone situation that she felt awful about getting him in trouble, which was why she'd come to his room to apologise. But he wasn't there and she'd dozed off while waiting for him.

Now they were in bed. Together. His arm around her waist, heavy and comforting. Their legs tangled together under the covers. Their lips within kissing distance.

Bee leaned forward and kissed him. She got his chin more than his lips.

But Arhan woke up. His dream-filled eyes went from slight confusion to smoky passion. He pulled her forward the scant two inches that separated them and whispered, 'Morning.'

Bee felt delicious shivers run down her spine at the throaty timbre of his sleep-scratchy voice. 'Morning.'

'You look pretty.'

She rolled her eyes as she tried to disengage her legs from his under the covers. 'Liar.'

He pulled her across the covers and on top of him, and she squealed as she shoved hair out of her eyes and glared at him in mock affront.

'Hey! Be careful.'

He grinned and kissed her deeply.

She stilled.

'Is that warning enough?' He talked against her lips.

It was all very hot.

'I need to brush my teeth.' She said while trying to open her mouth as little as possible.

But when his fingers snaked under her T-shirt and started tracing patterns across her back, she tried to remember why brushing one's teeth was important. His calloused fingers felt so good on her bare skin. Was her back really that sensitive? She wiggled closer and straddled him.

Arhan gave her a look that made her burn. He lifted her shirt over her head and threw it. Bee sighed. Morning cuddles were taking on a whole new meaning with this man. She bent and looped her arms around his neck and they kissed. A morning cuddle of a kiss. Fresh and sweet and hot.

When he turned and pressed her down on the bed, Bee went willingly, running her hands up his back. It was firm, scarred. She wanted to see those scars.

He sucked on the pulse hammering hard at her throat and she bit him on his shoulder. Arhan smoothed her hair, framing her head and kissed her. Deeply, invading her, taking her tongue and demanding a frantic response.

Bee's dreamy slide into pleasure turned into a wild ride when he took off her bra and cupped her breasts, rubbing his beard on their sensitive tips. She writhed and rubbed restlessly against him.

'You like that?' he murmured.

She didn't have the energy to nod. So he did it again.

Bee moaned, an essentially seductive sound that drove his arousal to the stratosphere. He took her roving hands to the front of his track pants and she gripped him. Hard and sure. He closed his eyes in blessed relief.

Then she stroked him and Arhan shuddered.

They kissed again, wild and desperate, urgently taking off their remaining clothes. Arhan sucked her breasts and Bee felt herself melting right into the bed. She pulled him closer, her legs intertwining around his hip, their bodies brushing against each other for the first time without clothes. It felt marvellous.

Then, three things happened in quick succession.

The phone rang.

The alarm clock went off—a Linkin Park number.

And there was a strident knock on the door.

'Fuck!' Arhan cursed at her belly button before giving it a quick kiss.

Bee wanted more. She twisted her fingers into his hair and said, 'Make them go away. Now.'

'I have a pre-breakfast meeting. I think I'm late.'

Her eyes narrowed in disbelief. 'You're going to leave me here? Now? Like this?'

He crushed her into him and spoke in her ear, unbelievably hot. 'You think I want to go? You think I am that dumb?'

She pressed closer to him, core to core, and had the pleasure of watching him shudder again. 'Then don't go. Stay here. Ten minutes.'

'It's not going to be just ten minutes.' Now he looked affronted.

'It's not going to be anything, is it?'

Chester Bennington screamed about nothing mattering in the end.

Arhan sat up, looking like an adorably grumpy, deliciously naked bear. A very horny naked bear.

The knocking on the door continued. '*Haan, haan*! I am coming!' he snarled.

Bee drew the covers decorously over her shoulders until only her flushed face and tousled hair were visible. 'Well, I am not.' She grinned at her own joke.

Arhan growled and hauled her up in an impressive show of strength. 'You'll pay for that when I actually have the time to do something about it.'

'How?' She played with the curls at the nape of his neck.

Arhan nipped her earlobe and traced the shell of her ear. 'I'll do anything I want and you'll love it.'

Bee quivered. 'Someone is very cocky.' Then she added after a beat, 'Hey, that's two for me.'

'You seem to be in a very punny mood,' he joked and started getting dressed.

Bee sat there and watched Arhan struggle into his pants and contemplated the cruelties of life that only allowed her glimpses of the best butt ever!

—⋅✦ ✦⋅—

Bee paused her morning note-taking of the previous night's match for the column as her phone vibrated, indicating a call. It was Arhan.

'Hello, cocky,' she grinned goofily.

'Hello, trouble.'

'What's up?' She settled more comfortably into her chair, looking critically at her nails. They were chipped, the polish wearing off. She would have to get them done soon.

'Nothing much. The meeting went off okay. The boys are all excited about the quarter-finals. It's looking very positive for them.'

'Can I quote you on this?'

'Bee.'

She sighed noisily. 'I had to ask, you know? It's my job. So why did you call?'

'Is a reason required?'

'Yes.'

'Why?' He sounded curious. 'I thought women liked it when men called them for no reason whatsoever.'

'We do like it. But then we miss it when it doesn't happen anymore and we start asking for it and we get told we are nags. So no, thank you. I don't need pointless conversation in the middle of the day.'

'Who hurt you so badly?'

She sat up in her chair. She couldn't believe that he'd understood her wariness just by her tone. She shook her head to clear her thoughts.

Not the time for this conversation.

'I didn't know you multitasked as a counsellor too,' she said instead.

'Fine, you win. There is a reason I called.'

Why were men who admitted they were wrong so undeniably sexy?

'What?'

'Inspector Thapar came to see me yesterday.'

Her heart sank. 'I see.'

'Yeah . . . He told me some extremely interesting things about Akshar.'

Bee instantly perked up. 'What things?'

'Can't tell you over the phone, babe.'

'Don't "babe" me, cocky. Fine. If not over the phone then where? When?'

'I don't know. We're doing a session at the nets. One of the guys wants to practise bouncers and I am helping out with that. Then we have a team counselling meeting scheduled for four in the afternoon. After that, I am flying out to Chandigarh with Akshar's body. They finally released it.'

Bee suddenly felt horrible about her selfish motives. 'Shit, Arhan. I'm so sorry.'

'It's fine. It's my job.'

'No, it isn't,' Bee thought, but she didn't correct him. 'Do you want me to come with you?'

Arhan sighed audibly. 'I'll take a rain check on that. I don't think funerals are the most appropriate choice for a first date.'

'How cute. *Kitna* romantic.'

Arhan chuckled at her sarcasm. 'Romance-shomance will have to wait for a bit, Bee. The next two days are insane. Practice sessions, meetings and then chalking out a strategy to beat the Sri Lankans. It's a huge task.'

'You're right, the coming days are going to be chaotic,' Bee said slowly. 'I've decided to investigate those burner phones.'

'Don't do anything dumb and don't get in trouble.'

'You didn't say don't break the law, AK. Are you learning or just a wimp?'

'I know you, that's all. But . . .' His hesitation was palpable.

'But what?'

'I don't even know your real name.'

Her jaw dropped at his comment. 'If I tell you my name, I'm going to have to——' But better sense prevailed and she bit her tongue from finishing the crass statement. 'I have work. Don't you have work?'

'I do. There is a very hot masseuse here who is flirting with me.'

'Have fun with her,' Bee said waspishly and ended the call while Arhan's laughter roared over the line. Two fuming seconds later, she redialled and said, 'If you let that hot masseuse touch you, it will end very badly for you.'

'Is that a threat? How badly will it go? Will there be whips and chains? Handcuffs?'

She groaned. 'You're sick, Arhan Kapoor. And I hate you.'

'No,' he disputed her cheerfully. 'You don't hate me. You like me. Just as I like you. So stop being jealous and go back to work. I'll text you when I can.'

Her silence was mutiny itself.

'Okay, Bee?'

'Fine,' she said. 'But I still want proof that no hot masseuses come near your sexy butt.'

'What about my sexy—'

He was still laughing when she hung up. But she was smiling too and it felt good. Given the bizarre and downright scary circumstances they had found themselves in, it felt good to laugh and be light of heart with a sweet, interesting man who understood her.

—◆ ◆—

The quarter-finals were to be played in Dharamshala, followed by the semis in Mohali. The grounds were a few hours away from each other, but there was some hard terrain to cover.

Eight of the competing sixteen teams had made it through. And they were all practising hard on the available grounds. The players also gave the natives a thrill when they went shopping or wandered the local points of interest.

Australia beat New Zealand convincingly in the first quarter-final —215-4, 155 all out—with just one controversial and contested ball. This match was followed by Pakistan killing the surprise entrants, Ireland. The wicket held after a hard day's batting and Ireland's gutsy 190 was not enough to deter the Pakistani batting attack.

Great cricket was being played under exemplary conditions and the crowds and viewers worldwide were getting their money's worth. The weather too was lovely, cooperative. Temperatures were a balmy 18 degrees and there was no mist or fog to obscure vision. Bad light did not interrupt play in the mountains even once.

Bee watched it all from the press box with her friends, Dheera and Harry; Sholes, for some inexplicable reason, was holed up in his room. Bee was a little intrigued as to why the cricket-crazy Sholes opted to watch the matches from the confines of his room.

Arhan had told her about the 'conversation' he'd had with Akshar the night the good doctor died, and she also wanted to talk to him about it. She was positive it wasn't anything since the cops weren't looking in his direction, but what was the harm in checking, right?

The trip to Dharamshala had been uneventful. She hadn't managed to catch up with Arhan in Chandigarh since he'd arrived a night before the rest of them with the body.

Bee had spent the last two evenings talking to her parents and the Maharani, so she'd been unable to hang out with her friends, especially Sholes.

Kalavati was still upset about her daughter and worried about Bee's whereabouts when they had tea the following evening after Pakistan's QF win.

'I was with Dheera,' Bee lied. 'She had an upset stomach and wanted me around. It was late and I didn't want to disturb you so I didn't leave a message.'

'That's all right, my dear. You're a good friend. A good daughter. I see you talking daily with your parents and I feel comforted.'

The Maharani rubbed a hand over her tired eyes and Bee noticed the fine lines that crowned them. The Maharani might look a well-preserved forty-five, but her real age was at least fifteen years more if the internet was to be believed.

Bee reached out her hand and gently squeezed the Maharani's wrist. The diamond bracelet felt cold to the touch. She remembered Ujwala's mocking words.

'It's all fake.'

'Your daughter will come around too, Ranisa. She's grieving right now. She hates the world. You can't blame her for being depressed and upset, can you?' She tried to keep her tone non-confrontational. No point in distressing the lady even more.

'I understand her grief. I am her mother after all. But I am a queen too, and she is a princess of the royal family, but I guess she has forgotten that in mourning her love. Appearances are everything, Bee, aren't they?' It was Kalavati's favourite refrain.

Bee nodded sympathetically.

'I have told her so many times to not roam around in her dead husband's shorts while the tourist walks are conducted at the palace, but does she listen? Just yesterday someone posted a picture of her in those ridiculous shorts, with a caption that read "Grieving Princess's Un-fab Wardrobe".'

Bee winced. 'That's awful, Ranisa.'

'Yes.' The Maharani's voice broke at the last syllable. 'It is awful. And disrespectful of the hundreds of years of tradition and honour that our family has proudly upheld. I just don't know what to do with her.'

'She needs time. That's all. She will be the daughter you love again soon.'

Bee tried to infuse hope and enthusiasm in her voice, even though she had her own doubts. The drunk woman she'd met in Kolkata looked like she knew exactly what she was doing—embarrassing her royal mother.

Bee wondered again at the kind of relationship the two of them shared and was snapped out of her reverie when the Maharani kept her cup down and wiped delicately at her eyes with a tissue.

'You're such a comfort to me, Bee. Such a source of strength. It might sound absurd but I feel grateful to that burglar for breaking into your room in Jaipur.'

'Me too,' she agreed. 'After all, it could have been Dheera here, enjoying Jacuzzi bathtubs and this really lovely Oolong tea.'

'Somehow,' the Maharani said in a wise tone, 'I doubt that, my dear. You were meant to be here. Now tell me about you and Arhan. I hear he is squiring you about town when he isn't discovering dead bodies.'

'Where did you hear that?' She was unable to hide her amazement at the forthright question.

'You have your sources, my dear. I have mine. Now spill.'

Bee blushed and protested so much that the Maharani tactfully left the matter alone. But their conversation made Bee realise that the Maharani knew more than she let on.

She knows everything.

It was a strangely disquieting thought. She hoped Arhan was having a better time dealing with Akshar's family.

On his plane ride to Chandigarh, Arhan discovered that dead bodies made for terrible companions. The thirty-minute-long chartered plane ride from Dharamshala to Chandigarh had been the most uncomfortable flight of his life. He would have been happy to pass on the task to anyone else, but there was no one.

This, coupled with his innate sense of responsibility, meant that Arhan had pretty much volunteered for this terrible task. One he immediately regretted.

Akshar's brother, Jatinder, met him at the airport with a special hearse. They didn't speak on the forty-minute ride to Akshar's home in the city.

Arhan had nothing to say.

'I'm so sorry for your loss,' he told Akshar's wife Jessica on reaching their house.

She stood in her widow whites, surrounded by family and friends, blank and apathetic in her grief. Her two young kids, aged eight and six, clung to her sari *pallu*.

Arhan was hollow with misery and confusion.

'I'm so sorry,' Arhan told Akshar's father.

The man looked broken. No one should have to watch their child's funeral. Shekhawat Sr hugged Arhan tight, holding on as if to a life raft.

Arhan was given a room to wash up and change for the funeral. He was invited to eat, but he had no appetite.

He did, however, have a mission. He needed to know if Thapar was right.

When he was done with his bath, he sent a quick catch-up text to Bee and wandered towards Akshar's study. He was able to gain access since everyone in the house was occupied with the body and the cremation.

The study was locked so Arhan looked both ways down the deserted corridor before breaking the lock with a resounding kick. The office held worn furniture and pictures; sunlit windows allowed him a view of the condolence committee settling in.

The sounds of wailing and weeping hurt his heart and head. He wished Bee were here standing next to him, squeezing his hand. Popping bubble wrap or talking about cricket stats.

Arhan loped over to the computer terminal and powered it on. It was password-protected. Luckily, given Akshar's penchant for forgetting the password on his official computer, Arhan had been granted access to it. He just hoped the man had used the same password on his home computer too—coLumbiadoc55$.

Crossing his fingers, he typed in the letters. The screen blinked to life.

Arhan glanced at the files on the desktop. Work stuff, a pictures folder, a few music and video programmes. Standard stuff.

He then accessed Akshar's email. His inbox was overflowing with unread emails dating back to the last three months. He hit refresh and waited for the new mails to download.

In the meantime, Arhan dug deeper, accessing files and folders on the other drives. There were three of them and in the F drive, in an innocuous folder named Jessica Bills, he hit pay dirt.

There was a subfolder titled 'Rummy' which detailed payments made to the website he was supposed to be indebted to. A separate excel sheet showed figures wagered, won and lost. The losses were not huge, but they had escalated over time.

His credit card bills were horrifying. All his cards were maxed out, each payment made past the due date for astronomical amounts.

There was also an entire folder dedicated to a woman named 'Big Tits Sasha'. Sleazy pictures and horny emails that they'd been writing each other for the past six months that Akshar, the lovesick client, had saved on his home computer.

The idiot!

Lastly, there was a balloon payment scheme for an apartment in Delhi's Vasant Vihar. A duplex, no less. Big Tits Sasha had been set up in style by her married Romeo.

When Arhan came across the videos, he decided to give them a pass, sickened by it all.

From what Thapar had told him, Arhan knew the police had all this information. It was the information they didn't have that he was interested in.

Online poker debts needed to be paid almost as quickly as regular gambling debts. In some cases, they kept ballooning the payments with the promise of more and higher wins. People ended up bankrupt in the end. Or injured. Or dead.

And yet no one in Akshar's family had suspected a thing. His PF, monthly investments and expenses were paid for from his salary until the last month.

He'd cashed in his bonus last year for an expensive holiday to Switzerland with his family. Arhan remembered this because Akshar had been so excited to show the pictures on his new iPad.

Then where the hell had the physio got the money to set his mistress up in a love nest in the uber posh Vasant Vihar? All the while supporting a gambling addiction that ran into lakhs of rupees at last count?

What was this bank account that his Amex card was linked to?

Arhan didn't have to search for long before he found a poorly hidden folder with details of a joint bank account in the name of Akshar and Sasha Shekhawat, which held fifty lakh rupees. The deposits had been made over a period of three months and had come from Suisse Francais National Bank in Geneva.

The amount had been withdrawn exactly three days ago, the credit card paid out for the bare minimum.

The computer pinged, signalling the end of email download on Akshar's official address. Arhan checked it automatically.

The last one interested him the most. It was from Bee's reporter friend, Karan Sholekar.

The body of the email was empty. The subject stated 'I know what you've done. We need to talk.'

It was dated the day before yesterday. The day of Akshar's murder.

Arhan heard footsteps pounding on the hardwood floor and hurriedly turned off the machine. He rushed out into the corridor, shutting the study door softly behind him. His brain churned with endless possibilities.

'Bhai, are you ready?' Jatinder asked him.

'*Haan*,' Arhan answered. 'I am ready.'

Then he went to cremate the body of a man he'd thought of as a friend but who, it turned out, had successfully lied to him for almost the entire time they'd known each other.

The next day was the first of the quarter-finals. Everyone was waiting for the Aussie batsmen to walk on to the field. The sun was shining pleasantly since it was a day game. The other QF would be played under lights later in the evening.

It was going to be a long day of cricket and the coffee and curses in the press box were already flowing hot.

At half-time, Bee looked fondly around the press room. Dheera was yelling at her son in a mix of Bangla and English over some mischief he'd committed. Harry was digging into the *chole bhature* like it was his last meal.

Bee saw the familiar faces of the people she had come to know pretty well over the last few days. Being in close quarters for extended periods of time like Big Boss housemates fostered a kind of camaraderie that was hard to find in other places.

She waved to the *Delhi Times* reporter, a sweet, young bespectacled geek who had asked her out when they'd first met. She'd refused him gently.

Bee didn't date co-workers, the media, sportspersons or anyone related to any of the above in general. Her last disastrous relationship had been with a friend—a good friend—who had, it turned out, been passing the time while she had fallen fathoms deep in love with him.

He had hurt her, like Arhan had so accurately observed.

Then what are you doing with Assistant Coach Arhan Kapoor?

Bee didn't want to delve too deeply into self-analysis because then she would have to talk to Dheera who would give her the 'asshole attraction' lecture all over again and she didn't need that, thank you very much.

What she needed was some action, a distraction.

Bee texted her brother. 'How do I go about finding out who owns a SIM card?'

The reply was instantaneous. 'Why would you need to do that? What are you involved in now, sis?'

Bee rolled her eyes and huffed out a breath. Why was it impossible for anyone to take her seriously? 'Nothing. Just curious. Never mind.'

Aggy replied, 'I don't believe that for a second. But if you want to know the details of a SIM card, you need to check with the service provider. Usually buyer information is registered with them.'

Bee pondered for a minute before turning to Dheera. 'We need to talk.'

Dheera gave her a blank look. 'We're talking now.'

Bee gave Harry, who was texting sweet nothings to his fiancée in Jharkhand, a significant look.

'We need to *talk*,' she repeated.

Harry looked up at that exact moment and said, 'Hey, what do you want to talk about?'

Dheera shrugged. 'Female problems. You want in?'

Harry grimaced. 'I miss Sholes, man. He would never let you guys torture me like this.'

'Where is he, anyway?' Bee looked around the room again.

The QFs were important, more important than the round-robin stage, since they were basically elimination matches. India making it to the quarters was a dream run for this team, one that had made even the press box start Bleeding Blue. Sholes was a true-blue patriotic professional; he wouldn't miss this match for anything.

'His phone was switched off when I got on the bus. He disappeared somewhere last night. Didn't even show up for dinner.'

Dheera grinned. 'It has to be a cheerleader.'

'Please,' Harry snorted. 'Sholes is happily married. He has a loving wife. Asmita is hot and they just had a baby. He isn't going to mess that up for some match bait. It's ridiculous to think that.'

'But not impossible,' Bee murmured.

'Nothing is,' Dheera chimed in.

'I hate this. I want Sholes,' Harry announced.

The stadium roared as the fielders took their positions and the batsmen jogged to the middle. The commentators started with the importance of the game.

South Africa versus West Indies was always a humdinger with neither side willing to give an inch.

'It's a tragedy, *yaar,*' Harry said as the *Delhi Times* reporter wandered over to their corner and smiled tentatively at Bee.

Bee smiled back politely.

'Akshar shouldn't have died in the middle of the tournament,' Harry said mournfully. 'It's messing the team up. See how Chandranaraine is peering off into the distance instead of vomiting. That's his thing, man! Every time he vomits before a match, he gets wickets in the first spell.'

'That's disgusting,' Dheera said.

'I tried to call Lakhani and his tail for a quote before India's match,' the *Times* guy chimed in. 'But they said "Fuck off" and slammed the phone on me. Bloody—'

'Hey, the match has begun,' Bee said, smiling brightly. 'Let's all watch it, yes?'

The reporter shut up immediately.

Dheera looked at Bee and said, 'Okay, let's talk now.'

'Not here.'

Both of them stared at the men engrossed in the proceedings and oblivious to the world around them, and slipped out noiselessly.

In Dheera's room, Bee spilled the beans about finding the burner phones, talking to Arhan on the night of Akshar's murder, her disastrous interview with Thapar and what Aggy had just told her about finding the SIM details.

'You're in trouble,' Dheera said, deadpan.

Bee nodded miserably. 'I am. And I need help. You're the only one I can think of to get me out of this, Dhee.'

'I didn't think you'd ever admit to needing help, Bee,' Dheera teased. She thought about it for a long, tense moment. Then she texted someone and finally said, 'Let's find a café with Wi-Fi. I don't want this to be easily traced back to us. '

So Bee found herself sitting in a café at the other end of Dharamshala. They settled in with iced teas and their laptops.

Dheera started a video call with her nephew's friend who called himself DDLJSRKRaj. The guy who appeared on the screen was barely twenty and looked like the epitome of a computer nerd. He even wore a T-shirt that said 'I Make Nerd Look Cool'. Behind him was a whiteboard full of squiggly numbers that made no sense to Bee or Dheera.

He perked up at Dheera's smile.

'Hello, DDLJSRKRaj.'

He leaned back on his chair and said, 'Please. Call me Raj.' He even dropped his voice like the superstar did when he spoke to women. 'Which one of you fine ladies needs my help?'

Bee leaned in and he sat up straighter.

'Hi, Raj,' she said. 'I'm the one who wants your help. Dheera here is just the middle . . . person.'

'That's cool.' The nerd gulped.

'I'm very grateful that you've agreed to help us out on such short notice, Raj.' Bee smiled warmly.

Dheera pinched her thigh under the table as the boy's ears turned pink from all the flattery.

Bee leaned back, taking her tank-top cleavage with her.

Raj turned business-like. 'So, what can I help you with?'

'We would love for you to tell us how to trace the owner of a SIM card,' Bee said briskly.

'Okay. Why?'

'Is that really necessary for you to know?'

'Not really. But if you're going to hack into the servers of a service provider, you need to be absolutely untraceable. And you need to know what you're doing once you get in there.'

'We were hoping you could help us out with those details without, you know, getting caught.'

Raj looked thoughtful. 'I could do it for you. I'd need the SIM card, of course.'

Bee shook her head instantly. 'No way, kid. Absolutely not. I don't have the time to express courier it to you. Besides,' she added with determination, 'there's no way I'm cool with a minor breaking the law on my behalf.'

'Hey!' Raj was affronted. 'First off, you don't need to send it to me physically. I just need the details on the card and the phone number. Secondly, this is what I do. It's what I am known for. And I am not a kid. I'm twenty-one, okay! And I dig cougars.' He included both of them in his appreciative glance.

Bee grinned, flattered despite herself. 'You look fourteen. And you're a total sweetheart.'

'Come on, Raj. Help us out please?' Dheera said. But she too looked pleased as she shook her long mane of hair.

'The SIM would have a record of most of the service provider activity on your phone. Latest messages, contacts, calls too. Nowadays with cloud support, people forget that SIM cards also store your contact information and messages. In fact, when Motorola first invented the cell phone, they did it so that —'

'Raj, honey. We have a deadline here,' Dheera interrupted him gently. 'Can you help us out or not?'

'I could try. But it would really be better to use an off-grid PC for this sort of thing. You feel me?'

Bee resisted the urge to roll her eyes. Raj looked like the nerd physicist on a very popular sitcom and talked like he was from Jersey. What was he trying to prove?

'I feel you, Raj. So there's no way that I could do it myself?'

Raj shook his head. 'Not really, no.'

She casually took a sip of her iced tea, backtracking a little. 'Then would you be willing to do it for us?'

The kid looked conflicted and a little wary. 'You just said you didn't want me to do it.'

'I did but I wouldn't be asking if it wasn't important, Raj. It's for a good cause, a really good cause. Trust me,' Bee rushed to reassure him while Dheera pinched her hard on the thigh. 'You'd be helping us save lives and expose a major conspiracy if my hunch is right.'

'It's going to cost you,' Raj warned her.

'We have money,' Bee said without blinking an eye. She was sure Arhan, the CEO of a major chain of sugar factories, could cough up the money if she promised him outrageous sexual favours. *Fuck!* What the hell are you thinking, Bee? This is your score, your story. I'll find a way to pay Raj *somehow*.

'We also get the friends and family discount, don't we?' Dheera asked sweetly. 'Considering how highly my nephew talks of you.'

Raj grinned and adjusted his glasses. 'Of course, Dheera Aunty.'

Dheera's eyes narrowed at the term.

Bee squeezed her hand under the table and said sweetly, 'That's awesome, Raj. Tell me what you need and we can get this show going.'

Raj nodded and turned his attention to his laptop. 'All right. I am guessing you have the SIM card in question?'

Bee nodded. 'I do.'

'All right, here's what I need,' Raj began authoritatively.

As the boy wonder hacked into the server in Andhra Pradesh, Bee hoped with all her heart that her hunch would not end up landing her, her best friend or the nerd in jail!

26

Arhan was having the greatest dream ever.

It was the World Cup finals and he was walking in to bat at his favourite position—No. 3. The run chase was on—1 down for the loss of 53, 270 more to go. It was a day-night game at his favourite pitch—Wanderers, Johannesburg. Reverse swing action could be expected at this time of the day, with the ball turning.

He was dressed in India blue with the tricolour on his helmet. His bat, a comforting familiar extension of his arm, his spikes springing into the grass on the field as he middled to the pitch.

That feeling . . . of holding that bat, wearing that cap and that uniform. It was unbeatable. It was everything.

At that moment, he was Arhan Kapoor, star batsman for India. Playing the World Cup.

He blinked once to shake the sweat and lights out of his eyes and looked around the crowd. Somewhere in the screaming stands was his family. Bee was there too. Cheering for him, watching him take guard. Watching him watch the paceman barrel down like a freight train.

He gripped his bat tighter, watched the ball . . . come on, come on, come on . . . and when he deemed it perfect, Arhan swung his bat. The ball made contact. Thwack! His body swung with the momentum, shoulders, torso, hands and legs in perfect alignment, his footwork, excellent.

He knew as the ball flew away, he knew . . .

It soared, soared, soared over the slips, mid-on . . . the fielder at deep cover. It soared over his outstretched hands into the stands. The stands where the screaming fans were cheering for him—AK! AK!

The commentator yelled, 'And he scores! It's a six! What a sublime shot. Perfect timing, precision work. Played like a master.'

Arhan walked forward with the confidence of a king. His heart thumping, adrenaline pumping, he could do this all day long. He could win this match.

And then . . .

There was furious knocking on the door. Pounding, really.

Arhan sat up. His dream brutally shattered, abruptly jerked from a deep sleep. A deep, comforting sleep. Groggily, he checked the time on his travel clock: 2:49 a.m.

Who could it be?

He stumbled out of bed, stubbing his toe at the edge. He cursed under his breath and opened the door.

There stood Bee, practically vibrating with excitement. 'Thank god, that hotel security guard is not here. I've been banging on the door for the past five minutes,' she whispered, brushing past him into the room.

Arhan blinked hard, his mind still foggy. 'What are you doing here? What's going on?'

'We have a lead. A solid, *solid* lead. I am a hundred per cent sure about it.'

'What lead? What are you talking about? Why aren't you asleep? Hey, don't turn on the lights! Ah fuck, Bee!' Arhan sat on his bed, closing his eyes shut against the sudden glare from the bright lights in the room.

He turned his piercing glare on her as he finally opened his eyes.

'Dammit, Bee. It's three o'clock in the morning. I have had a rough week! Spare me.'

Bee gave him a cool look from the bed where she had comfortably settled in, powering on her laptop. 'I'm going to give you a pass because you've really had a terrible week and it *is* 3 a.m., but you're going to want to hear this. Trust me.'

'It couldn't wait until morning?'

He walked, yawning widely, scratching his belly, and slumped next to her. Barely awake.

She sighed, giving his scratchy beard a quick kiss. 'Sorry. But no, it can't.'

And so Bee filled him in on how the nerd had hacked into the servers to find the store where the SIM cards were sold. Bee had then called the store manager and, using her charm and wiles, gleaned a description of the person who had bought the SIM cards. A nondescript man in a black hoodie had purchased six SIM cards in all!

Arhan looked at her in wary surprise. 'How did you do all that?'

Bee beamed. 'I'm a damn good reporter!'

'I bet the guy who bought all those SIM cards gave one to Akshar,' Bee said triumphantly. 'I am reasonably sure it was he who was meeting Akshar at the hotel in Jaipur when I met you.'

'You mean when you assaulted me.'

Bee sighed loudly. 'How many times will you bring it up?'

'It still hurts when I sneeze.' Arhan gave her a droll look.

'I'm so terribly sorry, Mr Kapoor, that I broke your nose.' She grinned sheepishly.

'You don't look sorry at all.'

'You know what?' Bee said softly, throwing caution to the wind and opening herself to the possibility of actual hurt. 'I'm not.'

Arhan looked at her for a single charged moment. 'Neither am I.'

Then he kissed her. Soft and sweet at first, but more urgently as the seconds ticked away. As he was getting to the good part, she slid away from him. She was secretly pleased he looked as whacked out as she felt.

'So now what?' He nodded at the computer. 'We still don't know his identity or what they were doing with the SIM cards.'

'Actually . . .' Bee typed in a few commands on her laptop and a page opened up. 'Voila!'

Arhan leaned forward. He took the laptop from her and stared at the screen which displayed messages.

'These are the last few messages exchanged using the burner phones,' Bee clarified.

Arhan moved the cursor over the first message. It was dated the day the tournament began.

Payment initiated. Let the games begin.

He swore under his breath and looked at the text.

The 15th over. Get him out. Third ball should be good. He clicked on the next one.

Last ball. Make it a six. Crowd-pleaser.

'Fuck,' he said quietly.

'Does this mean what I think it means?' Bee asked tentatively.

'If you're thinking of a match-fixing scandal, then, yeah . . . that's exactly what this means.'

'Hai Bhagwan!' Bee whispered as her worst suspicion was confirmed. She laid her suddenly dizzy head on Arhan's shoulder.

They both stared at the flickering screen that displayed the damning truth: the Indian team's physiotherapist was spot-fixing the World Cup T20 matches!

'You can't report any of this!' Arhan said instinctively.

Bee jerked her head up, nearly taking his chin out in the process.

He stared patiently at her.

She couldn't believe how utterly serious he looked. 'I beg your pardon?'

'I said you can't report any of this,' he repeated. 'This is not media fodder. Not yet. I need to . . . I need to talk to someone . . . The cops, I think. We need to let the authorities handle this and I can't have you haring off and printing shit before I do that.'

Bee took a deep breath, remembered the ODI batting average of Adam Gilchrist—96.9—and felt her anger fade the tiniest bit. 'I thought we were beyond this. That you trusted me.'

Arhan rubbed a weary hand over his beard. 'I do,' he said quietly. 'But I also can't forget that you are brave and smart and ambitious. All of which are great qualities—qualities I love about you. God, you so easily learned how to be a hacker today.' He shuddered. 'But you fuck up the curve, Bee. You know what I mean?'

'I know what you mean. I know exactly what you mean. And now I'd like to go back to bed. My bed.' She'd learned the art of being coldly regal from her time with the Maharani. It was paying off.

He looked stoically at her. 'Nope. You're not leaving like that. No more filmy exits, woman.'

'Watch me.'

Bee ploughed her elbow into his stomach and tried to scramble off the bed, but he pinned her down, his legs stilling her thrashing knees to keep them from doing damage to strategic body parts.

Arhan kissed her button nose while her eyes spit holy fire at him.

Next, he aimed for her mouth, but she turned her face away. He nuzzled his nose against her jaw. It was a tender gesture. She hated that she found herself melting at it. Hated that she was considering staying just because he was being sweet to her and had called her smart and ambitious without sounding pissed off.

'I trust you, Bee. You have to know that by now,' he said quietly. 'It's why I didn't tell Thapar about the fucking burner phone in the first place. Because *you* had the other one. But you can't report it, not yet. Surely you're professional enough to understand this requires deeper investigation?' he whispered, hoarsely.

'And you have to understand, I am sensitive to your situation, Arhan. I know what a story like this requires. Timing is everything here. And the timing's just not right. Yet.'

Arhan gave her a thoughtful look. 'What does a story like this require, Bee?'

Bee started counting off the elements of the story. 'It needs the act, the what. Then it needs the when and the where.' She pointed at the SIM cards. 'I have all that now. But I still don't have two pieces of the story.'

'The who,' Arhan supplied wryly. 'The people involved.'

'And the reason I love true crime so much. Motive,' Bee said. 'The why. Why do all this with a team that's already devastated and on the verge of being wrecked? But do you know what this story needs the most?'

'What?' Arhan was cautious.

Bee smiled and kissed his lean chin. 'A hero,' she said softly. 'Care to be mine?'

They both stared at each other, a little out of breath, as they unpacked yet another layer of intimacy between them.

'I can't decide if you're serious or messing with me so I don't get in the way of your investigation.' He pulled her up to a sitting position and spoke without rancour.

'Can't it be both?' Her good humour was back, all thoughts of leaving his bed gone.

'Now can I please tell you what I found at Akshar's place? It ties very neatly into this spot-fixing theory we have stumbled on to.' Arhan rubbed her shoulders.

'We didn't *stumble* on to anything,' she corrected him loftily. 'I was investigating. I made this happen.'

He wisely swallowed his chuckle at her indignation. 'Fine, you made this happen. Now can we please talk like rational adults?'

'Right. Focusing now. What did you learn?'

He took her through the scene at Akshar's study. The records, the pornography (in which she showed extraordinary interest), the joint bank account and finally the email that Karan Sholekar had sent Akshar just hours before his death.

'Putting that email in context with Sholes showing Akshar his laptop, I am reasonably sure that he knows about the match-fixing,' Arhan ended slowly. 'Or he has doubts.'

'We need to talk to Sholes then,' Bee said firmly. 'See for ourselves what data he has collected. Maybe he can shed some light on this mysterious man. The SIM card buyer.'

'We are going to do absolutely nothing until the morning,' Arhan said just as firmly, 'when we hand over all this evidence to the police, along with the phones. And then we tell my bosses about the spot-fixing problem and let them handle it all.'

'But . . .'

Arhan gave her a quiet look. 'You've been attacked. *Twice.* A man is dead, possibly murdered. These are dangerous people. You're not messing with them, Bee. I will not allow it.'

'Allow it?' she sputtered. 'You can't *allow* . . .'

'I am deathly scared for you. So yeah, I'd rather keep you safe than hurt. Is that a problem?' It was such a reasonable demand she couldn't argue with him.

'But . . .' Her lips made the most adorable pout. 'I just want to talk to Sholes.'

'And you can,' Arhan said, 'once the authorities are done talking to him. Don't override me on this, Bee. Please.'

Bee said nothing, but the glint in her eyes faded into disappointment. He moved in closer to her, framing her face between his palms, and studied her with a fierce look in his usually glowering eyes. A look that was simultaneously solemn and a little heartbreaking in its intensity.

It made her own eyes smart.

'You matter to me, Bee. I don't want to risk you or have you risk yourself for this. Okay?'

'Okay.' She smiled and they looked at each other, hands entwined, hearts in sync for this one moment. A perfect moment in an otherwise crazy night.

The next morning, when Arhan fished for Bee under the covers, he couldn't find her.

She was gone . . . and so was her laptop.

He had a sinking feeling he knew exactly where she was.

27

Bee couldn't sleep. Arhan's words kept buzzing in her head. Comforting and infinitely needed.

'You matter to me.'

It wasn't a declaration of everlasting love. But it meant so much more because it was real. It was heartfelt.

But knowing that he cared, although amazingly comforting, wasn't enough for her. Other questions kept her awake. In fact, knowing he cared for her gave her the courage to consider this problem from all angles . . . because it affected Arhan and Arhan mattered to her.

She kept coming back to Karan Sholekar, her friend.

What does Sholes know? How did he figure out all this? Is he a part of this scheme? What is the scheme anyway? Is it to ensure India's victory? Because the team isn't playing well at all! How do the mysterious hoodie guy and Akshar tie into all this?

Finally, Bee couldn't stand it anymore. She left Arhan's bed, giving his acutely vulnerable and adorable face one last regretful glance. It sucked that she was falling for him big-time in the middle of all this madness.

But dammit, this was important too. She wanted to talk to Sholes before the cops got to him. He was her friend. She felt duty bound to help him if he was caught up in something dangerous.

And, okay, who was she kidding? She wanted to score the story as well.

There is no harm in being ambitious, it is there? Not if it means saving a friend and a hot hero-in-the-making in the process. Two birds, one stone and all that.

Bee went up to her room, ensuring that the Maharani was safely ensconced in her boudoir.

She pulled on a fresh pair of jeans, grabbed her tote, shoved her laptop in and exited.

The ride to the hotel where the press were put up by the ICCB would take twenty minutes and five hundred rupees. Bee paid without arguing. She didn't have time to waste.

At best, she had an hour before Arhan woke up and realised what she'd done.

At worst, he'd already be there with the cops by the time she reached the hotel. She knew he might never forgive her for this, but that was a chance she was willing to take.

Besides, if he liked her, he had to like her for who she was.

And she was a newshound.

The fates were on her side as, fifteen minutes later, she snuck into the hotel just as the sun was turning the night sky golden.

Bee didn't bother the front desk staff since she knew exactly where she was going. She flashed her press pass and they let her through. She went to the elevator bank and punched in Dheera's floor number.

She knew Sholes and Harry would be on the same floor.

On exiting the lift, Bee looked both ways down the corridor. It was deserted and there was no CCTV camera. A small miracle!

Now came the hard part. She needed to get into Sholes' room without letting him know she was there.

The easiest thing to do would be to ask Harry or even Dhee for his number, but she didn't want to involve them in this messy, possibly illegal, affair. Another reason she couldn't go to Dheera—her friend would definitely call Bee's parents if she knew the whole murderous scope of the story.

There was no way Bee was giving up her story. Ergo, she was in this alone.

Taking a deep breath, Bee walked to the end of the long corridor where she figured the room service station was located. There was a small storeroom next to the station and Bee could see the on-duty busboy curled up on a rattan mat, head pillowed on his arms, sound asleep.

Crossing her fingers, she knelt next to him and shook him awake. Gently.

The boy, for he was not more than seventeen or eighteen, came awake with a startled jerk. He looked wildly at her and she smiled, throwing her hands up.

'Good morning, sir,' she said, putting on her best Tamil accent after quickly reading the name Ramanujam on his tag.

'Yes, madam?' he asked, as he jumped up now, guiltily glancing at the mat where he'd been caught napping on the job. 'Anything you want?'

'Yes, sir.' Then she spoke in rapid-fire Tamil. 'I'd like to get inside my boyfriend's room. He is sleeping and doesn't remember our breakfast date. We are both journalists, you see?'

The boy blushed at the term 'boyfriend'. 'Yes, madam. I can understand.'

'I would love your help in getting inside his room. Except I've forgotten which room it is. Maybe it's 408 or 409 or something else.'

Bee bit her lip and summoned up a confused-exhausted expression. It wasn't that hard. Life had been nothing but confusing and exhausting recently.

'Can you please help me?' She reached over and squeezed the boy's thin wrist. He snatched it away as if she'd burned him. 'Please.'

He nodded, a mop of black curls flying around his too-young, too-thin face.

Bee took out a hundred-rupee note and gave it to the boy. 'Thank you,' she said with relief.

The boy extracted a bunch of keys from his ill-fitting pants pocket and went up to 408 at the other end of the corridor.

'Please be quiet, madam,' he instructed her. 'We don't want the guests waking up, no?'

Bee mimed zipping her lips shut.

The boy opened the door and they peered cautiously inside for just a second. They could make out two pairs of slippers in the doorway. Wrong room. Bee squashed the ick factor at what she was doing, invading other people's privacy like this. She prayed to whichever god looked after investigative reporters to forgive her this sin.

The busboy hurriedly shut the door and they moved on to the next one. It was locked from the inside and the boy shrugged. Bee hoped Sholes was not in there.

'Are you sure you can't remember the room number, madam?' The boy's discomfort forced him to ask.

She bit the inside of her cheek hard so tears spurted. 'I'm sorry, sir. This is wrong and I am wasting your time. I'll just leave.'

'No, no. Let's try this one.' The boy inserted the key to room number 404. It was unlocked even though it boasted a DND sign. The door opened with the merest of creaks.

She winced as the sound echoed like a gunshot in the silent corridor. They peered inside.

Bee spied Sholes' jacket discarded on the nearest chair.

She beamed at the busboy. 'That's his jacket,' she said in Tamil.

The busboy smiled back. 'Super, madam!'

Bee gave him a quick peck on his cheek and slipped inside. 'Thank you so much, sir. I'll never forget this,' she promised him.

'Me too, madam.' The boy was properly bashful, even though she could see the pleased grin on his mouth. 'You better go inside now before someone sees you.'

In the near distance, they could hear the wail of police sirens.

The noise was extremely disconcerting and reminded Bee of her true purpose in coming here. She smiled once more at the busboy and shut the door on his face. Mission accomplished.

The curtains were drawn, so light only spilled from the small bedside lamp. The room smelled a funny, like something rotten kept out in the sun, but Bee had hung out enough in Harry and Sholes' rooms to know that they weren't pros in the hygiene department.

Bee checked Sholes' jacket and found the detritus of the last match day—a crumpled cigarette packet, peanut wrappers, a ticket for a local pawnshop, pens and tissue papers filled with stream-of-consciousness ramblings, all of which would make its way into his articles the next day.

It was weird though that the paper was full of Sholes' thoughts on India's quarter-final match.

Sholes had not attended that match.

Bee skirted the bed, where she could see his face—eyes closed, sleeping soundly.

She went to the closet and pulled his out backpack. His laptop was not in its customary sleeve. She looked inside the closet; it wasn't there either.

Sholes didn't even stir as she tiptoed over to the table and found only room service menus.

Where the fuck is his laptop?

She guessed it was time to wake Sholes up, the whole exercise with the busboy being pointless. She said morosely, 'Sholes. Yo, Sholes. It's me, Bee. Wake up.'

Sholes didn't stir.

Bee skirted the bed again and shook him awake. 'Sholes, wake up. It's Bee. I need your help.'

He still didn't wake up.

Bee's heart pounded in her ears as fear congealed like mud in her stomach.

'Sholes,' she whispered, shakily. 'Sholes, please wake up.'

No response whatsoever.

With terrible foreboding, she flicked the covers back from Sholes' inert form.

Bee swallowed the scream that threatened to explode out of her. She stuffed her knuckles in her mouth.

There lay Sholes. In a pool of his own blood, piss, sweat and poop. He had been stabbed repeatedly in the chest. She could see his innards gaping through his rib cage.

Bee retched, adding to the foul smell and the mess on the bed, bending double in undisguised panic. She spied a piece of paper sticking out from under the carpet's edge at the corner of the bed.

She picked it up on autopilot, intent only on getting out.

There was no way she could be found here. The cops would crucify her. Her career would be over.

Arhan would kill her.

Arhan!

Nausea crawled up her throat and Bee rushed into the bathroom and vomited everything she had ever eaten. Then she quickly and with great presence of mind used her sleeve to clean her fingerprints from the flush.

Feeling shit scared, shaken and completely out of her depth, Bee conceded Arhan had a point.

She pulled her phone out with shaking fingers and texted him. 'You're right. We need to tell the cops now.'

She crawled up to the washbasin that still had bits of shaving cream stuck to the edges. Bee felt sick again. She swallowed down the bile and splashed cold, cold water on her face.

She needed to get out of here. *Now.* There was no time to waste.

After wiping her prints off the basin, Bee marched out, carefully averting her eyes from the corpse that used to be her friend, and opened the door.

Outside stood Chief Inspector Paramjit Thapar. Gun in hand, a terrified Ramanujam by his side.

'Good morning, Ms Vishwanathan,' Thapar said calmly.

Bee felt faint. 'Morning, Inspector.' She prayed to all the gods that her voice didn't sound as weak as her legs felt. 'What are you doing here?'

'I got an anonymous tip, madam. From someone concerned about Karan Sholekar's whereabouts. The better question is what are you doing here? In his room?'

Bee couldn't help it. She slid a guilty glance over her shoulder. 'I . . .' Her aching brain could not come up with a believable reason.

'If you'll excuse me?' Thapar squeezed himself into the room. He immediately spied the stiff body.

The cop smiled thinly. 'You know, right?'

He unsnapped a pair of handcuffs from his back pocket and her eyes strayed to their shiny glint.

Bee gulped and felt sicker than ever. Bile tasted as awful going down as it did coming up. She prayed that she wouldn't vomit anymore. 'What do I know?'

Paramjit Thapar held the cuffs out to her. 'You're under arrest on suspicion of the murders of Akshar Shekhawat and Karan Sholekar.'

Sweat ran down her temple as the cuffs were snapped on and, at last, Bee vomited horribly all over Thapar's immaculately polished loafers.

—·◆ ◆·—

Arhan pounced on his phone the minute it rang. It showed an unfamiliar local number. Tape from the previous match and reams of pages with stats were strewn on his desk. But they might as well have been in French for all the sense they made to him.

'Arhan Kapoor,' he barked, his mind on Bee's whereabouts instead of on the post-match analysis.

'Arhan?'

He closed his eyes at the simple relief pouring through him at the sound of her voice.

She is alive. Praise Babaji! I am going to fucking murder her!

'Bee, where the fuck—' he began.

'I am in trouble,' she said softly. In a voice he hadn't heard from her before. She sounded afraid, Arhan realised with nasty disquiet. Well and truly scared.

'Are you okay? Are you hurt?'

'No,' she answered. And then, 'So you haven't seen your phone or anything?'

'No, I'm offline. I wanted to concentrate on the quarter-final tape and where we could improve.'

She chuckled. It was a strange, watery sound. 'Of course, you're the hero coach.'

'Bee, talk to me. I am freaking out here.'

'I'm under arrest, Arhan,' she said dully. 'They think I killed Akshar and Sholes . . . Oh, and Sholes is dead.'

Arhan spent the better part of the morning with his phone stuck to his ear.

The second he'd heard Bee was under arrest he'd called his family lawyer and asked him for the best way to proceed. His advice was to find a local lawyer and get Bee out on bail before things became sticky.

He'd waited anxiously, impatiently, till the man came back with a name. All the while, he'd been fielding calls from the media, his team and his bosses, telling them all to back off. It was a mistake. All lies.

He'd swallowed his hurt and anger, and the sheer abuse of trust on Bee's part, and stuck to his conviction. Bee hadn't murdered anyone. He couldn't imagine the woman he knew to be capable of such a thing.

Yes, she sometimes lied and had all the tenacity and finesse of a fucking hound, but she was no murderer.

Arhan struggled into the first decent pair of pants he could find that were not jeans and took just enough time to shave. These law-and-order types appreciated scruffiness the same as they did a terrorist. He should know, he'd spent time with them before.

He knew it was extremely bad luck to shave in the middle of a tournament, a tournament that India was still a part of—however crooked the whole situation was, but this was Bee.

She was in jail, probably being tortured to confess to crimes she didn't commit. He'd seen enough Hindi movies to know what the third-degree treatment looked like. And the special branch was bound to be worse.

Besides, he wanted her free so *he* could kill her for doing this to him!

—◆ ◆—

The local lawyer was surprised to see Arhan at his residence, but the call from the Punjab Governor's office had silenced him. He'd opened his office an hour early and was now preparing the documents that would get Bee released on bail.

It was strange, but Maharani Kalavati Devi had also insisted on coming to the lawyer's office with Arhan, minus Kartar Singh, her bodyguard.

Arhan shot the perfectly poised woman a sideward glance as he massaged his aching neck and wondered if maybe he could take over the typing from Advocate Slowpoke.

The Maharani looked deeply distressed.

'Sir,' she said in her mellifluous velvet-over-steel voice. 'Bee is like a daughter to me. I would much appreciate it if you could hurry up this process. Now.'

The lawyer knew who she was, which made him obsequious. 'Maharani Sahiba, I understand the problem. But, you see, this is a double murder, *na*? The police are not going to let it go that easily. In fact, it is a surprise they haven't remanded her to the city with all her belongings, even her clothes, locked in evidence.'

Arhan tapped his booted foot and drummed his fingers on his knees. His jacket was continuously vibrating with all the unanswered calls on his phone. He wasn't interested in anything but the man in front of him.

For once, just this once, cricket would have to wait.

'Where would the bond money come from?' the lawyer inquired.

'Me,' Arhan said before the Maharani could open her mouth. He extracted his chequebook, signed a leaf and gave it to the lawyer. 'Make it happen. Now . . . Please,' he added as an afterthought.

The lawyer looked at the blank cheque and nodded. He adjusted his collar and blew out a breath, his eyes taking on a greedy gleam. Arhan would have punched him if he was not the only one capable of getting Bee out of jail.

Hang on, Bee.

The Maharani gave Arhan's hand a squeeze. Her fingers were ice-cold from the air-conditioning in the lawyer's office as well as from the chilling terror of the situation.

'Don't worry,' she said quietly. 'I have a farmhouse on the outskirts of Chandigarh. You must take Bee there till this whole matter is cleared up. Her safety is paramount.'

Arhan gave her a grateful look. 'Thank you, ma'am. That sounds like a doable plan.' Then he added with a rueful grin. 'If she agrees to it, that is.'

The Maharani's squeeze this time was firmer. 'Make her,' she said.

'It is done, ji,' the lawyer said, whipping out sheets of paper from his printer. 'Let's go to the district court and get the required stamp papers to notarize these.'

And so it was past lunchtime when Arhan drove pell-mell through the town, the Maharani's coiffure in danger of being windblown, and parked haphazardly on the pavement outside the main police station.

He exited the car, brandishing the sheaf of papers like a sword so the havaldars would let him through.

'Where is Thapar sahab?' he asked. A sub-inspector pointed towards a pair of pocket doors through which he could see a dimly lit room.

Arhan strode inside as if he owned the place and the Maharani followed, a regal shadow.

The cop was wearing unwrinkled blue cotton today, Arhan noted in a dispassionate corner of his mind.

He thumped the sheaf of papers on the table.

The lawyer arrived finally, wheezing and huffing, loosening the collar of his starched shirt, his robes still flapping around him.

He smiled at the SI on duty and said, 'Kumawat sirji, *kya haal?*'

The SI shrugged and chewed *paan*. *'Theek hai.'*

'Where is she?' Arhan addressed Thapar. He didn't even acknowledge the others.

'She's where she belongs for now,' Thapar replied. 'Behind bars.'

Arhan's face closed up, muscle by muscle until only a single one ticked in his jaw. His eyes were hideously empty.

It spoke volumes for Thapar's grit that he merely gave the man a polite look. 'Is there anything you wanted?'

Arhan resisted the caveman-like homicidal impulse coursing through him that demanded he haul Thapar over the desk one-handed and choke him for being so cavalier about Bee.

An innocent woman was behind bars.

A woman who's broken your trust. And a promise to you.

But that was not important right now. He had to get her out first. He nodded at the papers and the lawyer and said, 'Talk.'

The lawyer announced that Bee should be released into Arhan's custody since a judge had already granted bail. Thapar's displeasure was evident by the tightening of his thin mouth. But he didn't say a word. He only waved a hand to the SI who stood up on wobbling legs, saluted him and went off to do his bidding.

Arhan started to follow the SI.

'Mr Kapoor.' Thapar's steely voice stopped him. 'You need to sign some forms. You and the lawyer need to stay here and take care of the legalities. Maybe the lady can escort Bee out.'

'The lady,' Arhan said through gritted teeth, 'is the maharani of Jaigarh, Her Royal Highness Kalavati Devi Chauhan. So mind your tongue, Inspector.'

'I beg your pardon, Your Highness,' Thapar said with a touch of instant suavity. He bowed deeply, jack-knifing from his seat. 'I didn't recognise you without your trademark diamond earrings.'

The Maharani inclined her head a mere half-inch. An insulting acknowledgement of the lowly peasant. 'I was in too much of a hurry to get to Bee to fuss with them, Inspector. Now, if you'd be so kind as to take me to my dear girl, we would appreciate that.'

Thapar had no choice but to accede to her request.

The Maharani smiled reassuringly at Arhan. 'Don't worry, my boy. I'll make sure she comes to no harm. You just get done here.'

Arhan turned back to the inspector and said, 'Where are these fucking forms you need me to sign?'

Thapar gave the freely perspiring lawyer a sympathetic smile. 'He is one of your more difficult clients, isn't he?'

The lawyer didn't say a word but his heavenward look spoke volumes.

Arhan resisted the urge to knock out his own lawyer.

'My dear.' The Maharani wrapped her bony knuckles around the filthy bars of the cell and immediately stepped back. 'My dear girl, this is a terrible place to be.'

Bee shrugged as she stretched, stiffened muscles creaking in protest. While she'd gone into her mind palace and tried to find connections between everything that had happened so far, her body had atrophied from sitting in one position for so long.

She wondered how long she'd spent in here. Wondered how arrest records showed up on journalists' CVs.

'You shouldn't have come down here, Ranisa. This is no place for you.' Bee walked forward, shaking the numbness from her legs.

'You are in trouble. Of course, I will come. I promised your parents that you would be utterly safe in my care.' The Maharani gave the filthy, urine-stained walls a disparaging glance. 'Your current surroundings are less than pleasant, my dear. We must have you released post-haste.'

Sunita, the sour-looking policewoman, unlocked the cell door with keys that clanged loudly. 'Go,' she spat out in Hindi. 'Your bail's been posted.' Then she gave Bee a venomous look. '*Kutiya.*'

Bee walked out, head held high and said, very clearly, when she passed the lady havaldar. '*Tu bhi.*'

The Maharani pretended not to hear her as she sailed regally before the freed prisoner.

'You have all your stuff with you?' Arhan asked Bee the second he saw her come out of the lockup. She signed for her personal belongings, minus the burner phones, her personal phone and her laptop, which had been impounded as evidence.

Bee nodded, her heart pounding in sheer relief as she saw Arhan. Spiffed up, in formal clothes, like he'd been the night they'd kissed for the very first time. And with pretty much the same smouldering, glowering expression.

He looked like a powder keg ready to go off.

'It's all here,' she said as solemnly as possible. She didn't want to say or do anything that would result in him getting arrested for violence against women, even if the woman was a self-destructive maniac named Bee Vishwanathan!

'Good.' He took her elbow and almost shoved her out of the station.

She didn't ask him to watch it. She was tripping over her own feet to get out.

'Ms Vishwanathan . . . Bee,' Thapar called out as he also walked out with them, wearing classy Wayfarers.

'Yes?' It was Arhan who snapped the question.

'You wouldn't do anything stupid like leave town without informing us, would you?'

Bee smiled sweetly. 'I'll add you to my Google Calendar. Would that suffice?'

'It would if I knew what it was.' Thapar looked puzzled.

Bee smiled, sweeter still. 'Look it up.'

Then she ran down the steps before she could do some serious damage to those Wayfarers.

Bee watched, leaning against the still-hot hood of the SUV as Arhan conferred for a few minutes with the cops, her hands in the pockets of her jeans. Something crinkled against the seams of the coin pocket and she pulled it out.

It was the paper she'd shoved into her pants in Sholes' room, which the cops had somehow missed while searching her. She nearly called out to the inspector to give him the evidence when curiosity, that perfidious cat, got the better of her and she took a closer, surreptitious look at it.

It seemed to be an address with a vault number. The company's name was Shree Ram Warehousing and Storage, and the address was mid-way to Chandigarh, in a small town on the outskirts.

As Arhan and the Maharani walked up, Bee quickly smoothed her hands back into her pockets and hugged the Maharani. Tight.

'Thank you,' she told the older woman. 'I was losing my mind in there. Thank you for showing up so quickly.'

The Maharani ran a gentle hand down her hair and squeezed her arm. 'Think nothing of it, my dear.' She sighed. 'I am used to hauling recalcitrant daughters out of police stations.'

'I bet Princess Ujwala never killed anyone.'

'Neither did you,' Arhan said shortly.

Something hard and stone-like melted in her chest at his words. He didn't doubt her for a second, she could see it clear as day in his eyes.

Bee didn't smile or say something cheeky or make a sarcastic comment.

This was important.

She just looked at him. He stared steadily back at her.

Her heart flip-flopped at the utter trust he had in her, the confidence he radiated. The ease with which he had just paid her bail of two lakh rupees without blinking.

He was a man—a hero—to die for and he didn't even know it.

'Well,' the Maharani interrupted their charged, intensely private moment. 'We should all proceed to my farmhouse. No time to waste.'

Bee shrugged, went on her toes and whispered in Arhan's ears as she hugged him. 'We have to go somewhere else. We need to ditch her.'

Arhan gave her a look of consternation but he said, 'Why don't we drop you back at the hotel, Ranisa, so the press doesn't have a field day and we can then go to the safe house?'

The Maharani looked taken aback for a second, something like ruthlessness radiating from her otherwise warm eyes. Then she smiled and Bee knew it was just a trick of the light. 'Of course. Appearances are everything.'

Bee hugged the old woman again. 'Thank you,' she said.

'Don't thank me. Arhan did all the work. He's your hero.'

'Yes,' Bee said softly. 'Yes, he is.'

Bee held her hand out to Arhan while he helped the Maharani into the SUV.

'What?' he asked, more than a bite of temper in his voice.

'I need to call Dhee. I need to call home before I make you do something that could potentially get us arrested again.'

'Why?' he bit out.

Looking around, Bee quickly handed the crumpled paper to Arhan. 'I found this *in* Sholes' hand. He was holding it when he . . .' She swallowed. Unable to finish the thought.

Bee sighed when Arhan did nothing. He continued to stare steadily at her. 'Forget it. I'm sorry.' She tried to withdraw her hand when he took the paper.

Then he gave her another pointed look. 'You're sure you want to do this?'

Bee teared up as she recalled with 4K Ultra HD clarity Sholes' slack mouth. 'I have to,' she whispered. 'You don't. I understand that now.'

Her words seemed to trip something in him. Seeing her tears, Arhan handed his phone over without a word.

An hour later, they were on their way out of Dharamshala after dropping the Maharani off at the hotel.

Bee was still on the phone with Dheera, after having consoled her parents with promises of an in-depth video chat very, very soon.

'Babe,' Dheera said miserably, once Bee informed her of making bail and being turned over to Arhan's custody, 'I don't know how to tell you this but you're fired.'

Bee sighed, looking out at the speeding scenery. 'I know.'

She'd figured it out in the hours she'd spent in jail that Satyarth—her very lenient boss who'd allowed her to get away with some extremely questionable shit because she was a good writer who *knew* cricket and had elevated the status of their fringe website with her recent columns—was going to fire her.

Because even Satyarth had to draw the line somewhere. Murder suspect was apparently it.

She did not blame him. In fact, she was surprised he'd not fired her sooner. She only hoped his generosity would run to writing her a reference letter someday.

'I tried to talk him out of it, but—'

'Listen to me, Dhee. Don't even think of helping me,' Bee spoke harshly, harsher than she had intended. 'This whole thing is on me. I won't take you or anyone else down with me.' 'I agree,' Dheera said miserably. 'I have two kids to think of and my foolish husband who is a law-abiding citizen. I can't afford to jeopardise my life for this. And Bee . . .' Dheera sniffed. 'Neither can you!'

Bee said formally, 'Thank you for understanding. I'll talk to you later.'

She ended the call and placed the phone on the dashboard, exhausted beyond words.

Arhan shot her a cool look.

He wanted to reach out and touch her soft cheek which still carried the tiniest speck of jail cell grime. But he was afraid he would never let her go if he did. She looked tiny and breakable and like no one's idea of a murderer.

Anger at Thapar's callousness boiled in him all over again.

It sucked that he was mad on her behalf while being so unspeakably mad at her.

Arhan swore softly, fluidly.

'Thank you,' Bee whispered.

'Don't thank me.'

'Why not?'

'Because I don't need it.' Arhan kept his gaze trained on the road ahead as all the hurt and anger he'd successfully repressed came rushing back with the force of a tsunami.

'Arhan.' Bee touched his arm.

He shook it off.

She shot him a hurt look. 'I know you're offended—'

'You don't know anything. You don't care about anything, Bee. So shut up.' He ground the gears with a ferociousness.

But, a few minutes later, Arhan did something that almost made Bee's heart stop.

He extracted a pile of bubble wrap from his jacket pocket and handed it to her. Silently.

Bee took it from him with shaking fingers.

I will not cry in front of this man. I will not cry . . . dammit!

Bee popped with all her might.

Pop. Pop. Pop.

'Why would you lie to me?' he asked softly when she was done. 'Why did you go to see Sholekar after you swore to me you wouldn't?'

Bee had no answer. 'Because I suck.'

'Yes,' he said with so much grimness her heart stuttered again. 'You suck.'

She swallowed back a sob and pushed a wayward strand of her hair back. She also turned in her seat and looked imploringly at him. 'I will apologise for the rest of my life even if you won't forgive me now.'

'The apology means nothing if you don't keep your word, Bee. I don't know if I trust you when you don't keep your word.'

She couldn't argue with the ineffable logic. Besides, he looked as miserable, as tired, as she felt.

'I will apologise for lying to you. For sneaking out on you. And for causing everyone to worry when they needed it the least. But, Arhan.' She squeezed his hand on the gear shift. Hard enough that he was forced to look at her. 'This is who I really am,' she said with injured dignity. 'I chase after news stories even when it's not good for me, personally or professionally. I hate cricket with a passion even though I resort to reciting cricket stats when anxious. I haven't had a successful relationship because I am too ambitious and loud and aggressive and men hate that. I ask prominent politicians what brand of condom they use when discussing their stand on sex education in schools. I am not good at doing what I am told to do. I suck and there are parts of me I'll change but not this.'

'I don't want you to change, Bee. Just consider your physical safety, if you can, before you consider a damn headline,' he bit off. 'And, just for the record, I am not perfect either. I'm tenacious as fuck, hyper competitive. I have a mean temper and I eat *gulab jamuns* by the kilo on my cheat day. I hate being CEO but I'll do it because it's the right thing for my family.'

He gave her a grim look. 'I am helping you for the same reason.'

She wiped a single tear and sniffed. 'I know that. You really are the hero India doesn't know it needs.'

He was quiet as he consulted the GPS and they turned left on an off-ramp that would take them to their destination. Then he asked, 'Will you at least promise not to lie to me anymore and call me for help the second you need it?'

Bee sucked in a sobbing breath. 'Will you come if I ask?'

Arhan sighed. 'I came today, didn't I? And I was mad enough to kill you.'

'Okay, then.'

She sniffed and looked blindly out the window. A welter of feelings assaulted her as she contemplated the lovely, completely novel idea of someone caring about her enough to come whenever she needed them, even when they were mad enough to kill her.

Apart from her family and Dheera, she had not really encountered many people who would do that for her.

'Arhan?'

'Yeah?'

'I'll come too. If you need anything,' she vowed.

He entwined their fingers on the gear shift.

'By the way, which politician did you embarrass by asking about condoms?' he asked, lifting the mood.

She gave him a chagrined look. 'You don't want to know.'

'Oh, but I do.'

So Bee spilled more of her secrets to the man who'd earned them.

29

Shree Ram Warehousing and Storage was on the outskirts of a nondescript, rundown town with a generic Punjabi name, a few hundred kilometres from Chandigarh.

It was nearly 9 p.m. when they pulled into the so-called parking lot of the facility and found it overflowing with trash from the nearby dump. They also found a semi-respectable Honda languishing in a corner.

Arhan parked next to it.

They exited the car and Bee held her tote in the crook of her arm, smoothed back her hair and attempted to look like she hadn't spent the day in jail.

It almost worked.

'Let me do the talking,' Arhan told her as he took the piece of paper that Bee gave him.

She huffed out a breath and didn't answer. Since he'd just saved her ass *and* paid for it, she owed it to him . . . just this once.

They entered the door marked 'Offis' and noticed the creaking ceiling fan before anything else. It dangled precariously and killed whatever air there was in the small room every time it finished a dying rotation. Behind the dust- and file-covered table, a small figure sat perched on a chair.

'Ji?' the figure inquired.

Bee squinted as she tried to make out who the speaker was.

Arhan smiled easily as he moved forward, hand outstretched, and the figure rose, a small man with thin hands.

'Good afternoon, manager sahab,' Arhan said and then rattled off something in rapid Punjabi.

The manager replied. Money exchanged hands, as did the piece of paper Bee had given Arhan. More money exchanged hands.

Bee resisted the urge to sneeze while she tried to breathe the dust-laden air.

The manager looked at Bee and said, '*Namaste, bhabhiji.*'

Bee smiled back politely.

Arhan slipped a casual arm around her waist.

They walked out of the 'offis' and the manager led them to a unit in the middle of the stark compound. The facility was desolate inside. Clearly, it didn't get a lot of business in the middle of nowhere.

Arhan whispered in her ear. 'This place is owned by the construction mafia. They supposedly built the place for public use. But, of course, no one ever uses it. Instead, the mafia is able to stash their own shit here in plain sight.'

Bee understood then. The desolation was intentional.

The manager opened one of the ten-feet-tall concrete units and led them inside. The air smelled like dead rats, dog pee and something fouler.

Bee gagged. Arhan squeezed her waist in warning.

The manager dragged out a small steel suitcase. Held it out to Arhan and smiled, a smarmy movement of his mouth that Bee immediately wanted to punch.

Arhan dug into his wallet and extended another five-hundred-rupee note. He then took the suitcase, quite suddenly, jerking the guy forward in the process.

'If anybody asks, we weren't here. Understood, manager sahab?' His voice was perfectly reasonable while he bent the 'offis' manager's thumb back.

Bee's lust snake slithered back to life at the casual display of strength.

Oh, she was so screwed!

The manager nodded rapidly, making a series of squeaks.

Arhan smiled broadly and broke into Punjabi again as they walked back.

The manager massaged his fingers and gave Arhan baleful looks but he smiled and pretended beautifully.

Bee clutched the suitcase as if it held the secrets to her universe and, in all probability, it did.

When they reached the SUV, she tried to do the right thing. The proper thing for the assistant coach of the Indian cricket team.

'You should go back.' She nodded at the unused Honda. 'I can drive that thing to the Maharani's safe house. This is not good for your career.'

'I know,' he said, opening the driver's door. 'I'm either going to end up in a mental institution or the hospital if I stick with you.'

'Then you shouldn't be here.'

He got into the car and, placing his hands on the wheel, stared out the windshield, his lips a thin, righteous line of anger and determination.

Bee counted to ten, then slid into the passenger seat.

Arhan started the car and drove them away from Shree Ram Warehousing and Storage Facility in total silence.

—◆ ◆—

They had been driving for what seemed like forever. In leaving Dharamshala, day had turned to night. Now it was well past dinner time as they crossed over into Haryana. Bee's head lolled against the window as Arhan kept to the speed limit. They blended into outward-bound traffic on the highway, whizzing by buses, cars, trucks and a couple of bullock carts. All the while, Arhan drove cautiously, never crossing the speed limit.

The silence in the car spoke volumes, but Bee didn't want to be the first to break it, the roiling-coiling sensation growing in her stomach. Eventually, her eyes drifted shut.

At the back of her mind, in a vaguely concrete way, Bee knew she was beyond tired. She hadn't had a proper meal or sleep for almost twenty hours. Finally, the blessed narcotic of sleep dragged her in its undertow and she dozed off.

Her last conscious thought was of Arhan's face, stoic, peaked and hero-like.

Was it any wonder she was almost in love with him?

—◆ ◆—

Halfway into the state of Haryana Arhan decided they were safe enough and began to look for hotel accommodation. He didn't want to end up in an extremely shady place, and five-star luxury was out of the question for now.

He sneaked a quick look at his snoozing passenger.

Bee's hand was lax against the door handle, palm up and he could make out the deep grooves that hugging the handle had left against her soft skin.

It made him feel more helpless than any tears she might have shed.

She'd been such a trooper. Not complaining, not even talking, so he could focus on driving. Idly, he wondered about everything that had happened to them in the last couple of days. The two murders and the information on the mysterious man buying the six SIM cards.

He was a little surprised that they weren't being chased by the villains already. So far, Bee's attacker in the hoodie had turned up everywhere Bee was, seeming to find her with just enough ease to make Arhan think someone must be supplying him with the information.

Maybe Akshar's and the journalist's deaths had put a dent in his plans and he had backed off.

But Arhan had a hunch—a gut instinct that had served him well during his playing days—that it was not going to be that easy.

Arhan knew as much as the next player that they were all vulnerable to the lure of cold, hard cash. That fixers and bookies played a siren song of booze, boobs and unlimited moola to hook you in, and then hung you out to dry once you were caught on film.

You were theirs once they filmed you.

He wondered if anyone else, apart from Akshar, was a ringer for the match fixers. One insider was a given in match-fixing situations, unpalatable as it was. And Akshar was dead now.

Could there be more? Was that possible?

Arhan gave the innocuous steel suitcase that occupied pride of place in the backseat a thoughtful glance.

That thing better give them some answers. Or they were screwed with the cops. They needed more information than they currently had to gain some leverage.

And to stay alive.

—◆ ◆ ◆—

Bee woke up like she always did. All at once, as if one moment her brain was dead to the world and the next it was electrocuted awake. But although her brain might wake into consciousness, it would still be a while before it generated coherent thought.

And so her first emotion was panic.

Where am I?

Her surroundings seemed unfamiliar. Oppressive. Dark. The blanket on her leg was scratchy; nothing like the three-hundred thread count cotton she'd recently become used to. The pillow was lumpy and she felt a sense of being alienated.

On the heels of that first thread of panic came the next thought.

Arhan.

Bee shot up, dislodging the rough blanket and looked for him, wide-eyed. It was dark. She could only make out vague shapes.

But no Arhan. The panic came again in waves. He couldn't have just left her in some random place.

This is Arhan we are talking about.

Sense trickled through, subsiding the scream that rose to the back of her throat.

A sound alerted her to a door opening and she swung around wildly for a makeshift weapon.

Bee found a rock-hard pillow and she held it threateningly in both hands as someone stepped in and switched on the lights. She threw the pillow at the figure before he had a chance to defend himself.

'Aaaahh!' Arhan screamed and his curse rebounded off the walls.

The brown package he was holding dropped to the floor, spilling *rotis* and rice, spattering the walls with dal. Ruining his Jordan 5s in the process.

He looked in utter shock at the mess on his expensive shoes. Then at her.

His expression was priceless. Like he'd been dropped into a strange world and knew nothing about the language, the people or the customs. Just pure shock.

'What the fuck?' His voice sounded startled too.

Giggles that Bee was trying to suppress burst forth in a torrent. They spilled out of her, a high-pitched squeaky sound that wouldn't stop, even when she clamped a hand on her mouth. Her eyes were shining, dancing with mirth as she took in the sight of an utterly nonplussed, clueless Arhan Kapoor.

It *was* priceless.

Arhan's initial lethargy cleared up and he narrowed his eyes at her. A muscle ticked in his jaw. A sure-fire sign of danger.

Bee scrambled to the edge of the bed, one hand clamped to her mouth, the other scrabbling for purchase on the wall. Tears were streaming from her eyes with the force of her laughter.

Arhan took a few steps forward, his shoes squelching unpleasantly on the plain mosaic. The sound was loud in the dead of the night.

Abruptly, he sat down on the edge of the bed and toed off his shoes. Bee craned to look over his shoulder and then squealed when he shot one long hand out and neatly caught a fistful of her T-shirt.

She scrambled into his lap, shuddering soundlessly. She hadn't realised when her giggles had turned into actual tears. She started wiping at her streaming eyes with shaking hands.

'I'm sorry.' She hiccupped. 'I don't know what's wrong with me.'

'It's okay,' Arhan replied, awkwardly patting her on the back. 'It's okay, Bee. I'm here.'

It took a lot of caresses and even more endearments before she calmed down. Bee sniffled and wiped her squishy nose.

Arhan kissed it.

'I'm a mess.'

'I know. You're a hot, annoying, terrible, walking, talking catastrophe.' He punctuated each word with a kiss. On cheeks, sticky with tears. On her forehead. On her eyelids, gritty from crying.

'You're my mess.'

At his heartfelt words something spread like fire inside her, spreading outwards everywhere he touched, everywhere he didn't.

Her breath turned shallow, uneven . . . thick with desire. Desire that had never been far away, buried under conversation and being arrested. It was a basic, human need that wouldn't go away. Not even in the face of dire danger. It took over from the hysteria and grief from moments ago, annihilating them.

Bee kissed Arhan as her resistance melted, just like her heart did around him.

She kissed him with all her heart. With everything she had.

Their tongues melded, but he did nothing apart from gently letting his lips, teeth and tongue touch hers. He even maintained a scant distance between their bodies.

It made her crazier than ever. This kiss was soft, seeking. It offered gentleness and wonder. Bee couldn't hold it in anymore. She hugged him around the neck, pulling him close to her.

It seemed as if a switch tripped inside him. He swung her into his arms as she squealed against his mouth. Her hands tightened around him as the world tilted for her.

He pushed her against the bed, nuzzling her cheeks, her chin, as she played with the ends of his hair.

Then he suddenly stopped and watched her, hovering over her. She lay there, staring back at him, arms limp at her sides, unable to move for the look in his eyes. Black and consuming and so . . . aware.

Aware of the way her toes were curling in a sudden onset of shyness. Of the single lock of hair on her forehead that he wanted to move aside. Of the hint of lace against her soft breasts that he imagined tasting.

She pulled him closer, holding the collars of his shirt, wanting to be one with him because the world had gone crazy and he was saving her. He was always saving her.

Their legs tangled as he landed on top of her, softly, and she laughed, made breathless by the crush of his weight.

Arhan kissed her and the laughter fled leaving the air around them encased in bubble wrap. Thick with desire and stormy emotions neither wanted to name.

She sighed against his mouth as his hand moved under her T-shirt and his palm rested on her bare stomach. Her skin tingled, hot and deliciously aroused.

She arched into his touch and his hand slid higher to the curve of her breast. Bee raised her hand and placed it on his chest, on his left breastbone. His heart beat as if he was going for a century with the next six. Thud, thud, thud, the sound echoing against her palm, inside her head, pounding in her blood.

She opened his buttons, one by one, and shucked off his shirt. He helped her with one hand, the other one still exploring her. His muscles gleamed in the harsh glaring light of the seedy motel.

'This isn't where . . .' he began, as the first stirrings of sanity hit him.

'I know.' Bee sat up, almost dislodging him in the process, and took off her own shirt. His jaw dropped at her fantasy of a bra. It was sheer grey with pink roses in strategic places.

And—holy god!—a front clasp.

Arhan swallowed. He reached a shaking hand and cupped the warm weight of her. All the blood in his body seemed to have pooled in his pants as he looked at the sexy, inviting woman in his arms.

He struggled to draw a deep breath. 'I didn't know they made these here.' She swallowed too and the movement pushed more of her into his hand. Her nipple peaked and he rubbed against it.

She made a soft sound. Agreement? Surrender? He couldn't make out.

'It's from abroad. My cousin—' She stopped talking when he flicked open her bra with his free hand and cupped both her breasts.

Then he leaned in closer and whispered in her ear, 'Are you sure?'

Bee gulped but her throat remained dry. She'd never felt like this. It had just been sex before. This felt like something else. Something more.

She leaned back and tugged his head down to her breast in response to his question. Arhan fell on her like a starving beast. Sensations thrummed through her, making her nerveless and weak, as she was pushed back on the bed, her legs turning to water even though she wasn't standing.

He made her weak. Made her need. Made her want.

Arhan kissed and tasted every inch of her, getting rid of every stitch of clothing she wore, stopping at the matching lace panties that had him going cross-eyed.

He left those on.

The way he stared at her lacy panties, Bee felt exposed, naked and open in a way she hadn't ever been with a man.

'Aren't you going to . . .' She gestured to his trousers.

He shrugged, stomach muscles rippling with power. And she felt more heat snake through her. He was such a hot specimen, no wonder she was this nervous. This scared her.

'Be my guest.'

So Bee touched him, taking her own sweet time. She kissed his chest, his shoulders, the scar on his back he'd got as a child when he'd fallen on a coffee table taking a catch while playing in the living room.

She moved on to his spine, the indentations down his back. She ran a single finger over them.

Arhan sucked in a hot breath and caught her by the hair, dragging her around so he could kiss her mindless, his hands streaking everywhere they could.

Bee got rid of his belt next and unzipped his pants and then . . . giggled! He wore the cutest Batman boxers.

Arhan smiled, a self-conscious grin that made her heart trip all over again.

'I'm Bat-man . . . get it?' he said, boyishly scratching the back of his head.

'I get it!' Bee smiled wide.

His vulnerability tripped a wire inside her, escalating this snarling need of hers into something else. Something more. She wanted him. She wanted the sweet, sweet pleasure of making love with the man she loved. She wanted to know things about him she wouldn't have known otherwise. Wanted to keep him safe, and love him so hard it hurt.

She gripped him hard and stroked him from base to tip. 'I really hope you have condoms.'

Arhan gripped her hair just a bit tighter. 'I do.'

'Take off your pants,' she ordered.

He complied so fast that she chuckled again. Then they were side by side and he was kissing her through her lacy panties, taking his time with her. It was all colours and sounds in her head.

When he pushed her panties down, she kicked them off and he replaced his lips with his fingers. The sound in her mind grew louder. Like a freight train approaching a signal. She felt a rush so deep, it shook her to her core. Bee closed her eyes relishing every sensation. Arhan put on a condom and then spread her legs wider and crawled up, looking at her flushed face.

He waited for her to open her eyes, which Bee did slowly, looking dazed, as if turned inside out. And that's when he slid into her, so she would understand what they were doing. What this was.

He entwined their fingers and placed them on the pillow by her head as he went in deep, so deep he wondered if he would ever return to reality. Her breath hitched, their bodies rubbing in delicious friction with the movement, and her eyes were lost, glassy in a world of their own as she rode it out. Her orgasm hit her and she cried out softly. His climax tackled his spine and he felt like he would explode as she encouraged him with tiny sounds. Inaudible. Roaring. A meshing of bodies and hearts and pulses.

He hoped she understood he was making her his.

And at the last moment, when his vision blurred, he knew she was making him hers too.

30

Arhan woke up from the best sleep of his life, after the best orgasm of his life, only when Bee shook him awake.

He couldn't remember what he had been dreaming about, but it was something that made him smile, even in his sleep. Probably Bee. Probably sex. Most probably sex with Bee.

When the sleep cleared from his eyes and he saw her on the other side of the bed, leaning over him, he figured sex with Bee in real life far surpassed sex with Bee in a dream.

He reached out and draped her over himself.

She thumped his chest, shoving hair from her eyes.

'Hey,' he rumbled.

Then he leaned in, burying his head in the side of her neck, drawing deeply. She smelled warm and lovely. Like a melted bar of Cadbury Silk left in the foil, that sticky-sweet, tantalizing scent of chocolate and milk and sheer happiness. She smelled edible.

Bee stilled.

When Arhan's lips travelled south of her neck, she tugged his head back up and said, 'Food.'

'Hmmm.' He bit her on the cheek, a quick exacting bite. 'Hell, yes.'

Arhan moved over her with intent and she was suddenly, achingly, aware of him. Desire shot liquid fire into her veins, as insidious and seductive as his sleepy-dreamy eyes.

'No.' She couldn't help the laugh that tumbled out of her. 'Actual food. *Roti. Sabzi. Dal. Achaar.*'

He shot her a droll look. 'Do I look like the waiter at a *dhaba*?'

She pinched his sexy behind and he tackled her beneath him, pinning her with ridiculous ease.

She said, 'We need to eat. Actual food, not each other. Take a shower and let's look at that suitcase.'

Arhan's descent stilled. Everything that had been shoved into a convenient corner of his mind came tumbling to the fore. He became completely and totally serious. All laughter and passion leached out of him in a flash.

'I forgot to ask you before. Are you hurt anywhere?'

'What? From the sex?'

'No.' He shook his head. 'From before. The arrest and . . .'

Bee shrugged. 'I'm fine. I thought I might have suffered whiplash from the seatbelt but it was probably just terror taking over my body. I'm okay now.' She smiled, a small, careful smile. 'I'm just epically hungry.'

'I did get us food.'

They looked at the congealed mess on the floor.

Bee wrinkled her nose in distaste. 'We should call someone and have that cleaned up.'

Arhan gave her a look of dismay. 'But we'll have to put on clothes for that.'

'That is the plan.'

Arhan leaned in close and inhaled her as if he couldn't live without breathing her in. It was so incredibly touching. Bee sighed. It was sinful; she had no business feeling this content when lives were at stake. She put her arms around him cautiously and was comforted. He had such a solid, strong presence.

And he was so good at taking care of her even though she didn't need taking care of. But she enjoyed being squished against him. It was a novel experience having an actual conversation after sex, one that did not make her feel awkward or flustered.

Who knew, not all men were clueless jerks.

'But I like you naked. You look so good. You feel so . . .'

Arhan cupped her breast and it fit in his rough palm perfectly, as if it was made for just this.

She could feel her resistance melting, drip by drip, so she pushed his hand away from her and said, 'Focus, mister. We are in the middle of a crisis situation here.'

He rubbed his erection against her thigh. 'That we most certainly are.'

Bee chuckled. The man was insane, but in a good way.

'Not this situation, which, by the way, is very impressive.'

Bee gave him a quick kiss. One of those casual kisses that couples who'd been together for ages shared because it telegraphed tenderness and affection and the need to get a move on, all in two seconds.

'But I meant the situation in the real world where I'm wanted for the murders of my friend *and* your friend.' She was so proud of the way her voice didn't crack.

Arhan ran a comforting hand up and down her back. 'I haven't said this yet, but I am sorry. About Sholes . . . about all of it.'

Bee shrugged. 'It's not your fault. Your friend's dead too.'

The mood changed from light and playful to painfully real. A reality where they were being hunted and the T20 World Cup was fixed.

'Okay.' Arhan nearly dislodged Bee as he sat up. 'You get into the shower and I'll get the bellboy to clean up in here and ask about the food situation. It must be close to ten am now,' he said, looking at his watch. 'Shit! India's playing.'

Bee sighed. His face was so full of distress, so openly upset.

When she had met him first, she never imagined that Arhan could be vulnerable, emotional. But he was.

She felt awful that she was responsible for him missing the game. He didn't deserve to be in this predicament. This was all on her.

'Listen,' she said in a small, determined voice, unable to face him. 'I really think you should drive back now. You'll reach well in time to catch the flight back with the team, after the match. They need you.'

Arhan said nothing.

Bee continued with real remorse. 'I am so epically sorry. This whole mess is my fault. You wouldn't be here in the first place if I hadn't been so arrogant as to break a media gag order and try and see the freaking captain right before the opening match. I should have known how important pre-game night was and not bothered you guys. You should have had me thrown in jail then and there.'

'I was going to, but you broke my nose, remember?' Arhan said, trying to lighten the mood.

She huffed out a miserable breath. 'All the more reason for you to stay away from me . . . And I am sorry for tagging along with the Maharani and making your life more miserable and disrupting the team and—'

'Hey, hey, hey!' Arhan cupped her chin in his hand and forced her to make eye contact. 'Where's all this coming from?'

She was miserable and guilty. Contrite. It didn't look as good on her as he'd imagined it would.

'You could get fired for helping me.' Bee's voice broke at last. 'You're already missing out on helping a team that needs you, its lynchpin. I know how much this job, this chance, means to you, what you've done to get here, and I am taking it away from you and —'

'You make it seem as if I have no will, no brains, of my own.' He was so matter-of-fact that she stopped speaking.

'What?'

'I am here because I *want* to be here, Bee. If I didn't, I would have paid your bail and gone the hell back to the team that needs me. I thought you realised this back at the storage facility.'

She had but she really did not want him to miss out on the chance of a lifetime because of her. 'But —'

He shut her mouth gently. 'Don't question my motives and overanalyse this. Just accept it. We're in this together. I am not going anywhere till this is over and you're safe.'

And what about after? She was tempted to ask him. But she didn't. She was afraid of his answer.

So Bee just nodded and said, 'I'll go shower now.'

He ran a hand up her thigh. She fought the urge to shiver.

'Wish I could join you.'

'Next time,' she said.

'Next time.'

He meant it as a promise and she understood that.

— ◆ ◆ —

Bee took a relaxing albeit cold shower since highway hotels didn't exactly have running hot water. She felt extremely alert and refreshed as she dried herself off on the holey excuse of a Turkish towel provided for the guests.

Her body was awake and alive in places she'd never thought possible and she was in a very positive frame of mind, everything considered.

Bee caught sight of herself in the tiny mirror perched on an acrylic stand. Her eyes were tiger-bright, her skin flushed from more than a good scrubbing and her face . . . shit, she looked like how she felt on the inside.

Glowing.

Bee scrunched her face into a more sober expression, since she didn't want Arhan freaking out because of her crazy-happy face, and walked out.

He was talking to the bellboy, and the floor was mercifully clean. The bellboy's eyes bugged out as they caught sight of Bee in a large men's shirt, which came down to her slim thighs, and nothing else.

She smiled graciously at him. No point in being embarrassed.

The teenage boy grinned nervously back at her, dropped his eyes to his feet and exited as fast as he could.

Arhan, on the other hand, gave her a slow thorough survey as he leaned back against the locked door. Her hair was stringy, staining the dark shirt wet as water dripped down, and her face was rosy, flushed. Beautiful without any makeup at all.

'Giving Sunny Leone a run for her money, are we?'

'Care to reenact that shower scene from *Ragini MMS* later?' She struck her hip out in a provocative pose and then spoiled it all by laughing.

Arhan caught her by the waist and nuzzled her neck, ready for round two.

But his stomach rumbled loudly. Embarrassingly loud.

Bee chuckled and stepped out of his embrace. 'I hope you gave that boy instructions for food.'

Arhan nodded. 'He is going to run to the fields of Ludhiana to get *sarson* to make the *saag*. All in the hope of seeing your sexy legs one more time.'

She rolled her eyes and padded over to where they'd stashed the metal suitcase. As she bent down, Bee became aware of exactly how much of her was visible underneath the shirt.

'You should wear some pants,' Arhan muttered, gathering her jeans close to his chest and throwing them at her.

She straightened with the suitcase in her hand and then had to bend down again to pick up the jeans. Giving him a generous view of her breasts.

Arhan shoved his hands into his pockets. 'I'll take a shower and you get started on this, will you?'

Because she had half an idea why he was so jumpy around her, Bee deliberately brushed up against him as he walked by her and had the incredible pleasure of seeing him take a deep breath, as if he needed to control himself around her.

This was better than any declarations of love.

As Arhan busied himself in the bathroom, Bee sat down on the rumpled bed, settling against the lumpy pillows and the sorry excuse of a headboard, and unlocked the suitcase.

It didn't have a combination lock—thank god for small mercies—and so she was able to extract the heavy laptop from its felt casing without any difficulty. She also found a phone-charging cable and quickly plugged in Arhan's dead phone.

Next, she booted up the laptop and waited for the password prompt but instead a video filled the screen.

It was Sholes, looking directly at her through the camera.

Bee sat up straight.

'If you're watching this video,' Sholes said, 'it means you've found my laptop. Either I am already dead or in no condition to inform the proper authorities or my good friends, Dheera, Harry and Bee. They work for . . .' He went on to name their respective publications.

Then he said those damning words. 'If you're watching this video, you know what I know . . . this T20 World Cup is fixed.'

Sholes paused and took a deep breath. 'I have found evidence of spot- and match-fixing.'

Bee put a trembling hand to her mouth as tears filled her eyes. It really was Sholes, in his customary starched shirt, glasses dangling from a chain around his neck. So serious, so earnest. He'd been an excellent newshound, so good at his job.

No wonder he'd discovered the match-fixing angle much before she had.

'You can search my laptop and find evidence that shows how particular balls were played a certain way by batsmen, how important catches were dropped by fielders and how a few crucial balls bowled by competent bowlers changed the face of each game, all leading to a predetermined conclusion. I hope you catch the bastards who did this, starting with Akshar Shekhawat, and hang them out to dry in Tihar. I hope you have the luck I guess I didn't. God bless.'

The video blinked off and the screen turned blank before the screensaver came on.

It was a picture of the four of them taken on the first day of the tournament at the Sawai Mansingh Stadium.

Bee swallowed valiantly against the grief that threatened to erupt in useless tears.

Bee started cruising through the folders on the desktop as she waited for the phone to charge.

She found an Excel spreadsheet and a detailed story in a Word doc that chronicled the fate of each match played until the first quarter-final, with special mentions of particular balls or overs.

The last sweep shot in the first match that India had won had been let go by a Bangladeshi on the take. There was a picture of him smoking weed with a guy in a black hoodie.

The story continued with proof of about 50 per cent of the matches being fixed. Not glaringly, not so obvious that questions could be raised. But just enough.

Just enough to raise the stakes higher for one team whose odds were long to begin with.

Just enough to turn ordinary matches into sensational chases and get the bookies excited.

Just enough to have India scrape by on a win-lose-win graph in the group league and then have the round robin stitched up nicely from the other side.

Sholes had painstakingly jotted down bookie figures and the odds against each team in every match. And, as things stood right now, the odds of India winning the T20 World Cup were 30–1. Still, inconceivably, they were somehow in the running for the finals.

Bee scrolled through the figures and the spreadsheets, trying to find a link, a connection that could tie all of this to someone other than Akshar. It was a given that in a situation like this, more than one team member was involved in the fixing.

It hurt her heart, her brain, to think of the insider who was not only cheating sixteen earnest, dedicated people—his teammates—but also the country of an honest chance to regain glory.

Was it someone in the management? Could it be . . .

She shook her head vigorously even as the thought formed in her head.

No, Arhan had no need to fix the damn game to regain his glory. He had more honour and pride in his little finger than a lot of people did in their whole bodies.

But maybe the other boss? There had been news of Salil Achrekar's injury sparking a sort of outrage in a meeting. Maybe someone else had commanded the man to play in order to profit from his injury.

Arhan's phone beeped as it came back to life. There were several frantic messages, including for her from Dheera and the Maharani and since she'd already spoken to Dheera, she decided to call the Maharani first.

The woman had been kind enough to help Arhan bail her out of jail, and she'd left thirteen messages, each of them increasingly haughty in tone—the Maharani's way of showing concern.

Bee hit dial and the phone rang exactly once before the Maharani answered. 'Maharani Kalavati here.'

'Ranisa, it's me, Bee.'

'Bee! Where *are* you? I called the safe house in Chandigarh two hours ago and the staff told me you hadn't arrived yet. Arhan's phone was also switched off! It's most worrying, my dear. Where are you?' she repeated.

'I'm fine, Maharani.' Bee shifted the laptop from her knees on to the bed and stood. The floor was wet where the boy had cleaned the floor. Her toes contracted from the cold. She skirted the area and began pacing.

'We're holed up in a safe place till we can figure out what to do next.'

'We?' The Maharani sounded gently curious. 'Who's we? Who's with you?'

'Arhan, Ranisa.'

'My god, child.' The woman was blank with shock.

Bee spoke quickly before the Maharani started poking holes in the flimsy story she'd concocted. 'Is Thapar very angry about us skipping town?'

'He is *livid*, Bee,' Kalavati replied grimly. 'I suggest you come back immediately and apologise to him before he arrests you both!'

Arhan came out of the bathroom and switched on the dinky TV.

Of course, the sports channel broadcasting the match came on. The crowd was cheering madly.

Arhan sat down at the edge of the bed. He watched Nazir Imran, one of the middle-order batsmen from Pakistan, walk to the middle of the pitch and loft a shot straight to deep cover. The crowd roared.

Arhan closed his eyes as if he were in pain.

Bee hurt for him. 'We'll be back soon, Ranisa. Please don't worry about us. We're on the trail of something solid here.'

'And where exactly are you, dear child?'

'In a hotel somewhere in Haryana. On the national highway.'

Arhan threw his hands up in a gesture of acute frustration, a look of disbelief blending with the palpable pain.

She winced and shrugged. 'Sorry,' she mouthed.

'Oh. That's a bit too far, my dear. And you're both alone so . . .'

'Don't worry about us. We're going to be fine. We'll be back by tomorrow.' Bee pressed the call end button.

Arhan shook his head and continued watching the match. He gripped his thighs and stared at the TV screen.

Bee had no way of consoling him so she just sat beside him and kept her mouth shut. After ten minutes of watching each ball, her head aching and dizzy with hunger and exhaustion and unanswered complicated questions, Bee turned to Arhan. He dropped a light kiss on the top of her head.

'Don't think so loudly. You're giving me a motherfucking migraine.'

Bee rolled her eyes. 'I know you want to be in the dressing room right now.'

Arhan didn't lie. He nodded. 'I do.'

Her heart contracted with guilt and jealousy at the yearning in his eyes. He looked like he really, really missed being in the thick of the action.

'But I also want to be with you. Here. Now,' he spoke as if reading her mind.

Bee dropped her eyes back to the match, her set face giving her away.

Arhan turned her around to face him, tipped her chin up and said clearly, 'I promise I am not lying. Or just being nice to you. I really do want to be with you. You . . . you're important. I don't have fancy words. I am not a writer like you. But when I thought of you in jail, possibly being manhandled by Thapar, I wanted to burn the station down.'

Her jaw dropped open. He'd said it so matter-of-factly.

'Let's not do that,' she said weakly. 'Let's not burn police stations . . . ever.'

He smiled, a small smile that was incongruous considering the conversation they were having. 'Let's also not feel unnecessarily guilty, okay? Did you find anything on the laptop?'

Bee nodded, even as tears filled her eyes. She took a deep, shaky breath and willed them away. 'There's a video. Sholes left it for the finder of the laptop. You need to watch it. See if it makes more sense to you. Maybe you know something that I don't.'

'Trust me, you know more than I do.' He stretched across the bed that was queen-sized at best and dragged the laptop towards him. 'I wouldn't have been able to connect the dots like you have, Bee.'

She flushed, shooting him a surprised look from underneath her lashes but he'd made the comment in an offhand manner and was now as deeply absorbed in the laptop as he'd been in the match.

Bee turned her attention back to the TV and watched as Suresh floored a straight drive with all the ease of a seasoned batsman.

She blinked back morbid tears, determined to not think badly of any of the lovely sportsmen she'd spent so much time with. None of them could be the insider in this horrid match-fixing mess.

—·◆ ◆·—

A jubilant India stormed into the semis with three balls to spare, shrieking and hooting like frisky jackals.

The stadium in Dharamshala was sheer pandemonium. People were yelling, hooting, cheering, even their seedy motel saw a few whistles emerge from room windows.

The whole country was celebrating as the segment anchor tried to talk over the din of celebrations.

Arhan placed the laptop aside. He gave the TV a bleak, defeated look.

'I don't know,' he said. 'I don't know if they won it fair and square or if they were messed with. I don't know and it is killing me.'

'We'll figure it out, Arhan. I promise.'

He gave her the same bleak look. 'It began as just a story for you. This game. This scandal. Juicy headlines. Maybe a few journalism awards. But this is my life. These are the lives of the men who wear the India blue and saunter on to the field. These are the lives of everyone who works to make that happen, riding on the expectations of more than a billion people. This is more than my career, Bee.'

She tamped down the righteous hurt and indignation that wanted to spill out at his criticism. She wasn't going to lash out at him when he was already feeling so disheartened.

'I understand where you're coming from, but believe me when I say this.' Her voice was as level as she could manage. 'Sholes is dead. *Dead*. I'll never play Candy Crush on his phone again. Never have him call me by my real name again. I'll never get to hug him again. He was my friend . . . and I was arrested for his murder. That makes this personal. Getting to the bottom of this is more than just a story. For me too, it's more than my career.'

She was hurt now.

Did last night mean nothing to him or is he just really good at pushing my buttons?

'I thought that somewhere along the way, when we slept together, you'd . . .'

'I need you,' he said baldly.

She got up from the bed but he caught her by the waist and buried his head in her stomach, wrapping his arms firmly around her so she couldn't move even if she wanted to.

She stood rigid, immobile, in his arms.

'Damn you,' she whispered, squirming to get away. He hugged her closer.

'After papa's death, my kneejerk reaction has been to not trust anyone,' he whispered against her skin. 'To constantly question their motives, their agendas. I am usually tough in most situations because I'm the only one handling them.'

'But you're not the only one here, Arhan,' she reminded him. 'I'm here too. We are in this together.'

He looked up from the haven of her arms and said, 'This . . . This is new to me.'

'So you say mean things to test me? To figure out my motives? To see whether I'll stay or leave? That's fucked up, Arhan.'

He sounded so forlorn when he said, 'Tell me about it. But you won't go, will you? Will you, Bee?'

Bee had no answer to that painfully honest question, so she just gathered him close again and stroked his hair softly.

When he pulled her into his lap she went without any resistance. When he kissed her lips and cheeks, the soft skin abraded by his tongue, she wrapped her arms around his neck tightly and hung on for dear life.

And when he took her in a frenzy of need and unconfessed emotion she tried to keep from telling him the truth.

I think I'm falling in love with you.

32

'I want my toothbrush.'

Arhan grunted, rolled over and made a snuffling sound that would have been cute under other circumstances.

Bee shook his shoulders. Hard. Hard enough to wake him up. 'Arhan, I want my toothbrush.'

'Mmmm!' His indistinct mutter and the quick way he shifted his head towards her, gathering her around the waist, turned her already silly brain to mush.

Then he let out a snore. A tiny one. Garlic-onion-scented breath wafted between them.

Bee wrinkled her nose in acute distaste. She wasn't going back to sleep without brushing her teeth. She needed to maintain some routines in the midst of her upended sleep schedule.

'Arhan.' She shook him harder now. 'Wake up, please.'

He curled closer to her and kissed her where her shoulder met her neck. Dead weight, beloved and so sexy with his scruffy stubble scratching against her bare skin.

Bee decided she was depraved if she could think about his sexy stubble instead of personal hygiene. She leaned down and kissed his earlobe before giving it a good bite.

Arhan woke up in a hurry, arousal and sleepiness warring in his eyes. The sleepiness cleared a bit as he saw her and reached for her with intent.

She stopped him with a firm hand on his bare chest.

'My toothbrush.'

'Wha-what?'

I will not melt at that gruff voice.

'I need my toothbrush, Arhan. That delicious lunch we had contained pungent items and I need to brush my teeth. It's been almost two days

since I last brushed and I refuse to deal with onion breath any longer.'
She shuddered in pure horror.

'Huh? So brush your teeth? We have toothpaste in the bathroom.'

She rolled her eyes. His incomprehension was not cute anymore. She needed action. 'I am not doing that till I get my toothbrush. It's probably fallen in the car. I searched my bag and couldn't find it. Can we please go get it?'

'Why were you carrying a toothbrush in your backpa—' He stopped mid-way realising there was no good answer. This was Bee he was talking to. The woman carried a roll of bubble wrap with her, a toothbrush was nothing compared to that. Instead, he asked, 'How do you know it's fallen in the car? Maybe it fell in the parking lot of that warehouse facility'

Bee shuddered again, horror evident in her warm eyes.

How was it that he could want her, even now, even after having had her? It was a thirst that refused to be satiated. A thirst that kept building and building. He'd never experienced wanting on a scale like this.

Bee poked him again in the arm. 'You're not paying any attention to me.'

Arhan sighed, a deep gust of breath. He rubbed his chest, scratched it absently and hunted for his shirt. It had fallen on the floor, where she'd thrown it in her frenzy to get to his skin. He shrugged it on, his muscles coiling and bunching at the action.

Bee ogled at him shamelessly.

'What?' he demanded once he was done with the buttons. 'You like what you see?'

She grabbed him and kissed him, onion breath and all. And then tweaked his nose. 'I like. A lot. Now my toothbrush, please.'

'A shower sounds so much better. It's much more hygienic, Bee.' She had to give him points for earnestness. 'Soap. Water.'

'Naked,' she said.

'Exactly.'

He nuzzled her neck and then kissed her on the nose. 'God, I—'

'Yeah?'

Arhan shook his head and slid off the bed with obvious reluctance. Bee scrambled off too and walked on tiptoe to where they'd stashed their shoes.

'Get back in bed,' he said as he slipped on his shoes and pocketed the car keys.

'Why? I am coming with you.'

'It's late and this is Haryana, not Mumbai. Get back in bed. Stay there. I'll get the damn toothbrush.'

There was that hard, implacable cast to his face she'd seen lots of times. The one that brooked no argument. The one that made her blood boil because he was being a chauvinistic ass.

'But . . .'

'You want your toothbrush, I'll get you your fucking toothbrush. But I won't have you walking down the parking lot of a seedy motel while the police are looking for you since you blew across state lines. Understand?'

Bee didn't answer. Her glare was mutiny enough.

'Do you understand me, Bee?'

She huffed out an indignant breath and nodded stiffly.

'Lock the door behind me and open it only when I say so, okay?'

'You'll do well as a RAW agent, Arhan Kapoor.'

Arhan grinned. 'I'd definitely seduce state secrets out of you.'

With that cheeky remark, Arhan walked out the door, shutting it securely behind him. He chuckled because he heard the muffled curse Bee let out, knowing he'd won this round.

He'd probably have to pay for it later, possibly in bed, possibly naked, but he was cool with that. It was fun making Bee mad.

Arhan jogged out of the entrance and into the deserted parking lot.

The receptionist was sleeping, his head on the desk, against the keyboard. He was going to wake up with one hell of a pillow-face.

Arhan easily located his car and unlocked it. Then he switched on the internal light and poked his head under the dash on the passenger side. He located something lime green. He reached out and picked it up.

It was a *Monster High* toothbrush with a safety cap.

Arhan couldn't help it. He laughed out loud. The woman was crazy. Adorably crazy. He was going to have so much fun getting to know her better. Getting to know everything about her.

Right at the heels of that thought came another, unpleasant one.

How would he get the opportunity to know her at all when he lived in Punjab and she lived in Mumbai?

This tournament would end one way or another, and then everyone would go back home. She would leave for Mumbai and he would head back home for a month-long break before meeting his team again in Bengaluru for a training camp for the upcoming series against South Africa.

He had responsibilities galore waiting for him when he went back to Punjab. Sure, she was currently jobless so she could come with him as his . . . what? Girlfriend? Significant other? Personal assistant?

Thinking about this quagmire was depressing, so he decided to focus on the now and worry about tomorrow, well, tomorrow.

Arhan locked up behind him on autopilot and pocketed the toothbrush carefully, ensuring the cap was still on. The other end of the brush was a green, fanged female with a crown on her head. It was sharp and poked at him through the cloth.

He stepped back inside and saw the receptionist still sleeping soundly over the keyboard, lucky chump.

Suddenly, someone stepped up to him, wrapped his throat in a chokehold before he could blink and laid a gun to his temple.

'Say one word and I will blow your head off like I did that bastard receptionist's. Okay?'

Arhan scrabbled against his throat for a second but as the attacker's words penetrated his brain, he let his hands fall limply to the side.

'Give me your fucking car keys.'

'Left . . . left . . .' Arhan tried to talk through the restricted oxygen supply.

He desperately tried to remember the three self-defence classes he'd been forced to attend with the team. There was something about kicking the shin or the knee in order to unbalance the attacker and then running as fast as you can.

The attacker reached into Arhan's left pocket and extracted the keys.

'Your only weapon is gone, so don't even think about trying to escape me, AK. I'll put a bullet in you. And then I'll put one in her too. After I fuck her up. Do you want that?'

Arhan shook his head. He would die before he let this bastard harm Bee.

'Good. I'm glad we understand each other. Which room are you in?'

Arhan clenched his fists as he tried to keep the curses in.

'Do you like your fingers, AK? How much do you like them?'

The cold touch of the gun's metal against his right hand galvanised Arhan into action.

He scrabbled against the chokehold and the attacker just tightened his grip until Arhan began to see black spots, gasping soundlessly.

The attacker was just slightly shorter than him, a negligible difference, but his hold on Arhan's throat was so sure, so strong, that Arhan couldn't even move to headbutt the man's nose.

All his self-defence lessons flew out of the window and he was powerless against a man who knew exactly how to hurt him.

It was a terrible position to be in.

'I know the number, but I had to shoot the bastard before I could get directions.'

Arhan closed his eyes as a suffocating wave of guilt swamped him. Someone had died because of him. Because of them. Oh God!

'Left or right?'

Arhan jerked his head to the left.

'Nice try, hero.' The attacker pressed the trigger and Arhan jumped and almost crapped his pants as a silenced bullet embedded itself in the space between his feet. He had to lock his muscles together in order not to tremble.

'Next time, that will be your toe. Now which side, left or right?'

Arhan jerked his head to the right.

'Let's walk slow and easy, okay? No sudden movements. No more *heropanti*. Or I will shoot you dead. *Samjhe?*'

Arhan nodded in a hurry.

'Slow and easy, okay?'

They started walking, a shuffling version of a couple, as Arhan baby-stepped in order to compensate for the lack of oxygen and the man currently trying to choke him.

The movement poked the sharp end of the toothbrush against his thigh and he tried to slide his hand inside his pocket as stealthily as possible but they were pressed up too close to each other for the attacker to not notice the slightest change in movement.

Arhan would have to pick the right moment.

'You know, you two are fucking crazy.' The attacker pressed the silencer closer to Arhan's temple, drilling it in so he could feel the cold of the metal. 'I didn't think you'd have the balls to go to Shree Ram without telling the authorities.'

Arhan didn't answer. He barely had enough air to breathe.

'I wanted to take you out a long time ago. Way back that night in Kolkata. I was going to come for you after I finished with her. I just knew you'd cause me headaches.'

The man cranked his hold tighter. Arhan tried desperately to dig his nails into the man's hands to get him to ease off.

'Motherfucker.'

The low curse in Hindi rebounded in Arhan's head as he led his assailant straight towards Bee. They stopped at the right door—202.

'What do you do now? Knock?'

Arhan shook his head.

'Then what? Sing a Govinda song?' The snigger added to the rage boiling in Arhan.

Arhan's eyes flashed, the attacker eased the pressure a bit, and he rasped out, 'I tell her it's me.'

'Great. Do that. And don't even try and make a run for it. I'll shoot you in the knees and make you watch what I do to her. I promise.'

And because Arhan believed him, he raised his shaking hand and knocked three times before rasping out, 'It's me. Open the door.'

'Arhan?' Bee called out, anxiety turning her voice pitchy.

'Yeah, it's me.'

The attacker nodded encouragingly.

The gun pressed closer to his temple and, in a very filmy move, Arhan felt a strip of sweat run down his temple, caressing the muzzle, and straight down his jaw.

His heart hammered in triple time and he prayed to Waheguru that Bee would somehow develop some hitherto unknown sense of premonition and arm herself before she opened the door.

Just like she'd done the last time.

Bee is logical. She is smart and she'd waited for my code. Double-checked it.
He tried to reassure himself.

Please God, please, let me get Bee out of this one ...

The door opened wide as Bee said, 'About time you got back, Kapoor.'

Her face froze. Her eyes went wide with fear and she gripped the handle of the door tightly.

She stood there and looked with blank terror at the scene before her—Arhan, the attacker and the gun.

'Hello, Bee,' the mysterious man said. 'We meet again.'

33

Bee couldn't think past the gun. It was long, black and shiny and had a matte-finished silencer.

No thoughts formed in her brain as she saw Arhan being held in a chokehold by her attacker. The gun to his temple made her heart beat faster.

Thapar would know the name and make of this gun. Thapar would know what to do here. Why didn't we involve him from the beginning?

'Let us in,' Bee's nightmare commanded.

Bee moved to the side and Arhan and the attacker shuffled in awkwardly. She tried to snap her brain into working, formulating a plan that would lead to Arhan being freed but the gun was so big, so shiny, so close to his skin.

It would take no time for the mysterious man to pull the trigger and then . . . and then . . .

Bee started to hyperventilate, gasping, shattering the hypnotic stillness of the room.

'I know about your bubble wrap,' the attacker spoke.

He pressed the muzzle into Arhan's mouth now, forcing his lips to shape around it. The attacker caressed the trigger lovingly, stroking it with a fingertip.

Bee swayed on the spot, waves of panic assailing her, making it difficult for her to see straight, locking her into a rictus of terror.

'Get yourself under control or I swear to god I will blow his brains out.'

Bee sank to the ground.

Arhan's pupils widened. He scrabbled against the attacker's hold and could do absolutely nothing except flail in place.

'Stop moving now, Coach Sir,' the attacker snarled, 'or I will shoot her before you. It won't be pretty.'

Arhan stilled immediately and let his hands dangle at his sides, sliding one into his pocket.

Bee crab-walked and hit the side of the bed, her hair falling all over her panic-stricken face, out of control and in trouble. Her gasps turned into sobs.

The attacker almost bit off Arhan's ear as he spoke, 'Tell her to shut up. Tell her to shut the fuck up. I don't want any noise from her.'

Bee stuffed her hand into her mouth to keep the sobs in while tears poured from her eyes in a steady, endless stream. She couldn't think, couldn't breathe . . . All she knew was that she was going to watch Arhan die.

This monster was going to kill the man she loved and she had no idea how to stop him. She had words but words stood no chance against a bullet. But she had to try anyway.

'Please,' Bee whispered, closing her eyes. 'Please, let him go. We'll give you whatever you want.'

'You should have thought of that before picking up something that didn't belong to you.' The attacker tacked on a rude epithet in the end.

Arhan jerked, an instinctive reflex of outrage at having someone he deeply cared about being insulted. He could feel himself going dizzy, weak from the steady lack of oxygen.

The only good thing was that Bee's histrionics had the bastard sufficiently occupied and distracted so he had managed a solid grip on Bee's toothbrush. He had to hold on, gauge his moment . . . and not pass out.

Arhan breathed through his mouth, focusing on what he had to do.

'You two have given me so much trouble. Even today, not being where you were supposed to be. I am so glad I finally got the order to kill you.'

Bee's head snapped up at the word 'order'. Arhan noted the razor sharpness in her but the bastard kept gloating. Clearly, he was not as smart as he made himself out to be.

'Order?' Bee asked quietly. 'So you have a boss too? Someone who is even worse than you are, you *choot*?'

The said *choot* yanked Arhan to his toes, jerking his head back.

Arhan flailed around, face contorted with pain.

'You don't talk to me that way unless you want me snapping Coach's neck off. Believe me, I am only supposed to kill you. The *how* part is entirely up to me. And I would love to do it this way. Watching Zakeer die was such a pleasure . . .'

Bee's eyes sharpened even more and she wiped some of her tears away. 'What are you talking about?'

'Nothing. Now let's get on with ending this, shall we?'

Arhan had been allowed to drop back on to his feet. He jerked his head wildly to the left, trying hard to head-butt the bastard.

Bee didn't get his message at first but then she blurted out, 'So you don't want the laptop then? You just have to kill us? Those are your orders?'

'What laptop?'

Bee smiled. She had him hooked. 'Let the coach go and I'll give it to you.'

'Hand it over or I will kill him.'

'You're going to kill us anyway. Why make it easy for you?'

'That's true.'

The attacker levelled the gun at her. But Arhan winked at her. It was the only distraction he needed. Arhan seized the moment.

Bee watched everything happen as if in slow motion.

The attacker moved to squeeze the trigger . . . but Arhan took something out of his pants pocket and jabbed it straight into the man's eye. It made a squishing, squelching sound as it sunk in.

The man toppled to the floor with a scream.

Arhan grabbed the gun and reached for Bee in a bruising hold.

'It's okay,' Arhan rasped out. 'It's okay. We're okay.'

He was stroking her hair, her face, her back, heavy shudders running through him, the gun trembling in his hand.

Bee focused on Arhan. He was okay! The attacker was groaning on the floor, a lime green object poking out of his right eye, blood pooling around him, coating him and his black hoodie.

Her eyes widened as she looked at Arhan with awe. 'Is that . . . is that my *toothbrush*?'

—•◆ ◆•—

'Who do you work for?'

'Fuck you.'

'How did you find us?'

'Fuck. You.'

'Who else from the Indian team is involved in this mess?'

'Fuck—'

'Yeah, me.' Arhan massaged his throat again and took a sip of water.

His insides felt like they'd been through a blender and Bee did not look much better. As it was, his anger was on a choke chain that was straining at the ends. It wanted out now.

It wanted to hurt this bastard.

'You need to ask the right questions, Arhan.' Bee squeezed his hand and slipped an arm around his waist. He gathered her close and they both stared at the murderer. His driving licence had revealed his name to be Bhavanchandar Pal.

Bhavanchandar Pal was laid spread-eagled, his hands and legs tied to the four ends of the bed with bedsheets. Bee was an expert at tying knots from her days of rappelling down the wall to sneak out of the house when she was in college.

Pal glared at them with malevolence emanating from his good eye.

Bee had to resist the urge to swallow. This man would now surely kill them if he was let free. Just because they'd bested him.

'What is the right question, then?' Arhan spoke carefully. Gently touching her like she was made of spun glass.

The sight of Bhavanchandar Pal pointing a gun at Bee would never leave his consciousness.

'How much did you get paid?' Bee asked Bhavanchandar.

Bhavanchandar kept silent.

Arhan trembled, his body surging with the need to physically hurt the bastard. He shouldn't be breathing. He'd killed Zakeer. He'd killed Akshar, making his wife a widow. He wanted to . . .

'Who contacted you? How did you get this job?'

'I am not going to tell you anything.'

'Here's the deal,' Bee said firmly.

Bee made a soothing motion down Arhan's back and he tried to regulate the violence of his thoughts.

'You need a doctor right fucking now,' she said implacably. 'I'll call one if you tell us everything we need to know. Or I'm calling the police.'

Pal snickered. 'They will arrest you and your boyfriend for violating the law.'

'They'll let us go when we hand you over to them. We'll make a deal.'

'So you want me to make one with you instead?'

'No,' Bee spoke so softly. 'I want you to say no, so we leave you blind in one eye and at the mercy of the police.'

Arhan gave her a startled glance; she sounded dead serious. His trigger finger twitched. There were so many places he could shoot the bastard without killing him.

'Yeah.' Arhan nodded. 'I am okay with that. I might even put a bullet in your kneecap for trying to kill me. Just as a thank you.'

Bee turned to him in alarm as Bhavanchandar Pal tried to thrash against the bare mattresses. He couldn't move much; the knots held.

When Arhan pointed the gun at him, he stilled. His bleeding eye seemed to bleed hatred.

'Fuck you,' Bhavanchandar said again.

'You say that one more time and I will blow your toe off. You like your toes, bhai?'

Bhavanchandar glared at Bee. Bee glared at Arhan.

Arhan glared at both of them. 'He traumatised me, you know,' he muttered.

'I am trying to make a deal here,' Bee muttered back.

'We should leave him to Thapar.'

'And then Sholes' killer walks free because his boss will cut him loose and run.'

'How do you know that?'

'Because it's what I would do,' she answered simply.

Since her logic was inescapable, Arhan turned back and trained the gun on the bastard assassin.

'Do you want to live with one eye as a free man or do you want to spend the rest of your natural life counting the bars of your jail cell?'

Bee picked up Arhan's phone and held it in one hand.

Bhavanchandar glared some more, the area around his bleeding eye looking gory and grotesque, a character out of a Rohit Shetty film. It was a wonder he hadn't passed out from the blood loss yet.

'Fine. Fuck it. What do you want to know?'

Bee quickly searched for a local doctor online and dialled the number given on the website. The man answered and she asked him to come to their hotel room.

'We have thirty minutes before he gets here,' she said.

Arhan handed over the gun to Bee and started stuffing all their things into a bag.

Bee started recording a voice note and settled down on the single chair in the room.

'Start talking, motherfucker,' she said quietly. 'How did you get this job?'

'I was contacted by email on the dark web.'

'Who contacted you? It would be better if you told this in story form. Beginning to end,' ordered Bee.

'Well, it was simple actually. They were looking for someone with my skill set to murder Zakeer Hussain and make it look like an accident. I put up my resume and references and I was emailed the job offer. I took it up.'

Arhan's eyes widened at the sheer normalcy of ordering a hit.

Bee swallowed. 'How did you . . . how did you do it?'

The man shrugged. 'I watched the man for a month. I knew he was going to go away on a holiday soon with his new wife. I just had to catch him alone somewhere. I did it when he went hand-gliding. His neck snapping looked more realistic, you know . . .' Bhavanchandar smiled in reminiscence.

Arhan's breath hissed out as he whipped his head and gave the assassin a murderous look.

Bee stared at him. Back off, her eyes indicated.

He started wiping their prints from the room, like Bee had instructed.

'What next? How did you get involved with the match-fixing?' Bee asked, the perfect reporter.

'The boss contacted me again, more money. *Lamba kaam*. Needed to keep some people sweet, blackmail them with photos . . . set up a few phones and get a communication chain rolling. Standard procedure.'

'Standard procedure?'

Bhavanchandar elaborated on the MO then, explaining the logic behind burner phones and prepaid numbers and false addresses. Explaining the idea of nailing the physiotherapist when his weakness for gambling and Big Tits Sasha was discovered.

He also named the other member in the Indian team involved in the scam. It broke Arhan's heart to learn Garry Marshall's indifference was a calculated act to allow for this horrible scam to unfold under his regime.

The plan was simple—gather dedicated bookies who were looking for cash and start manipulating the numbers, all the while manipulating the players as well. The outcome of each match was pre-determined and the game played in accordance.

Bee was right.

It wasn't India's win they wanted; it was India winning like *heroes* . . . impossibly driving the odds against them, so that whoever was at the very end of this long con stood to make a shitload of money at the finals.

Bee felt sicker as she heard the whole sorry story, the tiny strings that had been set up to snare gullible players and staff.

The way Akshar's death had come about. Stealing the xylazine had apparently been the boss's idea.

'And Sholekar?' Bee asked.

Pal made a dismissive movement. 'Karan Sholekar was a complication. *Toh usko uda dia!*'

That left . . .

'Me,' Bee murmured. 'I am the only one left now.'

'Yeah. Your contract wasn't approved till tonight. Who knows, you could have been spared if you hadn't holed up here.'

'*Jhooth.*'

The man shrugged and then grimaced as the movement jarred his eye.

'Do you know who your boss is?'

Bee knew the answer to that question but she still had to ask.

'If I knew who it was, I would have squeezed them for a lot more money, wouldn't I?'

Arhan reached over and lightly touched the toothbrush. Bhavanchandar Pal screamed in mortal agony.

'People will hear,' Bee hissed.

'I don't want to leave him here. I want him dead.'

'That's not our call.' She could see murder in Arhan's eyes and she hoped her sane voice would prevail through the righteous violence swirling in him. 'Arhan, that's not our call. Please.'

Arhan eased his knee off the bed and looked at her.

'What now?'

Bee looked steadily at him. 'Now we go to Mumbai and end this.'

34

Aghora 'Aggy' Vishwanathan was having a very good time. It involved a well-known actress, a can of whipped cream and a bed.

So when the knocking started, just as the actress started unbuttoning her nurse's uniform, he twitched in reflex. Inside and out.

The knocking continued even though the actress stayed in position, whipped cream in one hand.

Aghora cursed as he struggled through layers of sleep and dreams, and reluctantly came awake. He rubbed his eyes and searched for the woman on the bed, disappointment colouring his face as he realised it was only a dream.

Except for the knocking. That was pretty effing real.

Aghora checked the time. The clock glowed 3.50 a.m.

Who the hell is banging on my door at this ungodly hour?

He ambled out of his bedroom and crossed the 10 feet of the living room to open the door.

'Who the fuck—Bee!' Aggy's jaw dropped as he pulled his sister and hugged her tightly.

Bee hugged him back, just as hard, her arms wrapping around her beanpole and she breathed in the familiar scent of detergent, coffee and chemicals on him. She wrinkled her nose. She could also smell the cigarette he'd smoked before bed.

Aggy let her go just far enough to look down at her and shake her shoulders.

'Do you have any idea what you've put Amma and Appa through? They are apeshit scared for you. The cops showed up asking about you and Amma started crying. I wasn't there to handle it because, as usual, I was conducting my experiments here,' he said making air quotes around the word experiments.

Bee knew all about her brother's 'experiments' and she also knew that apart from a select few, which excluded her parents, no one else knew about them.

'Yeah, yeah . . . I know what you've been up to. That is why I am here,' she said.

'What have you done now, Brigha?'

Bee winced at the censuring tone. 'I can explain everything as soon as we come in.'

'We?'

She stepped back and caught Arhan's wrist, pulling him forward.

Aggy narrowed his eyes at the casual ease of the gesture.

'I'll . . .' Bee glanced at Arhan's grim face, 'We'll tell you everything. I just need to know, are you going to turn us in to the cops?'

Aggy glared at her. '*Podi,* Bee! How can you ask me that?'

'It's a fair assumption on her part,' Arhan said. 'You might be a law-abiding citizen who wants to do the right thing.'

'I am a brother,' Aggy snarled. 'Her brother. And, as her brother, I know she can speak for herself so why don't you pipe down, Coach Sir?'

Bee slapped a hand on both their chests before they butted heads like colliding bulls, the air heavy with testosterone and repressed violence.

Everyone was on edge and she had just one chance to diffuse this situation.

'Stop it, please. Both of you.' She turned to give Arhan an imploring look. 'Arhan, we need Aggy. He is the only one I trust here. And Aggy, Arhan and I are in this together. So you can't go all protective *bhai* on him.'

'I don't know what the fuck you're talking about.'

'If you calm down,' she told her glaring brother, her *younger* brother, who seemed to think that superior height and weight meant superior intellect. 'I will explain the whole situation to you. And, of course, you're not calling the cops. Sorry for asking that.'

Abruptly, all the anger melted from her brother's face and he looked so intensely worried. She had to wonder what the cops had made her family go through.

What *Aggy* himself must've gone through on her behalf.

Wondered if this was the right thing to do or was she taking this crusade way too far.

Sholes' soulless eyes stared at her, printed on the back of her eyelids. Innocent, knowing. His words echoed in her head. *I am already dead.*

No, she had to do this for him. His death couldn't go unavenged.

Arhan wisely kept his mouth shut as Bee stepped forward into her brother's arms and they hugged again for the longest time. She went up on her toes and talked to him in a low tone in Tamil.

Arhan couldn't make out anything except Amma, Appa and it freaked him out, made him a bit envious and a whole lot jealous.

To get a handle on his insane emotions he glanced around the tiny room. Thankfully, this place wasn't under police surveillance yet because, apparently, Aggy was 'house-sitting' for a friend who was off studying some lost tribe in the Amazon.

It was closer to a decrepit studio than an actual apartment, with peeling paint and sparse furnishings and a small CRT TV (with an antenna!) that looked like it was going to breathe its last any second now.

There was also a huge lamp in the shape of a snake. The genius friend of the scientist brother had questionable taste in furniture.

Arhan could feel Aghora's eyes on him, distrusting and questioning. But he clearly loved his sister. It was evident in the rapt, disapproving expression on his face as Bee continued talking in Tamil, switching to English abruptly. 'And then the assailant showed up at our hotel room and we ended up with a shitload of information we desperately needed.'

Aggy jerked his head in the direction of the sofa and steered Bee towards it.

'How exactly did he find you guys when the cops didn't?'

Bee shrugged. 'I am not exactly sure.' But she averted her eyes from Aggy, a move Arhan noted. 'I assume criminals are smarter than cops.'

'Such faith you have in our khaki force.'

'Actually, now that I think about it, I do trust Thapar.' Bee frowned in contemplation.

'Yeah. Even though Thapar is a dog, a vicious sniffer hound,' Arhan said bluntly.

They'd all situated on to the sagging couch where Arhan sat as far away from the brother as possible, while the brother sat as close to his sister as possible.

'He will still arrest your ass when he finds you, Bee,' Aggy said. 'You're in violation of the terms of your bail apparently.'

Bee was contrite. 'I know.'

'How did you manage to sneak into Mumbai?'

Bee flushed and grinned and shot Arhan an adoring, affectionate look. It filled Arhan's cold, mistrusting heart with warmth. 'Tell him about the sugar truck, Arhan.'

'What's to tell?' Arhan was uncomfortable being in the spotlight.

Aggy smiled too, nastily. 'Yeah, I'd love to know about the "sugar" truck.'

Arhan nailed him with his own little smile. 'I own a few sugar cane processing units, and one of the largest sugar manufacturing plants in the country,' Arhan spoke casually, 'I made a call and asked for one of my vehicles to be redirected to Chandigarh airport. We boarded a freight plane that my company had chartered to deliver a large consignment of goods to a subsidiary outlet here in Mumbai.'

'Right.' The brother had no choice but to nod.

'And we rode in a barrel of sugar to the airport.' Bee grinned at the memory and Arhan wisely chose to not say a word more.

As he looked at Aghora, he saw him do the same. They had a moment of perfect communion. This woman was important to both of them and they weren't going to hurt her.

Or let her get hurt.

Some of the tension eased out of the room.

—·◆ ◆·—

'You are insane and so is your theory,' Aggy said three hours later, wiping the last of the instant noodles clean from his bowl.

Arhan was still on his second helping while Bee had eaten just one bowl.

Sholes' laptop was open and Aghora's opinion had been taken on the verification of the fixes. He'd woefully seen the pattern too, predicting when the next big stunt was coming by the end of the round robin.

He was extremely pissed as well. Someone had messed with the sanctity of his favourite game.

'It's all we have at this point, isn't it?'

'And what if India doesn't make it to the finals?'

Arhan shrugged. 'Even if the match isn't fixed, I have faith in my boys. They should win if they stick to the strategy we discussed.'

'I hope it was your idea to stick Irfan in instead of Achrekar.'

'I wanted Achrekar out from the beginning because of his shoulder.' Arhan was justifiably bitter. 'But management overruled me on this one . . . like they have on a lot of things since I became the assistant coach.'

Bee gave him a concerned look. 'Are you even allowed to talk about all this with him?'

Arhan shrugged. 'I've gone rogue now. I bet they've already lined up my replacement and will announce it at a press con tomorrow morning.'

Bee reached over, giving his arm a squeeze. 'You'll be a goddamn hero soon. No one's taking your beloved job away from you.'

The strangest haunted look entered his beetle black eyes and he said nothing to her.

'Are you guys planning on using disguises to get inside Wankhede? The police would have circulated red alert posters of the both of you to every constable in town.' Aggy frowned.

'We'll figure something out,' Bee said.

'We have a bigger problem to tackle before that,' Arhan said grimly.

'What now?' Aggy demanded.

'I have to call up Hasmukh Kanstiya and tender my resignation.'

'Why?' Bee cried in distress.

'Because,' Arhan spoke in a tone like death warmed over. 'The team needs an assistant coach and they have to fly in my replacement today. He has to gel with the team.'

He clenched his fists. 'They're going to lose it. First Zak, then Akshar. Now me.'

Bee shook her head. 'No, they aren't losing you, Arhan. You are going to go back to your team. This way, if something happens,' she gulped. 'Well, you'll be in the clear.'

Arhan stared at her like she'd lost her mind.

Aggy chuckled.

They both looked at him like he'd lost his mind.

'What's funny?' Bee asked furiously.

'I never thought of you as the self-sacrificing, martyr type, Bee.' Aggy shrugged. 'But it's nice to see you care about someone so much.'

Bee scuffed the floor with her toe, refusing to make eye contact with either of them. 'I am not a martyr. But I am a decent person.'

'So am I,' Arhan said gently. 'Besides,' he ran a hand through his stubble, 'I am going to be of more help to the team outside than inside, cheering them on.'

—◆ ◆—

Arhan couldn't sleep. He tossed and turned on the lumpy coir mat that Bee's brother had thoughtfully provided as bedding for him, along with a stony pillow. The ceiling fan whirred on at full speed.

Arhan hadn't contacted his family because he knew that even a halfway-intelligent cop would have bugged their phones. The only way he'd been able to redirect the Chandigarh truck and not get caught was because he remembered the direct number of the manager in charge of operations in the north zone.

It was sheer luck they'd managed to sneak into Mumbai undetected.

He honestly didn't care so much about his job right this minute as he cared about keeping Bee safe.

He knew a thing or two about how big business worked . . . how food chains worked. And the match-fixing ring was a well-run food chain. If Bhavanchandar 'Bastard' Pal didn't finish the job he'd been sent to do, then someone else would be hired for more money and so on and so forth until someone did finish them.

Their plan was daring and audacious and had to work for both of them to live safely and well into the future.

The future . . .

Arhan turned on his side and stared at the streaks of dawn lighting up the grey sky.

Time had lost all meaning for him in the last few days. Things had happened at the speed of light, one after the other, and it seemed like centuries had passed instead of mere days.

The worst part was accepting the murderous, violent side to himself. The predator that wanted to protect what was his. And Bee was his.

Arhan shut his eyes. He saw Bhavanchandar moving to fire the gun at Bee and his protective instincts had risen to the surface, stabbing Bhavanchandar in the eye with a fricking toothbrush. Then, he'd rushed to her side, weaving, lumbering and gathering her close to him. Breathing right for the first time in hours, centuries, millennia . . .

Arhan knew he loved her then. It made no sense but he loved her.

It was the only reason he had stayed when all he'd wanted was to leave, gathering his team close to him and running the hell away from this godawful tournament.

Love had indeed turned him into a fool.

There was a rustle against the mattress and a second later, he felt Bee's warmth. Her arms came around him and she pressed herself against him. Tight. So terribly tight that he became instantly horny.

'I can't sleep,' she whispered. 'I keep thinking about that pyscho coming after you . . .' She swallowed and moved closer to him.

He gripped her hands tight and said, 'It's going to be fine. I promise you.'

'What if he'd killed you?'

He felt the hot rush of her tears on his skin and turned to her, gathering her close and brushing the hair off her cheeks.

She had a red nose, terrified eyes, and her lips were trembling from the effort of not sobbing out loud.

'What do you do when you're panicking and you don't have bubble wrap or cricket facts?'

'I lose it,' she whispered.

'Then lose it,' he whispered, framing her face with both hands. 'I'll be there to find you when you're done.'

Her hands tightened around him, squeezing his chest. 'Aren't you scared too?'

He smiled, a tough-as-nails smile that wobbled slightly at the end, and threw his leg over hers in an innately protective gesture.

'I'm a Punjabi. Scared is for other people, not us.'

'You're insane, the lot of you.'

'I am . . .'

Arhan stopped talking and kissed her. Long and soft, a sweet meeting of the lips that asked for nothing but tenderness.

Bee kissed him back, slowly . . . taking her time with each press of her lips against his.

He could feel her calm down, bit by bit, as they kissed. The terror, the fear, leaving her body as she felt the solid warmth of his. The length of his legs against hers, his calloused palms rubbing her back under her T-shirt, moving lower.

Bee yanked his hand up and murmured, 'Aggy's sleeping in the other room. We can't fool around.'

'Too bad. I think fooling around will work much better than cricket facts and bubble wrap.'

She shrugged and rubbed her palm over his chest and felt his body react.

'Next time.'

Arhan opened his eyes and she sucked in a breath. He wondered if she saw in his eyes what he wanted her to see. What he couldn't say.

Bee kissed his nose and then returned to his mouth. 'We can continue with this remedy for now.'

So they did.

35

Wankhede Stadium was located in the heart of South Mumbai, the cultural, political and financial hub of the city.

Local trains gave one a fascinating glimpse of the massive structure as they pulled into Churchgate station and, at night, when games were on, floodlights illuminated the street and beyond.

Often youngsters could be found perched in nearby trees or on building terraces to watch the matches, especially when India was playing.

Wankhede was where the latest chief minister of Maharashtra had been sworn in to an elite audience of 5,000, an unprecedented event in state politics.

Wankhede was also the stadium where MS Dhoni had smashed a six to a roar of more than one billion people and won India the 2011 World Cup.

Wankhede *was* cricket as much as Eden Gardens, the MCG or the Oval were.

In a country obsessed with cricket, Wankhede symbolised the best and brightest moments of the sport.

It was only fitting that the final of the T20 World Cup would be played here.

—·◆ ◆·—

Arhan and Bee boarded a local train at Andheri with pre-paid coupons purchased by Aggy and kept shy of the ticket conductors at all times.

They reached Churchgate an hour later and walked to Wankhede, a good half-an-hour's walk that they had memorised.

On their recce, they looked at the external structure and gleaned facts from trusty Wikipedia. They looked at the exits and entrances, noted passenger flow, traffic patterns and signal intervals.

They noted everything on paper since digital footprints could not be trusted. They had fresh coconut water opposite Gate B and chatted with the friendly boy who ran the stall.

Yes, the cops had a traffic lockdown planned for the day of the match. It was going to eat into his business, of course, but the fuckers wouldn't understand that, would they?

No, he didn't know what time the security vans would arrive; it was different for each match.

Yes, he was friendly with a few cops and knew their routine. Some of them favoured coconut water over cutting *chai* because it was a healthier alternative and worked so effectively during summer. It wasn't the case during winter months, of course, but still his regulars came.

Yes, the Marine Lines Police Station, the Churchgate Police Station *and* the traffic police for South Mumbai would all provide security.

Bee felt terrible about lying to the young boy and gave him five hundred rupees which she could ill-afford while Arhan pretended to take pictures with his swanky new cellphone that also had a new number. Bee's brother had a friend help out with that.

Arhan had revised his opinion of the Mohawked geek as he'd watched him handle his perky sister and calm her down, pointing her in the right direction, all without alarming or patronising her.

Handling Bee was an art and Aggy had mastered it. Plus, the man hadn't killed Arhan when he'd woken up at ten in the morning and seen his sister slumbering cosily with the guy.

Arhan gave him credit for all of that.

They rode back in a crowded train till Andheri and caught a rickshaw back to Aggy's current residence.

Bee put her head on Arhan's shoulder and said, 'I wish I could go home. See Amma, Appa.'

'You will, soon.'

'I wish you could go back to the team too.'

Arhan was quiet for a long time. Then he said slowly, 'I'm just grateful they gave me a leave of absence instead of accepting my resignation.'

Hasmukh Kanstiya had been incensed when Arhan had called him and resigned as the assistant coach. Talking to Garry would have made no difference, as Arhan well knew. The man did not coach or run the team; Kanstiya and Arhan did.

Kanstiya had cursed Arhan and his family for generations, on both sides. Bee had winced as the curses increased in volume, sounding distraught and ballistic. In the end, he had grudgingly accepted Arhan's leave of absence when the assistant coach had lied and said his mother was in the hospital with a heart murmur.

Kanstiya had, of course, wasted no time in reminding Arhan of the great sacrifice Sachin and Kohli had made when they'd played after tragedy had struck their families.

Arhan had been very firm and polite and asked Kanstiya to not emotionally blackmail him when he had only one parent remaining.

Kanstiya was pissed, but he expected Arhan back ASAP.

Bee took that as a win.

Arhan saw it for what it was—leverage that Kanstiya would hold over his head whenever he needed a whipping boy from here on out.

But it was all for a good cause, so he manned up and accepted the olive branch.

'I know,' Bee said, tightening her grip on his arm and giving him a peck on the cheek, not caring about the autorickshaw driver's stare. She said nothing else but her silence spoke volumes.

That night Aggy's friend's ancient TV telecast the India-South Africa semi-final in all its black and white glory.

Arhan and Aggy were parked in front of the couch with cans of beer and munchies.

Bee was pounding out her thoughts for the series of articles she was intending to write exposing the whole sorry match-fixing scandal, trying to make sense of it all, for herself, for the world.

Trying to honour her friend Sholes' death.

Getting it all out on the page made her feel a little closer to her friends since she couldn't reach out to them and pour out her fears.

Besides, she needed some alone time and work was as good an excuse as any to get her thoughts in order before she could present them to Arhan.

After almost three hours of copious notes, with pull-quotes, quips, subs and possible article headlines, and a list of the various sources she would need to contact and interview in order to get her background straight on a matter as weighty as this, Bee marched out of the bedroom and stood in front of the relic of a TV, hands on hips.

The two men winced in unison and craned their heads on either side of her.

Aggy murmured, 'Move, Bee.'

'I know what we have to do,' she said.

'Do about what?' Arhan cursed under his breath as the TV emitted noises that meant the opposition had done something right. 'Babe, could you move, please.'

'*Babe*,' Bee addressed him tartly, 'you really want to know what I am going to do.'

'What?'

'Remember how you said these match-fixing rings were like food chains? Well, we need to go up the food chain.'

Aggy frowned. 'What does that mean?'

'Ask him,' Bee pointed at Arhan. 'He knows all about how criminal organisations work. Apparently, they are like regular businesses with a hierarchy and everything.'

Arhan again gestured at Bee to move. She rolled her eyes and sat down on the floor. She whipped out the burner phone she'd found on Bhavanchandar Pal once Arhan had TKO'd his ass.

Arhan finally paid attention to her. 'What are you doing, Bee?' He looked horrified.

'You told me I have to tell you when I need you. And that I shouldn't put my life in unnecessary danger. Well, I'm telling you now that I need you and I am putting my life in *necessary* danger.'

Bee gestured with the phone towards the TV. 'Two birds. One stone.'

Arhan narrowed his eyes. 'Okay . . .'

Bee continued, 'I'm going to text the mastermind as the assassin to tell them that Bee Vishwanathan is dead and that I, the attacker, want double the payment on the day of the finals. Face-to-face. I will promise to show proof of death as well. This gets me the who and the why all in one shot. It's a genius plan, isn't it?'

Arhan stopped breathing.

She didn't look insane. She didn't look demented. In fact, she looked very much like the Bee who had cried and come apart in his arms just this morning. But she sure was talking like a crazy person.

Aggy sighed and cursed really loudly.

Arhan looked at him.

The brother gave him a look of sheer misery. 'If you stick around longer, worrying about her will kill you.'

Arhan whipped his head towards Bee.

She was sitting in the same pose, holding the phone and looking coolly at him, as if she hadn't just talked about making contact with a cold-blooded murderer.

'Can I just say, for the record, what a spectacularly disastrous idea this is,' Arhan said.

Aggy's voice was mournful as he joined in, 'Exactly.'

Bee sighed and reached out to touch both of them, one hand on each of their knees. She looked scared and somehow determined at the same time. 'You could talk me out of it. You matter more to me than some story,' she admitted in a small voice.

Arhan closed his eyes. Aggy looked like he was in pain.

They looked at each other. Another moment of silent communion.

'Do it,' they said simultaneously.

36

Paramjit Thapar was in the middle of career suicide.

His main suspect in a double murder case had fled the state after posting bail and he had no fucking clue how to find her. It was incredible, but she'd just vanished into thin air. Along with her boyfriend who had narrowly missed becoming a murder suspect himself. It was insane that the prime suspect in a double murder would willingly break the law the second she was released on bail, but that's exactly what Bee Vishwanathan had done.

If Thapar didn't know better, he would have thought they were trained spies or assassins who did this sort of shit on a regular basis.

But he *did* know better. He had the considerable resources of the Indian police force at his disposal so he'd tracked the pair of them to a storage facility outside Chandigarh. The man who owned the warehouse had willingly spilled all the details.

Apparently, Bee and Arhan had come in with no luggage and left with a suitcase from the warehouse locker. A few hours after they'd left, another car had driven up to the lot. A man in a black hoodie had bribed the manager into telling him everything about this particular locker—a man whose description matched the one Bee had given him the night of her attack in Kolkata.

Thapar wondered if maybe she'd been right all along. That there was something bigger going on here that he couldn't fathom or pinpoint.

He remembered the crazy things she'd said to him when he'd interrogated her after the arrest.

'Akshar Shekhawat was involved in a match-fixing scam with someone who tried to attack me, whose phone I picked up by accident the day the tournament began. A guy in a black hoodie.'

What if it really was as simple as that? She'd just picked up the wrong guy's phone and had been sucked into a vortex of conspiracy, murder and scamming the nation out of crores of rupees? It wasn't as if he was convinced beyond reasonable doubt that she had committed the murders.

None of this, of course, excused Brigha Vishwanathan's escape into the great void.

He was going to arrest her and put her in jail for violation of a court order . . . and for the aggravation she'd caused him.

This murder investigation had turned up no clues, save that Akshar had been accepting bribes for quite a while before the World Cup had even begun.

The dead journalist had a missing laptop and Thapar knew exactly who had it.

He just wished he could find their whereabouts.

The families of both Arhan and Brigha knew nothing—Mrs Vishwanathan was distraught at the idea of her daughter becoming a fugitive from the law—and neither did their friends.

Dheera Chakravorty had last heard from Brigha after she'd been released on bail and had had no contact with her since then.

Arhan's brother had not received any communication from him after the phone call in Chennai and a routine email the next day. Kanstiya had stonewalled him on the team front; not that he blamed the poor guy for trying to keep the team sane in the middle of this catastrophe.

But Thapar had another reason for wanting to find cricket's own Bunty *aur* Babli.

If someone had followed them to Shree Ram Warehousing and Storage, chances were that someone would attempt something again.

All things considered, he didn't want that silly reporter becoming collateral damage if it could be avoided.

Or, for that matter, Arhan Kapoor, that national fucking treasure, who most certainly was not back in his *pind*, mourning the death of a beloved grandmother while his mother recovered from a stroke. Or whatever lame excuse he'd given!

One of Thapar's flunkies came forward with a heavy package just as he considered tapping out another Wills Gold and smoking his fifth cigarette of the day.

His superiors were regularly *maroing* his *gaand* since Akshar Shekhawat represented the Boys in Blue. He needed to solve this case ASAP!

'What?' he barked, as the constable placed the heavy package on his table in the dingy police station in Chandigarh.

The TV at the front desk was playing highlights of India's drubbing of South Africa in the semi-finals on mute.

India would now face Australia in the finals.

'A package for you, sir.'

Paramjit looked at the neat label that was printed instead of handwritten. The package had been couriered, marked 'Express Delivery'. He removed his car key from his pocket and slit it open, cutting through bubble wrap, remembering Bee's insane fixation.

Inside was a Dell laptop with a note on top.

He removed the handwritten postcard-sized note and read it quickly. Then he read it again.

Param cursed. Long and loud and with particular viciousness.

Inspector Thapar

I am sending you this laptop as a gesture of good faith and to let you know that I am alive, if not exactly well.

I would also like to tell you that we are on the verge of a breakthrough with the case and will meet you as soon as the cup is handed over to the winning team.

I know I have caused you a lot of trouble and made your life more difficult than necessary but once you know the whole story, you'll understand.

Yours sincerely

Bee

PS: My gazette papers came through, finally. Hope you have that in your records.

PPS: See if you can trace a Bhavanchandar Pal who would have been admitted to a medical facility in Haryana with a toothbrush in his right eye.

Paramjit noted the date on the paper—yesterday. The parcel had been overnighted to him.

He looked at the constable who was staring at him with slight apprehension.

'Sir?' the constable asked. 'What's the matter, sir?'

'I need to know where this parcel came from. I need to know when the next flight from Chandigarh to Mumbai is. I need to be on that flight!'

Then he opened the laptop and punched the power button.

The dead journalist's face filled the screen.

Paramjit was cool, calm and collected. Like he always was in the middle of a chase.

He'd arrived in Mumbai in the early hours of the morning the day before the finals after getting the necessary permissions from his superiors. On the flight, he had put together a crack team culled from the CBI, the local police force and an emergency response team trained in scenarios that included ordnance disposal.

They were thirty men in total, manning different parts of the stadium, with him at the helm of it all in the program control room. Every square inch of the ground and the bleachers was under surveillance.

Communication was on a private channel and kept to a bare minimum.

Plus, he knew where his suspect was. He knew what the quarry looked like and the identikit artists had given him a decent idea of how much disguise and camouflage could change them.

Thapar ground the butt of his smoked-out Wills under the heel of his shoe and shaded his eyes from the glaring sun.

It was early evening and the crowd at Wankhede was filling up fast. All the tickets had been sold out so his team had leaned hard on the booking agents, online and offline, and finally struck gold this morning.

So far, their suspects had not been spotted.

They had been smart, evading the reach of the law, travelling incognito to Mumbai avoiding the airports and railway stations. Every state cop had a red alert circular bearing the names Bee Vishwanathan and Arhan Kapoor.

They'd even been smart in sending the parcel from a dead-end address where no one lived in a low-rental area in Andheri. The cell number given had also been disconnected.

Then, they'd stumbled.

They'd booked two tickets to the finals through an online booking portal using Arhan's special privilege account and Bee's credit card. The alert had popped up last night, screaming red.

Since it was such a solid golden lead, the authorities had no choice but to follow it.

Their seats were in the middle of the Sunil Gavaskar Stand. Row K, numbers 45 and 46. Two policemen in plainclothes were manning those seats at all times, and five more were in the immediate vicinity.

All the ticket checkers had been supplied with Bee's and Arhan's photos and their superiors had been informed as well.

Param suspected this red flag was as deliberate as the rest of their actions had been, including running away from the police and crossing state lines.

Bee Vishwanathan, he was coming to believe, was one sharp cookie. As was Arhan Kapoor.

The PCR director trawled from one camera to another, as Param had instructed him, while his assistants put together pre-match packages that would be relayed to the studios.

They were checking feed, text and data and making sure the control room was shipshape before the match began broadcasting.

The time was now 6.05 p.m.

Half the stadium was full, people settling in with their popcorn and Cokes and *samosas*, their bags tucked under the seats while they hunted desperately for water.

Stadiums had strict rules on what could and couldn't be carried in. You couldn't carry food and beverage items from outside and if it was a bag beyond a specific size, you had to deposit it in a locker, at your own risk.

Religious sites, stadiums and airports were the three most at-risk venues in any country. The first for very obvious reasons, and the other two for maximum impact.

Thapar hoped Arhan had enough sense to keep Bee away from the stadium while there were orders for her immediate arrest. Even though they had bought tickets in such an open manner and were probably considering showing up to expose the person responsible for the chaos and carnage that was this year's World Cup.

He admired the woman's moxie.

Prison clothes would not suit her and, after everything she'd done, no judge in the country was going to grant her bail.

'Don't come here,' he murmured to himself.

'Shall I move to the Gavaskar stand again?'

'Sure.'

The PCR director pressed buttons on his console and the Gavaskar stand came into HD focus. The seats were almost entirely occupied, and the two policemen were chugging on Coke, their eyes shifting constantly while they chilled on the government's dime.

Even though his job was on the line again, Param wanted those two seats to remain empty for the duration of the match.

The time was now 06:09 p.m.

37

'This is such a mistake,' Arhan grumbled even as he zipped Bee up in her UCLA hoodie adding a bright lime green cap a few hours before match time.

He pulled the bill of the cap forward so it partially obscured her face and tapped it affectionately. 'I am guessing your favourite colour is green?'

She shrugged and looked at herself in the mirror. 'I like green. It's Hulk's colour. It works for Mark Ruffalo.'

She almost pulled off the *Gully Boy* getup in her baggy sweatshirt, cargo pants and running shoes.

He grinned. 'Not an Eric Bana fan, then?'

'Nah. Although, Hector was a dreamboat.' As a dreamy expression suffused her features, Arhan felt another wave of love hit him . . . Just like the waves against the rocks at Marine Drive. They'd spent last night at the promenade, watching the waves crash over and over . . . silent, together, complete.

'There's a lot about you I still don't know, isn't it?' Arhan murmured as he checked her out in Aggy's cracked mirror.

'Does it matter?'

He carefully, calculatingly, refused to think about the future, what tomorrow held.

Today was all they had.

And after today, they'd . . .

Arhan squared his shoulders, straining under the fake GAP sweatshirt and baggy pants that complemented hers. He wore Adidas shoes and had grown his beard out, adding to the fake beard he wore.

He was almost impossible to recognise. To Bee, he seemed a thinner, scruffier version of the sexy Arhan Kapoor. But just as appealing.

Bee pulled him closer, went on her toes and kissed him soundly. He kissed her back, with enthusiasm.

When their lips broke apart, he asked, 'What was that for?'

'That was for luck. Don't get killed. Don't get caught. Come-back-to-me luck.'

'I should be doing that, shouldn't I?'

She smiled. A soft, special smile that almost, almost, made him believe she felt more for him than she was letting on.

He wanted to ask her.

What is this thing going on between us? Are we in a relationship? Do you love me like I love you? Could we be in a relationship?

But since he wasn't a guest on *Koffee with Karan*, he bottled up his confused, conflicted, overwhelming feelings like a proper Punjabi *munda* and kissed her hard. This time their kiss had a flavour of desperation and her eyes were the tiniest bit dazed as he let her go. Her knees felt weak so she held on to his waist.

'Don't get killed,' Arhan said. 'Don't get caught. Come back to me. That was a good luck kiss too.'

'Come up with some original lines.' She punched him lightly on the arm. But he hoped she knew he was dead serious.

'I told you, you're the writer. I don't have fancy words.'

'These work too.'

'Sending that laptop to Thapar was such a mistake,' he muttered as he slung a messenger bag over his shoulder. 'If he is smart he will be tracking us right now to this address and we'll be arrested any minute.'

Bee shrugged. 'I used an anonymous email address and we used the defunct flat in the next building for the sender information. Besides, Aggy is relatively in the clear by leaving for that conference in Gujarat. They have questioned him already when he was home with Amma and Appa. We are as safe as we could possibly be.'

Then, right on cue, her phone rang. It was her brother.

'Yeah?' she said. 'Yes, we are good. Getting ready to leave. We're going to hail a cab today. It's a better trail. Then when we get there, we'll get in and make the call. Yes, we purchased the tickets on my card itself. Thank god for online booking and Arhan's special privilege access which they haven't revoked yet.'

She listened for a minute to what her brother had to say. 'Yeah,' Bee said. 'We are sure. I want to do this. It's the right thing to do. The reporter in me wants this story, the friend in me wants Sholes' death to mean something. But mostly I want justice for the way the game you two love has been corrupted.'

She smiled in a weird, scary way that had Arhan's breath backing up in his throat. She looked ready for battle.

This was an insane plan with a 90 per cent chance of jail or worse, and that was the least of what could happen to them. And she was positively jumping with excitement.

How messed up was she that she needed this constant adrenaline rush to feel alive? Did he really not know her at all? Was the bubble wrap just the surface of her problems?

When she hung up after the goodbyes were done, he asked her, 'Who's your therapist?'

Bee grinned. 'Dheera. She's so good at calming me down when I'm about to lose it. She gave me the bubble wrap idea when I went after a fellow reporter with a stapler for calling me an opportunistic slut and sleeping my way to an interview with Shreenath Patil.'

'There are so many things I don't understand about that statement, I don't even want to get into it. I just want to know one thing.'

'Yes, Arhan?'

Was he a sap because he loved hearing her say his name?

'Are you scared?' he demanded quietly. 'Right now, are you scared? Because I am. I should protect you and take care of you and make sure nothing happens to you but I am scared of everything we are going to do. And I don't want anything to happen to you but I don't want anything to happen to me either.'

'And you think I do?'

Arhan nodded at the pink phone in her hand. 'Just now, when you were talking to your brother . . . you seemed gung-ho, like the thrill of it is all that matters. Like you don't care that we are endangering our lives and going to get in even further trouble with the law, with our families, with our former bosses.'

'I care about the law, our families and justice.' At his blank look, she added, 'I also care about doing the right thing and exposing evildoers and upholding the news reporters' oath.'

'What? Like the Hippocratic oath?'

'No. The Brighabhujaambaa oath. You shall always seek the truth because someone has to.'

Bee paused and took a deep breath. 'And I am terrified, for you, for me . . . God, for you because I don't want anything to happen to you because of me. I don't want your chances of coaching India to be jeopardised because you're caught up in a scandal all thanks to me. I don't want you to regret meeting me. You have no idea how scared I am that you'll regret —'

He clapped a hand on her mouth, which kept moving for moments after he'd silenced her.

Arhan's eyes dimmed and then glowed as if someone had flipped a switch. 'You talk so much. Most of it makes little sense. But I still can't live without you, Brighabhujaambaa Vishwanathan. Now I totally understand why you legally changed your name.'

She nodded, then pointed at his hand. He removed his hand and she said, 'Me too. I can't live without you, I mean. And I talk sense all the time.'

'You use a Monster High toothbrush, *kudiye*.' Arhan grinned. 'With a sharp, pointy end. That is a health hazard.'

'It saved your sexy ass, AK. Don't you forget that.'

For good measure, she slapped said sexy ass and he yelped and then chuckled.

Then they exited the small apartment they'd called home for the past few days and walked out. . . Two mysterious people blending into the mass of humanity that was Mumbai.

'Hey.' Bee smiled and tapped the shoulder of a girl dressed in shorts and a crop top in the parking lot farthest from the stadium.

The girl turned around, a can of pepper spray in her hand.

'Chill out, please,' Bee said, springing back a couple of steps. 'I was wondering if you wanted to trade seats with me.'

'Who the fuck are you that I should do that?'

'No one. But the seats are really good. Gavaskar stand. Row K. Almost in the front.'

The girl's kohl-lined eyes narrowed and she chewed vigorously on gum that smelled vaguely of Nicorette. 'Why would you want to trade good seats for crap ones?'

Bee sighed. 'I get bored in matches, my boyfriend loves them. Making out is not possible in the front, no? It's cool if you don't want to. I get it.'

The girl chewed some more, going smack-smack-smack.

Sweat dripped down Bee's spine, pooling at the waistband of her pants. She really hoped the girl wanted the seats.

'Fine,' she said, tipping her glares down her nose and looking at Bee. 'But I want to see yours first.'

Bee showed her the tickets; they were authentic. The exchange was made and the girl tucked the new tickets in her pocket and walked away, shaking her head.

Bee held the new tickets in her hand. They were on the opposite side, farther up at the back. Not the best seats in the world.

But they would do for the purposes of this mission.

She called up Arhan using another phone that Aggy had procured for them. 'I got them. I got the tickets.'

'You did?'

Bee overlooked the slight disappointment in his voice and continued, 'I'll meet you in five. Are you in position?'

Arhan sighed. 'Yes, I am.'

Bee ended the call.

—◆◆—

Arhan tapped his feet impatiently, standing in one of the long queues snaking into the stadium. He'd picked a random queue to blend in. He had absolutely no intention of entering the stadium for now.

That would come later.

The time was now 6.15 p.m.

The match was scheduled to begin at 8 p.m.

Entry to the gates would shut twenty minutes prior to the start of the match to give people enough time to settle down.

It also gave the players time to get accustomed to the crowd.

He remembered the Ashes 2005 test at Edgbaston that he'd attended with his family. The madness had been supreme then, the chaos extreme. The fans had gone absolutely nuts the more Australia collapsed. He too had cheered on the English team like crazy, his voice going hoarse, completely losing it on the last day when England won the test match and the series.

His own team was out there now. Without their assistant coach.

Fuck. Fuck. Fuck!

He was so irresponsible and selfish!

He'd abandoned them when they needed him the most and was instead helping a madwoman with a vendetta.

Except . . . he was helping them too and he knew it.

Whether India won or lost this match, he was ensuring the survival of the team and the game and that was all that mattered. More than this team, more than his career, more than the cup.

It was messed up that he could rationalise it so well in his head.

Before he spiralled any further, he spotted Bee's green cap.

Anger, fear, and apprehension congealed in a sick mess in his guts, twisting and knotting. Arhan got out of the queue and jogged up to her. The queue surged forward, pressing into the tiny smidgeon of space vacated by him.

The noise was deafening already—screams of 'India, India' and conversations ranging from India's chances to wild predictions on match outcomes and everything in between, all punctuated by the myriad ringtones of phones and camera clicks.

'Are we good?'

She showed him the tickets.

He looked them over. They'd do. 'Yeah. These are okay.'

'I know.'

Arhan hesitated.

Bee touched his arm. 'You can leave if you want to. You should.'

'Will you come with me?' There was real desperation in his eyes as he held on to her elbow, gripping her tightly. 'We can stop this right now. Go up to Thapar and you can turn yourself in. He'll take it forward.'

'I know.'

'But you're not going to do that.'

Bee sighed and closed her eyes. 'I'm sorry. You were right. This is a story for me too. I need to see it through to the end. You can hate me if you want.'

Arhan's eyes dulled and his hand dropped from her elbow.

'It's sad that you would even think that after everything we've been through.' Then his face hardened under the beard and he said, 'All right, let's do it.'

Bee steeled herself and extracted her new pink phone and texted the only number available on the burner phone.

'Confirm meet. Hotel Cornet Plaza. Outside Gate 4. 7 p.m.'

Bee pressed send and waited for the delivery confirmation to come through.

She only dared to give Arhan a sideways glance. He looked so defeated, so alone.

But this was her job, her career. This was about justice in its purest form. And she did not want to sacrifice it for a man, however much she loved him. Millions of women had not burned their bras for Bee to choose domestic bliss over doing the right thing.

Bee swallowed a lump the size of a cricket ball down her throat and focused on the job at hand.

The phone buzzed with a text notification.

I'll be there.

Arhan gave her a grim look, which Bee knew was reflected on her face.

'Shall we?' He offered her his arm.

She nodded.

They started walking towards the busiest gate of the stadium, Gate 4, which had access from the local train station and pedestrian crossing —the main reason they'd chosen it. They blended in easily with crowds waiting to enter the stadium for the most exciting game of the year.

It was organised chaos at its finest. And the best form of protection.

The crowd surged forward, as if in a great wave. Arhan and Bee held hands and melted into the darkness closing in from the skies, turning away from the stadium into a small lane that no one would notice unless they were actively looking for it.

38

Inspector Paramjit Thapar was disappointed.

The Idiot Duo hadn't shown up so far, and he doubted they would now.

It didn't make any sense.

Whatever their plan was, it had obviously been scrapped seeing the extra security. He wasn't surprised but he had expected at least a cursory appearance, if nothing else.

'Do we have a visual?' Param demanded.

'We are searching, sir,' a terrified lackey murmured.

Not fast enough.

Right then, as if the fates were having the last laugh at his expense, his phone rang. Param thumbed it open with a sinking heart.

'What the fuck, Thapar?' His boss yelled right in his ear. 'I put you in charge of security to defuse the situation. Not to convert it into a military standoff. Why do you have all this extra personnel stationed all around the stadium?'

'Because, sir,' Paramjit began calmly, 'we have reason to believe that our absconding fugitives, Arhan Kapoor and Bee Vishwanathan, are around here somewhere. Bringing them in is our top priority.'

The boss took a heaving breath. 'Handle this mess right now or I will make you push papers in Timbuktu for the rest of your miserable career.'

Param answered in the affirmative before switching his walkie on again. 'What's the status? All units report now.'

Various 'No sirs' could be heard and Param felt sick. His career really was fucking over.

Suddenly, his walkie crackled to life again. 'Sir, this is Unit 13, Sujit reporting in. We have a suspect in custody.'

'Who is it?'

Sujit responded in a mix of Hindi and English. '*Pata nai*, sir. *Ladki hai*. She showed up with the tickets purchased on Bee Vishwanathan's credit card. Accomplice *lagti hai*, sir.'

Param heard a cultured female voice spewing obscenities and the channel cut off communication. He pressed a button and said, 'Where are you, Sujit?'

'Gavaskar Stand. Row 14.' Sujit was slightly breathless. 'Madam, please stay calm.'

Param would have asked for video confirmation if he knew how to work the spaceship console. He grabbed his walkie and took off at a dead run.

The sixteen TV screens in the PCR showed scenes of absolute chaos as people settled into the stadium.

'You bloody fools!' Param was cold, cold as ice.

His anger was so absolute that he couldn't contain it with mere words.

'Fuck!'

The girl with the Nicorette gum glared at the two men restraining her and said, 'I know my rights. You guys are going to get *fired* for this.'

Param held up a hand. 'Sorry for the inconvenience, ma'am. But we can't take any chances today. We're looking for two suspects, a man and a woman.' Param whipped out the Mumbai Police flyer with Arhan's and Bee's photos with the caption 'WANTED' in bold red letters at the top. 'Have you seen either of these people?'

The girl nodded angrily. 'Yeah. That's the woman who gave me these tickets in exchange for mine.'

Param nodded thoughtfully. 'Where are your seats, ma'am?'

The girl laughed. 'She fucked with you. She's on the other side. Tendulkar stand, Row Q. Numbers 67, 68. Now let me go.'

Param looked at the thousands of people around the stadium and cursed mentally. The Idiot Duo had turned out to be smarter than he had anticipated.

'Fuck.'

'Let's go,' he told his team grimly, already jumping seats and weaving his way through the throng. It took them ten minutes, ten precious minutes they did not have, to get to the right stands.

And when they did, Param was half-expecting a gorilla in an India blue jersey to end his career on a spectacular low. What he got was something more unexpected.

In the stands, sitting calmly, munching popcorn was Aghora Vishwanathan.

39

Hotel Cornet Plaza was in a sleazy location with a sleazy name. In its heyday, back in the 1990s, it had been the preferred rendezvous point for fading film stars, sportsmen and businessmen and their mistresses. It was close to Churchgate station and the stadium, and was far from the local police station.

In the last decade though it had fallen prey to Airbnb's couple-friendly deals and was in a state of drab decay. So much so that nearby locals avoided its dark exterior like the haunted house it had become.

The road leading up to the property was full of overgrown trees, two large dumpsters overflowing with refuse and a blown streetlight that flickered in ghostly shadows. What made this place perfect for Bee and Arhan was that it had only one entrance and exit, so no one could try any funny business.

'Do you think Aghora got to the stands on time?' Bee mused out loud. 'We have to thank your brother's friend for arranging entry for him on such short notice.'

'We will.' Arhan squeezed her elbow. 'Later.'

'Thanks for suggesting the drop location,' Bee said gratefully, as they neared the hotel's entrance.

Arhan gave her a wry look. 'Drop location? Who are you, Villainelle?'

Bee shrugged. 'I always thought I gave off Eve energy but I'll take Villainelle.'

Arhan stopped dead in the middle of the road. His face was half in the shadows courtesy of the streetlight. He was sombre, almost funereal.

'Bee, there's still time. We can turn ourselves in. I can afford the best legal help we will undoubtedly need. You don't have to avenge your friend's death. It's not on you,' he spoke with thrumming urgency.

Tears pricked Bee's eyes. Tears of regret and anxiety and the hot familiar feeling she'd faced throughout her life, throughout her career. Disappointment.

She cupped Arhan's jaw in trembling hands. 'All my life, certainly after I started working in the media, people have underestimated me. Managers, editors, my colleagues. Well,' she smiled thinly, 'not Dhee. But most people. No one thinks I'm capable of fulfilling my ambitions. Of breaking a truly important story. No one.'

Then she added the sad, unvarnished truth. 'Not even you, Arhan.'

Arhan sighed.

'And you know what the saddest part is? I love you,' she said softly. 'I'm in love with you. Because you have always tried to do the right thing no matter how hard it was.'

She stepped back from him and the look she gave him was both sorrowful and mournful. 'I just wish you could see that I'm trying to do the right thing here too.'

Arhan grimaced. 'Bee, I —'

He made to touch her hand when he jerked. Once. Slowly, as if he was convulsing.

Bee heard the sound a second too late. A sort of clicking sound, like a lock coughing into place. And she smelled cordite and the copper stench of fresh blood.

Bee gasped as Arhan toppled towards her in slow motion. She caught him in her arms reflexively and immediately spun around so she was in the line of fire. The move made her dizzy but it did the job.

Arhan was safe now.

Bee felt a rush of something warm and sticky coat her fingers. A sob rushed out of her throat.

'Stop,' she screamed. 'Don't shoot.'

'Don't worry, my dear,' an all-too-familiar voice rang out in the eerily quiet street. 'I'm not going to kill him.'

Bee turned around, Arhan a dead weight. His breathing laboured.

He can't be dead! He just can't.

'Hello, Bee,' Maharani Kalavati Devi said pleasantly as she dragged a gagged and bound Dheera by the hair with her.

Kartar Singh held an effective pistol with a silencer. He had it pointed at Arhan.

'You've disappointed me, Bee,' Kalavati said in a perfect facsimile of a sorrowful voice while her beady eyes promised holy retribution. 'Terribly so.'

Bee's head spun as she tried to make sense of it all.

'Hello, Inspector,' Aghora said, standing up with his hands in the air, like the good little suspect he was.

'You're under arrest,' Param said flatly. 'For aiding and abetting wanted criminals. For disturbing the peace. For impersonating said criminals. And for aggravating me for no fucking reason. Arrest him,' he ordered.

Aghora held his arms out. 'You need to talk to them.'

Param's eyes narrowed. 'You know where they are?'

Aghora swallowed. He was a young man in his mid-twenties. He shouldn't be ruining his life over whatever clusterfuck this was. But family, it got to you, one way or the other.

'I don't,' he admitted. 'But I have something better.'

'What?' Param was wary. 'What the fuck do you have that could be of use to me?'

Aghora held up a smartphone with a blinking dot on the screen. 'I have GPS.'

The Maharani was resplendent in a lavender chiffon sari bedecked in *mukaish* and lace, diamonds glittering at her throat and ears, glinting at the wrists that held Dheera captive.

'You shot Arhan. You kidnapped my friend,' Bee tried to talk like she wasn't losing her mind. It was barely possible.

'Did you really think I was foolish enough to believe that a ridiculous hitman wanted to meet me in person to hand over proof of death?' Kalavati jerked Dheera's shoulder. 'She's just insurance so you don't try something even more idiotic.'

Bee closed her eyes. She had been foolish enough to think exactly that.

'So what's your plan now? Kill all of us and cry crocodile tears when the cops come?'

The Maharani shrugged delicately. 'If there's one thing I've learned in my wretched life, it's how to cry convincingly. Some of it might even be real.' Kalavati gave her a sad smile. 'But I must say, you really are an extraordinary young woman, putting all this mess together. I wish my daughter was more like you. Right down to getting Arhan for herself.'

'I don't understand,' Bee said feelingly.

'I know.' There was such remorse in the Maharani's voice. She sounded almost concerned. Almost. 'I know you don't. No one does.'

'But ... why?' Bee fairly screamed out the word. 'Why did you do all this? You are literally a fucking queen!'

The Maharani shrugged. 'What else was I to do when my daughter married a sportsman who had loads of money on paper but nothing in his bank account? Endorsements and player contracts are complex things with no immediate pay out, aren't they?'

Her eyes hardened. 'She should have married Arhan. Like I wanted her to. She should have married the businessman who could have saved us. Saved my legacy.'

'What? Ar-Arhan?' Bee couldn't get his name out. She flashed back to when the Maharani had said Arhan would have made her a good son-in-law.

What she had thought was idle conversation was actually real. Why wouldn't Arhan have said a word to her about Ujwala? Especially after the woman had practically attacked her in Kolkata . . .

Bee's eyes were on the gun but her throat was dry with fear. She was acutely conscious of the blood seeping out of Arhan. Of Dhee's tear-stained, frantic eyes, her silent screams.

The Maharani nodded. 'Arhan could have married Ujwala before she fell in love with Zakeer. He would have saved my palace, my Kunwarji's home, from being turned into a national heritage monument that's now open to the *common public*.' The Maharani's lips thinned. 'Like they are even fit to enter!'

She nodded at Kartar Singh. The man pulled the trigger.

Bee watched as the bullet made for her, grazing her arm because she hadn't moved at all, she was in such shock. And then pain, bright and intense and mind-numbing, consumed her.

Bee screamed.

———◆　◆———

'Cornet Plaza is right around the corner. On the next road,' Param's deputy informed him breathlessly as they patched Aghora's phone into the police computer to better track the GPS.

'Alert all units. We go in fully prepared and armed.'

Aghora gave him a grim look, looking oddly at home in the zip ties he wore around his wrists. 'It's faster if you run. It will take you three minutes.' He gave the potbellied deputy a doubtful look. 'Not you.'

The deputy raised his hand to smack the mouthy kid but Param shook his head.

Adrenalin poured through Param's spine, straightening it, leaving him clear-headed. 'We'll go on foot. Karan, Jeet, Arjun and Angad, you're with me.' He chose the swiftest, fittest, youngest men on the squad. 'The rest of you, follow Inspector Waghle's command and provide backup.'

Thapar was already suited in a bulletproof vest, so he tucked his walkie-talkie into one of the pockets and checked the safety of his standard-issue pistol.

Then he gave Aghora a death stare. 'You better be right about your sister's whereabouts. Or the penalty for obstructing an ongoing investigation will result in you never seeing daylight again.'

'Save my sister. Save Arhan,' Aghora said simply. 'Be the hero.'

Param started running, using the handheld GPS device as his guide. He was three minutes away from Gate 4 and the turn to Hotel Cornet Plaza.

———◆　◆———

'Don't make a fuss, dear,' the Maharani admonished Bee. 'It is only a flesh wound. If I wanted to kill you, you'd be dead by now.'

Dheera struggled against the Maharani's hold, wretched sounds emanating from her gagged mouth.

Bee clutched her arm and sank down, tears leaking out of her eyes. Arhan lay collapsed next to her, his breathing even.

'You're a monster,' Bee whispered, hurt physically and emotionally.

'I am the queen of a dying estate that nothing but extraordinary sums of money can save,' Kalavati said bitterly, dragging Dheera as she walked forward. 'Money no one could provide for me. I needed Zakeer to disappear.'

'Because he was the lynchpin holding the team together and his death would weaken them emotionally and strategically,' Bee surmised.

Kalavati didn't nod. 'Be still, dear. I'm talking to your friend,' she addressed Dheera, yanking tighter on her neck. Dheera's eyes almost rolled into the back of her head. She stopped clawing for escape.

'So you contracted Bhavanchandar Pal to take him out?' The pain was making Bee dizzy but she knew the only way they were going to stay alive was by engaging this woman. She had to make her talk.

Kalavati nodded. 'You can get anything you want online nowadays, can't you?'

Bee's blood ran cold at the casual words. 'You could have stopped there. With Zakeer out of the picture.'

'I could have,' the Maharani answered thoughtfully. 'But the drama and chaos following his death provided me an opportunity.'

'Two birds,' Bee said slowly. 'One stone. You would use Bhavanchandar Pal to blackmail the players, spot fix the matches and make your fortune. And with Zakeer gone, your daughter would have no choice but to come back home to you.'

'I had to ensure my estate was protected. And my daughter was protected from her own worst impulses. It was just business,' the Maharani said in a matter-of-fact way. As if she weren't talking about murder, conspiracy to commit murder, and swindling people out of crores of rupees.

'Why did you befriend me then?' That was the only thing Bee couldn't truly understand. 'If you were planning to kill me.'

The Maharani shrugged. 'I was never *planning* on killing you, Bee.' She smiled; it was terrible. 'You must believe that.'

'But?' Bee prompted her while she clutched her bleeding arm.

'But I wanted the burner phone back. And I wasn't sure you had it. Not until the night Akshar was killed. Then I knew. I wasn't even sure in Kolkata when that fool Bhavan tried to come after you. Men.' Kalavati spat out the word.

'Why did you kill Akshar?'

'Karan Sholekar somehow found out he was helping fix the matches and Akshar was getting paranoid. Unbalanced. He was going to talk, I just knew it. So I had Bhavan finish him off.'

Bee felt the pain travel up and down, radiating in all directions until she was a vortex of pain, of sheer agony that had no end. It was nothing compared to how sickly Arhan looked next to her.

With the end to her scheme in sight, the previously pale-looking Maharani seemed to have a new-found strength, a rush of adrenaline she didn't usually possess. She yanked tighter on Dheera's throat while the latter started kicking as she was slowly suffocated.

'I'd hoped you would stop if you were distracted by romancing Arhan. But you didn't. You even involved him in your crusade. I thought having you arrested would calm you down. So I had one of my people back home make that anonymous phone call to Thapar regarding that wretched journalist. I thought you'd be frightened enough to accept my help and go to my safe house.'

The Maharani sighed. A genuinely troubled sigh.

'Bhavan would have found you at the safe house, taken the phone and left you unconscious. That was all. You wouldn't have been hurt if you had just listened to me, my dear.'

'Don't call me "dear".'

The ever-loyal Kartar squeezed off a round at the ground near Arhan. Bee screamed.

'Now I know the police will be here in a second so this is just . . . goodbye. I am sorry, Bee. You really are a very lovely girl. I have so enjoyed our time together.'

There was a look of such abject sorrow on her face that Bee was almost tempted to believe her.

'The jewellery! Ujwala was right, wasn't she?' Bee murmured as sudden inspiration struck her. 'It's all paste and stones. It's all fake.'

The Maharani gave her a sad smile. 'I sold the last of it to pay that incompetent idiot Bhavanchandar. What a waste that turned out to be.'

Then she took a deep breath, let go of Dheera and nodded at Kartar.

He shot Dheera point-blank on her left shoulder. Dheera slumped down without a whimper.

Bee screamed.

'Appearances are everything, Bee. You know how strongly I believe that.'

'You won't get away with this, you know.'

'I will.' The Maharani took the gun from her bodyguard and pointed it at Bee. 'After all, no one's going to believe a queen would do something as common as taking a life. Right?'

Kalavati trained her sight on Bee's head, squeezing one eye shut just as she'd been taught by Kunwarji all those years ago on their second date. Her shoulders were level, her breath steady.

She exhaled slowly just as she caressed the trigger.

Arhan didn't believe much in God. When his father had died and left him in charge of the mess that was his family and business, and he'd been forced to abandon his game, had understood . . . God was arbitrary.

He needlessly inflicted pain and suffering on people just because He could. There was no fairness in the world. And you had to look out for yourself.

So it was a wonder that the same God decided he should live, instead of bleeding to death slowly on a dark and grisly Mumbai street.

Painful, ghostly consciousness rushed back into him at the same instant that he heard Bee scream.

Unbelievably, he heard Maharani Kalavati Devi murmur, 'Appearances are everything, Bee.'

His brain was not working at full capacity but he opened his eyes, vision wavering, without lifting his bent head, enough to make out a few things.

Dheera was lying prone at the Maharani's feet.

Fucking hell!

Kartar Singh was right beside his immaculately dressed mistress who was holding a gun and talking of taking a life as being a common thing. Most of all, Arhan was aware of Bee by his side.

Vibrating with anger, passion, fear. Life.

Arhan judged his moment. He knew it would be his last.

Just as the Maharani finished her speech, he rose with a grunt, his back a cacophony of fire and pain.

The Maharani's eyes widened because she now had two targets to choose from. She hesitated as she met his eyes, as she saw him, the boy who'd spent a summer in her *haveli*.

It was the merest second. Kartar Singh was already in position, poised to take Arhan down. He'd even taken the step forward.

It was all Arhan had.

Arhan lunged forward, faster than when he had to save his wicket from a run-out. Faster than the pace length he bowled. Faster than the path of an oncoming bullet.

He leaped over Dheera's prone form and butted the royal Maharani's chin with the side of his head. The pain seared.

The Maharani screamed.

Bee screamed.

Kartar screamed.

And then, mercifully, came other sounds. Police sirens. A commanding voice yelling at them that they were under arrest, to stay where they were.

Arhan collapsed over the Maharani, her slight body bending under his massive weight.

But Arhan didn't care. He didn't care about the rough hands yanking him away from the homicidal queen. He didn't care about the pain blinding his extremities one by one.

He only had eyes for Bee.

She was crying. Copiously. Loudly. Struggling because she saw him. And he was alive. And so was she.

It was over.

Fireworks lit up the sky as Wankhede Stadium, indeed the whole city, roared. The World Cup final was on and it was India's to lose.

Arhan awoke to the smell of disinfectant and blood.

His body was moving, shaking, jerking and he didn't know where Bee was. He swung his eyes open and saw her.

She said calmly, 'You're going to be fine. The bullet went through and through. We're taking you to the hospital now in the ambulance. You're going to be just fine.'

He nodded or at least tried to nod. He winced instead. He knew there was something important he had to tell her, crucial. But he couldn't remember what.

—∙◆ ◆∙—

Bee woke up with a gasp. She smelled disinfectant, but thankfully no blood.

Opening her eyes cautiously she looked around, trying to orient herself with her surroundings. The walls were a greying yellow and the bed was not the soft bed of the five-star luxury she had become accustomed to.

Bee paled, swallowed. She remembered everything.

It hurt. Everything hurt.

'Hello, Bee,' Inspector Paramjit Thapar murmured, coming into focus.

He looked like hell, eyes red-rimmed, hair standing up in tufts as if he'd gripped and tried to pull it out. He still wore his bulletproof vest, although it seemed to have been loosened now.

'How's Arhan?' she croaked. 'Is he okay?'

Is he alive?

'I'm here,' Arhan murmured.

She turned her head to see him on the bed next to her. Hooked up to IVs and with tubes running down his chest. But his eyes were open and they were levelled at her with an all-too-familiar expression.

'I love you too,' Arhan said.

He held out his taped hand from under the bedclothes. 'Okay?'

Bee's heartrate sped up on the monitor. A single tear streaked down her cheek.

'This is all very touching,' Param said wryly.

Arhan ignored his comment and said softly, 'Don't cry, Bee.'

'I don't have bubble wrap here,' she murmured.

'When we get out I'll build a bubble wrap factory for you,' he promised her solemnly.

Bee sniffed. 'I think I'm going to prison for a long time.' She looked at Param for confirmation.

'You're a national hero,' Param said tonelessly. He did not look like he agreed with the assessment.

'Both of you,' he included Arhan in his statement. 'You've helped bring down a deadly criminal organisation and nab a wanted murderer on at least sixteen counts in three states.' He gave them a myopic glare. 'While nearly getting killed in the process.'

Arhan cleared his throat and gave him a pointed look.

'The department, the cricket board, other concerned organisations . . . and I,' Param added reluctantly, 'all of us are very grateful for your persistence and cooperation.'

Bee gave a watery chuckle and wiped fruitlessly at more tears. 'I've become a gushing faucet. And you're thanking me. I must be dead.'

Arhan squeezed her hand. 'Don't say that. Don't talk like that.'

Bee gave him a haunted look. She couldn't get the image of the Maharani pressing the trigger out of her mind.

'The Maharani!' she asked. 'What about her?'

'We have her on all counts. A full confession,' Param said grimly. 'She wants representation. Ujwala is flying down with a lawyer. Your boyfriend called her.' He pinned Arhan with a disapproving glare.

Bee sighed. 'Of course you did.'

Arhan's eyes were flat. 'I had to. Ujwala is a friend, even if her mother is a devious, manipulative, psychopathic megalomaniac.'

Arhan's hand tightened around Bee's, where an IV was pumping meds into her system.

'So—'

'Yeah, I kno—'

The spoke together.

'I'll leave you two now. I'll also hold the doctors off for five minutes and give you some privacy,' Param murmured, melting out of the room.

Neither Bee nor Arhan heard him leave the room. Neither cared.

Bee's eyes flashed with some of her old fire and she tried to tug her hand away from Arhan's.

His hold tightened.

'I'm sorry,' she said, crying in earnest.

'You should be. I almost died out there tonight.'

She glared at him. 'So did I. When that fucking monster shot you,' she whispered, inelegantly wiping away snot from her nose. 'I almost died too.'

'Then you know how it feels . . . It's like when I'm around you,' Arhan retorted, 'I am constantly waiting for you to do something monumentally dumb and it kills m—.'

'I won't do it again,' she swore fervently. 'I'll never do anything dumb again.'

'Bee, you didn't let me finish.' Arhan leaned in close, smelling of blood and sweat and antiseptic. But somehow, to Bee, he smelled like home. 'Even though the constant worrying kills me, I'm proud as fuck of you and of what we did tonight.'

Bee lost her breath.

Because he gave her that look. The look that spoke more clearly than any words could. The look that said *Okay, we are doing this. I am okay with you ruining my life because I love you.*

'But could we please never do anything like this again for the rest of our lives?' he added, smiling.

'I can't promise anything,' she managed through an aching throat. 'Although I will try.'

'I can live with that.' He shrugged just as the door opened.

People poured in. Her parents, her brother, Harry and medical staff.

Bee knew chaos was about to rain down on them yet again. Knew that her life was never going to be the same.

Knew this man was her fate.

So she whispered, 'You can't back out of this now, you know? This is forever.'

Arhan smiled as everything inside him that had been going ballistic instantly calmed down. All the terror, panic, anger and fear leached out of him as Bee's smiling face telegraphed all that she wasn't telling him yet.

Telegraphing the love she'd whispered to him right before the world had gone to hell. Making him believe that it hadn't just been adrenaline or fear . . . or a dream.

This is real. This is better than any game I could have played.

EPILOGUE

Bee's Journal Entry #22

It feels weird to write copy that no one else will read. Well, except the counsellor, if I decide to share this with Dr Mehta. And she did say during our last session that my anger and anxiety had become more manageable after Amma, Appa and I had an honest heart-to-heart about everything.

This is not world-ending weird. Not like how I used to feel after Patil-Gate. When I had so much to prove to the world, to myself . . . prove that I was a serious reporter with investigative chops.

I'm not so insecure anymore.

That's a nice change.

No, it's a lovely change.

Another lovely change? My new job. It isn't as glamorous as catching red-blooded killers, but assistant manager of corporate communications at Madisaar Maami's Kaapi has a nice ring to it. And working with my uncle has its perks too, like the afternoon off for a movie premiere.

Hmmm? What else do I need to share?

Dhee's almost done with her last round of physical therapy and has regained full motor function of her arm. I was so worried that eight weeks wouldn't be enough to get her in shape. But thankfully it was. She is Wonder Woman.

She isn't talking to me right now, and I don't blame her.

Arhan says I have to give her some time to process everything.

I miss her. She is my best friend after all. She almost died because of me. In her place, I would have asked another hitman to unalive me because I'd dared to place her in mortal danger. Life isn't like the movies though, is it? Some things don't survive a best friendship.

On a happier note, Arhan's here. It's his weekend to visit me in Chennai. I'll go to Chandigarh next month. It's Aunty's birthday and I have a surprise she's going to love. (It's concert tickets to Arijit Singh.)

I don't exactly hate Chennai or this long-distance thing, which is a surprise. Because, by God, I love Arhan. Sometimes, when we are video-calling and he is shirtless (at my request), or he is snoring next to me, I look at him and my fingers tremble. There is a small, puckered scar five inches off his chest, from where the bullet hit him, missing all the vital organs . . . thank God.

I want to trace it. But I don't. Because it's perverse and I am determined to not be morbid.

I have the world's bravest, sexiest former Ranji player to myself. And I'm not going to give him up for anything. One of these days, I'm even going to propose to him. Maybe next month when the whole family is together. It sure would make Amma and Appa happy. They know I am safe with Arhan.

One of the most important lessons I have learned with Dr Mehta is the power of gratitude. For the big and small things. To make a list every day so I know how much I really have.

I'm grateful I got a front-page by-line, even if it was my first and last.

I'm truly grateful that Arhan loves me.

I'm grateful he was given a full pardon and was asked to come back to take over as Head Coach!

I'm less grateful he refused because in the aftermath of the match-fixing scandal they sure could have used his rigid, Mr India type of courage. But, as he often says, Arhan knows his heart. After all, it picked me.

I'm grateful for my surprisingly challenging new job in a new city.

I'm grateful for family and friends, former and current.

I'm grateful for today.

I am done recalling stats and keeping score.

Arhan loves me and I love him. That's the only score I want to keep.

ACKNOWLEDGEMENTS

This book would not have been possible but for a random conversation I had with my aunt one day when we were travelling back from a theme park. She mused out loud, 'What if something bad happened in the world of cricket, Aarti?' And I ran with it.

Thanks also to Kitchu and Laxmi for being willing sounding boards as I hashed this plot out with them through the ride, non-stop.

Special thanks to Karths for giving me one of my favourite scenes ever to write—the Zulu. Bee and I love it so much!

To the lovely team at Bloomsbury and The Book Bakers' Suhail Mathur, thank you for giving me the space and bandwidth to make *Score!* shine through a freaking pandemic. Thanks, Prerna, Mekhala and every awesome person to work on this book.

ABOUT THE AUTHOR

Aarti V Raman is the author of more than thirty contemporary romance novels. She loves to write about hot-mess desi girls who bring strong, filthy rich and powerful heroes to their knees. A happy ever after is guaranteed but not without lots of angst, spice and thrills. When torturing her characters emotionally isn't enough, she puts them in actual danger! Aarti learned this trick after reading thousands of romance novels and decided to tell stories her way, starring characters who looked and sounded like her.

The Worst Daughter Ever has been optioned for a screen adaptation while her Millionaire Foes series is on a time capsule bound for the moon. Many of her books have hit the Amazon US and India Top 100 and Top 50 bestseller lists.

But what gives Aarti the most pride is knowing that she is living her own version of her favourite three words—happy ever after—thinking up more stories to entertain herself (and the romance-reading world) with her large and largely tolerant family.